Nicholas Frost

The Labyrinth
Tales of
entanglement,
escape

For purchasing information, go to:
www.mouthsofillusion.com / nfrost@odp.com.au

Cover design by Alicia Grady, Struck By Violet www.struckbyviolet.com

Typeset by BookPOD

ISBN: 978-0-6450137-4-0 (pbk) 978-0-6450137-5-7 (e-book)

 A catalogue record for this book is available from the National Library of Australia

The Labyrinth:
Tales of Entanglement, Escape

Also By This Writer

Awareness Alone penetrates to the heart of experience, the eternal dance of absolute awareness. Grasping that awareness is all we can ever be, beyond endless becoming born of desire and fear, we discover the miracle of our own borderless freedom.

The Wandering   Distanced from partner Marsha and her daughter Matty by physical and psychic wanderings into geographic places, historical scenes, other lives… the narrator Blank dances solo with his unavoidable other, claiming to alert her to opaque parts of his nature and to her own: on clinging and running, victim and perpetrator, freedom and fundamentalism, splitting and taking responsibility… and on Samsara, the trivial endless recurrence. *The Wandering* is Blank's ruminating travelogue, tainted-love diary, mythic karmic romance, meditation on being and becoming, conscience and commitment.

The Elusive: Four Novellas
The Adventures of Sally Bang charts an unruly anti-heroine's coming of age, and a ghost writer's need to possess. At sixteen there's insight and beauty that never come again, and within every adult is a wish to get it back. What is gained and lost with growing up, and whose story is it anyway? **Commitment** ensnares a standoffish narrator in relationship dilemmas, in a psychologic navel-gaze in cliffhanger style on the elusive as romance, the tango of intimacy and distance, conformism and the irrational. **In Search of Francesca Mars** exposes an artist's vision of a self-immolating media star who tilts at strange liberation, who toys with all who need to put her on a pedestal or drag her down. A close-skinned portrayal of ambition and use, the politics of giving, glamour and ugliness, the artifice of art, the problem of value. **Innocence** asks, who doesn't want innocence, no matter how obtuse the path? Dancer Libby Castro submits to powerful and needy people: husband, employer, spiritual mentor, analyst. Yet beyond her insouciant roles and lazy vacancies, she'll be no-one's shadow: a straw, a girl unmarked, woman alone…

Total Drama (Macmillan Education Australia, 2010) investigates the dynamics of interpersonal encounters and the core ingredients of drama through original scripts and exercises.

Contents

Don't Worry
About a Thing

The meditator Dust is steered into community work by the Divinology Church, where like Dante in *infernal circles* he trawls people's rubbish in *aberrant and miserifying scenes*. With sainted girlfriend Blue Wendy and ascetic Anna Rex, all underhinged by his Employer's *spidery cult*, we trace a *satire* on Dust's fabulations with the *need to evolve*, with the problem of who and how to be.

Don't Worry About a Thing

Creatures of the Lower Depths

A youngish man of thirty-five years sits alone with spine erect and eyes wide shut in the hallowed-hushed hall of his adopted Church, pondering in his capacious mind pathways to his happiness. Desperately shying from the niggling need to dwell on horrid human struggle and slither in inky lower depths, he conjures beatifical altitudes of wonder and awe. Let us join in as he sits, as if watching television in dumb show. 'I see strange forests and outcrops washed in a bubbled ocean of clear fluid. Like the pipes of some great organ, the vegetations of this primal forest sway in currents, and beaded light falls and flickers in sandy riffs on the ocean floor. And strangely there are no fish, but beads of invisible force seem to flitter and flicker on purposeful errands, and activity seems to thrive in this world of undersea winds and fronds and flowings and breezes. Then the camera's eye rises up and out – as if to burst through a barrier like a hard nut, into a realm of far greater scope but not of deeper beauty – as if a horizonless sky over the rump of ocean. And we see from up here that the ocean had been... the interior of a human brain, and its fluids are reason and sensing and love, its currents are of feeling and impulse and connectedness, and that it gambols at the behest of an unknown white invisible that is *awareness alone*... and all its things are tiny flutterings in this greatest ocean of pure knowing, pure intention... and untrammeled desire. *Who is this?* we wonder. It is everything and everyone... and yet it is no one... it is not human, it dreams the human, dreams universes out of itself. It *is* itself...'

...Yet just as light sweats its shadow, our meditator's conscience drags him from the beatific to forms less pleasing and reassuring - and he is as if alone in a darkened wood where the sun is silent, in some darkgreen world of tangling roots and trunks and fractal branches, where wild animals may carry him off and devour. Now he can't make sense, his efforts are distorted, he indulges separative thoughts by turns manic and depressed; he encounters a smorgasbord of sufferings, subtle and deep as this cluttering wood of becoming. And he panics, repeats: 'the thing is to be nothing at all, the thing is to be. But how to do, or not to do? Stay as you are, don't move a solitary hair. Outside these firmshut eyes eternity replaces all, swiftly, silently. Don't worry about a single thing...' Yet despite this brave auto-dictation he slithers further - into miasmas of chemicals and vegetations, of creatures gnawing and fumbling and grasping, beetling and clawing and multiplying in the gluey lower depths and folds of the Being. This forest is murder absolute! Nothing survives but by eating some other. How organisms claw at the sun, millimetre by millipedal millimetre in their ten billion-year woe. Yet, beyond all these forms we might have taken, out of the strands of time and endless circumstance, we are *human*. And what did *I* do with this gift, what did I make of it? I who bear all shapes and scars and horrors and hopes and ghosts and dreams of the lower ones embryoed in my bones, I who've been all creatures... *am yet a man,* a man without a notion of how lucky he is, enmeshed in the soap opera of himself, in these fractal dungeons he crawls and falls to, in microscopic weaving of beetling experience in this cosmic weal, imbibing his turgid lesson, trotting his consequence inch by inch, embedding his grinding bread-butter experience on the wheel without end. And all the while a tiny voice echoes from shafts of the deep: You are the light of the world! Why conjure wastes and hells and enchainments where there are none? Because you *can*? Play your games of weal and woe but come on home. Your patient Maker breathes and sighs; he's lonely for companions. But we circle, we entertain, flaunt stupidities to Uncle, we abusive creatures drunk on darkling drafts of the heart! We blunderers with hands over eyes, faecal-brained dunces and dupes, gulled nonces, railers against windmills, wishers and mourners and cursers and negatives and jilted jealous curmudgeons, lame and lampooned, smelly-evil and limbless; we groaning hypochondriacs, faustian calculators flatterers smoothies arrogants pretenders treachers liars simonists hypocrites pissy poets blockheads politicians prissy artistes proletarian poseurs pathetic and grim... we demented menopausal handicapped hating hoons and holy goons, lowly lost and damned! What is surer than suffering, bitter fruit of our clinging and grasping? Anxiety of love, love of death, cloying wants amounting to nothing, hate of authority, poison of memory, trauma of history... Yet, if we could just be waves in Impersonal Vast... we'd feel no suffering at all! If we ceased to grasp, if we *ceased*... Never being this body (that we rent) we'd cease to worry on a single little thing. Human toil 'd make no sense. Nothing to be but a throbbing *clearness*. Buildings'd be candy floss, bodies light, rocks mere thoughts. This lifetime: a blip on the eternal. How many do we need? Our mothers merely ghosted us. We won't ever evolve, won't cope, will crave no relationship, abandon all *novels* lamenting the bitter fruits of clinging, spread arms to the sun, breathe spacewinds of lung-emptiness... Who'd need a body or blood or sight or breath or bed or happiness, sleep or job or drink or food or books or mind or neuron pathways earth ecology past or future history thought or sentence, buildings parties plans or erudition, or even trees or beaches stones or sky? Don't need to fill it in, don't need to sin, don't need a thing, don't need to fill it all in... And damn the fabled 'paths to God'! Some want to drown in surrendering, some want to love this world to death; and what use is the greatest: that of helping? We meditators seek to vanish! Me, ego, believed it wanted to Help... But so deep did I study Holy Science that I was locked in wonder: where's any *limit* to you and me, what telescope, what hourglass can measure it? Are we cosmic breath that outward flows forever, or starlight of stars that gaseous burn the aeons? Are we vibration that dreamed a particle, a microsecond so brief it never was? This absolute thing, so total, total is She. *You don't know me, can't think me. I'm quick, you don't see me.* But still, still the meditator dreams to deposit tiny specks in the whiteness! See how he plants little flags, colonises little kingdoms. See how he 'sits and ponders'. Mmm, can any man be mute and absolute, cut off from streets and streams of the world? An idiot's question! And so one is raped by temptation to be a demi-god, a little Jack Horner in his corner, where not one notion, act or feeling, discovery or vista or kingdom is not plucked from the field and sometime claimed as his own as if he dug a mound of gold from the giving earth, locked it in great safes and hired a phalanx of soldiers to protect it from all comers. Let any man enter the Celestial Library and read a million volumes: does he own a single letter of them? Is there anything more teeth-grindingly insular than self? Is it possible *not to cling*? Should one not sever one's own head? And so this little ego, chained angel, arriviste, ignominious fumbler for light from which he came, chatters out the endless schizoid conversation of himself... 'Serve, serve the *Great* (he says) - for though at heart I am unsullied, nameless, unruffled, entire, yet must I be myriad rough things in this cocktail of becoming, this purgatory, must be the spawn of Satan in the bottom parts of hell! For though I am Light I wear the cloth of Ignorance. I am Oneness trapped in ten billion hearts! - one who ascends and descends the great Gyre, who dances the eternal binaries of soul and shadow. And cleverly, I'll not shun ignorance as evil, for without it where could be the good? Both river and sea am I, lone bird and sky, boundless fool in rags of form, subject and creator-god; yet do I wallow as creature, as man, as a fish who admits no water, forest mole allergic to the green, furtive mouse scurrying in night forests, sniffing his own obliteration...'

...In the panelled cushion-green meditation hall of the Church of Divinology, the meditator Dust's agglomerated accustomed thoughts are about to be brutally interrupted. Has his Employer seen he's sat on his backside too long? Sure enough.

The Organisation

- Dust... Dust! Open your eyes. Pay attention. Sit by here. Listen. I, the Employer, have a weighty little *job* for you. Our private research tells us there are people (besides you) who are in need. You may go forth and visit the places I have written on this list. Do all that is required there. And do not fail to get them to donate to our organisation for services rendered or for any perceived improvement in their welfare, not least as a mark of respect for your own efforts. I leave all means of delivery to you. Needless to say, these souls will not always welcome your presence. Report to me in writing at regular intervals. Here is a stipend for expenses: don't spend it at once. And do not neglect during this assignment, responsibilities you have to those who rely on you... They say you have a girlfriend. She has visited here?
- Um, she helps me, such as my needs are
- With money? That cannot be. Support yourself
- How might I do that?
- Cease complaining! I know you persist in thinking 'pristine living'

depends on your remaining inward without outer connection! If you persist in exclusive inner focus the world becomes ridiculous, wasteful, absurd. It is time to stub your toe on something solid. Go stub all your toes, mister 'Dust'! I remind you: why are you a member of our Church? Are you a freeloader? Dive in deep and solve the physical, sensory, emotional, intellectual, egoistic problem of being human. Don't be lazy! Don't avoid. Don't be defeatist or narrow-minded. Or superior, patronising, superficial, complacent. Nor for that matter angry or vengeful or treacherous or lying or blocking or cold in the heart... Are you paying attention? We offer the privilege to scrabble in Lower Depths. Let empyrean clear winds sail beyond your head - and torment you!

Not a fellow to be interrupted, one's Employer (though apparently I, Dust, am). Still, he employed one's assumed name for the first time. Most likely he flatters prior to wrenching the rug from under. He's a clever clever man but his precipitous steaming-up is an act, a deeply complicated one in which he exerts copious energy trying to appear like Everyday Joe with everyday feelings and needs. But didn't we long ago trawl all this mush? Didn't we long ago condemn the world as a vale of tears, child's sandpit of waste and confusion and illusion? Why crawl out of retirement? Me, lowly bookshop assistant, why bother me: I've done it all - more or less. Sirrah, don't fail to remember I am a voluntary scion of the Church of Divinology! I may walk out that door (as you've said yourself) at any time. And 'employers' pay wages, not miserly stipends. Yet the Employer always wants something hard in return: services rendered to the Church of Divinology! Why do people join these clubs? For comfort or validation, or a cure for inferiority, narcissism, laziness? My Employer will remind that in my case it was for *service*. There was a time when he vigorously pulled me in (after I'd 'asked for a job') as if I were the sole saviour of his organisation and the only prospect for its continued welfare (I saw through the little flattery trick, and he picked me straight away for a snob) - and then came a time when he seemed to all intents to be kicking me *out*. My ego was temporarily offended, I don't mind mentioning. Still, his actions invariably force one to reflect. Maybe it's always about threats of leaving? Could be his famous exit door is really the way in, not out... to be dragged kicking and screaming to embrace a 'bigger reality'? Worse, maybe I was trapped in a bigger prison than I recognised before I asked for sanctuary and solace in this little heaven-hole. But when *do* we ever get to leave? Answer: when we're ready, when we're *mature*. Who decides, and when? Man, this is Hotel California: you can check out any time you want, but you can never leave! Laugh, reader, but it suggests none of us can judge arrival at our own maturity - surely a relative term in this open-forever universe. Since I'm obtuse I claim not to mind this idea, though it scared the bejazus out of many Church members who actually chewed on it. And hordes left for that reason. As for being a 'freeloader' in the Church of Divinology: to the contrary, I fear my own ambition - which could be a good reason to rebuff worldly enterprise, although no doubt I'd prove a better operator than a lot of these amateurs rousting about. The Employer himself revels in inefficiency, which raises one's hackles. Watch how deliberately he muffles order and clarity in a dust-storm of activity, a lot of it devoted to making fools of we educated ones, we who were brought up to 'self-manage'. He's a great spider in a web, where not a thing gets done without his initiation or consent. Intelligent free-thinking people the world over would want to quietly throttle him. Which makes him quietly smile. As for being ridiculed in public (as he's done to me), for many this is unforgiveable sin. Many have suffered such treatment and walked out. Me, I'm a very calculating cuss and look for a day where I can get moral revenge, that is, the more one is abused the more one is inclined to find clever and subtle ways to win. And it is in the nature of this Employer's personality to inspire subtle acts of rebellion by demanding commitment. He is charismatic and powerful and indomitable, sure enough. But curiously he is also able to inspire *pity*, as a man who works day and night for grubby little goals that seem of no personal benefit to him. Why does he bother? It's as if there's nothing so fanatically important as this present little tad of business - here, now, today; yet he resolutely undermines any of our own pretensions to meaning and significance. We live on a razor's edge between meaning and unmeaning, between triviality and commitment, between 'being here' and being nowhere, between taking initiative and being treated as delinquent drones in a dumbshow of quotidian insignificance. And there's no option but to play out the *passive*.

And so it is. On a fine day you want to be here in the thick of it; the next you want to run a country mile down a country road, and you'd give your eyes for some kind of normalised boring predictability. But, but. This is not meant to be a slick modern enterprise, this church. And no serenity is permitted!

In this milieu I am led to cogitate on the actual idea of service. What's the difference between a useless action and a useful one? Are all acts useless or all useful? I assume it is my role to decide. Sadly the Employer thinks it isn't. Again, which bit of me is adult and which the child? Disturbing, how the Employer always manages to criticise on the very things we have mastered, that are not the least problem in our own eyes. I'm pretty sure he picks on people for the sake of it, that he 'does it scientifically' - though I'm never certain since I've no special buddies in the place to gossip with. Except maybe one thin girl called Anna Rex. Let's assume the Employer always knows what's best. Clearly he's been there and done it all himself. So: the longer you stay the more you mimic the Employer, the more you become him. How? There is a cosy passivist masochism that creeps in - which no doubt he is alert to as well. Dominant personality! The truth is, I *let* him be so. Easier to give in than to fight. This church is a dance academy where people dance only with the Employer: betimes a serene waltz, betimes a fiery tango. Dance the waltz of commitment and you're thrown out on your ear. Essay the tango of non-commitment and you're inexorably sucked in. Then punished. And if you merely commit to being uncommitted - you feel the pain of your lie, since the Employer stamps on all your toes at once, complaining that he just can't dance with you at all... There was one black guy who thought he'd be the perfect helper, would take on like Saint Anthony all things the devil could throw at him. He aimed to succeed by sheer goodwill (or skin-thickness) but the Employer sure enough found a way to derail him. The faithful fellow got an illness - and the Employer threw him out of the church in an instant. Then the black *died.* His ego was always such that he thought of out-humbling his Employer's worst treatment! And he failed, since the Employer then affected to *forget* him. Yet it is said: in one's failure always lies the possibility of success. So the theory goes... Bad treatment by the

Employer can seem so callous. All of us in this church harbour numerous examples. One never really gets over being ridiculed or lambasted, but we quietly lick our wounds and resolve to forget. And the next time... it's no easier! It *never* gets any easier. And this is the joke: you never will learn as long as you live. *You just get better at continual emotional failure.* Worst of all to bear are people he promotes over you to do his dirty work. These turn into sanctimonious little holier-than-thou tyrants, all in the service of humility. So, humility gets a shitty name. Another of his tricks! Your hero Dust of course won't fall for it. He'll maintain a healthy hatred of sycophants and poseurs. Hatred 'll keep him honest. And there's always pity, Dust's other refuge. Pity for poor saps around him who actually believe in what they're doing. But again, our Employer will wipe out us aloof types by making us pity *him*... as just a poor wee man who tried and tried to help all the ignorant strugglers of this struggly world. He's the Oscar-winner.

Come to think of it, the poor wee man must have once had a barrel of money to make this church a goer. Perhaps he's a businessman after all. But why spend all your businessy talent on spiritual healing? No, I get it: it's more evolved than lowly profit-making; this is Money for God. But why do things for 'God' when his creation morphs into such continual farce? Me, I long since concluded I needed to step outside Creation, retire to the Emptiness. My Employer's having none of it. In the end, he makes me do all things farcical and soul-destroying: not to prove the world is a farce, but to prove that my belief that the world is a farce - is a farce. I know it but play the game, knowing it's a game but not a game but *is* a game... (not). For like - ever. Give up, dude! You can't control a *thing*. Lesson one: Employer is god; he always wins. So get out there and do the right thing! And the only way you'll ever 'succeed' is to feel bad, to not 'get it' at all, to cry out for help, to be a loser. And so you fall back on your resource and try to clamber up again, and realise you are *never* the smart guy - because today's success is tomorrow's failure, today's learning tomorrow's unlearning. Act, my friend, in the ugly truth of your own nothingness - and be glad! Sound simple? Just you try it.

I'm hearing all you 'independent-mind' types: 'Get the hell out from that oiky paradigm, take the shackles from your shoes, pop the penance-bubble, get stoned, do the party-thing, live for the day and die tomorrow with a smile on your dial.' But there's this little problem called Forever. Called *Eternity*. All of this, is the eternity of *Now*. We have to be here since there's nowhere else to ever be. So how we act is all. There can be no thought of later, of tomorrow, of 'other'. Naturally we're not really acting at all since the fruits of our efforts are crushed to *dust* in the instant. And we can't even try to recognise this fact, since it requires reflection, philosophical reflection, and that is a no-no if you want to remain as *dust* (as it were) here in 'this ever-nothing, this nothing-now'. One could therefore say it doesn't matter a crap what you do! Party up, be the animal, be a divine drunk, have no *conscience*. But why bother being that either? Act of rebellion at our own nothingness? Most likely. Anyway, enough of this absurd esotericalism, which is precisely the sort of navel-gazing the Employer abhors. Let him do the ab(w)horing for us since he is our greater conscience... Greater conscience? Deep down we all suspect that one day he'll simply sell up, shut the shop, make himself available to no-one at all, ever again. And then we'll all regret we didn't do better. When we had the chance. That we didn't profit in this business of saving souls. Our own at least. Thereby remember: if the Employer treats you like shit, you should be flattered. Consider yourself flattered, Mister Dust. With your oh-so-pretentious name.

It's said the man (or woman) who needs no organisation is free to mortgage himself to one. Or that the man who needs no Hell is free to enter therein. Perhaps the man who needs no pride is free to indulge it, and the man who is free may wrap himself in chains. My Employer would retort: the man who feels no pain is free to *hurt*. Himself and others. Perhaps freedom is freedom to feel all pain? Anyway, one might simply shut up. Shuddup Dust! Because *service* here we come. Compassion here we come. Learning here we come. Atonement here we come. Yippee.

Limbo

In a beauteous house in the affluent borough of Epicurea dwell Marcus and Helena Pace with their two rather fine children Benjamin and

Cassandra, known to all as Ben and Cassie. Nearby is a park of great capacious trees that stand majestic in littered fields of asphodel. Here's an aspect as near-Elysian as one might hope in a world that clamours dirtily for real estate. Eminently but consciably rich, their cup is filled yet runneth not over. Of comforts and clarities is life designed, but with positive bounty extended to all, and the Paces are counted among one's best and surest friends. *Pace,* as we know, is Italian for peace - and such is the serendipitous neatness of a name for those whose presence in the world is marked by settled rightness, by privileged pedestaled acceptance of the quiet glories of being modernly human - that I tell you all civilisation is here, and all the darkling past of the world banished, so very greenly do creepers of peace lick o'er mossed walls, and sparkle in a new-mown summer's garden ringed by wooded fields of asphodel. How lightly doth time tick in the lighted galleried halls, the parloured cossetted rooms of a new-renaissance family benignly at one with itself. For even if cloudish winds of autumn do crake the bon-ed fingers of great trees, and e'en when grey-white winter chills the landscape's warmsap heart in shuddering blood of ice - even then do memories of unruffled rightness still the distant bells of distant death, and hold this family safe-harboured in walls of breathing comfort-stone, keeping eternal promise of springs and summers past and to come.

There is no doubt in the mind of Dust that he has been sent to the Paces so that a little gold-dust from their moneyed edifice might fall upon his sponsor, the shadowy Church of Divinology. Undoubtedly a Church must change to suit a changing world, and since one never really departs it, such is its tenderly pervasive spiritual perfume (and the psychic threat of its founder), it must minister to the needs of 'former clients' in new and original ways. His new incarnation is neatly framed as 'tutor of English literature to the family's children', and with a salesman's assurance he now ruminates that he might 'neglect to reference the Church in any way at all'. And sure enough (via some arcane Church members' gossip pipeline) our man Dust finds himself one fine morning in telephone conversation with Helena Pace herself, on the subject of Beckett and Joyce and Eliot and Woolf, as well as the vagarious tastes of precocious teens - a topic perhaps closer to Helena's heart. Dust is moved to acquit himself in the manner of one who takes the literary canon seriously and believes in the cultivation of mind through Art. Helena Pace is all charm, and Dust is duly invited to the residence on Saturday next to meet the children. And to meet her Husband.

Just as ocean's great waters end in little wavelets that tickle one's toes upon a sandy shore… and as we gaze to unguarded horizons and contemplate the loveliness of our own future - we may be blessed with feelings that the world is solely here for our personal benefit. People of such attractive roseate vision attract envious others in their turn, and out of yearning we fantasise that life might always be this: an Eden where the lion lieth down with the lamb, where cosy parties in panelled rooms, firelit communing, woodland walks, gamboling in fields, drinks on the terrace under autumn sunset, smell of new hay, girlish sweat, plush carpets and nuts, beads of rain on one's umbrella… are as natural as living itself. That our real purpose is to be artistes, connoisseurs, parties to the seasons, dancers of nature's soft ways, participants in the smile of time, custodians of pleasure-gardens in a vale of greenness called Life. In this sleep of life, sweet sleep of life…

On Saturday, at the civilisedly alert hour of ten, Dust is led into the sun-bathed glass atrium looking out to the garden of the Pace residence. There's a Vienna Secession table surrounded by matching chairs and a bookcase groaning with erudition. A young fellow whom he takes to be Benjamin fiddles with his tablet. A large white cat is curled plaisantly upon the table.

- Benny darling, this is Mister Dust. Aha! And Michelangelo no doubt seeks to share the morning's edification
- Hello Benny. Hello Michelangelo.
Dust sinks his fingers into the bottomless fur of the benign white one, who deigns to acquiesce by divine right of cats, and purrs like a Bentley.
- Mister Dust, Marcus naturally felt he was able to tutor the children, but feels they might prefer 'new influences'
- Mister, my sister is batty, just so you know
- Darling, Mister Dust will make his own observations.

At which point Daddy Marcus steps in. Extending his hand in the manner of a reasoning being who meets the inequitable inconveniences of life with sheer niceness, he greets the newcomer. Dust takes the hand, thereby donning the garb of new-trusted aide who tacitly accepts the Pace family status quo. One advantage of peace is that there seems not a thing else that can ever exist. No use to protest, for post perfection, nought else is really to be taken seriously. Still, Marcus Pace is aware of the world's tendency to be unstably unsure of itself, so whilst entertaining the usual light thought that he might play ambassador to his own rightness, he nevertheless affects to diminish his star a little in order to make a visitor feel included. He is even wont to induce a hint of a problem, of light familial disharmony, for the sake of 'keeping it real'. This has the effect of infusing a frisson of irony into the conversation - perhaps of 'shared enlightenment balanced on a razor's edge of enquiry into itself'? And what else may the visitor do but smile?

- Doctor Dust, I presume.
- Not a doctor, I confess.
- But you must be since you profess to profess. Now then, has Helena warned you of our offspring? Ben considers himself an authority on all things beyond his age. I counsel you to beware. And Cassie (I note she is not present) can be demanding in ways that might surprise
- Darling! Mister Dust understands you've foregone the privilege of tutoring your own children.
A party to their jest, Dust counter-smiles. - I'm sure they're wonderful.
At which remark the Paces make a little banter he assumes is for his benefit:
- Cassie is at the age where, mysteriously, the delights of the Smartphone and YouTube are superior to those of the Moderns, the Pre-Raphaelites and the Ancients
- Oh no, Marcus! Mister Dust, she's merely seventeen and impressionable. And dare I say wilful
- You're both way off, Mum and Dad. Cass is determined to be *certified*
- so she can garner more attention than me since I'm more talented and more likely to get into Oxford.

Into this roseate and self-buoyed atmosphere Benjamin's elder sister walks in… in a manner that begs to suggest she has surprised them all talking about her.

- Are we all talking about me? Evil people. Ooh, you must be Mister Dusty. Cool. You look a bit young though. I've decided to study *Waiting for Godot*. I hear it's totally nihilistically incomprehensible. Come to my boudoir. What shall we call you?
- Call me Dust
- Cassie, *Mister* Dust will work with you here
- Nonsense, Mummy. Come along, Dusty.

Pet dog to a seventeen year-old? Dust raises an eyebrow to Marcus and Helena and follows her out the door. The big messy room upstairs announces itself as the gloried abode of Cassie Pace. A picture of a mythic young woman clutching trails of red hair has pride of place, sitting between two long windows looking out to woods. Cassie announces this is 'her special picture' (Evelyn de Morgan, 1898) depicting Cassandra in front of the burning city of Troy.

- She had the gift of prophecy but shitty Apollo put a curse on her so no-one would believe her amazing predictions! See her red hair in curls (d'you like my red streaks?) blue eyes and fair white skin! She's beautiful intelligent charming desirable elegant friendly cute. (She ticks them off like a list) But, Monsewer Dust, she was considered to be insane...

Cassie offers up a sexy-conspiring look. 'You are henceforth to regard me as secretly loony' it says. And with that, she'll string out any persona she wants.

- So what do you think of mumsy and dadsy?
- Very nice. Very sane
- Tee hee, she says. - D'you like my outfit?

Garish contradiction seems the order of the day: green and red striped tights, green jerkin rather like a doublet, buckle shoes, bunch of rings and earrings, face powdered faintly white.

- Listen to this, Fusty. (She's written a thing down) 'Cassandra evokes the same awe, horror and pity as do schizophrenics - who combine deep true insight with utter helplessness, and who retreat into madness'. Waddaya think?
- Who's Apollo anyway?
- He's a big arrogant god, dunce teacher
- Oh yeah. Some kind of 'big daddy'?
- Dunno.
Or maybe she does.

Dust takes up the narrative: 'Harking no doubt to the squalls of tuneless guitar emanating from his daughter's room during her inaugural tutoring session, Marcus pops his head in. I deliver a cheesy smile that says: all is under control! I merely indulge my pupil's associative flair within the ambit of *Waiting For Godot*. When the evil volume is turned down, daddy lightly suggests I might stay for lunch. I clock he's keen for a competitive chat. For under all the sureness, all the confidence, all the irony, I perceive Marcus is prone to doubt. And dislikes it. Every person of intellect who comes to his realm shall be tested, ever so subtly. You see, only a conservative may deserve peace in this material world, one who is at the centre of the balance of things, a reasoned and reasonable human being against whom extremes are shown up for the evil they are. But there is never a reason to be smug - and Marcus Pace is too intelligent to be smug. Conservatism though, must contain all free radicals, all fly-aways, all contentiousness within its orb of reason. For behind the facade of success lies the beyond - of the unfulfilled, of the forest, of the *deep*. Is this 'beyond' the assassinator of perfection, the curser of peace, choker of the subtle limbo of success? I profess to have no idea. But I predict he'll pressure me to reveal some squished evidence of wild disorder within myself. Oh but I can do that: I can circle the wagons ten times with my war-paint and tomahawk and scalp him right where he thinks he's at without a sweat. Very 'umbly of course. *Strangeness* is the crazy-making feather I'll tickle him with, the simple canker I'll infest him with. But all this is nary the point. The point would be Cassie. Me being the new tutor and all, a debate is a chance to impress. At lunch it is Hostess Helena who casts the bait.

- So, Mister Dust. Why do you think our young feel the need to rattle the world by refusing its settled wisdom?
- Well, I'm not a psychologist, but I say we should offer young people the heart and soul of the problem at the outset, since at their age they're ruled by developing intellect in its absolutist phase. That way we avoid patronizing.
She glances at her husband. He delivers a faint smile.
- Do go on
- I've heard youth say: 'Why bother with anything, we are all going to die.' But you and I should coolly reason. I tell them: 'The real joke is, we are incapable of death. We are nothing but eternal. To whom does death supposedly occur? He who is beyond it, obviously'.
Helena fishes again. - Do you think our Cassie will appreciate your brand of reasoning?
- Why not? - though young people are pretty emotional. Or I might have overlooked bi-polar tendency or a suicide-wish.
Her eyes widen slightly. But Marcus chimes in.
- According to your reasoning, young people may all put up their feet, 'chill out' and play the guitar

- No, humankind is born to action. Choose your occupation carefully lest we waste our eternity

(He smiles again) - What action do you suggest?

- Empower them. Get them to see that if we want to visualise or do a single thing, all the infinite powers and forces of the unseen must gather to make it happen. By the same token, whatever little evil we do, the unseen utterly compensates. We should get them to see they are literally drowned in the power of consciousness. Grocking that, can be deeply liberating for certain young people

- Or dangerous

(Helena) - You mean exciting, Marcus

- Excitement is not necessarily what they require

(Keep talking, Dust) - Truth is, if they set out to do a thing, especially an unusual thing, opposing forces automatically gather about. If they want to be free for instance, the strong forces of unfreedom clamp down just as precipitately as a posse called up to hunt down offending blacks. Seek creative chaos and crushing order is there. We're truly invested in the small and crushingly smug

- And your point is?

- I explain to young people, the horrific and dark side of the world must be accepted into us. We must be open to all possibility. Me, I dip my head in the cupboards of the dark, into the pools, the wells, the mines, the alleys, the brothels, dungeons, pits, mental caves, torture chambers, grottoes, underworlds. No Marcus, I'm not naive - or rather, if I were I wouldn't mind. Still, can we live? I tell you, not as we are now

- You are perhaps a *provocateur,* Mister Dust.

I make sure not to squirm under his coolly mature gaze. Behind his eyes I see several binding things: the need to be candid, for this is his cocoon of reason; the need to patronize for this is his platform of legitimacy; the need to be slightly ironically incredulous since he is the custodian par excellence of settledness; and the need to empunish, since he's the one being challenged right now.

- Mister Dust is not being allowed to have his lunch, darling.

Sweet Helena defaults to lightly serious airbrushing. Pervading success and contentment may have made her wonder where to put all those sensibilities of hers - as if it were wrong to be too happy or confident, yet also wrong to be too serious or inconfident. She who today has made a light and perfect lunch, keeps a gaggle of feelings on a leash. Unlike her daughter.

The following week after Cassie's lesson Helena invites me to lunch once more, and I assume Marcus is behind it. The amateur psychologist role I've been thrust into by the parental team will now be used against me, for Marcus must transfer onto me - in the guise of a suitable light lesson - his impotence with both his women. After a suitable banter-entree on foods and sports, in which I'm cleverly led to express edgy views, Marcus deftly steers us to topics unsolved.

- Do you think perhaps we are a too-pampered breed here in our corner of the woods? I suppose you see, mister Dust, that without the acquisition of wealth by some, the many would not prosper?

- Mmm

- Acquirers of wealth in all conscience actually take thought for the ultimate good of the world. Why assume it is not their ultimate goal to give wealth away to those in need?

- I assume no such thing

- There's a certain peace to be gained from the satisfactions of giving, and of knowing that one's giving is appreciated, even when the actual giving is unknown to its receiver. D'you have children, mister Dust? (He'll be quite aware that I don't) Because the engineering of young souls is a delicate thing

- Particularly when they're the unwitting recipients of privilege, as in your child's case. Someone has to apprise them of the need to appreciate what they've got - without disturbing their perfect future, and such that they don't neglect to love their benefactor. But no matter, feeling good about giving is its own reward. Its own drug, almost

- A drug? Helena and I give anonymously to numerous charities. You hint we do it hedonistically?

- There's nothing wrong with getting a hit from giving. But the pleasure is bound to seek reinforcement. And if it is its own reward, then *ergo,* it's a drug one can't get enough of.

He scans the space about my head, as if to seek further clues as to one's oily and elusive identity. But elusive is potent.

- Which people have helped and instructed and watched over you in your life, mister Dust?
- Many. And I'm grateful for it
- And what do you see as the purpose of life?
- No doubt 'to continue as things have always been'
- Really? Does the world not need improving?
- Which 'world' do you want to improve?
- Whichever falls to me. Whichever I inherit
- What about worlds alien to your own? The tortured worlds of individuals in layers of ignorance and suffering, their hells and layers of hells, their diseased hauntings, their spaghetti dreams, their limbos of grinding repetition
- Those are precisely the people one seeks to help
- Or maybe deprivation helps them better? Or loss, failure, blind pain? Perhaps those evil things are what we all need
- Yes! Let us all wallow like pigs in the trough of despond
- Slough of despond
- Whatever you say, young teacher
- So, Marcus. Which members of society should wallow like pigs and which should not?
- We seek to pull ourselves up by any means
- I know people who seek to shred themselves
- All choice is motivated by desire for pleasure and aversion to suffering - whether we like it or not
- Ha ha
- Do *you* never let pleasure get in the way of good old-fashioned pain?
- No no. Let's banish pain from the world and then all will be perfect. For when we suffer no pain, we're no longer in need of pleasure. Then we can all share in the state of perfect mental peace. Except we'd all be fat and happy and stupid
- Aha. Even we who suffer no apparent pain may suffer it, Master Dust
- A subtler, classier class of suffering? Excellent. Perhaps you really do suspect there's no learning without suffering

- And perhaps you know nothing of who I am, or what I have been through, or what I seek, what I have given up, what I have achieved. Nor what good advice I might offer you
- Beware: your need to self-justify comes at the *expense* of perfect poise, perfect peace, perfect etcetera
- I perceive you are either peevish due to jealousy, or have never been acknowledged for your noble efforts in the world
- Or maybe I like the pain of being resistant, the pain of contradiction, the pain of being alive
- The pain of being an irritant on the conscience of a smug world?
- Whatever you like, Mister Pace.
(Helena) - Pickled gherkin, anyone?'

Dust masks his fear and inadequacy by all this competing and judging! Can we fathom the subtle strands and wires that fashion even a single human frame? Why try to judge the evolutionary paths and forces and influences that fellow souls are grappling with in the shadowy sides of themselves, that masquerade as ugly or stupid or obscure or egotistic or any of the filigrees of contradiction that make up 'human progress'? The experience of even a single person is a gyre of unutterable worlds and planes beyond the sensible. It is a gathering of limitless nuance, of causes and effects beyond grasp - except by tiny experience, thing by thing, moment by moment in this eternal dot-play of space and time. For when the conscious Lord emits himself it's forever; there is no summation, no cathartic point, no climax, only the unutterable freedom of doing and living and making and shaping and rearranging worlds without end, worlds without end, in this flicker-film of the borderless whiteness of sentient being. And here we are judging, we who make our little pinpricks on the face of eternity. And this is our limitation: all judgy thoughts speak only of themselves, judgments speak only of ourselves. While Dust suspects that Marcus Pace is a limited man in his Epicurean avowal of 'contentment as highest end', how could he predict the ways this man Pace is swept by the catenations of history and time and circumstance to other visions, washed up on other lonely shores that glimmer in the half-light of his evolving, of his loneliness; that this creature known as Pace is lost like flotsam on the cruel oceans of green eternity, in his Crusoe-like odyssey to the yet undiscovered far-flung atolls and islands of his history... Dust! Cultivate a bit of compassion.

Thus Dust 'counsels himself'. But Marcus Pace by his air of settledness unsettles him. Marcus is selfish to be at peace as he claims, since others including those close to him, are simply not. He steals their peace away with his smug peacey peace. Marxists would avow that all blessed contentment is at others' expense: peace is imposition, illusion in a vengeful chaotic world! This is childish reasoning, but such is Marcus' air of impenetrable reasonableness that Dust has no choice but to be peevish. *Cassie Pace, I imagine you naked. I'm coming to share your bed.* Stop it. But Dust sees that the equanimity of Helena Pace is less secure (she being a woman) and therefore he thinks on how he might push his ego in her direction. And she may be vulnerably-in-touch-with-herself sufficient to appreciate it. Dust starts to glean that it was she who ventured long ago to seek the mystic kiss of the unknown in the form of the Divinology Church. Can Dust thus wedge her against her husband, at least enough to expose a measure of her lurking criticism of him - or is she imperviously loyal to the solid Pace burgher-spirit? Dust has a brief to teach the children, and to his mind the brief includes upsetting the status quo. For what's teaching but upsetting? Still, his ego's pretty unconscious, hard-wired to *compete*. His conscience says it should be otherwise, and in fact his position is made impossible since he has to trust and obey the Employer. What to do? Play or not play the venal game of ignorance called life? Hover above the fray or join in? Can we really 'go beyond' without duping ourself or hacking out a great lump of ourself? Humans are born to action, and action means making big fucking mistakes and being a dope and loser and judgmental competitive prick and everything else! Compassion is for *airheads*. In terms of a profession it certainly is. But no, we must 'wear the garment of life lightly', do the best we can knowing we can't actually succeed at any damn thing. The story goes that Krishna the God enjoined his disciple Arjuna to assassinate all his brothers in war (which is as futile as it gets), and so the disciple had no choice but to act. But Krishna said it was 'fine as long as he surrendered to Him'. Dust claims he *does* that. Surrender that is. Anyway, how can you not surrender since life is *total*? No, the attitude is the thing. The attitude, the attitude...

It turns out Marcus bloody Pace survived their spiky discussion pretty well... so our ruffled Dust has a brainwave. In the presence of Helena (who wisely kept her counsel during the males' little joust) he suggests:
- Let me bring Cassie to a meditation event. I have associates who will talk to her, give her the settled wisdom she surely craves. You've done all you can, as her father, for now.

Marcus looks at Helena. How to decline such a thing in the presence of his wife? She looks at him and smiles. Encouragingly.

Yes, for the Paces, a delicate and glittering balance has been painstakingly achieved, and even though they do witness life's ironies, and are quick to admit how fortunate they are, and offer so very many things to charity and would be upset if their children took it all for granted... these cultivated people cannot suspect how the pretty streams of life merely disgorge in a limbo-field of sweet and ghostly flowers, that its only substance is time-and-death, that it is *blind*. Let the soul wander then musingly, through chocolate-box worlds, no matter that this physical field is nothing but a tiny crust, a carapace on the great unuttered crystal spheres of being. No matter. Onward. We shall deliver our cribbed selves unto our *children*, shall let our children replicate us...

Or not, if Dust can help it.

The Toilet Cleaner

In the great Unending Story, we must look to the past in order to know the present, and to the present in order to know the past... In another life (say a hundred and twenty years ago) Dust found himself in the role of Toilet Attendant in the cellars of Paris. Underneath all the romance of Sisley's chimney-potted boulevards, such a predicament would suit a man jealous of his soul's progress on the lone miles of the cosmic road: here, he can conjure the portrait of a humble young man doing tough penance in his attritional war on pride. Even today when he steps into a humble public convenience, Dust envisions a grander walk: down curvaceous steps to tiled rooms, where, like the Maitre D' in any Rive Droite establishment, he marks the standards of cleanliness and inwardly tut-tuts at those who contribute not a thing but body waste, who think it their right to disorder one's preferred clean-tiled universe. How arrogantly people say: 'others will clean up after me'. Truth to tell, this nameless long-ago drudge who shuffled in the tunnels of better peoples' lives, preferred his anonymity. The former Dust aimed to be as a shadow - and he withstood the flittering of eyes, averting of heads, harrumph of pity from patrons who entered his white palace to flush away their better class of shit. For it was on *his* tiles, in his bowls that the world left its mark. And how thoroughly, expertly, he cleansed it all. Doggedly he stuck to his Herculean labour: to accept this tainted cavern as his home. How else to fulfill his karmic duty to the Masters Upstairs! Twenty steps down from the street at L'Opera (as if descending to the Metro) lies a gleaming vestibule of gilt-fringed white, with two adjacent rooms ringed by ornate basins for the lavage of hands: one for ladies, the other for gentlemen. Corridors to left and right, each with booths, watched over by fish-eyed Parisiennes of a coarser strain who pocket one's copper coin in exchange for little serviettes. (The young man had to struggle for his place inside this women's domain) At the back, a little room for workers and a kettle-place for tea. Best of all: behind a cupboard a low door leading out to the Paris catacombs, to red-brick arched tombs that wound, wound their way to steps beneath a narrow street far off. A private exit to the air - to salve one's sense of daring adventure. Or at least, one's dignity.

Even today Dust stands hypnotised before a toilet bowl and watches yellow streams from the body of a man fritter down the hole on a journey of co-mingled wastes destined for the sea. Standing thus, he re-lives his struggles in semi-fetid rooms where he took in the dead breath of strangers and passed it on in his turn, all in the hope of embedding a feeling that we humans are 'as one'. It was a pleasant legend. Especially now it's over. But really, was it so bad? Was it not akin to a restaurant - with customers coming and going and waiters waiting on the great and good? Just the other end of the process, food out instead of in. We're all servants, sinners in the lord's hands, though some of us will look down on others and feel entitled. Poor fools, don't you *see* when you do, God makes a mark against your souls? Dust imagines he advised his patrons with civilised reason: 'We are equals, mon vieux! Shall we enjoy the irony? Is it not something from Balzac? Surely you recall me from the Café Royale in my erstwhile profession! Seven years amid that gilt and plush and now look at me: seven years penance for my sin! I, an educated man (so Dust hoped), am called up to wait upon you again. *Cubicle treize, monsieur? Ha ha.* Do I observe that *madame* has turned rather portly? (I do not mention my own little sin of gluttony…) Even in our nether world, madame, civilised people exist, no?' 'Mais certainment, monsieur Dust! One does not think to discover such as *you* in such a place. And will you not consent to meet my daughter? - who is sure to be be entertained by such an enigmatic man!' *Etceteraaa.* And Dust would step out in his mind by the low door into the catacombs, and would wander under the streets of Paris, a sentinel, a watcher, savant to whom stupendous things happen. Or not, such is the sombre irony of this superficial world. For this underrated man, the wishy pleasures of the mind are his solace… until cold tomorrow morning comes.

Yet in this nineteenth-century Parisian life, Dust fancies he did meet that rather forward mother's daughter. It occurred at the head of the curved stair to the convenience near the Palais Garnier… 'Anna Blum was of the haute bourgeoisie, very thin and rather absent, but intensely so - as if she resented being what she was, who abominated life under others' eyes, despised indeed the very factualities of living… ugh, this absurd lace-clad prison-house of civility, this 'belle-epoque' *civilisation.* And Dust saw her abrupt look of vulnerable sorrow, as if she 'wanted to be sorry for something', and realised she wanted to be sorry for herself, but somewhere had decided this was self-indulgence since discipline was needed instead. She never descended those stairs, he knew. (Had no need to, by the thin look of her) Mind you, none may escape toilets, mused Dust. And that is why one works here; they are great levellers. People are not aware of this philosophic fact but only of shame, shame for no reason at all. Anna Blum, I know you think it disciplined to self-starve, that it is your sweet and clever little way to have both discipline and death - both meaning and death's escape. For then we may stay aloof and 'everyone can go hang' - including mother, in whose image one must never be coined. Discipline and death are but 'the grand tradition of asceticism', the noble path. But there's one nagging little thing: who will ever notice you? Someone might... someone must! Perhaps *that* man will notice. The one who stands at the entrance to the... (underground convenience) and acts as if he watches nothing... and who spoke with my *mother*. Ugh, how bored I am, how I feel permanently *bled*. (And yet I never bleed as other women do) Mother wants me to attend luncheons and make me eat and meet a husband. But I am a lesbian! Yes, I shall be one of those since I despise fleshy-pink mustachioed men. Oh lord make me barren. Even the sunlight on the boulevard drizzling the dusted trees gives no pleasure. And my heavy-shod feet scuff impatiently at the gravel in the park, and I feel the bench hard against my bones as I sit motionless there, and know the world eyes my skeletal frame in strictured disgust. I shall *stand* then and be proud, shall let the four winds tug at the blacklace fringes of my unwomanly skirt. To stand is better, 'tis statuesque. I am tall, I am noble. *Je suis tragique.* Oh, nonsense! I shall simply practise the continence of loss and demise, *ma solution de facilité!*'

Dust (in this other life) has no qualms about dressing dapperly on the streets when not employed down below. Perhaps he exudes an odour of containment, of mysterious absorption that signals promise to certain women... in this case to Madame Blum, mother of the black-clad waif Anna. Dust could see all: that Anna was no great beauty and that she compensated with quiet fierceness, that in her mind a great struggle raged, and that this attracted him somewhat in the way of a man who has no plan to become entangled with women at all. That she also had no such plan made it easy then. But Madame has certain fixed ideas. One Sunday it happens that she invites Dust to promenade with she and her daughter in the Jardin de Luxembourg, with a view to viewing a flower show. Her manner suggests it to be the lightest thing in the world, and Dust sees no reason to refuse, and so it is. Amid the multicoloured blooms Dust and Anna Blum exchange glances, and the flowers offer suitable fodder for conversation between young new acquaintances. Madame at one point ventures to wonder if Mister Dust is 'a man of means'. Anna butts in to say it could not possibly matter - though Dust smilingly affirms that 'one is not without certain pretensions to the higher ordures'. This is quite enough to elicit a river of light conversation from Madame the match-maker, whose eye for detail registers such sudden protestations from her severe daughter to be veiled but sure signs of interest. Dust was referring of course not to material but spiritual pretensions, and Anna knew it, and Dust knew she knew it. Thus the afternoon passes pleasantly amid the flowers and gravelled lanes, by the pond and in the tropic house and at the tea-kiosk. At one point, a large flaxen-haired woman smiles and offers them blooms. Dust puts coins in her ample hand. She watches the group as they pass on. Dust effortlessly charms the Madame in the manner of one who has not a thing to lose, and stick-like Anna absorbs the irony of it. But it is Madame who neglects to see how a future match will be based not on physical but intellectual connection. For Anna feels it has been her singular achievement in her relationship with Mother never to reveal her true self. It is amazing that a child should think this way, when all her nature is laid out like the carcass of a great fish for the world to see. Mothers are more experienced in certain things than any child can ever know. Is it all spite then - this girl's feeling of being misunderstood, of being put upon by the world's ridiculous pretensions (as embodied by her mother) - an adulty version of spite that compensates for her childy fear of loss, fear of aloneness, fear of her own fascination with death, in a bourgeois milieu that values only the accoutrements of social positioning, commonsensical practicality and properness and proportion, in a belle-epoque world that is asleep to a berserk crazy-wild hopeless naked occult flame of the *esprit* that burns and blisters the bones of this repressed agitated woman for whom nature itself could provide no comfort, and who blunders on in a void toward some freakish future where only the slide unto death has any meaning or consolation?

- And will you take cream, monsieur? A moustachioed waiter at the Cafe Royale leans over the pale yellow tablecloth separating the lunch pair. His unctual manner prompts them both to smile discreetly. Dust and Anna Blum are unchaperoned this day, and the atmosphere between them seems natural. Both discover that together they create a sort of cocoon of irony; for her a welcome relief from the loneliness of her bony abrasive life, for him a holiday from his penance in the cellars. Has he apprised her yet of his actual occupation? The answer is yes. And simply by saying so, he offers her a frame for her own grand rebellion against the flesh. Today to reward him she actually nibbles at something resembling a cake. She has also tossed a dash of red (a scarf) over her accustomed black. Taste of red-bloodedness perhaps? Her long knees protrude with slight absurdity under their cosy table, as do her clumpy buckled shoes, and he neglects to let himself be embarrassed by it. For (the former) Dust is a man who feels compassion for all those idiocies and embarrassments of the world that he is not required by God to participate in. Poor Anna must never be allowed to seem a spinster, sipping her tea in gorgeous places like this. Dust requires her to be a sort of strange girlfriend cum sister - and in this understanding they can relax in their cocoon of irony. Anna Blum thinks on how she was shudderingly amazed at Dust's audacity in posing as a lavatory attendant, albeit at the Palais Garnier, and while she wonders 'what it says about one's mother and her attitude to me that she should introduce me to a man suspected of being a cleaner of a public convenience', Anna dimly senses that the protection of a haute bourgeoise upbringing might have its advantages. No matter, the two of them fall to enjoying their lunch in the company of the great and stuffy and pretentious and fashionable and falsely gay, here inside the Café Royale. And this elegant pink-silver room sends them on a ride of fancy into the occult and metaphysic, spiced by an otherworldly thrill of insolent rebellion amid the clink of spoons and teacups.

- You see, Anna, the thought that we are all mortal, that we are going to die, that all is waste, that we are eternal victims of change, always swept away, crying out in this vale of tears, seeking with hawk-like eyes the confirmation of our worst fears as we rush headlong toward the exit-tunnel of the void… is really *just a thought*
- A demanding one, no doubt

- We are creatures of habit, and we cling to thoughts, gather them up till they create a coherent narrative, something we can live by
- So a better narrative would be: we should seek a state that ends narrative altogether...
- True. How's this: we are eternal, so *don't worry about a thing*
- But if we practise *that* thought, then a thousand and one little fears will start to creep and knock at the door and catch us unawares and breathless, desperate to make us return to the old state of panic and dejection and self-sorrow
- But a thought is really *just* a thought, no matter how repetitive it is. This is surely the basis of all self-therapy - replacing one undesirable thought with another more desirable
- Can we go beyond thought?
- There is a thing indeed, that is forever beyond thought - and this is the Eternal. The remainder is: we must play the game of time and consequence and death, even though we are simultaneously deathless
- Where do we go?
- Nowhere
- Do we evolve?
- Not at all. So we might *relax*
- I do like you, mister lavatory cleaner
- And I appreciate you, miss cadaver aged twenty-two. ...Have you thought of Buddhism?
- There is something beguiling and beautiful about the East
- Mmm, all that *denial*
- And all that mushy *atonement*. In toilet basements. For sins imagined by *thought*. (She raises her eyebrow in quite a charming way) ...Who are we running from?
- You from Mummy, Me from the Masters Upstairs.
(A pause) - I'd marry you if you asked me, mister Dust
(Another pause) - I see how you take a risk in saying that. I'll think about it. I promise
- I might even eat cake, for your sake
- Now now Anna, don't do anything radical.
Thus, thin Anna Blum smiles at her new man, and sips her tea.

Glut and Lack

The present-day Dust, to fulfill his Contract must send dispatches to the Employer - in all their potential revealingness and embarrassingness. Though writing comes easily to him, he is understandably loath to report every little episode. His conscience finally wraps itself in a satiric but mournful tone of philosophic conjecture, akin to what we just read. He knows it'll disappoint the Boss - and it takes courage to persist with a man who takes precise steps to ridicule one's effort. Dust visualises the Employer pursing his lips and binning his file with a long-fingernailed mouse-tap. Shut up and do the WORK, he'll say. How sadly absurd are one's employees! What topic to please the Employer then, beyond atonements in underground toilets, shenanigans in past lives? Back to the List. Let's try this: *The Slavery of Glut and Lack.*

'...Since third-world countries are flooded with cheap junk food by the noble effort of multinationals to feed the impoverished classes, children everywhere - victims in the wombs of badly-nourished mothers who themselves sweated through an infancy of lack and need - are suddenly assailed by a river, a flood, an ocean, of fatty sugarious calorific burgerific cokified chocolated meaty processed sludge. And being human, they cannot resist. Twin devils called Glut and Lack, hitherto locked in deadly war inside a billion stomachs, cement their evil pact. The child grows up and balloons, slowly drowns in her own fat, is trapped in the cage of obesity, is harrassed by demons of diabetes and heart disease and cancer. The poor are now impressively fat, no longer skinny, but are victims still. Low self-esteem and depression follow, like night follows day. As civilisation develops apace, these are the diseases of progress. Still, at least we're faithful consumers who imbibe the dream. At least we contribute...

Messrs. Slobbe and Moon and Hippo sit thigh to thigh on their sofa in the underworld bottom flat of the Staan Building on Fernino Street, and think dully of the same woman (who trades under the name 'Blondie'). Slobbe flicks off some turgid TV doc on Third World Food and rubs his copious stomach. 'My Blondie's a real lap dancer!' He copped it sweet with this chick after the boys home-hired her for a sex party. That time, the fifteen-stone girly paraded about in nothing but a blond wig. The name stuck. But Blondie's nobody's floozie: her previous (drooling) victim, Hippo, third wheel in the Slobbe-Moon-Hippo brigade, didn't get over her neever. He's now keen to muscle back into his old flat after being ejected by Slobbe and Moon in a recent coup dey flat. And bugger it, he's 'ere again. Slothful slow-brained Slobbe, sconced on his sofa thinks vaguely of how to chuck out *both* Hippo and Moon and get Blondie to himself, just as Moon thinks sloppily of teaming up with Hippo 'gainst Slobbe etcetera… The chances of any of 'em making their claim stick are zero. One big thing these stooges have in common (besides Blondie, low self-esteem and failure) is… they like to *eat*. Here's the real ground for co-existence. The flat's a miracle of squalor resembling those rubbish-filled places on the TV news where dead bodies are found by neighbours after years of rotting. A sort of fat kudos is to be had here, bogan pride at being a dweller in this porridge mess. And being there awhile you start to regard it as a kind of sloven's artwork and you let it all be. At that point you become a settled-in team member. And let us not leave out *Sir Boris* the fat hairless dog. The humans joke that he's got multiple heads, but these are a result of the congealed personae of his several masters. Being even portlier than the humans, he's set up as scapegoat, or scape-dog. How do fat fuckers value their own worth? In their capacity to punish something fatter, is the answer. Sir Boris looks like a grinning sausage wrapped in tripe with a toothpick at each corner. Not pretty and he knows it. Veteran of many idle boots, it's hard to say whether punishment produced his horrid schizoid nature or the reverse. Mind you, maybe he enjoys to be booted and hollered at. Makes him feel important, loved even. But revenge is sweet when laughing-stock morphs into 'hell-hound'. Boris has a trick of getting open the lid on the all-important freezer in the basement and desecrating the contents by licking at a frozen bit for hours, gobbling it up then vomiting it in a corner of a bedroom. One time he flew at the neck of Slobbe's friend Fungus, took a bite out of him and sent him to hospital. Fungus nearly died of blood loss. Apparently Boris was avenging Slobbe for 'Blondie losing her fragile honour' at the hands of Fungus. That dog's seen it all. Low-life experience clings to him like ticks and fleas.

Dust enters his own narrative at the point where he stands before the Door of the three stooges at the very base of the dirty-rundown but imposing Staan Building on Fernino Street. Dust composes a face and knocks. There follows a skitter of feet along a passage and the raucous barking of a dog. Sir Boris claims to be in charge until the sound of a boot splatting his flesh and a whelping howl puts paid to this notion. 'Git out of it! It's the pizza guy, ya little shit!' The door swings wide, and here's the fellow Dust will shortly learn to be Slobbe, master of the 'ouse. There's a strange smell from within, like a hellish collusion of ten thousand farts. *Brought our dinner then?* The dog snarls by his master's feet. Dust notes a huge grubby green T-shirt, eye drooping slightly over a treble chin in which are embedded the hairy survivors of some mutilating shave. For some reason he wears shorts above knees that seem to fold downward in gloopy cascades. A pudgy red mitt grips the doorframe and he wheezes. - *Er,* says Dust. This is the moment where Dust wonders if his Employer supplied the wrong address, knows he hasn't and hates him for it. *Triple ham n' sausage steak and egg pizza with extra sausage etcetera? That's us.* Dust looks at Slobbe's little eyes, seeing far into dungeon-tunnels through which light never seeps. *Er, er no - not yet. But I'll get it for you,* Dust hears himself say. Slobbe wheezes like a bellows. - *Errr, we lost your order, and er I had to come and check it. That is, we lost your number.* Dust makes this up right on the spot. *Shall I come back in a few minutes?* In canyon-deep corridors of his head of meat, Slobbe appears to process this. – *Roight, 'urry up then.* Dust backs away and the dog comes at him, sputtering and snarling. - *Git in the 'ouse!* burbles the green man. Boris gives Dust the evil eye. - *I'll bite yer balls off, cunt,* it says. Dust backs away to the street, wondering where the nearest pizza joint might be. Chop up that *dog* and pizza-ise it, is his next thought. But Dust has not far to look. A mere four doors down Fernino Street is Welk and Co, purveyors of best pie and mash to the Queen, and undoubtedly the fount of all sustenance in the house of Slobbe and Co. Behind fogged windows the great junk menu looms above a steel counter, and several spatter-aproned men and women fist great piles of chips into bubbling lakes of battery oil, scoop it out, slubber it onto plains of white paper, top-dress it in rains of salt and slomp it over the counter to cries of: - Six 'addock an' scoops, forty steakburgers, two 'undred 'otdog fritters, four 'undred litres of coke. 'Ank you, sir. Next! And the lines of proles on the dirty lino raise their heads in hope that this order could be *their* treasure, the parcel they'll snatch up then skitter home through slimy brick streets to their hovels, hunters home with the kill, ready to feed their keening young with the fat-nectar of the good life. But the line merely shuffles obedient inside the shop, in this ornery damp-tired Monday evening in the rubbishy city. Dust stands in line, puts in his order as far as he can remember the words of Slobbe. And (creative touch) - a pile of chips on the 'ouse, guv'nor. Pizza guy at the far end shovels doughy pads into his hell-oven's maw. Dust receives his goods, fists an inexact money mound on the counter, ducks back out to brick-cold streets. Why the hell am I doing this? he asks himself again. At the bottom of the cavernous stairwell of the Staan building, Dust finds the door slightly ajar. He calls out. Where's the damnable dog? The sound of television burbles from within. And *that smell*. His nostrils for the first time apprehend its content: cocktail of socks and jocks and fat and gravy and batter and sweat and dog odour and sick and tobacco and staley beer and dust and breath and lowlife farty bedsheet bog-roll underpants... begins to append itself to his nasal cavity like sulphurous wind from a crematorium. The first dose is the keenest, richest, most poignant; and from thereon his soul begins to assimilate its strange sullied romance. For in the midst of anything - be it ever so evil, ever so sinful - a human being will *adapt*. This is the way of the world.

Dust takes up the tale: 'I'm in the hallway... From the back comes the sound of a flushing toilet. A youngish woman appears, waddling heavily on stilettos in my direction. Her bumpy thighs bulge under a leather mini, and yellowy blond hair is coifed upwards in a big mound. The lidded eyes are saucery, there are heavy rouged lips, and she walks with insouciant grandiosity like a woman whose body might be a public convenience, or a public picnic.
- 'Ullo sailor
I can't believe she said that. - Oh hi there. I brought your friends their dinner
- Yah. Bring it right in. You staying? More the merrier

- Uh…

- I'm Barbara. Blondie or Barbie if you like. (I offer a flaccid hand) - Mmm, a gent. You look all right. Bit of a spunk in yer quiet way? 'Come see me some time'. Unless you're a ponce. Not that I mind.

She comes close, thrusts her chest toward me. I inhale a cloying scent. Her fleshy be-ringed fingers linger.

- This way, sweetie.

I follow the swishy backside up to a red door. She flings it, rather theatrically. A TV blares.

- Fellers! Meet muh new *playmate.*

She points at me, framed in the doorway. At least four pairs of eyes lurch in my direction. I step uneasily forward, place the food on a low table strewn with cans and other rubbish.

- Hey there guys. Personal delivery.

Green-shirted Slobbe on the sofa curls his lip. - 'Bout time.

Another fellow with a moon-face as wide as a dinner plate, says: - Oo're you?

- Er, I'm Dust. I deliver Pizzas

- We c'n see that, says another big bloke in a crumbly armchair. - We c'n see it

- I invited him for a bite, says Blondie.

- Why? says Slobbe.

- Like the look of him, don't I. Looks intelligent. Polite and all. Ain't you, mister Dust?

- 'Z not havin' moi share, says the chair-guy.

- 'E won't ask, Hippo. He's sharin' mine

- *Grrrrr.* (The fat ugly dog seems keen to be involved as well)

- 'Old yer 'orses, Boris. (says Moon-face) - What we got then?

- Er, pizzas, fish and chips, sauce, coke. All good stuff. Heh heh.

Blondie mutes the TV, passes the grub about. Nobody lifts a finger. Her ample arse manoeuvres with studied care and all eyes watch it.

- Sit here with me, Dust.

And she feeds me herself. Dulcet sounds of chomping fill the room. Hippo's beady little eyes bore into me at intervals. Slobbe blinks at Blondie and mechanically stuffs matter in his mouth. Moon's face is fixed in a grin.

There's calculation in there somewhere. Boris's bloody green eyes glare at me as if I'm to be dessert. I don't eat much. Blondie notes it but says nothing.

- 'E don't eat much, says Moon, and belches.
- Keepin' his weight down, says Blondie. - You might take a leaf out of 'is book
- I ain't as fat as Hippo and Slobbe
- You ain't as pretty either
- Fuckin' bullsh-
- Stow it, Moonie. She's right, sorta (says Slobbe). We're all fat and fucken ugly. Blondie baby, go to the freezer and get us ice cream will ya. Two tubs. And some six-packs.
- Come with me Dust, says Blondie. They all glare at her. - Boys! I can't carry it all.

She and I exit the room, poked in the back by several pairs of eyes. She leads me to a low door at the very end of the apartment. We descend narrow steps. Her heels click on the concrete. She flicks on a light.
- Don't worry 'bout that lot. All jealous. Bark's worse than their bite. And not a decent-sized whanger between 'em. (She grins at me in the gloom)
- But you, you're pretty nice. Know quality when I see it... Wanna quick little fuck while we're down 'ere? No charge.

My mouth goes dry. Jesus! I'm actually aroused. When she says it, wildness seems as natural as breathing. She leans on a hip and waits. - *No, look. I'm er, fine. Better get the stuff.* She grazes my cheek with her finger. - *Suit yourself. Only a matter of time though eh, hot boy?* She turns away.
- *Beer's in that cooler. Ice cream in the big box.* There is a tall fridge against the wall and a great heavy-looking horizontal freezer beside it. I fumble about. She leans in and shoves me lightly with her crotch. - *Come along, Dusty.* I actually put my hands about her hips. Lush breasts beckon at my face... but she slithers away, clicks up the steps. And I follow, a cold tub in each hand.

Upstairs, the Footy Game That Never Ends burbles on the tele. Slobbe and Moon and Hippo suck on beer and slurp ice cream, and scungy Boris gets to shove his snout in half-empty tubs. Moon lights a dirty big cigar and waves it about. Is he mentally defective? After half an hour Blondie beckons me to the kitchen. It's a bomb-site too. We start to clear up.

- How d'you put up with it all?
- Free rent. Big tips for sex times three. Get used to it. The stink I mean. Maybe I wouldn't live anywhere else. Got no standards. Professional fucking losers, us
- Hail to those who add no value to the world
- What?
- Nothing. Poetry. No standards, eh?
- Don't tempt me to raise my bar, little boy. And maybe I should kick you out right now. But I'm human and I'm female. And you want me, right? (I look at her) Don't fool yourself, I'm fucking hot. And not as stupid as I come across
- I get it. You're not stupid at all. Where's the money come from?
- Slobbe's a forklift driver. Hippo works in some bakery. Moonie claims he makes dough playin' stocks and shares. Don't believe it. Drug-dealing more like
- They share you?
- Yeah, but one at a time. Plenty of room for a rugby team in here, mind. (She slips a finger over her crotch) Plus the back end
- Not a recipe for disaster?
- Sure is. Hippo wants to kill the other two but maybe he's too stupid. Takes it out on me. And I let him, yeah. Shocked? Don't be, 'cos the others 'll wanna rescue me. We get rid of Hip, an' I manage on two for a while. For a price. Then I go off with Hip someplace else and they come chasing. Fuckin' misery for all. Can't avoid it: I'm such a hot fat she-bitch, whadya gonna do?
- Why don't they all lose weight, scrub up, shape up, compete for you at a higher level?
- 'Cause we're actually one big happy slut family.

What does her tone say? Bitter irony or longing? I'll bet both. To compete for the lower depths, to drill for degradation paydirt, might be some humans' only claim to being special. And degradation wants so much more of itself. It's our dick drug, cunt drug, stomach drug, lung drug, degraded organ drug, ugliness drug. It's a dirty dirty aphrodisiac.

Suddenly I'm keen to be off. But Slobbe trundles in. Frowns at us chatting at the sink.

- Er, you can er - come over termorrer. We're doin' prawns. An' there's a thing on the tele. 'Bout animals in jungles.

Blondie goes to Slobbe and runs her fingers over his elephantine neck. They look at me, big unwieldy pair blocking the doorway. *Yeah, come tomorrow,* she says.

I fail to tell them I won't.

* * * *

It's termorrer. We're all sconced round the TV. Moon delivers some quips at others' expense.

- Waddya fink of the animals, Dusty? We like watching 'em eat each other. 'Specially hippos. Right, fatso? (No-one reacts) So where'd you get yer name, Dusty?

- I thought it up. It's ironic. Can't expect a man of thirty-five to be free of vanity. Though some might accuse me of lacking aspiration

- Who's accusing ya?

- My employer, possibly. He's my bigger conscience. Or rather I dump my conscience on him

- Yer a slave, mate. Make yer own decision!

Upon Moon's pontifications, Boris growls and bares his teeth like a Greek chorus.

- Why? I admit I have my issues and someone has to point them out. I don't like it, but we have to learn any way we can, right?

Slobbe peers at me. - So this employer bloke. He the head pizza guy, is he?

- Er, actually I've another job as well. In this other job the top guy asks me to 'help people', sort of. Get them on their feet. He's some kind of philosopher or social worker. Weird guy!

Moon narrows his slitty eyes. Hippo grins. - Sounds fucken weird

- He's very tricky, yeah. Puts me in all sorts of situations.

Blondie chimes in. - Like this one maybe?

- Uhhh no, this is some kind of serendipity. Accident, I mean. This is my pizza job.

Hippo farts loudly, flicks the TV volume up.

- Give it a rest, Fatso! says Slobbe. – Dust 'ere is *talkin'*. So what would he say, this bloke, about fat-arse losers like us?

- Oh no, he values everyone's pathway, everyone's choice

- He's a fuckin' loony then

- Nah, but Dusty's just itchin' to tell us what's what. (This Moon-guy is a real menace)

Blondie deposits herself conspicuously on Slobbe's lap and the others glare.

- We sure like to hear about other weirdos besides us. Don't we Slobbie? Dusty darling, tell us what he'd say if he was here now. Go on!

- Yeah. Spill it, Dust.

- I don't want to bore anyone... (Moon curls his lip) and I know we all have our issues. But he might say: What does it mean to be *alive*? We're all mostly blocked up. Dull notions, dull habits, junky food. And we repeat ourselves over and over, claim we want it to change, want it to be better but we're too lazy to do anything. We totally identify with the body. We fear that if the body dies then everything's gone. But aren't we more than just mobile sewers? Don't we admit that human beings exist mostly in their minds anyway? And that's good 'cause mind isn't 'fat', it takes up no space! Ha ha. (Everyone glares) ...So why eat and eat till we're bone ugly, even when we know it? We don't have the guts to live fully or freely. We let the slime in. Maybe our parents kicked our arses so often we just passed it down the line, automatic-like. We don't think about it. And we all have our story: depression, sadness, shredded self-esteem, loneliness, failure, loss, lack... Lack of what? Love. Not being noticed. And we're jealous at all those 'trim taut terrific' types. And we hate, we wanna destroy... But our death-wish is really a life-wish! And if we want to pick up the chicks... we might wanna slim down, go to the gym, feel better about ourselves... (They all stare) Yeah I know, my boss is kind of tough! I get in the firing line myself. Sorry people. Raving too much.

Blondie rescues. - There's a smidge of truth in all that, don't ya think, boys? We should listen

- If it was his own speech we might, mutters Moon.

- Yeah, made it all up, says Hippo.

Slobbe cuts in. - You dunno shit, Hippo. But then we're all too fucken thick. Bring that bloke round some time, mate. I'll feed 'im a keg or two, see what 'e sez *then*. Hey Blondie, let's you and me go to my room and 'discuss philosophy'. An' Dusty, come roun' termorrer. We'll 'ear another speech. Areeverderchy, gennlemen!

Blondie winks to me. - Bye, Dusty. See ya tomorrow.

The pair exit with hands clutching each other's backsides. Folks in this house are practised at winding each other up! Hippo turns up the TV loud. I don't hang round. And that fangy goggle-eyed Boris with his knobbly claws, dogs my heels as I head down the corridor.'

A couple of visits later, Dust turns up to hear from Blondie that the three fat tweedles have gone out to the Pig and Pauper, their local drinking hole. She wasn't invited to tag along. Are they giving her the shoulder because Dust's hanging about? You could be the last straw in our relationship, says Blondie. This makes Dust feel at ease. She invites him into her little cell. There's nothing but a bed. She comes in close in her fleshy white blouse and bulgy thighs and lips. Dust with sandpaper throat hints this might not be so clever, but she's a pro and knows where he's at, so lightly suggests they smoke a bit of meth first. Moon's the man I get it from, she says. It'll put us in the mood, no mistake. Dust has the sense there's a bit of a set-up... and he feels like not caring a damn. In the service of the Church, right? She pulls out a little pipe and they fill the cell with smoke. Dust loses the plot in the fog and haze. Following on, she smoothly gets him to fill her up as well. Full as a sow before I even grocked it! she says after. She smiles sweetly. Blame it on the meth. Her tongue is loosened. One bit where she says she 'knows Dust has a lot of dough but she'll never take advantage'... has him pondering. (Where'd she get the idea I have money?) He hears a squeaky creak in the corridor. Must be the dog, she says. In their cuddle bed she tells her stories. 'It was my wee thing as a kid to burrow down deep in my bed... I'd tuck in layers of blanket, maybe eight or nine, and leave an opening in each layer at both ends so I could crawl in a zigzag down down till I got to the mattress. I'd hide in my underworld cave of muffly silence and wonder if the big parent world out there 'd ever notice. I felt solitude, a kind of ending - and a feeling of itchy possibility, risk. I wanted to not be a child any more - but be a child forever'. This big girl's not stupid, thinks Dust. I'm gonna end up liking her. 'The fatsos 'll all be sucking up to you now sweetie. You're top of the heap', she says through soft-parted lips. Dust asks her if she plans to exit this dunghill, get a life. She tells him: Who are you to tell me I don't have one? Fair enough, he says. So they 'do it' again, this time involving her back end, because they can. Her eyes start to shine. You fit good, she whispers. See what a saint I am? Dust is careful to thank her. Despite her profession it's strangely innocent. Anybody tell me what's wrong with totally letting go? she says. Dust agrees. Time passes. He sees they are pretty slimy, suggests they get up, go out. She lets him guide, pliant as can be. At the front door Boris leers and snorts at them, but they pass into the night. It's raining. Down at the Pig and Pauper which she comes upon 'by happenstance' and pulls him into in her strap heels and sheer fur and half-bare arse, him half-proud at being her louche guy - with her densely calling out to the Slobbe brigade in their booth, who seem unsurprised (which Dust doesn't grock, drug-distracted as he is, and by the fug and the crowd), and the couple of shady girls hanging out with the Slobbe team, their table smothered in jugs and cigs and chips and shit... the next act of the little drama begins. Mister Moon gives a big smile like he wouldn't trust Dust as far as he could chuck him off a cliff. Dust is stonedly civil in return. *Treachers* exhibit the deepest need, he muses to himself. Well hell, Blondie is Moon's keeper, not him.

- What'd youze two get up to tonight, Blondie?
- Us? We had a philosophic conversation, Moonie
- Hear that, Hippo? Philosophik conversation.

The ladies at the table look at each other. Dust watches the black window behind their heads streak with rain. The blokes have evidently had a lot of drink by volume. Which no doubt exacerbates their several personalities. The chicks aren't fat, in fact they're quite shapely, clearly well paid. Blondie sure won't mix with them. She sits by Dust and fondles his hand under the table. It's alarming how Dust neglects to see what's coming next.

- I reckon, I *reckon*, (slobbers Moon) that this guy's got a load of dough. An' I reckon 'e don't pay one cent for his 'up-keep'. I reckon if yer payin' for goods and services yer don't expect 'em to be raked up by some other *bastard*.
The last word comes out with a spit and a hiss.
- Steady. Steady as she goes, says Slobbe.
- Wot's that? blubbers Hippo. - Stole? Stole fucken what?
- *Fuck off,* Moon. Fuck off all of yers, says Blondie.
The floozies stand up.
- Siddown, bitches. You can learn from this.

Moon has a jug in his fist. Dust goggles at him. Blondie's on her feet. Slobbe puts a heavy paw on Dust's chest, all protective like those cops who tried to look shocked when Lee Oswald got shot. Hippo jumps up, the table tips, he grabs Dust, pulls him sideways. Moon's jug clangs into Blondie's face, splattering content over the window. Dust is on the floor under the big guy. Hippo thumps him repeatedly in the face, shoves his knee in his genitals. Dust throws up with a lurch. Probably it's Slobbe who pulled Hippo off. Dust wouldn't know. There's screaming and cursing above. Table-edge comes down on Dust's neck and he's covered in detritus. Blondie falls on him. Apparently Moon runs for it and Hippo punches Slobbe, knocks a tooth out, runs for the street as well. The chicks are gone. Bouncers are there. Slobbe is shouting at them and gargling blood. Someone pulls Dust upright. He finds himself outside. Rain is bucketing down. He can hardly stand or walk. Slobbe takes hold, bundles him away down Fernino Street. In a certain alley Slobbe is attacked in turn; a 'large blond woman' now totters away, heels clattering, bottle dropping from her hand and splittering on the cobbles. The fat guy lies in a pile of rubbish, great bulgy head nestled in a greasy mound. Dust subsides into the gutter's brown streaming slush. Cold water soaks him through. Doesn't get up for a long time. Crawls home later sometime. Doesn't have a clue how.

The content of this episode in the dirty realm of the senses, is scantily reported to his Employer. For personal reasons.

The World of Anna Rex

'Never before had Anna Rex intimated to me where she lived, let alone invited me to dinner. Our relationship in the Divinology Church was somewhat casual since she and I co-inhabited a metaphysic sphere like seabirds over an ocean, our physical encounters confined to slightly strained esotericisms in the thaw after winters of silence in the meditation hall. Strain seems an apt word for the vibe of Anna Rex in her vice-like embrace of silent peace. I, Dust, have seen similar symptoms among many students of the esoteric (though I don't reflect on my own emotional status under ascetic draughts). The strain comes from this: how do we yoke the worldly and the unworldly? If you want to carry your hard-won silence into the world like a monk into a marketplace, you will invariably get a hefty shock. Each day you must take a conscious careful step out of the silence and into the noise, must straddle the ghostly and the corporeal, spurn impersonal blankness for the messy chaotic icky quotidian. This discourages gung-ho young players, but after a time even they realise that the universe is so infinitely unfathomably abrasive that our little silence is of no interest to it. Travellers in the void long to self-annihilate, and it makes of us schizophrenics to squander our absorption in the oceanic winds of life. And yet we also want to *live*. What mortal doesn't? But no mortal can see the face of God and live! We must therefore fool ourselves. In the foyer outside the silence-chamber we chat furtively over green tea. It's like having a ciggy outside the exam hall. Generally there's Anna and me or one or two other angular, weedy student-cum-helper types. Meditators live a life of which outsiders see nothing, and glazed years go by on the outside, like waves rolling in forever to a lonely coast. And maybe nothing ever happens except some fickle sense of inner progress, of sniffing a distant dream, of creeping forward hour upon hour toward some promised garden far away over a desert, a journey so personal and lonely that it is a wonder human beings can find any justification for it. We're like mysterious birds who migrate to far pavilions without the shadow of knowing why. Me, I claim to know why, in my poised intellect. (We're merely longing, and are forever gone.) And in these places and spaces designated 'spiritual' we wayfarers huddle together, rub bony shoulders, whisper of our thousandmile quests. What is there to say where silence is our language? Still, we talk because we're social beasts: we're complainers, needers, feelers of feelings; we're children, we're humans.

Anna Rex as a woman is all head and intellect, all bone and no flesh, and her angulated body speaks for itself. I don't comment, but know that every ounce of love she puts into thought is an ounce taken from her fleshly breast. Deep self-punishment, the ascetic pathway abandoned by Buddha himself, is her last cry against god. In women it is a refuge against nurture. Anna's peculiar bent, her bete grise, her perennial cold sore, her dry itch - is to accentuate the negative about herself. It's the only way to improve, she says. Meanwhile her ironic best is the microscopic attention she pays to *others'* health through spindly cures and pin-pointy remedies, directed at the most arcane possible level of theoretical health. And none of it involves putting food down your gullet, just so we're clear. She's the fierce carer who puts no tickets on herself. But when a person *hates,* we are bound to ask: what's the cause? Aren't we safe? Aren't we connected? Aren't we good enough? And why has she this night resolved to offer me a health-giving repast in her apartment? I suspect over time I've passed a subtle trust-test, perhaps by not reacting too pointedly to her abrasive ways. Perhaps she thinks I am steadfast. If I am, pity makes me so.

When I discover myself standing at the entrance to the Staan Building on Fernino Street, I'm moved to wonder at the magnetic strangeness of the world. You will recall this is the place where reside certain other tormented souls within the ambit of the Divinology Church. The lift is out of order, and I must ascend cold steps to the seventh floor. The bulbs at the landings flicker when I press the button then quickly fade like lamps in a mine. The walls are of double stripe: deep slime-green and dry-blood magenta. Doors shiffle by... and what do they hide? What secrets, privacies, estrangements, furtive knowings, silences, revelations, decay or hope ignored, life whispered, death sensed, ghosts of dwellers past and gone? The city whispers without, and a building sweats its secrets. Floor seven then. Anna's door. A weird notion pokes at me: am I the only man ever to enter here?

The little flat is spartan. Unkempt rows of books line walls which elsewhere support a desultory art-poster or two. A glimpse to the boudoir reveals a lone bed. There's a faint musty smell, her private odour. My host this evening though, is energetic: nervously sweetly conspiratorial, she enshrouds you in whatever is her latest obsession. All neurotically entertaining, and my role is clearly to tag along as spectator.

- Naturally Dust, we don't need any *church* per se, but I suppose these stolid rituals in our lives serve as pointers to the ineffable
- True. The forever ghost-dance of Being and Becoming must run its course
- Correct. So what is identity? Foucault avers there is no individual separate from his acts
- And yet who is it that is conscious of those acts?
- The Self is but a made-up idea, a vortex, a centre formed by magnetic force of acts, needs, desires. It is the detritus of experience swirling around a centre of memory. The all-pervading consciousness merely appears to individualise - by the force of personal journeyings, of 'yours' and 'mine'
- True again. And yet the self persists, saying 'this is me', and 'this is not me'. It is a *feeling* that can never go away. For instance, am I this seaweed casserole?
- I detect your aversion to seaweed casserole, Dust
- And I detect yours
- No no. I take nourishment from the enjoyments of others
- *If* they enjoy it, that is… Even better when *you* eat it too
- I shall, I shall
- What's food when *identity* is at stake, eh Anna?
- Quite. Derrida proved there's no personal identity that can't be deconstructed, since all identities are mere discourses and paradigms that feed themselves, producing a 'world' according to their own lights
- Yeah, I know that line: that positing a 'truth' begs all things *not* included in that truth, and that therefore invalidate it. Dot creates infinitude. Centre

creates margin. Subject creates object. Dualism proves non-existence. Yadda yadda. Will you *eat* something?

- I eat! I eat knowledge. I eat experience. I eat love. I eat strife and peace and horror and past and memory and desire. I eat a billion things. My unconscious mind has swallowed universes! And it bloats, and feeds me endless stupid dreams at night. But is there space for simplicity? Space for purity? Emptiness? Is there space for *me*?

- But you may be a victim of extremes, the victim of a duality-discourse. One that tacitly accepts *binaries*: complication versus simplicity, glut versus emptiness, dirty versus clean, alien versus self

- I certainly am no victim!

- Who the hell puts 'I' at the beginning of every sentence?! You do. And who the hell are 'you'?

- As I said, Foucault's and Derrida's -

- Bullshit to that

- Don't get upset, Dust. Mmm, this casserole is pretty good. You'll note I cooked it with my own hands. Yum

- I suppose I worry about you

- But don't! I have nothing to live for

- Karma. Can't wriggle out that easily

- Karma is an illusion kept in place by our fixation with it

- We all have a deep past, and we all have a deep future, so to speak. Sure, there never was anything but *now,* and now has no existence either... *But you... Anna Rex*

(She likes the flattery) - A mere name. Concatenation of ghost-atoms

- Yes, but a living breathing *being* who feels and knows and experiences, and who *collects* experience like iron filings to a magnet, and who cannot help doing so

- Because she has an ego. And ego must be erased

- But ego is also illusion. Am I right? *Who says* ego must be erased?

- The Self

- *You,* in other words.

Pause. The widowy woman gazes at me. - But are you going to fuck me, Dust?

(What?) - Errr... don't know

- You know it's why I asked you here! But I don't need your baby all at once. I want your cock and your tongue inside me first. At least one time. I want you! I'm not 'empty' at all. I have needs. Help me! But am I too thin for you? Should I eat for you, should I *gorge* for you? Shall I be your Rubens woman? Because I need to get another baby-life inside me, so that I can run away from the facts of my *own*. I want to perpetuate this rubbish-tip life forever! Must do my bit to perpetuate the ignorance of the human race. I must, I must!

This girl is *intense*. She really should eat more. It glues the brain cells together.

- All right Anna. You win. (Pause. We look at each other) I tell you, you win

- No Dust. I don't. But just stop telling me what I need. Now, let's talk about my toilet. I need it looked at. Can you fix toilets? After that I need to talk about the Church

- As you like

- Or perhaps you love me, Dust. Why come here otherwise?

- To fix your bog, apparently

- If you *really* loved me, you'd take note of my new reform effort. Because I *see* the error of my ways. I see how I alienate myself from the common weal. I am often ill. I vomit liquid. I shall vomit later. I am my own victim. Do you think I don't see it all, Dust? Do you think I haven't been told? And I *will* pass away. I know it

- Don't do that

- But I will, Dust. And why? Because I *am* a victim. I must play the victim. Because it is my stairway to heaven

- Who was the evil bad guy? Daddy or Mummy?

- No, nothing so simple. You and I must talk about the *Church*

- Don't wanna do that, Anna

- But you do. Because you came to my apartment. And you ate my food. And I want your baby

- Like hell you do. Lemme look at your toilet instead…

Anna Rex has her weird ways, as you can see. Before I get out of there that night at around two, and after she's plied me with claggy wine and made me drink it dry, she informs me that *the Employer was her lover.* For many months in fact. That she submitted to him in the best of faith believing that he had her deep interests at heart. Until, I glean, he took another lover. As you do. Though there's scant evidence of all this. But what is evidence when we need to create a reality-bed for ourself and need to lie in it? The golden rule: that the closer you get to the Employer and the more special you appear to him the more he will shaft you, do you over, gouge your impurities, bore at your karma like a drill into rock - may be lost on the woman Anna Rex. Hell hath no fury like a woman scorned! No doubt she plans to exploit my own ambivalence toward the church. But then why would she need my help or advice since she's already the immortal soul of emptiness? Speaking of *victims,* there are phobias that lurk in the dread depths of the psyche that bubble to the surface like methane gas from the bowels of the earth, that we (and others) cannot fail to inhale and get addled by. For Jews like Anna we assume the *Shoah* plus centuries of Ejection to be the cause of everything. But does it matter what the historic cause is? There is not a person on the earth who has not suffered Rejection, suffered the Abjection that is the true beginning of self-reflection, that is the beginning of a long crawl out of the night, out of the consuming holes of human unconsciousness... from the lowest, called shame, into guilt, into apathy, then grief, fear, desire, anger, pride; then on to courage, to neutrality, to willingness, to acceptance, to reason, to love; and at last to joy, to peace, to enlightenment... Such is Anna's dedication to the arts of rejection and abjection, she has relegated her own Jewishness to a historical accident. Such trifles as History she thrusts aside. Instead she wants to talk about *trust* - about how I am to be her chosen watcher, her mentor, the aide to her *future,* in her grand crusade back to health and healthy eating. For some people 'the measure of their development is the gap between the simple guileless wish and sneaky reality'. In other words, they lie. But perhaps I am too hard on her. The progress of a soul is like a great ragged army on the march: at the front are knights and generals resplendent in finery, who with fearless eye and valiant arm face the oncoming future with unshakeable firmness. And in the middle are foot soldiers whose weal is unglamorous, repetitive, plodding, who march to the unknown destination with heads lowered, communing with myriad aches and woes in the dull privacy of their breathing souls. At the rear are the parasitic hangers-on, the also-rans, the low-lifes, flotsam, carrion, prostitutes, thieves, shysters and users who ply their dirty trades oblivious to heroic leadership and noble purpose, miles beyond them on the road. Anna's favoured mouthpiece Derrida must surely have whispered to her of the infinitudinal incomprehensible complexity of life's conglomerated bits and strands and pathways, of the impossibility of gathering any of it into sense, conclusion, tied-up result; and hence of the foolishness of blaming other persons or things for your woes. One may as well blame the wind or the seven seas, or supernovae, or nebulae, or idle talk or thought or birth or feeling or nerves or germs or atoms or dream-shapes or the unutterable unconscious or the lost whispers of lovers and haters ten thousand aeons past… The truth is we are too impersonal, and yet too hopelessly personal. So we really *should not worry about a thing*. And we should eat.

Following the invitation to her boudoir under the guise of exhorting me to mentor her return to ampleness, Anna's real agenda starts to crystallise in the clearness of evil daylight. For she's a clinger, an obsessive, a nice girl who became a hater, an auto-violent who yet wriggles her bony fingers around love she's given up on, an airless soul who gasps: I must suffer more than is speakable so that I may become the Unspeakable, the Clear Light of Truth. She's a phoney ascetic with a bubbling love for the gossippy world, if only she'd admit to it. And now she's singled me out as her touchstone, her whipping boy who'll hold the cat-o-nine-tails that will lash her back to curmudgeonly health. I'm a man with proper flesh on his bones and to me she's a bloody attention-seeker - like all suicides, slow or quick. And I wonder if I can hide my disgust enough to be compassionate, can swallow her quirks enough to become a little influential with her - enough to swipe her out of her narcissistic bleeding and make her slightly *sensible*. And meanwhile, here is her real agenda: to enmesh me in her war against the Employer. The very best person to blame in your life is the one who is the perfect symbolic repository of all that you need to dig up and resolve in yourself. Now if that person had sex with you, thereby showing up your failure at motherhood and your hatred of your own barrenness, showing up your fear of engagement with the great laboratory of life, instead sublimating it to the laboratory of one's *mind* - and then by sitting on one's increasingly bony (not bonny) arse for so long in the effort to chase the dark hooligans of abject repression out of the grinning stadium of your psyche, and forgetting that you are a breathing gobbing shitting pissing crying laughing sensing chattering fool of a human being like everybody *else* - then you will have a million and one reasons to *hate his fucking guts.* As if he were dedicated solely to tricking you into feeling permanently bad about your life! And if you don't eat properly or at all (and if your brain tends to work on the whiff of an oily rag) you will inflate him to the status of devil incarnate, of bete noir, of eternal itch, of bad daddy and cold mummy and horrible husband, on top of treacherous ex-lover. That he might be a clever psychologist holding up a mirror to your own immature face is no longer to be swallowed, considering that in order to grow up one has to reject this embarrassing parental conception in favour of taking responsibility for oneself, and dwell instead in the cavernous cold abjection of one's own honesty. But Anna is suspended on a high wire because she has no mates, no helpers. She has only her *tormentor.* She is doubly abject, and really, she might die. All she has left now is to practise such denial that she whips herself into a superiority complex of such loftily tragical noble proportions that she shall probably starve to death before she greets the dawn. The dark before the dawn - the worstest time. I have long since exited her bed, but Anna Rex needs me now! ...The call comes at six am. Christ. I know who it is before I pick up. The hero in me might be flattered, but he's going to have his hell-ride.

- You know what, Dust? *Sex* is just another *control-trip* for that self-appointed guru in his so-called communal church. Along with criticism and ostracism. Followed by gossip and withholding favours. Systemic attack on our so-called weaknesses. But it's all about subtle conformism to *his* ego. Guess what, we can't have spiritual progress without him! We're just idiots, children! Me, I'm so naïve. And thank god I am. I didn't even question the motives of the guy who invented the *social experiment* I'm a guinea pig in
- Was he self-appointed? We all joined up

- Dust, listen! Look how many people walked out
- People walk out of lots of churches, and usually badmouth the place afterwards
- Do you wanna listen to me or not?
- Sorry. It's six in the morning. I left you four hours ago
- Don't you get up for the five am meditation nowadays?
- Are you kidding?
- And why take me into his bed? Next he'll be saying I *needed* it
- Well, why did you do it?
- Some people do it because they *like* someone
- Come off it. He never does a thing without ten reasons. He wants you to have a spiritual child. You could be flattered. He invested in you
- But we *shouldn't* be flattered, should we Dust? We should be *humble.* Fuck it! I hate fucking men! Especially posing as shitting spiritualists
- Hope you don't include me
- What if I did?
- I'd probably get off the phone
- Don't have a hissy fit. So you're saying I'm barren, I can't conceive - is that it?
- I'm not saying anything
- Typical male. Another fucking cop-out! CLICK.

That was call number one. I suspect I'm about to mislay my mobile. Do I *need* this kind of rough transference? Or might the Employer be dangling both of us by the same string? In the subtle world of spiritual dealings there are a ton of things at play we're barely aware of. If we *were* aware, we wouldn't need to deal with any of it. Here's the perennial trap for egotists (read spiritual students). Need to think we're in control, but never are. If you submit you're possibly holy. But who can do it? Who can be in control of submitting? Catch 22. I said it before: the Employers's strategy is to put you in such a bind that you give up trying to control *anything.* The heat in the kitchen is far too great for most, Anna included. Women don't like it anyway; they need 'love'. We men think we just need discipline. Both sexes are goners (though this is not about sex). Still, it's nice to know Anna is getting *fried.* Makes a change from me. Poor girl though, why so thin? Needs some love on her bones. I'll have to help. Suppose I'll 'ave to get fried too.

Two days later, her next call. More pacific this time. She's had time to cook up new strategems.

- Apologies for pulling your ear off last time, Dust. I know I'm an unstable girl at times, and I really should eat properly. In fact, I started a new meditation that I recall a better teacher taught me. And I've got a new food regimen worked out. Maybe you'll come over and discuss?
- Want me to do your shopping?
- Er, no no. Just come.

I end up at her doorway after bedtime. The strange grating sound of a parrot reaches my ear from a door down the corridor... Anna likes our meetings to be late-late. I assume it's to avoid the morning's clear reality-light. Though I wonder at this woman's ability to glibly self-analyse. She's dressed in some kind of black twenties retro number with tassels. She's also put on succulent make-up, and the effect is sort of Addams Family Flapper. Girls are scary who don't know how to dress. Anyway, pacified with green tea I pay court on the sofa as she glibs her latest.

- It seems to me, Dust, that if I am to resurrect my soul as it were, I should pay attention not only to the stomach but to the emotional self. So I've concluded since we last spoke that no food regimen is going to pay off unless I am at peace within myself. And the reason for any lack of peace despite my best meditational effort - is the little issue of *hypocrisy.*
A cloying wish to disturb her brittleness, wells up on cue. Resist.
- I have in fact written an article for publication. A newspaper and a magazine have shown keen interest. (My brow crinkles involuntarily) *You see,* Dust, you need to listen before you pass judgement! It takes the form - (she sighs) - it takes the form of my journal in which I expose my treatment at the hands of a *cult leader.* Yes Dust, that is what I am calling him. And you wouldn't disagree if you thought about it or were honest about it. The reality is, and here I must swallow pride, is that I was unable to compete against a deeply manipulative mind

- Anna, you're an adult
- All I want is for him to learn, and the public to learn, that his method creates victims, creates casualties. This has to be said!
- I'm not a victim or a casualty
- You fucking well are! And you *don't* possess the intellectual rigour to analyse it. I'm doing *you* a favour as well. We have a duty to fight intellectually against such a controlling ethos. Precisely because we're adults, we need to work it out for ourselves
- He's probably impregnable
- In that case Dust, he won't mind me publishing my criticism of his duplicity and his sexism and his faithlessness to women.
It occurs to me our Employer might relish the publicity.
- You? *You* are going to say this in the media?
And her face crumples. Oops. I just managed to hint she's less than a desirable woman. Shut up and listen to the neurosis, Dust, rather than holding your nose to a bad smell.
- Sorry Anna. But you're vulnerable, and you might get hurt.
(At this she shrivels) - But I'm hurt already. I'm the awful victim of brainwashing. Don't you believe we need self-reliance? Need non-attachment? What use is our obedience, what use our caring if it's abused? You know what I'm talking about, you say it yourself. I had a *miscarriage,* Dust! It was *his* child. It should have been a love child. He told me that was the reason we were together. He soothed me. I gave in. And I am still there! Still at his church. And I hate it. And I spread horrid vibrations about in his meditation hall! Is that the proper thing to do?
- Miscarriage. When?
- It doesn't matter. I've written the journal and they are going to publish
- Hmm. Maybe he felt sorry for you all along
- Just like you do
- Give me a *break.*
She attempts a pitying look instead.
- I was going to ask you to read it. I don't think you want to
- I'm tired. But yeah, show me anyway. I'll read it now in fact. But it had better all be true.
This remark startles her as well. Neurotic women! But she exits to her

study and returns with a wad of paper. I stand up, take it formally, say thank you. Take a moment to brush her cheek with my fingers.
- Sorry you had a hard time, Annie.

That melts her. She morphs now into solicitous aide, sitting beside on the sofa, bony knees together, glancing at me and offering querulous murmurings as I read. One bit of it begs my attention:

'The most significant event in participating in a church is the moment when we decide to leave. A church is nothing but a springboard to a fulfilled life elsewhere. At this moment we are no longer children but adults, and must make our failures and missteps alone. Do we run away? I have asked myself this many times. But it is better to die than to be humiliated. I never thought I would say this, being a spiritual student, but I realised I could not accept utter assault on my dignity for the sake of an unknown spiritual 'progress'. My progress in fact depends on my reclaiming my dignity, beyond all the unrequited caring and mindless obedience. Dignity is at the heart of it for me. I am a woman, and an intellectual, and a Jew, and I will not be told by any Gentile, by any male, that I am not good enough to be accorded dignity. Was I a fool to trust a powerful teacher? I am anorexic and need special support, and did not get it. Instead I was passed over for another woman (whose need was no doubt greater!) because I committed the crime of not bringing a child to term, a love child, a child conceived of my teacher. Yet he has in fact been my teacher in ways he will never know. He has taught me to trust - not in clever, demanding, manipulative people who think they can set the agenda for others' salvation - but to trust in my own resources, my own righteous anger, my own ability to fight. Even if I fail in this life, even if I die, I will have learnt that lesson. I shall not be passive. Because I am good enough. True, I am alone, but I am connected with my destiny. Though I feel unsafe, I take heart in the knowledge that no-one can help me but myself. No-one ever could, no-one ever will. I took my chances with this fickle world, and I walked on. I am free.'

- Well? What do you say to me?
- His church is too abrasive for some women. They want a milieu that

validates them. They want more love. It's not his style, though he can 'turn it on'. Maybe he wants you to hate him, and maybe that's the point. Still, you're brave. And I hope your anger sustains you.

Of course it won't. It will wear her out. But you can't say it. Hate will be her work, her spiritual *sadhana,* the hard stone she must slowly slowly wear away. It gives her her life and spirit but irradiates her as well. One day the Employer might dispel it all for her with a deft gesture, but that time will be long in coming. In the meantime she will have to drag that stone about with her, wheresoever she goes… Anna takes my hands in hers and fixes me with her glittery look.

- Dust. I have been having another thought. One day I want to start my own spiritual school. And I want you to join me. I want you to help me.

I don't recall with what niceties and nods and phrases I fobbed off Anna Rex before escaping into the night. Later, I wandered down Fernino Street. Anna doesn't want to cast away her fetishes. She is in love with them. Who can take them from her? The guru? I always chuckle that *Guru* in sanskrit means 'heavy'. I wonder if he's like those Mafia Heavies who relieve you of your life? Ha ha. No. Anna is going to be her own guru.

In the meantime, her assault on the world (with me as her proxy) is far from done.

Where Are You Going, Blue Wendy?

It is high time to speak of Blue Wendy, my real sort-of girlfriend. In what way real and sort-of? When Blue Wendy comes to my house she comes like a thief in the night: she is always en route, always with someplace else to go. She might sleep over, but she will do it dignifiedly on my couch. Soon though I will get her into my bed. That is, I will buy a queen bed and hope she will enter it. And she might, like a shy ship berthing in a port. Wendy will never be upset by my blatant attempts to win a married woman. She accepts affection like a bouquet, without fuss. My adolescent excuse is that I don't regard her as properly married. I make no mention of her pain-in-the-ass husband. One might be annoyed at Blue Wendy's studied dutifulness to the world's undesirables (like her husband) but there's no way to hold a grudge for long. Our dear Wendy worships and nurtures the possibilities in others, thrives on the vicissitudes of suffering and forbearance. Positivity shields her. She is a tower. She shivers and cries sometimes, then pulls her life together and goes on. Where is she going, Blue Wendy? Once it came to me: she travels nowhere, travels positively to nowhere. This is entirely the only possible answer. The wonder of it! And she has the survivor's knack. There's much to learn from her, I know it. Folks don't. They see her as none too bright, a fool even, but I know better. She's an idol to me. And she gives me her money. Why do I accept it? Because I must, and because she must give. In her dowdy clothes she's not so beautiful, is homely even, and she never lets herself scrub up as if out on a date. But soon I'll do it. I'll put her in shiny tight clothes that advertise her quite-decent rump and thighs, get her peasanty flaxen hair to curl about her shoulders like a corn-waterfall, and dress her in blue sapphire earrings, put red lippy on her so she'll smile a shy smile and come with me to a posh place... and with her big eyes will wonder why she's there... and she'll inwardly dream of being home, in her ticking forbearance, inside her unglamorous forty-year life that holds no promise. No promise save in the imaginings of her would-be paramour. Blue Wendy quietly manages this world but has no place in it. I'd offer her a place but don't know how. I always miss her and have no idea why. Perhaps she's my lost mother.

And I hate Blue Wendy's husband. Really I shouldn't, since I've no right to hate women's husbands, and since Gordon was an inexpungible member of the Divinology Church. Not that he was any asset to it, rather he was a drain on its patience. That church is littered with basket-souls who slunk off to their private life and weal like lumps of old asteroid blindly orbiting a cold-distant sun. Such that the whole reason Wendy goes anywhere is to be of service, she joined the church to support *him*. Service! Wendy has no metaphysic pretentions (unlike your writer) but like the great horse in Orwell's Animal Farm puts her shoulder to the karmic wheel and trudges her way. Wendy is ever keen to attach herself to compromised souls, to hang round the dying, the lying, the destitute. Her specialty is the Exploiters, the ones who calculate they can offload their sins on her and take their rise from her. All those Calculators and Betrayers, the ones with complicated layers. Now, all of us hate what reminds us of our worser selves - and this is one of the subtler spokes of the Divinology wheel, that ill-matched souls will be tied to hidden karmic wrestlings long after they've forgotten the reason, long after they've exited the officialdom of that church. Wendy anticipates all this, wraps her karmic tentacles about the real basket cases who'll give her a lifelong run for her money, give her plenty to chew on and to cry and fret about and fail with and be a doormat to - even get throttled by. One should be permanently annoyed with Blue Wendy and her stoical ways, but instead one inwardly defers to her, as if she'll carry away our sins. The only price is our ego, in the sense that we affirm she is a better person than any of us. Still, it's a relief to know there are heroes in this world, people deeper than us, more foreseeing, luminous. How would it be if fools like me were at the top of the evolution chain? A horror scenario. We need our teachers and mentors. Do we look forward to a day when we shall be leaders, shall take responsibility, shall stand alone and naked before our destiny? The answer is a quiet no. Rather we want to remain as children, to nestle under the bosom of the great… so let us suckle on the teat of great ones, let *them* be our best conscience, and in the meantime feign that we are needy victims indeed. Let us never grow up.

Husband Gordon has perfected a hundred and one ways to never grow up, and to test and torture his wife whereby he can straddle an exquisite razor's edge: to indulge his sadism yet confront his masochism. He must offer her a *reason* to be married to a poor fool who would like to love her (if only she would 'let him', that is) whilst hoping against hope that one day he might wean himself away from the victim that he is and stand on his own feet. Yet such is his terrible past, his karmic debt, that he must *allow* this perverse torture of marriage in order to admit to himself that he is somehow *worthy* of atonement, is somehow better than the *bastard* he secretly believes himself to be - and must resist the terrible temptation to flush himself away in the sewers of suicide! Alack, how finely poised is one's self-esteem in this world, that we may be miserable sinners yet do others a service - in that *they* may become dedicated to saving us through love! Welcome to the venal labyrinth of Gordon's mind. On one hand, we should marvel at the wonder and glory of the ways of the Lord in his infinite mercy and patience; on the other, one feels one might contribute to Gordon's welfare by explaining to him what a profound arsehole he is, just in case he missed anything. But ah, before taking the speck out of the other's eye we must take the plank from our own.

All our soap operas can seem meaningful when dressed in the raiment of 'the soul's journey'. And indeed that is why many people join churches and become navel-gazers par excellence, since it gives them a sense that their stupidities and dirtinesses are somehow clothed in slightly sullied gold, that the soul is a sweet rose merely covered by mud, that the debate they arc having is not rcally a narcissistic indulgence but a noble effort to face the exquisite dilemmas of being human. Such is the counterfeit of the mind that it is able to justify its own ignorance as the currency of *enlightenment*; that though it struggles in the tunnels of ignorance, yet is it blessed. That all its ways are somehow positive and meaningful; even abject stupidity and venality are part of the divine plan! And for sophisticated players of the game, ignorance is a beautiful justification for doing nothing. Enter husband Gordon. Folks like him are good fodder for burgeoning pseudo-professional new-age industries, industries supported by neurotically self-obsessed middle-class recipients of human progress who've basically not had enough that is nasty, brutish and short to worry on. Our Gordon also knows a rival when he sees one (me). Nothing spiritual about this I fear. If you are scrawny and slightly bow-legged and not so good-looking, like he is, you will no doubt compensate with cunning wit and keen sight. His first instinct is threat followed by bile followed by guile, all chugged along nicely by envy. Gordon's had a lot of practice. After all, if you don't stack up your sins, how can it be worth knocking them down - if and when that good journey of atonement ever actually begins. Besides, one's knees are far too boney, one's body too fragile to put on sackcloth and ashes just yet. But the thought is there, or rather the nuanced notion, or the dream in air, or some aspiration long buried. Lord help me, but I am a good person under all this tripe! I did not deserve this - the slime and smell my body makes, this angulated sandpaper chin of mine, these sunk eyes, this lank lifeless hair I curse in the mirror each day of my life. And I cry out against the self-fulfilling prophecy created by these mean and hungry looks!

I, Dust, suffer few such pangs, being altogether better made. Though I have my own issues, they reveal themselves not to the eyes of others. Nevertheless I suspect all of we human creatures are exactly the same. But so what? This doesn't mean that some of us have not seen the folly and error and have not corrected it, whereas others refuse to or are incapable of doing so, and who indulge in evil even when they know indulgence is of no use. Surely they made their own beds and now lie in them? Ugh. But this is where Wendy is superior to all of us. She does not transfer her own fear and jealousy onto the nearest unsuspecting idiot. Then again maybe her ego is as big as the planet she wants to enfold in her loving arms. Literally the 'earth mother'. I see how she might just be a tad annoying, how she might inspire sabotage. Husband Gordon needs Wendy all to himself to play his especial snotty games. But I notice that when she turns her gaze to *me* - and frankly I consider it to be her sweet weakness that she somehow sees in me an Eden, a promissory love, a holiday from her toils - that Gordon becomes suddenly very astute at apportioning blame for being cuckolded and scorned, like one of those hysterics who sees danger everywhere, who cries wolf at the cosmos before it so much as blows in their ear or disturbs their toupe. With his sunk little chest and his sideburns and his mock-heroistic craggy profile and his amateur Scholarship of the Soul and his little urine-puddles of mea culpa and his self-deluding monologues at anyone who'll listen (preferably strangers not yet inured to his ways) - he conducts the soap opera of his husbandy role with all the fake importance of a man who knows he has none, but protests at the corruption of his critics, and hates anyone who so much as catches the eye of his special Wendy-sow in her cage constructed so brilliantly by him the indulgent sow-master. 'Cause he's doing her a favour! A favour when he embezzles a tap-stream of money from her. A favour when he lies to her. A favour when he engineers his own woman affairs. When he claims he has a 'fatal disease'. When he convinces her he will have a 'short life'. When he comes on with his best fallback: his claim that he is 'testing' her, trying to provoke her to action, to get her to be decisive! To get her to hate him decisively! To get her to *reject* him like a cur in the dust for the good of her soul. What a martyr! He is dedicated to self-abasement, he is a shit, a heel, a cur, a mongrel, a loser. Kick me, he cries. Anything for a bit of attention, anything to fire up the old sour reasons he went to that Divinology church years ago: to get himself well lambasted by the famed Guru, since he heard the Guru had a reputation for kicking the arses of sinners like him, for sorting 'em out, for turning them into sinewed street fighters of the soul... See how tightly I loathe Gordon? It's me and 'im then: we should be like two mud-wrestling brothers in a circus who forever flail at each other, getting filthier and filthier the more we protest we are somehow cleaner than the other.

But he's still an *arsehole* - and I've made a new decision. To cajole Wendy away from her city cares, ergo out of Gordy's reach for a while. The old soul won't be deflected from her mournful path, but it won't stop me trying to be the spindle in her wheel. With wheedling guile I'll copy his scoundrelly games and get my trusty woman to come away. She, full-bodied gold-haired demeter, longed-for mother and wellspring, ample goddess who shyly embraces me though inaccessible as the hills of eldorado and untouchable as drifting dunes in a desert... Blue Wendy will come with me, drive the roads with me, sleep near me, bend her head to hear my woes. And I'll expend my hopes on the glassy rocks of your maiden eyes, you in your sweet sorrowed silence that breathes like heather in the hills, that lingers like shadows in the lee of sadness. You who are forever and never there for me. And what does this make me - a grasping ego-child, shitty as Gordon? Yes but no, I'm the finer more cultivated version: more insidious therefore. I'd be better for you! And maybe I'll uncover your secret agenda, secret love of domineering the world and all its parts that you quietly wrap in the mother arms of your superb ego. Why seek out all the horrors and hushed iniquities of the world, Blue Wendy, all its excesses and abominations, unless you fetishise them, unless you secretly long for them? We are not just supposed to forbear! To fail and laugh and scream and hate and adore - these are our stoppers out of the fizz bottle! that arrest our cringy self-absorption in the name of religiosity and narcissistic piety and all the hypocritic notions we humans have of being martyrs who take on the burden of sins, who carry the word of God on our lips, who lay ourselves bare in the name of forbearance. Clever humans: do you think you're resourceful enough, *egotistical* enough to take in all that god and nature can throw at you? You ragged atom, shriveled rat, speck of dust blithered on the wind: you are never significant. You, the funfair glomeration of myriad bits and byways, you the detritus of a great bloodying opera, cauldron of nature's experiment with its own howling laughter and tears, absurd plaything of worlds crashing and dying and birthing in instants, in aeons, in blank-waved seas that surge forever to unplugged horizons in the horror and funniness of creation's hooligan game with itself. A game that arrows through cosmic woods and fields and blunders over hills stretching to ends of borderless space and time and fortune forever, in a bacchanalian drunken game of shouting noise. You, girl, are a speck, a frolic, a moment, frittered thought, daunted shadow cast by a molecule of sunlight, ten billion years of nothing, sullen whiff of smoke from a devil's cigarette, lump of popcorn tossed to the floor in the back row of a movie slept through by God.

Sure sure, but Wendy suspects all that! and yet performs her little things, knows she drags the weight of total failure like the ragged cloak of an exiled empress behind her in this endless slush of living. She *knows*. And I'm an immature idiot. She knows what a risible farce it is to live, to play the human part in a universe that tears you asunder with every thought, every breath. To stand for 'continuity and sanity and clarity' amid worlds of blood that fling on the winds - in these groaning gales that lather today at the coasts of our faces, she and I, standing like ninepins, like reeds on this clifftop overlooking bellicose seas of flecked waves that trundle forever out of the blue-black fathoms of nowhere, into our lungs and our socketed eyes... we human creature-people, what are we? We are forgotten breath, thought-mist unknown, light that dissolved in the black nether of infinite space, tired of its fickle journey to nowhere. And yet... we are the impish upspring of a moment, clever forgetters of yesterdays, improvisors who twisted a new thing out of wretchedness, who gleaned seeds out of a dead field, who countenanced a snatch of singing like tiny birds in breathless vaults of the air. We are *here*. We are actually here... Wendy and me in our little cottage on the Southern coast, we talk of no such things. But it's the substance, the subtext, the aura of our being here. Her quietness speaks. It's the most precious thing. I love her like I love the land and the sea. She's really unknown to me. We walk on stony and sandy beaches in the freezing winter, wrapped like puffins under our coats and scarves, and her face chisels itself and her heavy hair fans backward in the stuttering wind. We advance slowly in the cold, observing wild things of the rocks, creatures of the pools, and the weed that lies like corpses slumped on Omaha beach rumped by scathing wind that howls *I'll never leave you be...* She and I become nothing, nothing special in this void. We lose contact with duty and agenda - which I tell her is really the point of our holiday respite. But she'll nary sleep with me, being married as she claims. And she doesn't even think on the absurdity of being with one who's not her husband and not bringing me under blankets into the caverns of her body in our private far gone cottage room above the sea. For Blue Wendy is so real, as real as you can ever be. Ah, she must be immortal.

Yet on our day at Tintagel she had a little turn in the heart, as if the brink of the land were sad and she were forced to fail a little just for its sake. I couldn't get her to face the cliff path. She is not a thin girl, is a little ponderous and can't be made to do a certain thing. But this stubbornness is good, hinting she is not just a wand to be waved, reed to be bent, horse to be ridden. And she knows I want her to forget her karmic weal and give herself to me. That I dare her to believe I'm worth it, as if glory could come from embracing just a wee devil-delighty bit of the world instead of it all. But again I'm immature. For she's seen all that, done all that. In fact she does it all the time by being there for all the people and the creatures. Wander no more, fair Wendy, tarry with me! Feel what it is to be consumed by love, by passion, by want. Drench in unquenchable feeling for one instant. Lose your steadfast sense, lose your cosmosity, humble pomposity. Get real, be mortal, fail... But these cliffs are resolute. They'll not be climbed.

And one day in a sea-town she went away with another man and passed the afternoon with him. They came back to the beach café where I was, and they smiled together as if satisfaction had passed between them, and he kissed her in front of me and said thank you and left. He was a youngish man in a long coat, and didn't seem especially dissolute or needy. But she'd obviously seen his soul and seen what he needed. Didn't mention what *she* needed. She never does. To be jealous would be an asinine thing, though I am and she knows it. She's all sorry for that too. And ineluctably we don't talk about it. Blue Wendy is not without price! and thereby not without ego. So I'm right, I'm right, and so what? I'm infantile, I told you. But I sense she wants me to persist with her: one thousand years of persisting. She'll never leave; besides, there's nowhere to go. Compared to Gordon I am her day of rest, and there is hope because she shared it with me. I won't get angry. She wouldn't respond anyway, though she'd think: 'why do you want to get inside me? I'm open, there's nothing hidden…' This is truly true and yet it's bullshit.

One afternoon as we come in sight of the cottage from our coast walk, we notice a car pull away up the track to the main road. Later in the parlour gloom she neglects to mention she knows it's Gordon's car. I toss off a cryptic remark or two, and so she unweariedly addresses the truth.

- Gordon is having a hard time, Dust
- So now we have to meet with him? We said no calls these two weeks
- Only once or twice, darling. Can't leave him totally in the dark
- Understood. But he needs to leave you be. That's the point of this
- It is, it is. Space for me and for you
- Wen, the point is he has to stand on his own
- We all have to stand on our own
- Not me. I want you.
She never looks at me when I challenge her. But she'll nod at first and later she'll look. The cure-all look. Not.
- Or perhaps he wants money?
- I gave it him before I left. All I could
- You know he'll never let you rest

- I know it, Dust. I know it. But as long as he's harassing me, he's not harassing someone else.

I've no riposte to her promiscuous wager with passivity. But in the moonlit night I wake to see a shadow hovering beside our window. I don't tell her. And in the morning when I go to fetch firewood I see Gordon's silhouette on a far headland. Again I say nothing… Fact repeated: taking shit for the sake of atonement is inverted egotism. And hanging around suffering and death and morbidity is egotism personified. Whatever we do is egoic, no way round it. Force of creation. No-brainer. I won't argue the toss with Blue Wendy but I'll sabotage one thing or the other. And she'll rush to put up with it. Like a giant snowball rolling down a mountainside, she'll gather up this fucking world and hug it all to herself. Let's see if I can do her a favour then!

* * * *

Today is clear and cold and we travel the high roads of the cliff-coast, dipping into cottagey hamlets and smiley beaches, but always out and on to lonelier places where sea hugs the headlands and sky spreadeagles over us like a gigantic mute negation to all our touristic trivia. It is getting past four pm and the light is fading. I'm driving. In the mirror I spy Gordon's older model blue Ford rounding the bend behind us. The road hugs bluffs to our right, avoiding grey raked sea and bulbous rocks to our left. Wendy's flaxen head is lowered, she's telling her beads. I slow to a crawl. She glances at me. Tough road, I say. Take care, she says. Then Gordon's grinning Ford grill is right behind. I brake suddenly. Wendy lurches at the dash. We're still. She looks back. Her husband's car can't back up on the narrow road. Wendy and I look at each other. There's a moment between us. Nothing and everything happened in that moment, I tell you. Gordon revs his motor, pulls beside, tries to squeeze past under the bluff. That's when I stepped on the gas and our car glanced forward, scraped him. We saw his upset face through the glass. He shoveled his car forward, tried to slither away. I tail-gated him. Wendy shouted: *Let him go! Let go, Dust!* Least, she thinks that's what she said. But Gordon's car slithered, clutched at the corner ahead, his wheel slid to the edge, a tail-light loomed over the gulf. We came in too fast, it's true. I threw the wheel, slugged the wall but did I clip him? Don't remember. Gordon's chassis ground over the lip of the cliff but he wouldn't slow, wouldn't see what was happening. His back wheel skitters into space, car tips, drops away. Wendy screams. Gordon in his casket frumps and clatters downward then turns over in space. I scram the car to stop, don't see any impact, but Wendy claimed she saw Gordy's car shunt side first into rocks sixty feet below and tip and crunch on its back just where the waves wrestle and gurgle-sputter upward out of sea holes under the rocks.

We agree we exited the car, hurried to the place. There was no immediate way down. I maintain that Wendy was not hysteric but calm. No-one came. I saw a way down. I tell you she wouldn't come with me. She could have, wasn't that hard. Maybe she was in shock. I made it to the bottom. The waves splattered me as I tried to force open the wrecked door. I tell you it was impossible. He wasn't moving at all. You'd expect that. I'd no idea he wasn't dead. Sure looked it. I couldn't face those sputtering spouts and backed off, crawled up the cliff. Wendy was wandering down the fucking road. I shouted but she wouldn't answer. I got in the car, came alongside. Her jacket was heaving like a balloon, hair bundles obscured her face. I got her in, she sat like a corpse. 'Nothing we can do! We'll get to the next hamlet.' I coaxed and coaxed. 'Get your mobile out. Call someone.' I swear I wanted to get us to the sea village, but something made me right-turn inland at a crossroad two miles ahead. I just kept driving into hills... We saw no-one. I was hypnotised by moor grasses bending crazily under the wind. The way that gale curled and howled over those moors, no creature, no weasel would want to stick his head up. My mind was gone really. Wendy sure said nothing, paralysed for one time in her coping coping life. I drove for an hour at least. It got totally dark. I'd had enough. We saw a light by the roadside, looked like a petrol station. I pulled in under its awning. Only then did I find the phone in her bag and call ambulance. No police. Didn't give a name. Told them where they should go. That was it. After that we didn't do a thing. I got a blanket out, put it over us. We fell asleep obviously. Hours might have gone by. We were woken by someone knocking on our window. Some grinning guy, who brought us indoors.

Dark-hair, looked Italian. Introduces us to his brother. His twin. Said they were the Alighieri Brothers. They fed us. Said they were car guys. Late that night the local radio was on. Report on a crash in Cornwall under the sea-cliffs. The guy and his brother seemed to put two and two together. I know because they looked at us in a spidery way, and later they had a little conference - and before we turned in they took our car and locked it in their garage. I lay beside Wendy. She didn't speak or move. And I didn't say a thing to her about the messages on her phone. The ones I saw she'd sent to Gordon at three pm today, just eight hours ago… Anyhow, I erased them. Decided to get rid of her phone later too.

Next morning was Sunday. They gave us breakfast, served petrol to one customer. The brother who called himself Dan. T. said: 'This is the empty part of Exmoor'. Sure looked quiet. Bleak is a better word. Wendy drifted off, up the road. Wasn't properly dressed and I wanted to rug her up. The other brother Domenico saw. *Let her go. She needs to be alone,* he said. I was glad to take his word for it. Later the two sat me down and we had words.

- We fix up your car, my friend.
- It's my er - wife's car
- No worries. We do panel beat, repaint, good as new
- Is it scratched up? I thought maybe it wasn't
- Sure sure. Scratched up. We fix. You relax. One hundred. Good price. You take it
- Okay… sure, sure. Very kind.
- No trouble, no trouble friend, said Dan T.

Two hours and it was done. I went in search of Wendy. Found her in a hedgerow a mile up the road in sad sunlight, and drove her back. At the garage the radio was on… What's the news? Domenico flicked it off. 'Nothing, nothing today. Listen, you stay few days. No problem, pay small rent, no problem.' Dan. T. nodded approval. I said okay. Wendy glared at me in a fleetingly evil way. The brothers saw it. So I took her away again, in the car for a while. We spotted a hill path, walked an hour, arrived at a grassy knoll overlooking some iron-age ruins in a high valley. She wouldn't talk. The winter breeze forked at us out of a clear sun-wan sky.

- Now talk to me, baby darling. The fact is, he's dead and we are not to blame. We are not going to take this on. These brothers heard about the crash: even as strangers they've sussed it all. And we're going to take their advice and stay out of it
- Stay out? You can't stay out of anything in this world, Dust. You either deal with it now or you deal with it later
- Wallow unnecessarily now or wallow unnecessarily later
- The police will be looking. I will not lie about being there
- You will. You will lie, Wendy. And it is going to be good for you to do it. And you are going to act all those lies out. Now you and me are gonna get our story straight
- I never will, Dust
- 'We were touring in the area. You texted Gordon earlier that day. Our car is now clean, fixed. The first you heard was a radio report next day'. D'you understand?
- Why are you being this way? Are you a stupid fool?
- Because he knew where we were. I saw your goddam text! Did you want him to follow us? Did you want to meet him?
- I won't betray him. I won't leave him!
- You already did. You already have
- I will tell the whole story. This is our soul's karma. This must *be*.

She sits there on her hill, with her head forward, white fingers clutched in semi-prayer, her bomber jacket puffed against the winter, solid thighs under, her estuary of heavy hair tossing in wind. And I know I won't ever let her get away with her version of the future.

- Fuck it Blue Wendy. You're going to be mine, you're going to love me. For one simple reason. I love you and I respect you and that fucker never did
- What the hell do you know about him and me?
- Are you insane? You *used* him. Used him like you use everybody and everything. For your satisfaction, for your grand fucking journey to god

or whatever you think it is. And I can respect it, really I can - but I won't accept your blundering bloody failure to face up to your own crummy ego! You are not going to let yourself down for some shitting crook who is too lazy to stand up and *live*. He got what he needed, he got the karrr-maa that was commm-ing!

She is on her feet and breathless, and she is heavier than me, stronger even, but I tell you I shoved her down on the grass on that hilltop and I took her clothes apart and I made sure she got the whole lot, the whole works, all of me, inside, all she deserved. And in the middle of it I told her: you will take me seriously, you will notice me, you will take me *seriously*. For me and for you.

We never called it rape, we're too advanced for that. Called it my 'moment'. She wouldn't ever own it, but in a future time might 'let it be what it was'… somehow. But not before she'd languished for minutes on that mound with her body unplugged and her flesh reddening in the wintry wind and then had sat up and kicked me as hard as she ever could and then run off and been pursued by me, bottom-naked, and had turned and punched me so hard, so satisfactorily hard, that I went down on the stones and nearly lost my skull on a big rock and was dazed but not enough to fail to see her run to a brook and throw her head in and hold it under so long that I staggered down and yanked her out and shoved her to the bank where she howled and cried and cried while I lay over her, shielded her from the stormwind that rattled through that iron-age valley as it had for twenty thousand years… as it wooshed and jibbered and cackled at the sobs of women and men in their betrayals… on this sodden unforgiven earth under the implacable palm of an alien god.

And I got her down and out of that high valley she was in, back onto the road. And we hadn't reckoned that the soul of Gordy was not for exiting the earth so easily. The Alighieris seemed to be waiting. They peeped at Wendy's destroyed face and my guilty one and nodded their two heads. Later they sat us down with wine in the kitchen. Dan T. said he heard 'that driver' was in a hospital in Exeter, in intensive care but alive. Wendy abruptly stood, but we three men were on our feet, surrounding her.

- We seen the car-damage, Signora. Don't make no silly moves. We seen a lot in our time. Your husband is no fool. Do as he tells
- This man is not my husband!
- It's okay. She's upset. The driver of the car is her legal husband. He followed us, drove off the cliff. Not our fault. I don't want to have to explain this to anyone
- You stay here. Long as you like. Talk over. Maybe go to hospital later. Finish. You are beautiful lady. Don't cause yourself no harm, see?

And Wendy looks at these sanguine brothers and wonders how they can be so understandingly wise. And feels a light shine out of them onto her. I see it as it happens. I know her. All women need to be embraced. Easier, if it's by non-threatening people who won't ask you to change. So we talk and drink into the night. She drifts in and out, but listens. We men self-talk in our machinations and our satisfied justice. I am not even ashamed of my attack on Wendy's body. She has to forbear no matter what. It's her duty-pact with herself and the miserable world. Maybe I should be shamed. But I feel remorselessly sorry for her. Our evil event won't change anything. And though no-one will ever topple this woman's utter obeisance to the inexorable Law, I know my task, before her future is lost. I need to nurture a tiny devil-seed… *Did you want me to will Gordon's injury, or his death - so that you could benefit by ministering to it?*

Next morning we say goodbye. The brothers shake our hands. There's equanimity in their faces. We drink it in. Wendy stares at them.

- See you again, then
- Next time you come by, we will not be here. We never were here. At all
- How do you mean?
- Life is like that. *Arrivederci.* Goodbye.

* * * *

- Dust, if you will admit that you're no better than him, then I will accept your criticism of my path
- So what are you doing here with me?

She replies with nothing as usual. Nothing verbal that is.

- And Wen, don't patronize by hinting you feel sorry for me. Or that you're doing me some kind of service. I'm immune to service.

Mmm, her woman eyes are hurt by that one. - And you're too wonderful to be patronized. Admit the beauty in me, Wendy, and just maybe you'll see it in yourself.

How can she resist such a challenge in the name of honesty? And why on earth haven't we got to this before? Because she keeps it in, all to herself in that closeted generous ego.

- I see the beauty in Gordon
- Bullshit you do.

Our cathartical conversation takes place in a field, last stop before we enter Exeter. In the hospital car park I deliver my best meaningful hug, and watch her go off to do her duty to her husband and get herself tangled and mangled by bureaucracy and blame and the beady eyes and bastardries of the system. I linger, and I see her diminish. She doesn't wave. I walk to the station, catch a train back to the city.

But I'm sad. Is one any better than Gordon? Ugh, guess not. Getting her angry is a law of diminishing returns. Why do I interfere really? I suspect Wendy feels time spent with me is ultimately an indulgence: I'm her little sleep, little holiday from toil, since in her world the quicker we experience badness the quicker we get rid of it. Yet the psychology of ego says all action is motivated by self-interest - which ultimately must be pursuit of pleasure - which is psychological hedonism. Still, it is said that 'emotional intelligence' is the ability to put off pleasure so that the reward reaped is magnified. Wendy's altruism is a drug then, with hope of a big payout. And I know she fears her own self-centredness. She denies she has it all *calculated* under that patina of soft silence. Ironies of an old soul! And I? I am an annoyance, a saboteur, one who tells himself we need indulgence and frippery and passion for the sake of liberty. That'd make me immature, but not passive. Driven by contempt and anger more like. Not a recipe for compassion but a bloody-minded demand that my world is shit and needs transforming. I guess people come to compassion when they've given up on pushing, when they lay their bodies down in the cosmic stream and let the current do the job… Wendy knows she can never avoid to act, so she acts out a compassion-play. Still, I admit I want what she has, and thereby grasp at her. (Even Gordy somewhere deep wants what she has.) Follow Wendy then? I suppose I ought to copy her. *Or maybe not.* Those Alighieri brothers… they were like a cool breath from nowhere, a real foil to Wendy's dogged path. Spontaneous tuned in mischievous irrepeatable, right on! Ghosts who deliver a parcel and vamoose. Really, she should love that. And somewhere I know she does.

In the weeks following, she sits around in Exeter ministering to her broken man. I glean that the police interviewed her. She avoids me, won't elaborate on the phone, especially not about Gordon. Perhaps he's more sacred than ever now, being close to the door of death. Trouble is he's going to recover. Her muted voice on the phone alerts me she's diverted to depression. I urge her back to the city. What can she do for the guy anyhow? Her florist's shop is ailing and her assistant is complaining. (I even call the assistant for gossip, claiming to be a concerned friend.) So, disingenuous query: why be depressed? Wendy's a professional sad-sack but this is other: this is the threat of the *unsolvable*. The fact I hit on her on that hilltop… add that to the truth about Gordon, how she secretly longed for me to shove him off that cliff! Dared to think she could tread a high-wire of guilt, or dig even deeper into the pit of herself and uncover *dirty shame*. Creative! For god's sake, she needs to cling on to her abrasive vortex of spiritual suffering, her big hotline to evolving. I see her thoughts: she's disappointed too. Wanted to venerate me as 'purer choice', till I proved as exploitative as Gordy. More, even. Her duty said she should cleave to me just because I want her. But with me she entertained a higher hope, a reward even. I turned out drudgy instead. (Failed her with my insistence on fucking.) I'll call her naïve but she'll quietly say: *maybe naivety is not such as bad thing.* No, Wendy! I strike at the core of your Bargain With Shit. Not sustainable! Can't be sad and resigned, can't rely on 'weltschmerz'. Duty is your concoction, your big mental jam. I'm going to tempt you to see me as better, or worse, than that. 'Cause I am, and she knows it. Licking up Gordon's shit ain't sexy any more. She has to engage with a higher pulse, a keener vision. I'm not her holiday, I'm her *confusion*. Such a malleable girl with all her devotion to raking up the karma muck. I'll bloody well use it against her. Cosy spiritual depression won't wash. It's going to be uncosy and wild and oily and contradictory! …But I forget: she suffers, god love her. If she gives up on Gordy her ego will tell her she failed. For what is duty if you don't do it? Stick to it like a dog with a bone, *die* with it. Maybe she really is crazy. No. Wendy, do the opposite. Disbelieve. Passion rules us. We're alive. And alive is eternity.

Finally she is back. I hasten to the shop. There she is dithering at the back, her ponderous frame bent over blooms. I buy one, put a coin in her hand and solemnly hand the bloom to her. Don't you see I love you in a pure and special way? says my look. You can have the riches *and* the flower. This wins a tiny smile. Later I ask her to a teahouse, where she and I will have a civilised chat. Yes, Gordon is on the mend but very slowly, and yes, the police asked a lot of questions but she answered just as I instructed. And she was happy to do so. I frown discreetly, avoiding to smile.

- I know it's no small thing to lie, Wendy. But this world just won't conform to our wants. And that is good. When we acknowledge it I mean. We're to blame only when we believe we are.
She nods at this sagery, smiles a little, then says:
- Dust, I've been thinking a lot. And really, thank you for everything. (Pause) Shall I tell you what I thought?
- Er, yes, do
- Well… I have been… thinking. One day at some later time - I will get a separation - from Gordon. We will become - just friends. And then… and then… I will think of marrying you. If you like.
This time she looks into my eyes. In fact, we gaze for a while.
- You see, on the hilltop -
- I'm sorry, Wendy. I really am. And I'm glad you kicked my arse. But -
- But you needed me. I truly get it. And I got so angry
- I'm glad you did. I'm glad
- But why?
- Because it's real. And fucking sexy
- I know it's real. But it's… it's…
- Wrong? Are you crazy?

- Yes, I am. I am
- I'm crazy about *you*. And I shouldn't be. But if you marry me out of duty or atonement or friendship or compassion or because you're sad or for any other reason except that you *want* me to strip you naked and spreadeagled on a deserted hilltop then fuck ourselves senseless… then I'll not do it. I won't do it. Won't marry you. So there.
Wendy's eyes widen. I try to appear satisfied with my statement.
- You're hard. That's what you are
- Whatever, I love you
- I don't love you!
- Yes you do.

Now her eyes moisten, and drip. Not hard to do it. But lady, this is *my* duty, my integrity, my high-wire tightrope. Getting you sad or angry *is* a law of diminishing return, but how to shift you? Do I have to use and use you? Blue Wendy, you makes it impossible for people not to do it. And this I cannot stand. The reader can call me selfish but I've my reasons. And now, I am going to do us both the honour of looking on the bright side. Blue Wendy is going to be mine some day… In the meantime, Lord deliver me from any more sanctity.

Furious

'Cassie Pace the teenage daughter took to meditation like a duck to water. She sat in lotus on a cushion in the middle of the big hall at Divinology Church for two hours and never twitched a muscle. Lived up to her peacey name. It surprised me. After it she said she felt like the 'high priestess in the temple of Apollo' - whatever that means. Hey dudes, check out my trance! She likes being looked at, the hot little teen in the funky outfit with goldy hair spreadeagled everywhere. Several male devotees seem to lurk about after the session for no reputable reason. But Cassie has a tendency to burble things when she's excited and there's a chance to impress. - Yeah, meditation is like, *cool*. I predict mental patients will do it and oppressed women will do it and kids with ADHD will do it 'cos you can fully zap your inner repressions in the virtual reality of brahman consciousness 'cos like the will-force is merging with the supermind and we're plugged into the cosmic sanctuary in the pituitary gland yeeaah, which checks right into the garden of peace, man. Woo-hoo. Talk about Waiting for Go Dot! Anybody got like a herbal tea or some shit?

Etcetera. I hustle her out into the streets, away from those drooping male members. It's dark out. She seems blissfully wired.

- And now, Dusty boy. We're gonna take *my* trip. Come on
- Slow down. How about a coffee?
- 'Kay. Then we go meet the Furies!
After the caffeine she's still raving, which appears to be her default mode in public places. The cool feeling I got bringing a chicky-babe into church is wearing off.

- You ever heard of Charlie Manson, Dusty? He had like a commune and it was Helter Skelter and the Apocalypse was gonna be coming and he had like loads of girls eating out of his hand who did anything he wanted! They all murdered Sharon Tate! He was neat. Man, this is gonna be groove-arse tonight. I'm showing a film. I did it at home on my computer.
- What? Where are we going?

In ten minutes we're downtown. She drags me down an alley. Under a blue light is a doorway with steps curving down to a cellar. Padded doors are ahead. A bouncer looms, curls his lip at Cassie. She pulls fifty-quid notes out of her jeans and shoves them in his shirtfront. Crikey girl. She yanks me bodily through the doors, and a wall of weirdy music and chatter and psychedelic light assaults my sense.

- Where's this?
- Come to the Furies' dressing room!

In the room behind the stage Cassie bursts into with a demented *Hiya dudes!* - is a collection of thin, angular Amy Winehouse gothic looking girls sitting about smoking, tapping smartphones, dabbing lurid paint on faces. These seem to be the Furies. The aura is formidable, self-contained. None of them particularly reacts to Cassie. It can hardly be cool to do so. She defaults to puffing up me as her special friend and mentor etcetera.

Silence. I give her the eye. But Cassie Pace don't take 'run away kiddo' for an answer.

- Hey, c'n I show my file on your laptop. It's got all the stuff I told you about
- What stuff? says a girl with blacked eyes and blood-red hair like snakes.
- Ya know: death and mayhem scenes and Sharon Tate and Manson and Himmler and ritual zombie porn sex and Satanists and Beat Poets and -
- Oh fuck yeah. Give it 'ere.
In it goes, and Cassie gives her drooling commentary until told to shut it by the snaky redhead.
- Okay, we'll think about putting it onscreen. Here's yer little present. (She drops a couple of pills into Cassie's hand) Now, if you'd like to fuck off we'll see yous in the hall. Keep her on a leash, will ya mister.
We exit. That went well, I remark. Don't let their shit fool you, she says. The Furies love me. Oh, and here's your share. Open mouth... Open, Dusty!
How to refuse? I do it. The little pill goes down.

The Furies are ramping it up on stage in the big room. Alex, Meg, Tisi and Dusa wanna fuck up our eardrums. Who's the sluttiest nuttiest girl band in all the world? *Helter Skelter!* Cassie shrieks and grabs my ears. We keel over, people stomp on our legs, knees flog about our heads. Cass puts her crotch in my face, gyres her arms in funky-wild style. *You may be a lover but you ain't no dan-cer!* Wriggles to the slam beat, shouts at my ear. *This party's beyond insanity! Where'll we be in ten ugga megabillion years? In the pit! Down the pit!* I get it: she's in hell-bliss, nowhere to put herself. Now the clothes are comin' off. People are going drug strange. Cassandra shouts the future and I believe her! No morals no remorse! Manson's girls slaughtered Sharon Tate and her 'migos and her tummy baby and din' feel a feckin thing. Richy Sharona got her desserts! In the deepy depth of a diver's suit my breath is rasping. If I carked it I wouldn't care. Impregnable. We're little planets breathing and milling in a sunless cosmos. Need humans to despise in my aloof solitude. We're the hell-sixties reborn! The pulse racks me like a knife through buttocks. My heart's banging. Light shoots out a million miles a second. Fuck I am STONED. *Now* is the death of time. Diamond on girl's finger, hardest rock out of *emptiness*. Get outa the thickened brain! Hello I love you won't you tell me yer name… Where's Cass? Fuck, promised mummydaddy I'd guard her body n' soul. The Furies spit thrash death, Cassie's video splats on the shimmer screen. Where's compassion in struggle-street? Beggars fight to eat and squillionaires piss on us from Bel Air mansions. *Izzat justice?* Need violence! Furies ain't happy till the big V rears its head. Some drunk goldilocks whacks a guy in the eye so he lunges at another dude who goes down just as goldy is told to feck off by some wired female who gets clunked and falls sidewise on a boofy feller who's lookin' for a fight 'cause he can't score chicks so chucks a punch and female gets face in the way and freaks out and kicks boofhead who resents personal space intrusion embalmed in pickling effect of alcohol blaaa… suddenly it's a RIOT and hooley dooley!' Dust is down under thundering feet and its panic and flail and those moles onstage ramp it it's out of hand the flames of riot are licking high the devil's got in and body piles gasp n' scream - NOW some cunt pulled the plug on the band the doors swing wide they're pushing bodies out the COPS are in it's lockdown and uuuuuh the punters got an enemy to curse now! It's a fucken party any law 'gainst having a time ya dickhead squares it's the sixties don't ya dig it WILD? Poor old plods don't dig being spat at - and there's Goldy Cass onstage screaming wacked obscenities and dribbling in a trance - clearly at the edge of socially apt, so the fuzz grab her and drag her out.

Dust follows on, has to retrieve her from the station after hours of 'vestigation and charges threatened after spitty insults at the Boys in Blue and texts to Marcus and Helena who turn up white-faced but *in control* and it's all super embarrassing.

- Your meditation class certainly had a calming effect, Mister Dust.

Dust is relieved when Cassie calls daddy a fucking dropkick. The family Pace climb into the Jag and disappear. Dust reflects that Marcus under his vastly reasonable veneer looked pretty furious. Result! High five.

But next day Dust has the inkling he might've a bit lost the plot on the saving of Cassie's soul. He rings the Pace number but hangs up when Marcus answers. Later he calls and Benjamin is there. Dust wants the goss. - Mister Dust. You're a corrupt influence! Daddy's a bit ruffled. Hold on. Helena comes on the line. Dust decides to be straight with her, more or less. Tells her there are things he can influence, things he can't, which prompts her to say none of it is his role at all, which makes him suddenly get jack of these people. Dust decides there's a hoary big thing to be dealt with in this family but must contain himself… so he'll turn up for Cassie's class the following week whether Helena says yea or not. Besides, the tricksy teen texted him to come. He learns she got in tight with the Fury Girls after the party and now they deign to be impressed. They want her to 'write', might even let her sing in the band. Write your *future*, they said. Now she feels significant dangerous radical all at once. She dreams up some lyric about Fake Materialism Fame LA Hollywood Warhol etcetera-you-name-it. Cassie is big on prophecies as we know. Trouble is, one or two of them ought to come true once in a way.

'Poor little rich girl on Sunset, riding her Corvette to Malibu.
She don't wanna be lazy famous, no no, or a
fake like 'Paris' in some magazine.
Daddy paves a road to paradise. Big white house on a hill.
Oil the wheels of a death machine. Your
wannabe princess - she wants to kill!
Gotta play roulette with your hearts. Cool wind in my hair. Paparazzi
swarming round, round. What's that smell? What's that sound?
'Give me what I want!' I said, I said. Don't tell me what *you* want.
Gonna be crazy famous, yeah. I don't care what you want, you want.
'Cause I'm richer than your money, honey. Sweeter than 'success'.
It's all unreal, this paradise. This loneliness…
It's the last ride on Sunset. Showdown at Malibu.
The wreck of a Corvette makes the papers in Hollywood.
All your fame, your lies, your money. What
can you give your princess now?
What can you really give? A reason to live?
I wanna reason. Wanna reason.

Poor little girl - on Sunset. She's crazy - did you forget, forget?
This is me on Sunset. Last ride to Malibu. This
is me. Daddy, this is me. This is me...'

Dust fixes up her syntax since he can't otherwise contain the breathy lusty nymph. It'd be his job anyway. Up in Cassie's room the teacher feels like a fugitive. Though they don't invite him to lunch the Paces are overweeningly polite. As Helena observes, Cassie is 'enjoying her creative writing'. Later she puts it to a hypnotic distortion riff on her electric guitar (which really is pretty good) and Dust suggests she might sing it to the elders. She runs to the Furies instead. They 'commandeer' it (steal it) and give it the lurid creepy treatment. Cass doesn't get to sing on the record at all. This insult she affects not to notice, because a week later she's invited by the Girls to ride out to the coast 'in their Big Yankee Thunderbird'. There'll be no boys, just us, they say. But Cassie demands that her tutor come with. Dust rejoices in her loyalty! He sees the Furies would never 've agreed unless they wanted her there. But how to inform the parents? Dust slides out of that one, leaves it to creative Cassie.

Dust records: 'The Furies Ride Out! It's a clear-sky Sunday. Alecto steers into the back country with no hint of a map or plan, along hedgy lanes she hogs without the least care for oncoming traffic. Where they got this damnable convertible no-one will say, but she's a big dreckless beautiful bird anyway. These Furies keep up a draining strident allegiance to their own imagery, and anyone without enthusiasm for sardonic irony can't stick 'em for long. I start to grock this trip is an homage to the content of Cassie's song. Though they don't say it, I see quicker than Cassie the black japes they're keen to indulge at her expense. Time for me to keep an eye on proceedings. The hags pay no attention to me, and since normal relationships with them are out of the question I bung on shades and settle into the back seat with a nonchalance that does me credit. Can you call the Furies artistes? In so far as they proclaim all art as plagiarism, excusing their blatant stealing of others' ideas as a necessary counterweight to cynically exploitative western capitalism, and assuming you will be flattered when they fling the idea back in your face with a ferocity that enables you to experience the bogus hollowness of your own allegiance to art - then yes, they are artistes.

After a string of narrow-lane misses to the tune of ungovernable mock curses from Alecto and which the others respond not a whit to since they're busy daubing make-up and fiddling phones and sucking on weed-ciggies, we trawl out and onto a highway, as screeds of gravel shoot out in our wake for special effect. The country suddenly opens up, and I guess we're heading west. All this seems a signal by bat-telegraph for the Goths to awaken. Their new recording of Cassie's song, all fried and twizzled in the pyre of the Furies' dark muse suddenly blasts from the speakers. Raucous voices leer up in unison, distorted by the wind-rush about the car as they fling words not their own at each others' faces, laughing as they go. I see Cassie feels compelled to join in though not really grocking her own song. This dismay she hides for a second or two before leaping up on the front seat and surfing and bouncing and wailing her arms at the sky. The hags all laugh and holler at this. There's nothing natural about these people! I get instantly pissed, and none too soon since Alecto elects to swerve the car about the whites of the centreline, and with sun blazing into her face Cassie reels and crashes backward into my lap and bangs her frizzy head on my mouth. I don't shout out how I nearly lost a fucking tooth. And they must have put something in her mouth earlier because she starts to act up in hysteric out-of-whack teen style which only boosts their saturnalian delight. Alecto puts foot to floor and the big Bird sways and rumbles down the blacktop. The Furies are up on their feet on seats now, and there's a moment where the copycat dare surpasses irony and flips into the death-accident zone because Medusa sprays her redsnake hair into the face of Alecto and the ship is flying blind. I reach forward, shove her sideways but she falls on Megaera who nearly tips over the low doors and under the white-banded wheels rippering up the streaming road. In the wind-gush she hangs on and kicks out at me but I grasp the foot and drag her in and her head slaps bluntly on the doorframe. *Stop the car!* I shout at Alecto, but she's already shoveled it sideways into gravel then into some lay-by and we're stationary before anyone knows what's what. Tisiphone leaps out, strides about like a chicken, points her finger at me and shouts: Get outa the car, cunt! You wanna assault my sister, you gotta deal with me! If it weren't for the studs and blades and safety pins all over her tartan jacket and her pasty face I think I'd have punched her in the head. But no. Because it's all an *act*. Meg puts her arms round Tisi and says: Don't worry about the bad man. He don't count, no way. Then Alecto lurches the car forward. They all scatter but Cassie's in front of it. The car clunks to a halt against her legs. Alecto laughs. I step round the car, yank open the door, grab her by the hair and rip her sidewise into the gravel. She screams. I hold on. The others descend on me. I don't give a shit.

- If hate and anarchy's your game, girls, then you won't object to my pulling a bit of your sister's hair out. Uh? Just a game, uh?

Uh-oh. The bloke called their bluff. They're reduced. *Let Alex go,* mutters Medusa. I let Alecto drop to the gravel. Cassie stares at me. I smile back. Next, I snatch the car keys and zip 'em in my jacket. Silence. Evil glances all round. It appears I've stepped over a line. Girly violence is not real violence, it's allusive and symbolical, don't you get that, Dust? They all move off towards a green field. Alex gets all the girly touches now, centre of cooing affection. And I see what they are: the self-referencing little asylum-world they've made and walled and pampered up for themselves because the rest of humanity will never give any quarter or even notice, this little gang of like-souls and their unholy heresy, their copycatty fundamentalista ante, their clever nihilist spite-anarchic irresponsible little circus - is all they'll *ever* have, before they wither in the tides of time and grow old. These girls just wanna have fun, and the big bad man stomped on it. That doesn't mean they won't deal it to a young tenderfoot called Cassie, including making her taste every bit of isolation and failure they go through and hate and vow revenge on the world for. But how big is their world? Tiny corral of sad girly creatures is the answer. Cassie tells me in steely tone to apologise. I wrinkle my nose. *Apologise,* she says. So we follow them to where they sit in a gaggle under a tree in their punky costumes. They eye me with their cake-black eyes.

- I'm sorry. Too rough. Lost my nerve. Maybe you can see why. How's the hair, Alex? Hey, don't give a crap about me, I've a duty to look after Cassandra.

Cassie twitches moodily then runs off into trees. Dusa gives her man-withering look.

- Let her go, man. Let her learn, do mad stuff. Let her fuck up, grow with her own kind

- That's just it. I worry about the parents. They pay me, believe it or not.

They exchange looks of unutterable scorn.

- Want our keys back now, Mister. Our keys, man

- Sure. But tell me one thing. What makes you so sure you've a right to stir it all up when you won't admit you've been given everything? No, not by parents and oldies (and don't dump me in that category) - but by *life*.

Sound like an oldie! Tisi's eyes glitter. She's the group's intellectual, good at storing abuse for future use.

- Why do anything without total commitment? If you're always protecting your little girl, what would be the fucken point of her existence? Why do parents bring babies in the world - for their own kicks? A doll to put on their mantelpiece, a pill for their own failure

- You'd let her die, would you? I bet *you* don't have the guts for it. And how long can you guys keep it up? The elaborate hate, I mean. Hard work I reckon

- It's ironic, you cock

- So you don't believe in it then?

Alex spots this flaw in their front.

- No. Till we die, till we turn to dust. Like your wanky name

(But this is lame) - And *you* like your bit of violence, don't ya?

This from Megaera, who needs to score points.

- Cute point, Meg. But I react to stupidity more than anything. And lies. And people being used

- Used? (Dusa) Used? We're the fallen angels, the daughters of night! We are used by god! We punish all the fools and hypocrites and arseholes and slimeballs and losers. But not for fun. Or yeah, maybe for fun. They need it! And if the law won't let us cut off their balls, we find other ways

- Very picturesque. (I don't tell her I like the sound of it)

- Cassie's one of us, you jerk. Needs to be hardened up
- I get it. I really do. Don't laugh. But listen: how'd you get to be so arrogantly certain?
- We tread a righteous path. We're right, Dust
- Yeah, like fundamentalists who think they've a right to take a life for their fucked-up peanut vision. It ain't moral, it's primitive
(Tisiphone) - You wank on about morality? This world is absolute murder. Dress it up how you like. Nothing lives except by murder
(Alecto) - We're on our own! We piss on god
And they all start chanting. - We piss on god! We piss on god!
- Don't need a reason for nothing, Dust
- Ugh. Not even Charles Manson said that. But it's what his girls said, his girl killers.
Now they start to laugh right at me, long and loud. I'll let 'em. But Cassie's nowhere about.
- Meantime, I'll go find Cassie
- Keys, Dust. Keys!
- Wait till I find her.
I turned away but got no further. I believe someone delivered a big blow to my neck. A big sodding lugging thump, because I lost consciousness.

* * * *

I remember waking up and my neck was killing me and there was a body and it was calling Dust, Dust. Cassie. We were like propped by a tree in what seemed a shadowy wood. Cassie's scraggy hair-mound was in my mouth and her body was spooned in mine. She wriggled and I saw she was tied to me and naked. I could see abrased skin on her back. My skin was exposed as well. An itching pain came from under. *Dust, I'm so cold. I've been calling at you for ages.* My hands seemed bound behind. Some sort of vine. I wriggled and we rolled sideways into leaves. The wind ruffled the leaves, and the big tree seemed to groan above. Severe pain in my backside. Seemed to be odd objects strewn about as if in a circle. Who did it? One guess. Cassie was sniveling. I think I told her: *be still, I'll try to get free.* I remember fiddling for minutes and then a frond broke and a hand came free. There were livid marks on my wrists. I tore at the binding on Cassie's wrists. Her fingers were spread round my penis. I got them away then ripped at the fronds binding us. She rolled off. I saw her ankles were strapped. Her head bumped on a stone. She cried. When I saw a stick protruding from her anus I realised what my own pain was. Pulling the stick out of me made it snap. Which made me *furious*. I took hold of Cassie's rump and yanked the stick out of her. She screamed. I untangled her feet and sat her up. She'd been drawn over with red marks. Lipstick. On her navel was smeared words and a heart. Mud was caked on her face and legs. A thing was scrawled on my torso. I pulled her to a stand and we stumbled about. We found bits of clothing hanging oddly from branches, as if draped in significant shapes. The bitches had left them. I almost thanked them. It took straining minutes to get jeans onto Cassie's bottom half, then to find a tiny stream and get her there and try to wash. Mud came off her but the lipstick wouldn't. *'Girly loves her daddy'* was scrawled on her breast. On my stomach they'd written *'Victim'*. My penis was scratched, like ritually. It stung. I felt the wind get up, riffle through the slow-darkening wood. Our shoes were nowhere. My purse was gone. I held her hands, smoothed her, gave a hug. We're gonna walk, I told her. We'll find a farm and someone will get us home. Bare feet made the going hard. Cassie said nothing. Presently we came to a track with tyre marks, followed it. The day was drawing on. Only once did she look at me. I felt sorry. Finally we emerged from the wood and into fields. In the distance was the outline of a house. We knocked at the door and I explained to a startled farmer and his wife that we'd been attacked and robbed. They gave us showers and snacks and took us at our request to a rail station. I asked them for fifty quid, to be sent to them when we reached the city along with shoes they'd loaned. I'm not sure they thought we were the full quid. Thank you for helping my daughter and me, I said. We waited on a lonely platform, Cassie and me, and boarded a train back to the city.

Back in my apartment, Cassandra gathered her wits and called the parents, claiming she was staying over with a girlfriend. We got food on the street, didn't talk. Later, she seemed to have no qualms about sharing my bed.

Took care not to touch me all the same. But in the still of night she nudged at me, turned on the lamp. We looked at each other.

- Sorry Dust. You helped me. You're my friend
- Any time, baby girl
- How are we going to get our *revenge?*
Her fuzz of hair and white face made a halo in the gloom. Cassie Pace is a survivor. Maybe she just shoves the horror away, mushes it into fantasy.
- Don't you hate them utterly, Dust?
- I'm as angry as fuck, but that's exactly what they want us to want. You can't teach people like them. They're already victims, sado-masochists. Need to get above it, Cass. Revenge is one thing we can't have, though I'd love to rub all their faces in shit
- You're doing me in. Don't be a loser
- Cassie, you saw how I was capable of violence, the way I attacked Alex. You didn't like it. She got her revenge on me already
- But they expect us to do it. That's how they *live*
- No, Cass. That little ritual they did on us is all they've got. We have to pity them
- You're bullshit, Dust!
She went silent, wrapped the covers about her. Who to blame now?

Next morning she's vamoosed. I end up phoning the house. Helena answers. And if I'd anticipated what Cassie had done, I absolutely wouldn't have called.
- Cassandra told us a bizarre story about being attacked and tied up in a forest. What do you say about this?
- Helena, calm down. I am not sure that she... that she...
And I swear I don't know how the moment happened, but she finished my sentence for me.
- *Is sane?* Is that what you are saying? That my daughter is mentally ill?
- Uh... I don't want to -
- Do you say she fantasises? Acts crazy to get attention? Is she on drugs? Who *are* these Fury people, Mister Dust? I ask you, is she unstable? Because that is precisely what my husband is saying
- Helena. I wouldn't take what your husb-

And she hangs up. This is the point I realise I've been gazumped. Fuck!
Helena and Marcus and Cassandra Pace have retreated to the security of
a lie, a clannish lie. Cassie will play the vulnerable sick-kid card and the
parents will swallow it. How easy now to define her, reclaim her, mould
her as their own! The sickness of insanity is the excuse they need to enfold
Cassie for good. Cassie Pace has no loyalty to me at all. Or perhaps she
is crazy? Here's a nasty bind, and suddenly I feel numb. Maybe time has
come to abort my plan to stir up the Paces. But oh, when I saw that little
girl I knew I had a *duty*, I knew Daddy would swallow her up. Hang on
- didn't she do the big schizo act against him? Is that over? Can't be, she's
just fobbing the prick off with another cunning stunt. And she hates
those Furies. I call that a win. Or maybe she was only ever the privileged
kiddy showing off, maybe primogeniture is in her bones and she'll end up
inheriting all that they are. All of it. But what the hell is truth and why does
it matter? Truth should be self-manifesting, self-evident, indestructible!
People should not remain asleep in this world.

...Next night my dream mind is in overdrive. I find myself sconced in
the Paces' sitting-room, pontificating inside one of those bombastic self-
fulfilling dreams that when we wake dump us as the shrivellised nothings
we really are. 'You people! What about your Cassie? All this bipolar
behaviour! She can sit still as a pin in my meditation hall but put her in
a creative or social space and she's a sodding anarchist. Sick? I say no!
Obsessed with mad because you're so boringly PC. It's criminal to limit
her. Why clone a child to yourself? If you're desperate for status quo,
pin your hopes on little Benjy who'll pop up to Oxford and turn into a
mindless credit to the family.' Marcus has retired with dignity to his toilet,
meanwhile Loyal Wyfe doesn't appear to be showing the proper decorum
to puff up his status. He's back, didn't empty his bladder. 'Egocentricity is
cute ain't it, like we're all gliding down a summer road in our Thunderbird
and the world opens like a scene from *La Dolce Vita*, laid on a plate.
Marcus-Helena, smug in your clever studied beauty, did you *create*
anything? *Little Jack Horner sat in his corner, eating his pudding and pie...*
Come Marcus, why the long face, man? Did you conjure up the wind and
sky and sea and stars, conjure up consciousness, immutable mind, the

infinite electric pathways of a human being? Where did you get all your gifts? Ask, damn it! Let's all laugh at the squelch to our egos. Respect, awe, are what you need. So much respect and awe that it drowns you in love. Don't be a bourgie. Be the empty and drunken god that you are!'

But I wake up. It all fades. Dreams, they balance the distortions of waking. I'm depressed.

Out of the Woods And I just underestimated Helena Pace. The Lady in Limbo engineered a lull in things, no doubt to cool it all off. Now I get the summons. At her doorstep she tells me her husband is out. Her clear-light look tells me this might be a good thing. We settle in her atrium on a wicker sofa. Winter sun dabs at our faces. Michelangelo the cat peers at us, white Sphinx on a table.

- I know you're with the Divinology Church, Dust
- I think I knew you knew. It's not all I am, though
- Be that as it may. (She pauses for gravitas) I have a thing to tell you that I never told a soul. I went to that church in my early married days. As you might know, I'm not unattractive to some. Your Employer took me in, and… I ended up in his bed. I longed to be one of his spiritual women. I wanted it so much and I already had Marcus! What is my problem? I thought. What exactly is wrong with me?
- You know as well as I do that Marcus for all his accomplishment can't give you all you want
- I don't want to say it
I see she wishes to possibly cry. But how to shake off the tragic-romantic pose she's cultivated many a year here in Limbo?
- Spit it out. You said it often enough to yourself
- I think… that Cassie may not be Marcus' child.
I suckle her hand, hold her gaze. No crying so far.
- Perhaps it doesn't matter to me, Dust.
She gazes. Does she want it to be true?
- All right, Helena. No matter what, Cassie's her own self. But no, she *is* the blood daughter of you and Marcus and you know it. But let her be the spirit child of you and the Employer.

Her face flickers to a smile. Behind that untouched sophistication she's a very sweet girl. She leans over, puts her cheek to mine... lets me kiss her on the lips. For longer than is proper. And deftly she averts her face. There is silence in the manse. I'm thinking of the bedroom. She knows it. We pause by a glittering pond of possibility. But she stands, leads me out, through the garden, into the woods. It's glisteningly quiet there. A patina of sunlight shimmers amid the trees. The goddess clings to my arm. She wants to talk.

- The days of the church were like a thrilling heaven to me. I wanted to break out, 'experience the mystic'. And sex. And the Employer was magnetic beyond my dreams! Marcus was suspicious, said it was my 'child phase'. Had his own big project for me to invest in. Always had to prove the rational was superior. I wanted him but it seemed as if I was being locked in. Now I see you're doing my unlocking for me. I want you to. I want Cassie to
- You feared being exposed and alone, took on his fears over the years. Spidery pact: feeling versus his sacred rationality. Me, I kind of wish you'd do something ugly, smash something.
She runs a patrician finger over my cheek, around my lips.
- Don't trust me though. I project my shit about
- Then let me soothe you, little boy
- Wish you'd been my mother. Or my wife.
She laughs... I should say merrily! Child, mother, cream-cake girl.
- And girls like you should lead, not dissemble. Teach him quietly, bit by bit. Be the goddess. You've got Cass to do the radical stuff. I'm glad you're what you are... with me, in these woods. I actually like this world occasionally. I might dream about you. Totally honest, Helena.
Helena wrinkles her succulent mouth. I want to eat all of it. She has ascended to a heraldic beauty in my eyes. She studiously arranges her little boy's hair, takes his arm, pulls him on. We walk in the winter calm. She wants me to talk.
- Question to ask is: how many times do you want to come back?
- To where, Dust?
- To this world! One part of us says: 'I'll want always to return here -

for the delicate flowers in my garden, for my child's smile, my husband's smooth chest, my superior cooking, my woods and gilded sunsets on the terrace, even for my melancholy dreams of leaving...' Another part will say: 'how long do I want this grind, this desperate growing up, this clamour for status, to be noticed, accepted, to be pregnant again, to fight to understand, to stop fearing (at a distance) the world's suffering, or my need to be left alone, to carve out my peace...' We're all in thrall to lower depths, enticing pools and crevices, sleep and death. I used to want to grapple with the *shadow*. Now I just have to acknowledge it, like the side of the moon where sunlight never falls. Take the heat out: it's all we need. Life does the rest, drives us kicking and screaming to things we don't want to grapple with

- There's such huge resistance
- Yeah, but some things are already yours like gifts from heaven: your accomplishments. You barely notice those
- And so many things in those dark pools make me recoil, that I don't want to touch
- But we shouldn't worry about spirit-sapping nuisances or even harsh phobias. They're our big clean-out. And if not now, when? They're out of our control anyway. Reaches of the Gyre we just can't know. Helena Pace, you are a serious hot *babe*. And I know you don't mind being flattered since you want to swim in the ocean of your feelings. But you need to risk! And you need to stop waiting.

She actually blushes, laughs like Cassie, then trippingly covers it up.

- Yet we only have ignorance forced out of us by the most bitter experiences!
- Better still, by clear understanding
- Fill me in, Yogi Dust
- Righto. You are nothing but the absolute awareness of utter being, the eternal real substance, here, forever now, forever *this*. You are yourself, you are pure feeling, you are the endless delight of creation. Your job is to know it, and to give up the absurd idea of your separate existence... Howzat?

Well explained, Dust! The cool light in her eyes says so. But she's an untouchable beauty, this Helena Pace. We entwine fingers in the midst of the breathing wood, share the vulnerable thrill of silence.

And then her phone goes off. Fumble in handbag. Husband on the line! Her eyes stab at the trees about her. But she listens to him… and his world impinges once again, and her expression settles into one she's long practised, the one that contains all the vibrating world… earnest, charming, mild, cool, dutiful, out of reach. We're over then, and life and duty beckon. Marcus didn't share in our holy communion, our holy science. Strange warp of intertwining worlds that never mix. Horses for courses. Would I ever want him to hear it all? Sure thing. As long as I could steal away his wife, and his daughter, in exchange.

* * * *

Back at home, I think of packaging my clear-eyed speech and sending it to the Employer. He asked for reports, right? No doubt he steered me into sucking the goods from Helena Pace. Does he want me to heal up all his women? Why do I get to do his karma for him? And why do I always need his seal of approval? Maybe I should claim I'm a 'superior' soul. Or am I really 'not good enough'? I bloody well should be, but fear it is otherwise. And does he want me always hoisted on the horns of this dilemma? I suspect it. 'If you're good enough to learn, you're good enough to get your ego beaten and stomped on.' Trouble is, who would *trust* people who give no quarter, who're always right, who mercilessly point out our inadequacies? So I put my head on the block… and send the report! Amazingly he replies. First time ever. Sailing closer to the wind! The gist: he is 'not faintly interested in so-called speculative philosophic discourse'. Period. 'Waste of church's valuable time… writer should focus on the needs of the benighted and suffering etcetera… Go back to the list you were given…' Yadda! And following this, he no doubt obliterates my missive. The Employer knows the silly ways of his spiritual children. We loathe him for it but he's quite right. Quit scribbling, Dust.

…On the other hand, I finally got the fucker to reply to me.'

Blood Brothers

In the brown brick alleys of the Western City industrial zone, the Dowson and Daughters meat-processing facility glowers like Buchenwald beside a green canal. Beyond is nebulous marshland, and all around brick edifices stick their blackneedle chimneys into the horizon, jabbing at the sky. The narrator Dust, in a fit of conscience, went to a labour exchange and took a job. The description written on a card said 'meat packer'. Next day in the early dawn he left his home and took the interminable fog-windowed bus journey to the West. Into the gated mouth of Dis.

Dust the vegetarian begins his time here. First duty of the day is the unloading of the vans. The air is freezing outside, and scarcely warmer inside the facility. Vans are backed up to the ramp, and he clambers inside them to pull the massive carcasses from metaled hooks into great fridges in the building. The killing has mercifully been done elsewhere, but the bones are sharp reminders. His numbed fingers regularly get cut. He fails to notice. The ramp is greasy with frost, and lugging forty kilos of bone and flesh can put one's back out. The job requires grit, not least to put away that slow undertowing grief at the slavering futility of the world. By tea break the feeling dissipates a little, only to be revived by *The Sun* and *News of The World* which Dust scans absently while slurping at a mug of grey tea or chewing on a gluey British scone. The upstairs canteen with its fogged barred windows looks out to the courtyard and great metal doors of the packing hall. Its inhabitants are irretrievably blacky and whitey lower class, unmercifully ignorant, stooped by the badness and monotony of work life in grimy industrial waste zones. Once Dust brought in *The Guardian*, cudgeled by some memory of a civilisation outside the gates of Dis, and was confronted by a black prole who remarked: *Waat de fock is yorr game, maan?* But Dust's annoyance soon segued to pity. He saw slow hysteria in the young man's eyes, his green-palmed Jamaican dignity and multi-coloured Rastafarian hat turned to a sick joke in the confines of this death farm in the brown wastes of West London. Welcome to England, mon.

Dust's diary takes up the narrative. 'One day a youngish guy comes into the place whom I'm told by the head Fleischer is on day parole from

Wormwood Scrubs where he's 'doing four years'. He pig-stuck a guy with a knife in a street brawl, they say. Parole now consists of work experience in a meat-packing facility, complete with knives. He shows up in white coat and plastic hat at the bench beside me this morning. I say hello, and he grins when I say my name. I have the feeling he thinks I'm some kind of actor. *I'm Lenny Doodle*, he tells me. We look at each other. A faint derision in his eyes seems to light a spark of reckoning between us, from separate reaches of the mental spectrum. Places like this level us out, do they not? We stand together at the steel bench in the long room with the blood-puddles, racked ovens, muddy plastic curtains, fluoro lights. Our job is to honey and roast the yummy hams, cut and wrap the succulent joints. Lenny sticks by me. His manner is part friendly-familiar, part standoffish suspicious, part derisive-ironic. What's his story? Not the time to ask. Should I say I know he's on parole? Presently I get the feeling he knows I know, but'll take his time to announce it official-like. After all, there's power in it. I silently wonder what it's like to be in nick for a crime. What's really the line between the innocent and the guilty? There but for the grace of god... Once I visited some drug prisoners in the soaked heat of Bangkok. They cheerfully told me they were in for twenty years. I took them bundles of cigarettes and they accepted with a quiet thank you. We make a living from these, they said. I ponder on the plight of the incarcerated, the victims, the abused, the dying, the needy, the hopeless, the depth-dwellers. I want to taste (not live) their crimey lives for an episode, feel a wee smidgin of how it is. I'm the voyeur, and like so many others the dirty side of nature is my fetish. I gaze at pictures of glam-murder victim Sharon Tate, poke inside the heads of Manson's killer-girls, noisomely crave the details of their I-dare-you slaughter. The best crimes tickle the fancy! And I fear my new mate Lenny (not his real name) will shortly discover how naïve I am.

One never meets 'Dowson's Daughters', and never the old man either. Perhaps they're nineteenth-century ghosts who haunt the yards and alleys and galleries of this meat-mill. Or do they live in gardened villas in sweeter neighbourhoods paid for by grim-weary plastic-headed quotidian day workers who fondle and fiddle the flesh of the dead into plastic packets… all for them? For the great proletariat of England, here is life in all its promise. Abandon health, all ye who enter here! Sometimes in the dim carcassed halls I imagine the laughter of these Dowson daughters in spotted dresses and petticoats tippling in and out of carriages under the wether eye of Father, ruddy Victorian with paunch and jowl, rough-handling men and money, ascending the social ladder with bulldog brashness, building England's satanic mills. For here is certainly one of those, the dross-floored bowel of the elsewhere-civilised… For in this ever-dying place, with its sawdusted slabs under, the hearts of the animal dead are bled in rivers, processed sans name or recognition for the tasting of blood-lovers, for the sustenance of the race, the promotion of life through the stomach and veins - for we the people who eat our own death, we fine civilised people… And only when these places, erased from human history like *Treblinka* and *Sobibor* - whose sodden ground whispers the cries of the dead and where lupins grow innocuously above, their soft heads swaying in spring winds that fritter through black-green forests… only then shall we know what such places mean. Laboratories of soul-dissection, chambers for snuffing breath, factories of erasure, schoolyards of blotting out, clinics and slabs of forgetting. For if we can kill and process a million creatures, we can kill and process a million people. Should be simple, it's just flesh. Obviously we need the nourishment. Genocide for nourishment, for the betterment of the goodly race. Let dumb animals feed the world then - and let dumb humans feed history.'

…Home late and likely overtired, and in morbid imagination or to feed an overweening superiority need, Dust has hit on a pertinent subject for his Employer's perusal. No philosophic rant required. 'The processing facility operates twenty-four-seven. Efficiency, deadlines, vigorously adhered to. Let's walk you through. Transports turn up continuously, and it is not unusual for them to arrive past midnight. Officials open the doors to the cattle trucks, shepherd the livestock onto platforms. Stock is of variable quality and has to be sorted. Smaller or older specimens are directed to marshalling areas to the left, and better-fed stronger stock to the right. Under searchlights our platform marshall makes decisions with a practised eye. Stock are generally disoriented, so appear to appreciate the speedy transition to dedicated areas following an inhospitable journey. It is understood that they will be cleaned and deloused before transitioning the short distance to their final quartering yards. While the general purpose of the facility is clear, it is understood that to unduly upset or unnerve stock has a discernible effect on efficiency. Specialists, overseen by dedicated forepersons, stand ready to receive the incoming quota. Clean process according to business-best practise is a source of satisfaction in our establishment, and, we trust, to the satisfaction of eager shareholders in our burgeoning industry. All care is taken to mitigate the impact that stock effluent, for example, might put on the environment to the detriment or other tenants in the area. Security and noise-reduction measures obtain for the same positive purpose. Phase two, after cleaning and delousing, involves the channelling of stock to bays deep within. This is done by 'trusted low-tech means' (prods and cattle dogs) but we venture to say efficiency is not measurably compromised thereby. In fact, unruly conduct is minimised by use of steel channels and cages. Stock undergo efficient stunning or gassing before 'the pieces' are removed for processing at adjacent workstations. Operators work quickly by hand to ensure hygienic dismemberment before portions are assigned their packaged form. Relevant cooking is undertaken, and following this step all corporeal material is inspected and designated 'fully processed'. Waste products such as effluent, bone, gristle, blood, hair and sundry items are assigned either to a storage facility at the premises' core or shipped to sites outside for use in agricultural support, namely fertiliser. All unused material is incinerated and earmarked for landfill, to be distributed hygienically according to government regulation. And this is how business activity is carried out at our nationalised socialised processing facility known as...*

[* *Sobibor*]

'Next day, back at Dowson and Daughters, I'm looking for something to make the morning's ham-basting session with Lenny go swimmingly.
- Maybe the only real prison is in the imagination?

Lenny smiles a coy smile. He has lately proved himself a wit and waggish philosopher of cynic bent, and while his charm is tinglingly entertaining, I'm vaguely uneased to discover his mastery at feeding people exactly what they want to hear. Lenny obsequiously defers to powers-that-be at our factory, but his conversation leaves one with the faint taste of being taken for a fool's ride. If one is bent like he toward the notion that the cosmos is an almighty scam perpetrated by those powers-that-be on the poor 'n' needy, then this factory of toil is a mere stage set for the exposition of his coyly grinning subversive sly negations, his *not me guv I ain't no interlectual* pissing from a height on all pretentious systematised fabricated normality. And so politely of course. Learned it all on the inside, yeah. Yet in a harsh self-promoting world Lenny is really a nobody, a carper on the sidelines, eternal knocker-naysayer, humble old-womanish whinger with but a youthful glinty eye and ready-clever turn of phrase.

- Oi was reading in moi lonely cell just this week, about a certain invention by a savvy eighteen-century feller called Jerry Benting
- Yeah?
- Ay panopticon
(He's proud of his word) - Sounds wacky
- My dear Dusty, 'tis a monstrosity. But the rulin' class thought their Christmases all came at once. Imagine if you will, a round structure consisting of a lot of levels where a single controller at the centre can check on ev'ry tom dick n' 'arry inmate, all in separate cells wiv no contact to each other or the world or any connection to the power bosses. Great for the insane, for unruly children and for crims like me!
- Jeremy *Bentham*, eh? The authorities won't want you reading that guff
- See that camera dere? Our great democracy has more of 'em than any country on the face of the plannit. Smile for the camera, Dusty
- Why'd you get put in jail, Len?
- Me? (Perish the thought he should ever be in jail) Doncha know? Stabbed some cunt in the guts. (Delivered for vicious effect)
- Why, though?
- Didn't like 'im

- But surely there are deeper reasons. Sociological ones?
- Yeah. I'm a social victim. But I'll never be cured.

Lenny mixes his registers as if Gielgud were conversing with the Artful Dodger. Pathetic Lenny has no education. In his world this panopticon thingy is erudition. Though he could have been an actor. Coulda woulda shoulda been a lot of things I guess, but crime got in the way. I smile and nod along with him, suitably nonchalant. And he likes a conspiring audience (of one) to nudge and wink at. Lenny's the master of his own goon-world and inside it is quite the clever-clogs. If I listen and ask questions, he assumes all the seedy experience he gained on the inside and in the thuggy druggy byways of his life is relevant to me and my welfare. In this meaty work-world of ours, workmates in our Mondy Tuesdy merry-go-round, we can sing his crappy little tune. Still, he won't fail to give me a rap on the knuckles once in a way, perhaps in the manner of how a master thinks a dog needs discipline. He's resourceful, old Len. Coulda been a parent and all.

- Don't touch that knife with the green 'andle. It's mine. Use vat one.

Me, I don't argue. Though the green-handled one was actually mine before he turned up.

Following his elaborate putting of people in their place according to primitive dog-teach-dog hierarchies learned on the inside and in gang world and in some deadshit school he used to drive the teachers crazy at, Lenny will for a quiet while work away at his new profession of roasting and basting with a glazed acceptance, as if to show he's an acceptable man in the important team in the big kitchen. His quiet empty expression and slow-fiddly shuffle up and down the hall are at odds with that other bristly-bravado subversive ante fellow... and suggest a sad little lag who craved routine and discipline all along. The alter-ego wants to be this humble-important little worker in the big factory that does important fings for the world like makin' 'am and bacon and stuff. And he does his shuffly part like a dutiful child. This other Lenny amazes me at first, until I see its pathos. And then I cry out inside for him, the little shit. I care about him, this dude with his sly crummy joke and his third-rate mocking grin, the nice-dumb bloke who wants to get out from behind the smartarsey survivor. He lost his life somewhere along the line and got a counterfeit of it. Now in the grinding factories and smut-alleys of England, here's a life of sorts for the offering.

The great business of knives he takes very seriously, seems to morph into chastising parent whenever we handle the knife sets. Is he conscious of the irony or not? I can't decide: some human pig nearly died squirming on the end of one of his blades. He'll grin in a knowing way but there's no cultivation in the mind behind. Me, I enjoy the joker, feel sorry for the dumdum - and so I dance some kind of act around him. One of these days he'll wise up to me and then I don't know if he'll be in control or not. Up in the canteen we don't communicate, as if he thinks of me as some embarrassing sibling he has to keep at arm's length while he's carefully educating lesser proles round about. And he's good with these types. Adopts a patronisingly avuncular mode and tells them evil stories of his chequered life, always inflated and always with a rough homily at the end as if he were a great churchman dispensing succour to the dull-eyed and sinful. There's usually a few eyeless bods about him, swimmering in the hot haze with their greasy mugs and sausages. I discern there's a reformer in Lenny somewhere, an elder brother, an uncle or dad, even a moraliser, self-chastiser. All the roles he never got to play. In this grotty nowhere uncivilised industrial hole in West London, he can be a legend in his own lunchtime…

And uh-oh, it's an uh-oh morning. Something unpleasant must've gone down back at Wormy Scrubs. Lenny is capable of dark surprise when The Saboteur rears his head. He's started to rave about 'Fascists', a catch-all term no doubt: how they rool the world, how nuffing ever changes, how 'one 'alf of the 'uman race wants to do fings an' the other 'alf wants to stop 'em from doin' it'. And where do I put myself on this scale, he asks, wielding a chopper over the bench. We both look inhuman in our aprons and plastic hairnets, perhaps making it easier for Lenny's parade of altered personalities to rear up.

- Me? I'm an anarchist. I sympathise with your frustrations
- But yer bourgie and yer educated, right Dust?
(I never fail to be reminded how alien his world is to mine) - Meaning?
- You'd rather be a boss than a worker, wouldn' ya?
- Er, wouldn't you?
- Rather be left alone, mate
- Things going badly at the Scrubs?
- Listen to 'im. 'The Scrubs'. What the fock would ye know, matey?
- I loathe all forms of control, I assure you. And I still resent things that people did to me in the past, though I shouldn't, since it's immature
- You're a sly cunt. Is that remark about you or about me?
- Whatever, Lenny, whatever. You brought it up
- Yeah. Fuckin' fascists. And they're good at hidin' it, mate.
His eyes glaze over. He appears to have thought of something else.
- Talk to me Lenny, by all means. But don't assume you and I have to defend ourselves all the time. It's a conversation. We share information, opinions, thoughts. No sweat
- Yeah yeah, righto *mum*. Them racks need filling up. Snap to it, Dusty.
Here's the childish paranoid as well as the closet authoritarian - in the mode of surly working-class father who wouldn't let his wife go to a night class. Now he drops a tray with an unholy clang. No doubt to see how it gets on my nerves. Yup, it gets right on 'em.
After tea-break he's back on the subject, but as if nothing at all were said previously. Mister Innocent and Reasonable has popped up.
- 'Fing is, right, I was reading about them Nazis in the Jewish 'Olocaust. Wasn't just them ya know. Was the gypsies, the mormons, the mentals, jehovahs - they all went in the oven. Like a ham roast, mate.
(I'm suddenly tired) - And your point would be?
(He won't like my tone) - Point would be, *point* would be - we're all somebody else's fuckin' lunch. Know who did the dirty work though, mate? Cunts like us. You and me. Right there. Shoveled 'em all in, dragged 'em out, chopped 'em up. You n' me
- Not me, Lenny. I never did any of that shit. Never would, never could
- So you think. So you *think*. But you'd do it if they made ya. You'd do it,

I know ya. You're hoity-toity, but you'd shove them fuckin' bodies in the oven too if they made ya, mate

(Now we've got to mister Insufferably Patronising) - People will do anything to survive, Len

- Yeah, see? Got ya there mate! Even when they know they're goners anyway. But people like you don't wanna think about it, do ya? All that dirt and shit

- Len, I've read a hundred books on The Shoah and seen a thousand documentaries. What do you want?

- Yeah, you read about it. You read about it. But you might've *been* there. Or maybe you were one of them officers. Maybe you're a reincarnated officer of the SS! Bad karma, mate!

- What? Let's drop it. It's an evil subject

- Nah, mate. I don't drop shit. I don't -

- Pass me the green-handled knife, will you? Yeah, that one

- Nah, that's mine. Use yer own. Listen, I face shit. I deal with it every day

- Do you Len? Do you now? What kind of 'karma' do *you* have, mate?

- Better 'n' yours, mate

(This is so effing childish) - Lenny, the way we are now, speaks of the way we were *then*. Why are you reading about the Holocaust? Maybe because you need to understand it. But maybe you can't, maybe nobody can. And sometimes unexpected stuff comes up, out of the blue. But not for no reason, Len. For a *reason,* mate.

Now I'm lecturing. But he is way ahead.

- Can't control it. That's it mate! Can't *control* it. So we don't 'ave responsibility. Can't fix it once it's done.

This is getting a long way from bacon and ham.

- If you believe that, you'll never get out of Wormwood Scrubs

- But if you try to *run away,* Dust, then you're no better. You're not superior at all

- I'm not running away from shit!

And I snatch at his infernal green-handled knife but he gets it first. And he gives me two sudden nicks in the palm of my hand like a cross. Redness oozes out onto the bench. He grins. See what I mean? his grin says. What the fuck? I say, and push at him. But he sways deftly sideways. Now looks me in the face. The grin is strange but intimate. - Wot if you got it somewhere else, eh Dust? And he runs that blade right up my arm. And a jagged gash starts to run crimson all at once like a wave of paint seeping under a door. I panic. I kick out at him. He pulls aside my apron and flicks at me again. This time it's the abdomen. I think it's the abdomen. Can't believe this is happening. Dirty plastic curtain glares at me. I'm on my knees. Feel a pain rush in my middle. Bluewhite lights. No-one's here. My hand is running. Red everywhere. Flickeringly I see Lenny shove something under the tap. It gushes. Now he stands over me. Wait! he says. Wait! And he hurries away through the thick plastic. I'm waiting, Len! Then someone else is there, someone big and wide. Startled grunts from the new guy. Stained aprons coming at me now… I forget the rest.

I wake in the ambulance. It's bumping grinding hot. Lenny's face. He's saying stuff like 'It's gonna be okay. We're goin' to a picnic (clinic). Lie back and relax. I'm here mate.' At the hospital there's a palaver. They wanna stitch me up. Men in white. Big needle hurts. Lenny keeps close. They tell him get out of the way. Smell of something acidy. Feel sick. Throw up at least once. People seem to crowd about. I lose it. Later I'm awake. Lenny's face again. Nurse says something soft. He makes sweet talk. I go back to black. Later still… this guy on the far side of the room seems to be reading a magazine. Hurries over.

- 'Allo mate! They stitched you up no worries. You did good! (And soon, hushed) - Hey Dusty, listen. You and me know it was an accident, right? I mean, in the sense I din' know what I was doing. You neever, right? Both in alien territ'ry. You got me riled, I cut ya. 'S bad. Shouldn't 've 'appened. Sorry okay? Learned a lesson. You an' me both eh!

And plenty of *etcetera*. I stopped caring, went to sleep… And two days pass by. Lenny visits from work. Been all over my case, ain't he. Good samaritan, faithful mate blaa. Gettin' quite a reputation. I say nothing to no-one. Because I can't be bothered, or not angry enough? This evening the doctor tells me I'm up for discharge. Lenny has to supervise all that. Sits by me, looks furtive, whispers.

- So mate. Yer going home. Listen. You're on the *team* now mate. Reckon this thing 'll toughen yez up eh? You been through it, like.

What's this? Now I'm initiated into his cloying thug-world, patronized with his fucking version of baptism by violence? (I'm sweating) Can't be so stupid. No, he understands all too well. I'll seek refuge in the ceiling then… One should really take more thought for the eternal and less of the trackless grind of this suffering world… So what use in laying charges? If he's the slightest teeniest bit smug about this incident, I won't let it go. But of course he is though he hides it. Thinks he's won some kind of point or, perish the thought, made a disciple. In some arcane way is he passing his knowledge on to me? - bleeding out a bit of karma, letting me share the mystery of his dice games with evil. Maybe there's respect somewhere! Well if there isn't yet, there will be when I'm done, because I'll have to use Threat. A word from me to the cops and he's done for. But the problem is, will he be equipped to care? This is the delicate delicate part: he might just use it to entrench the rebel and victim, to get more Damned. But isn't Lenny somehow angling to get *out* of his past? All right, I'll keep silent for now. He'll get to swagger under my sword of Damocles; maybe he's used to that drear sword, having felt it all his life. Wait though. In shifting ways, silence may work on us all.

Meantime Lenny has resolved to hug his enemy close. And I know the moment I ask him to get away from me he'll turn nasty. We're locked in. Makes me sick. (Sudden thought: why not ask my Employer for advice? Ha! Why did I never have *that* thought before?) Now I'm confined at home for several days. Lenny bowls in, hands me tabloids, feeds me fish and chips, smokes in my room. And wants to know who else lives in my building. (Crim's habit I guess) I don't tell him. - So why d'you live 'ere? Crummy gaff ain't it? I got contacts, mate. Hey, I got rid of that fucken green knife, he says one time. As if the knife were to blame all by itself. - Listen Dust, I ain't the world's cleverest cunt but I know I gotta do better. Sure, I'm streetwise an' know how to deal it to the fascists pigs, but I know there's more. You showed me it. How? Just 'cause you're there, 'cause of who you are. Cultivated and such. Into spiritual shit and such. You helped me, I can dig it. And now I gotta help you, put yer back on yer feet. Get it?

I get it, Len. You slashed me and I'm supposed to forget about it. Maybe maybe I will but you'll need to give a thing in return. Not sure what it is but it better be something 'cause *I* can be an intolerant cunt! I say none of this, but he can't be stupid enough to see I'm not thinking it, there in my bed under my quietised mummified expression. But then he looks at me with his hollow-eyed scrubby-beardy look and his earring and his fake chummy way, and I see the weight of his past haloed over him like a cancered ghost and I feel he is lost. Didn't need to be but is - and will blunder on like he is for another millennium in and out of Wormwood Scrubs or its bullying fascistic equivalent, always teetering over the chasm of insanity on his knife-edge of pseudo-normality and illegitimacy and his feckless bargain with optimism glossed up by those crummy fake grinning naïve eyes; that surly-lipped school kid who pelts stones at gold palaces he'll never get entry to because his spirit just won't let him.

I'll keep my mouth shut then. Though most of me doesn't want a bar of him. (And I hate my bloody Employer for dumping me in it! Now I'm blaming *him* like Lenny blames his knives.) And I know I have to *go through* all this. You know what hell is? It's commitment - to someone else's dunghill of shit pain fear and rubbish. My own I can tinker with, make deals with, but not someone else's. Because they're also-rans, fellow grim-riders, effaced losers shoveled behind cell doors of forgetting, rats in the rubbish of my karma who mirror my face back to me, backstreet nobodies, slum-dwelling blackface races, toilet cleaners, walmart grunts, shuttered wives, spinsters, old men, snotty kids at my old school, trolls and oiks and grubs and urchins and all the poor creatures of this sallow world. And when I don't want to help them I know how much I hate the world, how much I hate myself! With my vomit-past and my centreless mind and guilt-stricken litany of mistakes and lies avoidances fooleries half-truths mess-ups compromises and repeated failing-not-learning, lugged with me to this very last day out of Dickensian pits I can no more erase than a drunken tramp his ragged beer-swilled liver-killed hopelessness, or a criminal his stinking record of jabbing the bastards he blames the failure of his own wits on, with a long-blade knife he'd rather use if he were honest to cut his own throat from ear to ear and have done with it. What kind of integrity does it take to put up with being stabbed? Too damn much for me. Now I have to be the fecking martyr. Why do all the things we think we've sorted come back and bite us on the arse? You never know. You never know what's coming.

There are monks in the East who as they walk turn every breath into prayer, who with continual mindful acts want to bring god and world together... this karma path that fuses opposites, forbears and forgives and calms the heart, dissolves self-disappointment, makes us appreciate birth, lets us understand our descent to depths, to ego-prisons, to wells of confusion - these monks are saying to me: Brother, I am you, I serve you, I feed you, I give myself away to you. Not to the abstract ideal, to the sky and clouds and fluffy and nice - but to you. You with your smelly armpits and your mound of karma shit and your vindictiveness and your error and your sly violence and all of it. You. *But I, Dust, I can't do it. Ever. Because I don't believe I have to.* And my Lenny won't appreciate it anyway. There has to be a bargain here. He has to be made to ride over and meet me part-way. In some way Lenny has to pay, and then I will own my hardness. Even those savvy monks know hardness. Let the chips fall as they may. Man proposes and God disposes. It's really got nothing to do with me.

Here comes the moralist again: what good will more punishment do for Len? Does absolutely everything have to turn to shit before anyone actually changes? I believe it. But it depends whether he *feels* anything for me. He may, but no more than for anyone else on this dirty planet. No catharsis! Silly idea. But he's the one who needs a lesson, not me! Or what do I really know about him anyway? Maybe Lenny has long since embarked on a fragile game of coping, of sly redemption that walks a fine line of sardony, of unfeeling, of saving himself from the anguish pit by a healthy contempt, a self-protecting matter-of-fact insouciance that lets him straddle the margin of acceptance and rejection. Which gives him a nose for vulnerable stooges like me whom he can't help but exploit because of their very desire to help. He may not be educated but he's streetwise, and that counts in the subject of human morality. Conclusion: morality is variable, subject to conditions. A wee stab, a wee lesson. Not beyond old Lenny to deliver a bit of karma-easing, a chance for his victim to have a little think about why it all happened, and to relate it in his conscience to all the bullying and guilt-shame and self-doubt and 'I deserve it' loser talk he ever told himself (and that Lenny might have told himself too). Taste of the medicine like. Lenny gets a leg-up, victim gets a leg-up. Is Lenny the teacher then? I told you I was naïve, out of depth. So the message is: 'dump a little shit on someone! It's like you dump a little kindness'. And chances are the universe wants you to do it. Cute bargain. On the other hand, human nature says Lenny 'll want to claim kudos for whatever little pact he's made with himself. Not one to wanna get poked in the eye. He's fragile and won't, can't admit it. Not to me, not publicly. Actions must speak louder than words. He needs to get the initiative and keep it. Hey, he'll be all kindness, practise a little kindness on me and feel better about it. And I suppose I should let him. Should I be stern or kind? Neither. I'll cocoon myself up in naivety. Let that be my balm that lets me do nothing, that lets silence speak some more, lets time gnaw things away a bit. Because you never know… you never know what's coming next.

What came next is complicated. Our blood-brother affair is suddenly tampered with. That bloke he ran to after the stabbing, that worker by the name of Boyce, has his little suspicions. Lenny doesn't seem to have a lot of cachet in the world, because Boyce had his wee chat with management and they've come a-knocking one morning at my flat. The younger of the two gentlemen present asks smilingly if I am in any way keen to stay on, because he's concerned for my health in a dirty business and is keen to offer me a (substantial) little severance package. Might a man of my abilities not seek employ in a better field?

- What happened with Len then, fellers?
- You do know that's not his real name?
- What did Boyce say?
- We'd rather not discuss that
- He might have it wrong
- Friend Len will not be returning

- Unfair. He has tried to support me. Boyce obviously doesn't like him, though Len trusted him
- We'd have to doubt that
- He's on parole, you idiots
- No smoke without fire, Mister Dust.

The two men look at me. The speaker is younger, rather suave for a meatpacking executive. The other is grizzled with bushy eyebrows. He takes over.

- Taking a fall for Lenny is not a good idea, young feller, even if you feel it's your duty. I don't say you're naïve. We've told the people at the Scrubs he needs a 'calmer environment' to finish his work-parole. And Len might just appreciate our 'little gesture' - one of these days.

Ouch, my little bubble-world just got pricked again. The older fellow deftly took the weight off me. Wow! People are nowhere near as dull as you might think.

So. Lenny naturally turns up one more time. And makes it plain and clear that he pleaded with them fascist pigs for me to take *his* job. No matter that it's a deadshit job and that Len thereby offers a backhander. And no matter that his motives are embarrassingly transparent. Still, he grins about it. And his grin might just be friendly-nice or it might just be a big seedy comic ironic act. Or both at once. Hmm... the final takeout on all this? Only help people if they ask for it? Not exactly. Some people need help even if they don't know it, and they ask for it even when they don't know they're asking. And some people want your help even though they specifically say they don't, and some will go to any lengths to avoid receiving any kind of help including repeating their foolish crimes forever. Because if we stay in our doldrums, there's always the hope of some fresh wind of renewal. Our Len wants to hog all the acts of helping. It makes him feel superior in the absence of trust, in the absence of having any friends in this world. It's his own special method of redemption. And don't you frickin' mess with that, Mister Dust, or whatever yer poncy name is.'

Old Man on the Seventh Floor

Picture a room in a building in a city, inhabited by a youngish man of thirty-five years. He has lately moved here, into this old building of nine floors with its blood-magenta slime-green corridors. A desk and chair stand beside his fourth-floor window, that looks out to a winter garden. There is a ragged tree sodden with winter, and beneath it a place for children to play. Few children play there. The walls of the room are bare since he has not been here long. His solitary lamp is frosted white, and if we look we notice a glass and empty bottle on the desk's dark surface. Pen and papers are splayed out, and if you spy from the corner of your eye you'll likely see an unmade bed. The day is drawing to a close. A paragraph on the computer screen: *Picture a room in a building in a city...* is not yet swallowed by the screensaver. He has stepped out to the darkened passage. The window is slightly open and the curtain is tickled by suggestions of a wind from afar. Distant traffic. Other lives. This is the moment then, where the scene - unless held, framed, made to stand as symbol, as act, as moment - will pass to the oblivion of time's winter forest. In the great war of annihilation that is the life of the world, we die here... of hidden wounds.

But no, our young man is back from the toilet, and he slumps again in his computer chair. Silence. He has the creeping suspicion nothing happened while he was out of the room. Mental illness was to have been the subject of his nascent story. He draws a blank now. The mind seems overshadowed by random things. The gloried march of Fascist culture for one... The phrase *vermin and scheisse* pops to mind. Excess schnapps perhaps? Something is waiting. He looks out to the garden. The children's summer camp was hereabouts. The snows have quite vanquished it now. No need to dwell therein. No need. Underneath. Underneath. At the edge of Poland...

Our youngish man of thirty-five had reached a peculiar plateau of late. On this high plain it no longer seemed to matter to him whether he experienced 'this or that', or anything at all. He felt in fact that no-one really experiences, that no part of us is personal, that there is no place to be in this turning world. Was this the longed-for exit? He remembers he felt momentarily lighter. I should smother the ego, stop waiting for a thing to happen, stop hoping that people will care or note some service I might have done them... To observe then, quietly: the best trick for putting up with it all, for when you're feeling sorry for yourself. Remember, your name is *Blank*. You walk alone in the depths of a green-black forest. Presently you tie one end of a rope about your neck, and tie the other to a single branch of a single tree... But again you see, the problem is there's no separation between your life and any other. Everything is everything else. The soul is the body and the body is the soul. And if both are one, then neither exists. Nor Yin nor Yang really exist. Your death is just some kind of narrowing, the naming of a solitary narrative you always seek. Or death is but a wind that turned to the east, a heat that died of coolness, a day that died of evening, a girl who died of growing up, a body that died of change. Death is a soldier who died of a general's notion of battle, a mind that died of wisdom, a story that died of being told. Words that died in a hail of sentences, peace that died of its own silence, love that died of sharing, seed that died of being born into a world. Family that died of the decades, heart that died of pulsing, blood that died of flowing outward to the frozen earth. This death... is nothing but the prison of your imagination.

In time, Blank must admit his several wounds are not so much physical as emotional, and that the purpose of doing the further bidding of his Employer can no longer be postponed. He is to visit a very elderly gentleman who lives on the seventh floor of the Staan Building on Fernino Street - by extraordinary serendipity just three floors above where Blank now resides. But how to connect, and what to say? Perhaps the old fellow needs a nurse... or a cleaner.

Blank records the following: 'I should not be surprised that I've had more than I bargained for these last weeks - with this antique German called Moodzlinger. I have learned a lot: that here is a man who extracts his pound of flesh from the world just as it exacted the same of him, a man who seems to tread heavily in the fields of his fate, to enact a fussy and complicated dueling harangue with the past, to assail even the calamity of his birth. Moodzlinger sweats his hypochondria and his wounds, he advertises them, he flitters them about him, sorts them in little piles in the form of talismans and signs and sighs and whispers and grudges, of logics and conversations that should have been corrected, pathways that never should have failed. He fights battles long lost, conducts polemics long superceded, rakes over ground long squished in the holocaust of history, so that only grey soil and weeds are left where a childish but stern aspiration once was, peering trustingly out to the future through the little round glasses of a child of the Reich. And if one (such as I) shows the presence and patience to engage with it all, one might be rewarded by his judging you a serious person, worthy of complaining to, worthy of presuming upon - a willing witness to the intricate horrors of a hypochondriac mind that secures no place in the slippery-eel paths of the past, that is cheated of peace in the epoch, whose raison d'etre is to scour back some clamouring pride or dignity under the slap of life's evil... To be judged serious one must *deal* with such punctilious facts and placements and logics and rights and wrongs. This self-sorry hyperbolic shambolic wreck of a German, in whom some punctilious policeman in shiny boots who believes that history must move in sweeps, clean modellings and plannings, forever chases a gasse-dwelling ingrate of epicurean tastes, some overblown expectant bourgeois in his city-hole who cowers in the face of metallic death-reports, and whose dainty handkerchiefed mouth pouts in disdain at clomping battalions in the streets; it is he, who could never marry the cleanliness he sought with the messy odours of his own dark taste. Perhaps he is a spiritual Nazi. And likely a closet Jew.

But is he an ironist? A man who trawls his old polemics and arguments a thousand times will be suspicious if you have not performed the same punctilious duty to history as he. Not an ironist then. But personal history is nothing but neurosis, and a fact is nothing but a fetish wrapped in a gristle of years, of sour sorrow and wanting and failure, of *This might have been...* and *How could this be so?* There is no clean fact but that which is embryoed by the filthy smells of history, the dung and the bad breath of a thousand mortal thoughts, the pant-pissing sweat of the condemned, the erection-creamed delight of the persecutors. And the etheric wars, the pasting of your sins on the skies of deeper mental worlds, the splattering of your evil on the vaults of the spirit, and the chain gangs of unquiet ghosts who live again the sweated horror and machination and detritus of the soap-opera world past: here are the indelible prints of the wrestlings of races, the insurmountable stains of the graspings of ordinary ones who lived and lost and died in holocausts, in the scum-tides of fortune, in the raked bonefields of wars, in the blood rivers of falsified hope - and in the mousy scrabblings of the peace, peace that fell upon us out of exhaustion and luck, seen only by half-alive ones who dodged the skyfall of bullets, who greased into this future out of cracks and shitholes of the past, who now stem their guilt and shame with elixirs of purpose and deserving, of family and renewal and hoping, in a better Germany, in a brave new world where men might be human again, under skies somehow made pure again…

Can we weave simplicity out of a basket of sorrow-threads, wash a bedsheet clean white from black waters? Can you get sweet youth back, when youth was dragged away by jackbooted men, or turn about the fuming bull of history with an anaemic wave of a knotty blue-veined hand?

- So, yah. You are here for cleaning zis my apartment?
- I am, if you need the help
- Iff I need the help? I haf the world on my shoulders and I need help? Okay okay. So you can clean around my things
- Can I help you sort your things? Put them in order?
- You tell some joke
- Not exactly
- Okay, you are inexperienced. We start again. Under my supervision we work. What is your charge?
- Oh, just by the hour. Nothing big
- You are from some church, some religion? You do your duty?
- Oh! No, I rent on the fourth floor… Although, do you know of the Church of Divi -
- I never wass religious. It helps nobody at all. All right. You will start. Bring me my medications. In zis next room there is a box. Bring the box.

(I do it) *Gut*. Do you know how many cleffer pills are invented to stave off death?

The old man needs to spread about the odour of himself, and anyone who comes near must be a party to his stiff agony. Und why else would you come near? You haf a life of your own to live? Pah! In his daylong fetishing and putting and placement, in his cardigan and roll-up trousers and spectacles, I witness the spectral busy-posing of the man and his methodised filing, filing of spittled masticated experience. Many thoughts that come at a man can make him sick. He is owned and enslaved to images like Sisyphus to his rock, like the god whose liver is eaten by eagles. And though there *may be* purity and rest, who is fool enough to dream of these? History demonstrates how stupid they are; there can be none of that. *And yet I am glad of it!* - says Moodzlinger.

I have not mentioned the old man has a sub-tenant. It is a parrot, who keeps vigil in a shadowed corner of Moodzlinger's winter rooms. And I notice there is a thing Virgil (that is his name) says every day in the morning: *Ever lost... Ever lost... Ever lost*. I'm guessing it's like the carbon-copied conscience of the man his keeper. The bird is also heard to utter a curious phrase at evening, intoning it with a spectral slow-motion regret; something absurd, something like: *Sobby Bore... Sobby Bore... Sobby Bore...* emphasising the *Sob*, with the inflection falling away under a guttering cackle. Life is a *sobby bore* then? I bet it is for you, mister parrot.

Don't we all repeat endlessly the things we cannot understand? Aren't we all parrots in our ways? Today Moodzlinger and I perform the ritual of the photographs. This scene has been enacted time and again since I came. From a shoebox marked *fotografien*, Moodzlinger takes the first little stained picture in his fingers, scrutinises it for a silent minute, and lays it on a little table next to his chair. I wait, ready to place the photo in a second box of similar size, this one a blood-magenta colour, also marked *fotografien*. This requires patience. Most would find it maddening, but I find it mysterious, even soothing, and in the winter room I am inoculated by history, by the lure of Moodzlinger the German's secrets, by European shadows, by the sepia gloom of The War. Sometimes after prolonged silence, Moodzlinger starts to talk. His topic is usually the same.

- To cleanse, to purify, iss important activity for human beings, no? Do you clean your house, put your house in order, mister Blank? For me it giffs peace. At times. Actually I have this from mein vater. He was a fit man, clean-living man, a sporting man even... You know it was Olympic spirit that brought the world together in thirty-six? It helped uss deutsche volk to see how we need zis world to realise our dreams. I need you, my opponent, becoss without you I can find no greatness. Und is greatness a crime? Sport is sublimation of war. True, there must be winners and losers. But after, we shake hands in friendship. For we are civilised.

Moodzlinger has a way of stroking under his ample nose with his thumb. He ponders.

- It wass said so much about the Polish camps that those who are forced to do the most evil work, conscripted as slave labourers to be later killed, quickly lost all sense of morality. Why? Becoss the work is routine. Industrial machine is created. It functions. So. Even killing of fellow creatures gets routine. Mechanical work is unfeeling work. This is our part in great experiment, great sport of Life. What will stop machine? Our *conscience?* No. We destroy fellow-feeling under pressure of unmeaning, absurdism. Then self-respect is destroyed. Just as personal feeling allows feeling for other, loss of personal worth means destruction of worth of other. There is loss of contact with the source of oneself, which is the source of All, of all people... They say it is through separateness that we have moral conscience, since I compare myself to you and feel that if I hurt you someone will hurt me in my turn. That it is proper to cooperate, to let rules have their way. But I tell you: it is obeisance to *idea* that counts only, and when idea becomes necessity it is a *relief* to surrender to idea. Here then is the death of our separateness! How did this apply to people in charge of za camps? To the proud SS, the Fuhrers? Something at the core must be surrendered. Our separate identity is now super-ego. Duty idea obliterates separateness. And duty of history erases here and now, erases common feeling. Sense of mission, rightness, loyalty, logic, duty

- *this is the true feeling.* It is our noble burden. We are the chosen. We dispense work to those fit for it. Victors must be victors, vanquished must be vanquished. It is clean, it is sport. Let criminals carry out the blood work. Let them indulge, enjoy themselves even! They know where they go, they go down the chute also. If life is a toilet, let it flush. Let us erase all unclean memory. Masters alone shall be; let the masters retain no evil memories, suffer no trauma stress, let them witness nothing of it! Let the left hand know nothing of what the right is doing! We offer the death work to the damned. We could neffer with conscience play that role. We are the beautiful, the pure race. We do not get our gloves and uniforms dirty. We do not kill, we issue orders. So. And it is done. So. That it is done was proof that it should be done. That it could be done is proof that it should be done. It is inevitable history. It is Idea!'

Fucking hell.

- You see, mister Blank? Nowadays, we are so clever to make life prolong. Once we were not so fussy. Listen to me, what do you possess? You are happy vibrant man. You have everything? What does a man need in order to go to death?
- Beg your pardon?
- Why do you think I am waiting, instead of dying?
Out of nowhere, Virgil the parrot chimes in: - *Sobby bore! Sobby bore!*
- Shut up stupid parrot. Mein vater -
- *Sobby bore! Sobby bore! Sobby bore!*
- Do you wonder why zis parrot is alive? Because I stay my hand, I show mercy
- Leave the parrot alone. Focus on you
- Ah! You who are 'positive', you who are full of hope. I *deny.* I refuse hope, I tell you
- Look. Whatever is in your past, you have to let it come to the front - let it come till it can rear its head no more, till it loses its energy, till it subsides and gives up in front of your eyes. You have to kill it with patience. Why else would we bother to live? We have to clear out all the shit
- You want to tell *me*?
- I don't mind. I'm giving you good advice

- I say you should leave now
- Sorry. I listen to your fascistic denial shit. You can listen to me for two seconds. *Who is it* that experiences the thought, the memory? If you look you will see it is a timeless self, it is awareness. That's *you*. You cling to the evil of the past. Yes, it is insidious and repetitious, but *you* have invited all the ingredients of a soap opera you want to perpetuate. Certainly we are victims of circumstance, but do we have to be? You won't turn your face away, you're sentimentally attached. And you're ignorant because you think that the past constitutes yourself. What of memories that are gone, are they still 'you'? Oh, you will say they are unconscious and therefore puppeteer our behaviour. But I tell you if they don't arise in consciousness, then they are no concern of ours. And if they do arise, every day over and over, then we have to *do battle*. You know this! The real problem is, you think they are 'you and yours' and they are not. So what's the nature of the battle: self-pity, which is your problem and everybody's? No, it is subtler, cleverer. You need to realise how you accommodate the thoughts, how you give them energy, how you *cling*. You need to *observe* the soap opera with your real self - which is eternal, spaceless, unconfined. This is you, not some shit that happened in World War Two, Moodzlinger
- So you are psychologist. Not house cleaner after all. But I am not so stupid. I cling because I have to punish. I must do vigil to punish. You were never there, you cannot know
- I have my shit to deal with. I actually am a 'house cleaner'!
- You are pampered youth, child of peace. You do not know
- Nurse your little soap opera. Do it forever, die with it tucked under your pillow
- Who are you, fucking? What can you know?
- More than you'd think, Moodzlinger. For example, I wanna know what happened at *Sobibor*.
The old man seems to shrink away, to diminish in his chair. Did I time this correctly? Did he assume I never suspected it? But of course not.
- Were you there, Moodzlinger?
And he wants me to stab him now, pitilessly.
- Or was it your father who was there? Is it sorrow that's your problem… or shame?

And he starts to grunt, to sniff, then begins a strange whining sound through his nose. It is his version of crying, there in his stuffed chair… Our little soap opera proceeds to its penultimate scene. I do not denigrate it, it is important; but it is sentimental. I take hold of his shoulders, grip them. He quietens after a time. Moodzlinger is not entirely lacking in rehearsal. Rehearsal for his cathartic reveal.

- That will do for today. I'll come back tomorrow.

I am not so inexperienced! Let him wait.

Next day, there he is in his seat, looking expectant. And he is well-dressed, meticulously so. Virgil the parrot regards us with disdaining beak and fishy eye. I immediately feel a kind of sorry disgust, but I make his customary cup of tea with biscuit. He is being patient with me, and I with him. One mustn't spoil history for youthful zeal. Finally I sit down opposite.

- It was always about removal of za handicap. Always it was about cleansing, about brave new world. Yes, we Germans were spiritually weak but we believed in purity, in strength. We wanted a better world, free from corruption, weakness, ugliness

- The Nazis did us a favour - is that what you're saying?

He glances at me, grunts. - I do not say it.

- But you were a bourgeois. You were a sensitive child. Later, an artist even. How did the Nazis contaminate your dreams? Were they too rough? How did you feel about all those stiff shiny boots and uniforms?

- You provoke. But I tell you one story now. Listen. There is a man, brought up to believe in duty, fidelity, loyalty. A patriot, family man, good husband. Clean, disciplined, strong and determined, even good-looking; not unintelligent, forward-looking, hard-working. Other qualities also. Can we say that this was not a virtuous man, a worthy man?

- If this man were real, not a figment

- This man is real. And he had a wife, who is also faithful though prone to flightiness, a little unruly, a little romantic you see, in the uncontrollable sense - but loving and kind and virtuous and clever and funny. And somewhat of an artist, and lover of fine foods and wine and dress and décor. Though not rich, no no. She is faithful when war comes, she holds to her man who must do his duty. No matter what

- A classic tale, not at all uncommon

- The question is: do we need to atone for things outside our control

- You always have a choice, Moodzlinger. You may die, but you have choice

- Do people have a choice to die, or to suffer? You talk nonsense

- I don't care. But you mean victims, and you are one of those. You need to be, don't you, or else you would be a perpetrator. Bad guy.

(Does he see how I need to unhinge him this way?) - No! Do you not see how we cling to the normal in face of pressure, of madness -

- Or how we refuse to face truth in order that we may go on as before, and how that makes it all so much worse

- What difference does one man's little stupid protest make? What difference to history, to anything? Can you stop a great wave from surging to shore?

- If nothing and no-one makes any difference, then history itself makes no difference! Logic. We are not victims, Moodzlinger. We are creators. History is the little things that happen right now. Why else would you assume your precious body is so important?

- But it is important. We must fight

- Yes. Then fight. Your own little soap opera is so important! But the big big soap opera of human history - why assume it is any more important? Death takes everything. Everybody. Why agonize, why worry?

- We must fight!

- What kind of fight though? To remain the victim, the hard-done by? Or the fight to go beyond the whole fucking lot? Now there'd be a fight worth fighting! Even while you're still in the middle of it

- That is what I do. Every day

- You think you do

- Shut up, boy. Listen to me! There is a boy who lives with his mother, day after day behind a wall in a dark house in the woods. Down the road beyond the village is a camp. Daddy works there, we are not allowed to go there. There is smoke every day. We smell it. It makes us sick. My mother will not, cannot, believe it. One day she runs away. I do not find her. She comes back at night. She takes me. It is all rough, sudden. We are gone, in a lorry to the city, to some place. I don't recognise anything. Soon we are starving. Someone helps us. Our father comes one day much later. There is a scene in the kitchen. There is screaming. She has a knife, wants to kill. He throws her down. I hide away. He is gone. We go to find the infirmary. It is already bombed. Mummy is hysterical. I cling to her. She is in bed for weeks. A woman helps us. A neighbour I think. So we exist. Later, later, the war is over. We hear it on the radio

- Your father -

- I never see him. Ever again. Years later there are stories - that he is killed. Strung up. By a mob. Especial for him. Hanged. They say he was a commandant

- Possibly not. We all have to follow orders

- He was hanged up in front of the scum!

- Moodzlinger, he was not *you*. Think of your mother. She had truer instincts. You are closer to her.

The shadows in the room have deepened. Virgil the spectral parrot has nothing to say. But he shuffles, grips his perch, eyes me birdily as I, wanting relief, make for the door.

Moodzlinger's story sounds to me eerily like *The Boy in the Striped Pyjamas*. But what would I know? We all need fiction to coat the facts, to fit our emotional constructs. The key to it all is the lies we tell ourselves; this is how we live after all. Moodzlinger is right, I am a kind of youthful extremist. There were plenty of them in Nazi days. But I don't apologize, because history is but a phantom, a fabled concatenation of Nows. And it never fades unless we replace it - with clear uncontaminated sky, where we might fly outward into clear knowing: that we are none of these beckoning strands, these thoughts, these smells, these clinging dreams. Or perhaps, perhaps, the Nazi time and the *Shoah* privileged us all, gave us a benchmark, a bottoming-out of human experience, a nadir by which we may measure and expedite our souls' new-beckoning at the light, at a higher peace, at the unsentimental, the non-clinging, the free. But every desperate painful step, ten forward, nine back, trodden by Moodzlinger and his mother and father and me and all of us - not one of these steps can be retracted. I get that. But one sweet morning we might arrive at the fabulous idea that the very journey is a phantom too, a roiling sweating in the mud of our own dreams, a fevered clinging to our paradigms of self-importance, to a self-narrative that leads us like donkeys onward by the nose in self-contaminated fabrics of guilt and shame and sorrow. Our really-special real soap opera. Reader, don't get me wrong. I feel things, and deeply too. But there has to be a limit... And the fabled death of the body is never that limit. The next day, I return to Moodzlinger. I know he has clung to the idea of a final act, either by suicide or by natural cause, as the tempting end of his deep-invested drama. I claim my job is to show him death as just another dream-state, another escape, another excuse for turgid paralysis inside his opera of emotional victimhood. I am naïve but don't care. Innovators and rebels are naïve. Think of it as freshness. And I've nothing to lose. But my *disgust* wells up again - and this might be motivation enough to hack at the old man's rigidity. Yet he was a boy once, in his little round glasses, cleaving to his flouncy teary mother and his distant noble father with his Destiny, swallowing all that boy-propaganda for the leader and the army and the cause. All his days he believed in something, because Germans did, because that generation did, because people do, and he didn't notice how his dreams quietly morphed sideways into other dreams of equally suspect provenance, until he was all grown up and on the downward curve - and still unable to see into his own dream-factory of a mind and say: it is all relative, and therefore absurd, and who is the dreamer anyway? History made him, his generation made him, the tides of belief and war made him, and now his enshrinement of the Fascist ideal that crushes individuals in service to the forward march of a race, is nothing but guilt turned to aggression. For what did Moodzlinger ever do to help anyone or anything? So here he is today - in his cardigan in his chair in his gloomy flat with his parrot-conscience, and the world surging all about him in borderless fitful dream strands, and he *loves* to be shoaled on the reefs of yesterday, fishhooked on lines of soaked suffering, blinking in the flickerings of forgotten tears, the croakings of history, ghost repetitions of a billion thoughts: the cloaked night of experience, the clanking cattle train, the blockade-mind's clamped and glittering and booted fetishes, the rubbish dump of generations, the swamp of history made personal, made aching in his head and his teeth and his fingertips. He is the insect in the headlights, the quivering deer that awaits the killer, the lonely dog that drags itself from hearth to lay down and shiveringly die in the woods… perhaps in the green-black woods of Eastern Poland at the fag-end of a war. And all the souls he mourns there, that were ashed and buried under clods in the green-black forest - they rose again and marched forward, yes they did. They, the undead army of refugee souls, stamping forward on their white chalk road into the relief of higher worlds! But *you*, Moodzlinger, had to live. What a curse, what a loss! … Be at peace, Moodzlinger.

But this is the seventh floor, like hell's seventh circle, and self-violence will out. We'll acquit ourselves by its creed. And he is wily, this German: doesn't spill his guts all at once. Draws me close with talk of hope, talk of value and common sense and moving on to brighter futures, to sunlit lands, to purity through discipline at last. Dream of his youth fulfilled! He bends an ear to my words, and in my inexperience I fail to note his game. But gradually I see: here is the limit to the mortal man called Moodzlinger. He must pass on his life, transfer his bloated being to someone younger, shovel his baggage down the line into the repeating future. And if I really wanted to help this man, I'd have had the patience to care about him. Yes, a catharsis of some ilk is fitting, but his longed-for confession scene seems to have bloated him so. Ugh, so self-consciously narcissistic. Don't ever fool yourself, Blank: compassion is not your strong point. But his future is his, not mine. What use compassion in his thickened self-idolising world? In the abstract, at a distance, I am sorry for him. But face to face, compassion vanishes. I should help him *erase* himself then? No. Suicides should face the present, else in some soft future the act will eat them insidiously, and their loved ones too. The old man must face the cold slap of Now. Don't leave till tomorrow what you can do today, old man. But how he cleaves and cloys and feeds on me. How he wants me to hate him, wants me to feel *responsible* for hating him. How else to make me, the future, grasp your suffering than to amplify it at the last? How else to slip away yet prolong your oily-sweet agonized need inside a future world. Even with one solitary stranger-helper in a private melodrama in your grotty flat in some grave-dead building somewhere - a stranger who'll take forward the horror into his own heart and get the cancer of it: let *him* feel what it is to be abject. Let the arrogant future, the arrogant youth who wallow in their arrogant peace - let them feel how the past shredded, boned, slit and sucked one poor man; let the future feel the hate that he felt, the weltering sorrows he felt. Let contamination continue, let future clang out the past! And if I were a fool I'd have the nerve to gaze on the evil and let it seep in my heart. Thank god I'm not so young, not such a fool. But what is left me - to despise him instead? Perhaps a middle way: to gaze with dispassion, assist his demise according to his wish. To wash hands of feeling. To wash hands, to assist. Like Pilate did. Like the SS did. But no. Moodzlinger will hook me and fight for me. I'm to be his dirty deliverer.

And I'm made to wait. Next time I come he asks if I know 'a girl he discovered' who lives on his floor. Zis girl is private, a little unfriendly, possibly Jewish. Her name iss *Anna*. (Uuhh? I mumble that I may have bumped into her) Why does she not eat food? Is she wanting to pay for sins of the past? (This remark shocks, in its insouciant ignorance) But I have interest. I brought her to my house on pretext that my key was lost! Heh heh. I show her my memoir but she wants to run away. I must offer something, make her stay. Why don't you call at her door one time? Young people need one another. She can explain her past to you, maybe show you her tears…

What is this? Why bring Anna Rex into the equation? Does he want me to think he doesn't need me any more? …Next day he does a significant little thing. Asks me to place, with my trusted hands, all his ranks of pills into a row of special bottles. They must be deposited, one by one. I ask why he doesn't give them up. - Neffer. How can I? I must stay alive, he says.

A week goes by, so that I've supposedly forgotten the ritual of the pills, and this day he sits me down and with solemn tone informs me:
- I wish to thank you for all you have done for me. I have re-made my will. I name you, my friend, as sole recipient of my estate.
This causes a silence.
- Is it large? is the only thing I can say.
- It is my apartment. And there are two hundred thousand Euros in a Dresden bank.
- I do not deserve any of it - is the next thing I can think of.

I look in his eyes. He looks into mine.

- But certainly you do. I do not want it to be stolen by the government. If you are not happy, donate it to charity. Why not… to your *Church of Divinology?*

Ugh! How long has he known about the Church? I am sobered by this thought! I say not a thing more. Two days later he asks me to come again. He is solemn this time, seated in his chair, dressed as usual in his shirt and tie and cardigan. His round glasses glint whitely in the light. The parrot is beside him.

- Fetch me the bottle of wine on the table in the dining room. Bring the stem glass.

I do it. - I will not ask you to join me. I know it is not your way. Pour the glass now.

I do it. - Thank you. You may do this shopping errand for me. Come back after you have finished.

He gives a longish list. It takes me an hour. I return. He is in his chair. He appears to be asleep. The light glints in his glasses as before. The bottle is beside him. I step closer. A small stream of vomit extends from his chin, down his shirt and into his lap. The eyes are slightly open. The parrot paces agitatedly in his cage, his claws grappling at the bar. Moodzlinger is gone.

I was a fool to think I could ever help the German. To pass on his silent grief to another generation may soothe him, but the truth is we must die alone, unheralded. Otherwise we tempt the future to vomit us back up. Have the guts to be no-one and nothing. Take your sorrows into the void, which is not a void but another new marketplace for the great barter of clinging and letting, of longing and stillness, egoic and impersonal. If we want to be born we must take the consequences. Even at this elevated human level of ours, we still don't have a choice. (One day we surely will.) Fear and hatred and depression and confusion are still our bedfellows, our dancing ghosts, our daily bread. We have to learn to let them go. But yes, I was a fool to think I could divest the old man of his investment in sorrowed shame and victimhood. Or perhaps after the long long night it only takes a moment: a breath, clear sunlight in the morning, an unexpected ride out, a change of scene, a helping hand, a clear new face, a childlike voice, a cheery smile, a brand new day. A holiday.

I flatter myself. Moodzlinger is really nothing if not the architect of his own myth. In each successive iteration, each lifetime in the gyre of his Becoming, his narcissist's soap opera invests itself in new climaxes, and the trickle of suicide blossoms to a fountain and to a flood that seeks to drown the world. The next Adolf Hitler, ladies and gentlemen! Not notorious yet, Moodzlinger is the closet killer of cell-armies of love and esteem, of races of peace molecules; this tyrant of veins and heart, this despot of the mind in his gyre-rut of victim seeking revenge. Oh well, at least there's a passion there. Passion for the ages.

* * * *

So here I stand, in the ticking room of Moodzlinger. The parrot Virgil twitches, clicks his beak. Presently there's a knock at the door. I hesitate, open. There's no-one. A distant door clicks in the blood-green corridor. I know it's her. Hovering a minute later at her door, I know I'm being *played*. I knock, and she feigns surprise. We stand in her room, embarrassed. She's afraid, this thin woman.

- Do you know what's happened, Anna?
- What do you mean?
- Moodzlinger is deceased. Not an hour ago.

She says not a thing. She in her stick jeans and little black top with no stomach under. And her eyes close, and she twists and totters backward. I lay her to the sofa. Her angular wrists seem to snatch away. She arises but this time falls into me. She holds on. We witness a struggle within. Her fine   black hair shreds under my mouth. Her faint musty odour surrounds. She shovels herself close. The eye sockets are wet. Her sharp knee bruises my thigh. We slide downward. Her legs part. She nuzzles at me, pushes her lips in mine. I let her. She shovels my hand in her jeans. I find the place. Face screws up, jaw creaks. She gyrates her hips. Fingernails in my shoulders. She seems to choke… She goes limp. I wait. Stroke the hair… make her look at me. The eyes are black. Anna Rex has no idea what to feel.

- Sorry, Dust
- Don't apologise. Let things be as they are
- Can't even have an orgasm… to celebrate.

We lie. Minutes shift away, abandon us both. If we could let things be as they are, the problems of this world would be solved. Now she pushes away, stands. I take her hand in mine. Silence. In time, we let ourselves shuffle down the corridor, into Moodzlinger's flat. The old man is quiet in the chair. Anna stares and stares. The little parrot claws at his perch. I want to run away. There is absolutely no-one but us. Suddenly it's she who heads for the door. And I'm blocking her.
- Anna. We're required to deal with this
- Fuck you. Fuck him. Fuck it all!
I hold on. She lets out a scream. I shove a hand over her mouth. Who heard?
- Don't! Listen! It's a death. People die. That's it…
- What the fuck would you know, gentile?
- What?
- D'you know who he was? What he is, why he did this? Why he did it *to me?*
- Wait. By that reasoning he did it to me as well
- You? Who are you?
- I was his assistant. I was here
- You? Did he put you in his will?
- Why d'you want to know that?
- Did he?!
- He claims he did, yeah.
She heaves herself over to a desk, drags at its drawer. It clutters to the floor. She flurries about, grabs a folder, waves it.
- Did he sign over his insurance to you? Sign over his life? (She flings the papers at the wall) Did he make you administer his little pills? Did he laugh and curse at you when you protested? Did he call you a goddam Jew

who wanted his money? Is it *your* fingerprints all over his flat? And did he make you feel *sorry* when he told you all his sufferings? Because maybe he made it all up! Maybe *he's* the SS bastard!

I kneel down to her, hold on. She is crying, in fits and gulps.

The Freezer

Anna Rex is perched on the rim of the bath. The old man's shaving bits and plasticated toilet aids are dumped in it.
- I tried to care. Why would I? I tell you I came to help. I felt nothing. He asked me to edit his memoir. Wanted it published. Why the hell would he want that? Dust, I tell you I made an effort!
- And you 'failed'. Is that it?
- You don't *know* what Jews carry around. I tried to face it!
- You *need* to fail, don't you? All that intelligence and drive and you need to kill it. What are you starving for, Anna - the dead? Life's a cruel rort ain't it? We nurture wounds of the past and nobody cares. Because we're *all* fellow travellers on the cattle train to the death camp. We *live* by not caring, we live by spite of others and their suffering. A competition! - to win our little space of hurt and spite in a milling crowd of spiting souls. Our battle to spite. You wanted to raise up Moodzlinger, treat him as your own, use him to nurture your *own* horror project. But you cared and don't want to admit it. Because to care for one of your own kind would be to admit defeat. The *real* horror project is to admit you're not alone in being a victim, you're not special any more, you're one of the horde, you're an also-ran. You have to join the slaughtered crowd, menagerie of ghosts, fields of the unquiet dead. You have to serve *them*. But it's all too big. I don't blame you: it means you'd no longer live for yourself, that you breathe in and swallow all sins, put your arms around the horror of life, embarrassingly stand and fall with the rest! You're a cog in the wheel of suffering, a statistic in the death camps, the forgotten refugee, the unmarked, the unknown, the detritus, the dust of history. You're the little boy Moodzlinger with his little glasses who got crushed by a great wave of hate!

Too far, too far. Her eyes are bulging.

- And so you wanna starve. Why not cut your throat quick? What's this slow drawn-out protest of yours ever gonna do?
- He was a fucking Nazi, you cunt
- A 'Jewish Nazi' then! So what?
- Here I am then! I kill myself! I do it now!

Anna Rex rushes into the kitchenette, slugs open a drawer. It clangs and skiffles on the floor. Scoops up a sharp object, raises it high. I'm at her, almost snap her bony wrist. The knife flies out. By strange event it sticks in the wall and shivers there. She drops away to the floor... as she is wont to do.

Rough is the only way you can communicate with Anna Rex. She believes in violence, to the soul and mind and body. I see why meditation is her grand compensation. One might call it her great lie if one had no compassion. At this moment I discover I have a little bit of it. Let her project on me then... But I need help. *Blue Wendy* must come. Only she has arms capacious enough for extremes like this. I can't let Rex out of my sight, and the old man is still here in the flesh. So I call up... And Wendy barely speaks. No, she doesn't care to help today. Has her shop to run, has delicate flowers to nurture.

- I won't ask for anything again. The Staan Building. Floor seven, unit seven. Please.

Another lie. She clicks me off. Wendy's learning to be hard! Don't learn that now, baby... But Anna is crawling about with a rag in her hand.

- Anna?
- I'm cleaning. I want no trace to be left. (I hold her) Leave me alone! Don't touch me, I'm so embarrassed, so stupid. Let me clean it all up. Let me finish it...

She seems 'weirdly resilient' now. Suicide bandwagon run out of tunes? But wait... what's the point in cleaning Moodzlinger's apartment?

- Do you suspect the authorities will think we're involved in his death? Anna?
- They're not going to know anything
- Wait. Stop. Think about it

- Leave me. This is my karma

- You're not even accurate there. We share the karma, you and me. All about sharing, ain't it? Your shit, my shit, his shit, everybody's shit! You and I are getting out of here and we're going to think…

It took an effort to get her out. I dragged her to a place called *Past Caring*. We trussed her up in the moth-eaten fur I grabbed from her flat, her 'cure-all coat' we call it. Makes her look gothically cool like a seventies London waif. I got her drinking green tea, got her smoking. She even ate half a biscuit.

- It was always my thing not to get involved with people and their suffering. I ran away from my family. Despised my mum, how overbearing she was. If you feel sorry for people in this world you get nothing but pain. How can feeling help? The world's a railway station, people and creatures come and go. Nothing changes. I have to make a choice: worrying for others distracts from my personal evolution. My battle's for self-reliance, emotional detachment. Better than all this shitty obeisance to peoples' endless wants

- Yeah, but past evil's not just ours, it's shared. Maybe it's an opportunity. I think you saw that with Moodzlinger. We don't need to 'die again and again'; we can go beyond. Why fear to care? My friend Blue Wendy has it sussed: she faces what she fears… though she overdoes it like crazy! Opposite to you.

There in the booth Anna puts her weary cheek on my shoulder. (It's always a bit gothic with her.)

- You and me then, Dust? You and me always… (Pause) And who's this Blue Wendy?

- Er… spiritual student

- But how d'you know her?

- Used to be in our Church. Helped her deal with her wacko husband, also a 'church member'

- Mmm. Maybe I'll interview 'em for my media hate campaign

- Anna, I've asked her to come. To help. She may be there now. We should go back.

123

She surveys me with icy, incisive calm - the severe girl with her cutty black hair and angulated face. I grind my teeth.

- All right Dusty. Let's go get cured - by your Lady friend.

Crouched on the step of the Staan building on Fernino street in her crappy blue anorak, is my solid-thighed girl. Her heavy hair spreadeagles in the wind. Hands are clasped, eyes lowered. She looks up, sees the pair of us. I kiss her face, whisper *thank you*. The women regard each other. Anna offers a hand. If Wendy wonders who this stick-waif might be she doesn't show it. The building's lift is frozen so it's a slow tramp to the seventh floor. (Time for these girls to wonder where they stand in my little world: for Anna to wonder why this Wendy 'asks no questions'; for Wendy to glance all her questions at me, and for me to nod assurances.) But Anna face turns stricken as we approach the Door. The suicide is in his chair - with his bulk, his vomit-soiled cardigan, clumped shoes, thinned-out white hair, round opaque glasses, pill bottles... Wendy eyes it all up in an instant, and there's a strange gratitude in her eyes. Why did I doubt you? she looks to me and seems to say.

- Is he your relative, Anna?
- Sort of. An acquaintance. I mean a friend. I served him. That is, he took me as his helper. Actually it was like father-daughter.
And she seems relieved to admit it.
- How long has he been gone?
- A few hours. I wasn't here. Dust was.
Wendy makes no enquiry as to my relationship with the dead man.
- Would you like to call the authorities?
- I don't... think we could... should... do that.
I know Anna's about to weep.
- It's all got complicated, Wendy. You see -
But Anna stings.
- *I* will tell it!

Which makes the parrot start up. *Sobby bore! Sobby bore! Sobby bore! Sobby bore!* The little guy shrieks, his little claws clutch at the bars. *Ever lost! Ever lost!* (The weird clarity of his words!) *Sobby   bore! Mother!*

Father! Mother! Father! This bird's seen and heard far too much. Wendy goes to the cage, puts her mouth close, whispers. The bird hesitates. Wendy takes off her jacket, drapes it over the bars. There's a dangling quiet. Only the scuffing of claws is heard within... We sit in semi-circle around the dead man. Wendy is calm. Anna seems ready to confess to this stranger.

- What do you want to tell us, Anna?
- Moodzlinger dumped his feelings on me. No doubt he had horrors to deal with, but he wanted me to feel every one of them. He's a *parasite*. He named me as recipient in his will - 'reward' for publication of his memoir
- Would you like to publish it?
- He turned over his life insurance to me! Got me to co-sign the policy. Sick joke! I don't wanna go to jail
- But why -
- He did basically the same to me, Wendy. The will, etcetera. Anna and my fingerprints are over everything. Literally and figuratively. Including all those pills that killed him! We look like conspirators. It looks bad
- And Moodzlinger asked in his will that we formally bury him! And I discovered his birth certificate. He claims to be half-Jewish!
(Now I seem like a glib little team member) - We shouldn't wipe those fingerprints. That looks worse. The police really should be called but it's compromising
- But you can simply say to the authorities you don't want anything of Moodzlinger's!
- My conscience is clear in terms of helping him, but if we exposed the inner workings of our relationship, the authorities would give us no end of trouble...
Wendy ponders my subtle reasoning.
- You can show them you've nothing to hide. Otherwise, why would you continue to put fingerprints all over the flat? Anna?
- He was senile. We appear to have forced him to sign things
- Is there evidence he was senile? He wrote a memoir. You know the law will eventually support you
- Moodzlinger is a manipulator. He wants to get me in *deep karmic shit*

- Dust? What do you say to this?

(Careful tone here) - I'm not sure Anna's wrong about that

- I have to dispose of the body! You have to help me, Dust! You're in it up to your neck

- Cut the paranoia, Anna. I helped him a bit, that's all

- I'll burn his will. I'll burn his life insurance

- There'll be official copies!

The thin girl is on her feet.

- I'll burn his fucking memoir! I'll burn the house down! Dust, do it! Get his body out. You're the *man*. And why is this *woman* here?

Wendy takes hold of her. She won't let go. Anna softens by degrees. The stranger sits her down, holds her hands.

- Let me tell you something, Anna. Dust didn't tell me he was mixed up in this. But in fact - I *knew* this man. I knew his name was Moodzlinger. We met at the Church of Divinology. You have to know he was once a committed member. He certainly knows the Employer.

Anna stares at her. And so do I.

- So the Employer put him up to it? That's it, then. The Employer sucked *me* into his death-world

- Wait. It doesn't matter if he did or didn't. This is *where you are*. Right here. And Dust and me are here. You know us both, don't you? Even if you don't recognise us as friends, we're here.

This speech creates a silence. And I cannot help but compare the two of them. Anna. Wendy. 'The one who incinerates and the one who waters'... nervous and peaceable, nerve versus sinew. Intellectual and healer. Hater and compassioner. Rebel and accepter. My glib little categories! These are beings with stories as long as creation itself, who trail old fortune behind them like the star trails of comets; journeying always, changing and failing and wishing in every place of love and woe, in every season now forgotten, every puppet-show that god tossed in their paths. Like oxen to the wheel or geese in the sky, they nurture their lives and grow and die. I've known them both for centuries. And I miss them, even as we sit here now. Even as we live I'm nostalgic for we three. This is the moment of déjà vu; we've all been here before, around this campfire, leaning in to weigh and ponder some weighty issue that falls to us, in this breathing present, in this stilled pond of time.

Now it's Wendy who talks.

- There is a story, about a girl called Anna K. who lived in Krakow in 1942. She was a nanny to little children of bourgeois families, and was young and slim with neat brown hair and trim clothes. It is said there was an appealing sparkle in her round eyes, for Anna K. was remarked on by many in her neighbourhood. But one day the government resolved to separate the undesirables, and she was arrested by special police at her apartment and placed on a truck that took her to a facility where she waited days in a crowded room, not given enough to eat or drink or offered toilet facilities commensurate with her dignity. From there she was placed on a rail transport with crowds of others, rough-handled by soldiers and made to stand precariously for more days in a darkened wagon that seemed to roll and rumble and sway endlessly under her feet, and she knew nothing and no-one except the smell of a weeping frau and her goggle-eyed child six inches from her face. And in the midnight when they stopped at a platform in a remote place and she was made to disembark with people spilling and milling in confusion and exhaustion all about her, it was surely a strange relief to feel a soft night wind on her cheek, although the rest of her felt utterly wooden and corrupted. She was led to a place and asked to remove her soiled clothing, then told to walk quickly to some other place where she'd be offered a bath and proper food. She goes along a pathway flanked by uniformed men and dogs. She is ushered into a chamber which fills so quickly and so tightly that her feet barely touch the floor. The iron doors clang shut and suddenly her chest is burning and she finds herself choking for air. She loses all knowledge of this world. Her body is taken and incinerated, her bones are crushed to powder and shoveled into bags and dumped in a pit in a forest. Grass and lupins and shrubs are planted over her so that no-one will know that such filth as Anna K. had ever been... As to her soul, it won't be erased so easily. It keeps memories it does not know it has. In a future time it begins to play on the muted strings of the past a ragged tune of inexplicable phobias of persecution and self-loathing. She is never safe, never good enough, always alone. She is a social problem, family problem, curse to herself. She has no guide but still must find her way. There are false starts and a string of suicides, slow or quick. Every sin of the fathers is visited on her. But I tell you - Anna K. is not a historical fiction or the child of someone else. She is always here, always with us. And she is always herself. And she must take the consequence of being herself. Forever.

Silence. Finally:

- Did Moodzlinger tell you this story?

- No, Anna. I made it up.

Anna stares at both of us. Tears seep in her eyes.

- Moodzlinger needed you. And needs you still. You can help him even in death. You can face *his* past, give meaning to his life. And maybe your own.

The parrot begins to croak again, then to squeal. Wendy opens up the cage, takes little Virgil and places him on her arm. And he sits still there, eyeing us in the gloom.

- Maybe he wanted to give you his money. Maybe he really did care

- I don't know. I just have to think. Think what to do. Dust? Think

(Wendy) - We shall have to call the authorities

- Wendy, Anna is going to decide what we do

- I hardly think -

- She will decide!

Wendy drops her eyes. But Anna heard my tone, and she turns steely. She knows she can *use* me now.

- The Employer's not going to manipulate me any more. Dust, you promised to help. And you will.

Our collusion moment. Anna and I stare at each other.

- Umm, there is a *freezer* in the base of this building. I'll get a van. On Monday. We'll take the body to the country. Bury it. End of story. We burn the rest. Memoir, insurance, will.

- No! You two are crazy!

- Don't you see, Wendy? Moodzlinger tempted Dust and me to exploit him, take his money. And so we won't. The *Employer* tempted us to fall into the trap, and we won't. This is our pure solution.

But Wendy glares at me, enough to make me quail. (Oh, why can't she and me ever be happy!)

\- I won't be a party to -

\- Dust and I need your help to carry him

\- No, no need. *Blondie* will do it.

The two of them look at me now. (You fuckwit, Dust!)

\- Blondie. Er, Barbara. She lives on floor one. She's a friend

(Wendy) - Some friend!

I can hear Anna's brain grinding. What's this - Blondie? Who *is* this Dust guy loyal to? But Wendy begins to smile. She's seen the grubby knot I just made for myself. Ugh, I'm a fool. The Employer has his claws in, in a new and novel way! The Women of the World have got me. I can't wriggle any which way. I'm a bug on a skewer. Shit-karma just got me. I can't think. How'll this work out? Now Wendy's brow registers cloudier weather, and Anna's lip curls. She's about to wedge me, skewer me against Wendy... I'm an anarchist, Dust baby. Nothing to lose.

\- Yeah. Let's do *the freezer.* Like you say. This Blondie's obviously someone we can all *trust.* Strong, is she?

Don't dump your swag on me, bitch! is my next thought. Say it. No don't.

\- Take ownership of this, Anna. It's all I ask

\- *You* take ownership, Dust. You.

Wendy might be enjoying this thieves' contretemps, but she's all integrity.

\- I'm going to leave you both now. Not because I want to, but I can't help you any more. I'm very sorry.

Suddenly I feel the loneliness. It's like cancer. I don't ever want you to go, Wendy! Is this one more thing squandered on our forever road? Wendy eases Virgil back in his cage. She takes her jacket. She's at the door.

\- Wendy? (She looks) Thank you. I will call you. Tomorrow. For sure

\- I'm sure you will.

And she's gone. Blue Wendy, in her blue anorak.

Now we're alone. Anna is all irony and smiles. How I hate you, Anna Rex. I don't want your life entangled with me one second more.

\- I'll go talk to Barbara...

* * * *

Blondie is ominously alone in the malodorous apartment at the bottom of the Staan building. But she's eaten something ugly and her mind isn't present in any manner I recognise. The unworldly saga of Moodzlinger is taken in without surprise. This is an evil omen. Although to tell her at all, is a sign there *was* something real between us. I never doubted her! - though she makes no reference to that ugly fracas in the pub... just another incident in the sodden weal of these bottom dwellers, I realise.

- So I'll come tonight with my friend Anna? I'll text at, say two am? Stay awake for me Blondie, please? If the lift works we'll get you to help. It'll be in your freezer for one day only, then we take it away, finish. Are you okay?
- Baby, I'm super okay. And you - are a crazy badass.

I thought, I'll get *your* body out of this stenchful dump one day too. Strangely, the lift was working that night. Anna and I got cloths and wiped every last bit of the apartment then collected Moodzlinger's papers in a case. Anna said, 'No-one knows me in this building. Does anyone else know you? I shitting well hope not, Dust.' We had the bright idea of employing the old guy's collapsible wheelchair, found in a cupboard. When Blondie shuffled in that night Anna couldn't believe her eyes. Blondie looked like she'd imbibed a thing that removed her mind. But we shovelled the old man into the lift. Why was the damn thing working? Blondie led us down the corridor to her cellar. Croaking snorts and snores could be heard from behind doors. We got to the steps, manhandled him down. Low-curdled growls disembogued from the darkness. Sir Boris! We removed an entire layer of frozen food, heaved him into the giant locker, made him comfortable, put the food back and with numbed fingers closed up. 'There's no lock,' Blondie said in a voice that seemed to condemn us all.

Back at Anna's apartment we both slid under the shower. The thin girl pulled me into her bed. We clung naked to each other for some hours. She shivered from time to time. I never slept. Next day I made half-cocked enquiries at a van-hire firm. We were worn out. As evening came on, Blondie showed up at Anna's door. Like two filthy conspirators we ushered her in. She was no longer stoned; her eyes registered consternation.

- I just got home. Sir Boris the dog got hold of him. Half dragged him out. Can't believe he did it. Licked him up. Thawed him. Wanted to eat him! Can't fuckin' believe it. No-one saw. Except maybe Moon. I locked the cellar. It was fucking shit. What you gonna do? Ugh. Uughh!

Anna emits a kind of howl, clumps to the floor, buries her face in the carpet like a Muslim.

- Come and get me! I did it! Arrest me now. I did it!

And she shakes with ridiculing laughter. I pull Blondie out and down the corridor.

- I'm sorry. I screwed this up

- You know I'll help, Dust. But I can't be there when the boys find out

- No! Look, we'll bring him back, put him in his bed - or his bath. That'll be it. Fuck, that's it. That's the end...

A look comes over Blondie's face. One I never really saw before, an old old look - as if she has witnessed all the tripe and shit and stupidity all the world's people can dish up, forever. And doesn't entertain a single bar of it. I feel like a stupid child.

- Okay Mister Dust, one more time. What's to lose? Nothing.

Six hours later, in the dark, she and I have done the job. Anna is left right out. The body is laid out on the bed. At the end, Blondie says:

- Got an appointment with Mister Moon. Mustn't keep him waiting

- I just saw... there are bite marks

- No, Dust. Just on his clothes. *You* are gonna sort it out from here. (She scans me) And no... I ain't gonna do away with Boris. Not even for you, Dust. Though I'd do quite a few things for ya - most of 'em dirty. (We look at each other) 'Cause he'd be Moonie's dog. And I ain't gonna upset Moonie, not on any account. So this is bye bye, mister Dust.'

The next day, the man known as Dust dumps a suitcase full of papers in a bin somewhere in the city. Later, he starts to make arrangements to depart the Staan Building on Fernino Street for good. Anna Rex lies low like a stoat in her hole. She's ready to bolt. Blue Wendy will not answer her phone, not for money or loving lies. And Virgil the parrot is left alone in the apartment with the putrefying body of Moodzlinger, no doubt to holler and squawk until some neighbour complains to the landlord. As one eventually will.

Don't Worry About a Thing

'Profligates who ruin their lives by desecrating the means by which life is sustained, will be mauled by ferocious dogs.' Out of the blue this little Dante Quote appears before the dream eyes of Dust. His conscience is not at rest. He's developing the creeping feeling that all things that befall him are known to some great-seeing Eye somewhere. Retribution, regurgitation, repetition - they linger in this world like the smell of decay and bludgeon out one's fate. Moodzlinger the suicide is supposed to have moved on to a deeper hell… and why should anyone care about the circumstance of a mere corpse? And has it been found yet? That scumbag Moon surely saw a body in his freezer. Will he take it out on Dust? On ever-ready Blondie he certainly will, in subtle and iterative ways. Dust has ushered new   foul karma into the world's cesspool. How to ever rescue Blondie now? She'll never rescue herself - or perhaps she's not that kind of a fool… And how *did* the Employer get his nose into Dust's loused-up woman games? Don't you be a mug. He's the devil-exploiter. He knows all, sees all…

But for how long eh? Like paper scraps thrown by kids from a passing train and caught by the wind, rumours have lately come swirling around the Head of the Divinology Church. Now arrives a strange excitement, a queer sweating in not a few hearts, as if of *liberation*. Can it be the Employer is finally leaving? Dust reported to him in detail on Lenny the Crim, but gave only bones (lies, in other words) about the saga of Moodzlinger the German. Dust is nothing if not selective with his truth. Next day in a newspaper he comes across a rant by one Anna Rex on the iniquities of the Church of Divinology. Dust feels dingily smeared by her mention of 'sources in support of the truth'. The monkey on one's shoulder won't be shaken off! How it morphs into the forms of Other People! Even when the Employer's exit will come, Dust knows nobody will be off the hook, and the gut-eating question is: just *how*. One week after Anna's publication, rumours crystallise that the Employer has 'left for good'. Whether this means 'disappeared' or 'dead', no-one is game to say. That very day, Dust receives a letter by post. He recognises the Employer's distinctive crawling hand.

'Dear Mister Dust, unfortunately I am no longer in a position to summarily discharge my worldly duties. Since you have proved yourself a tenacious member of our Organisation, I wonder if you would do me a last favour - the disposing of a coffin, at a location in Devon - of an old friend of mine who has lately passed away. Kindly collect address and instruction from my secretary. I advise you to select a companion for this task: you may need moral support. You will require a vehicle, for which I kindly ask you to shoulder the cost. With my regards, etc. ----- Founder-Employer, National Church of Divinology. PS: I urge you to remember... the toils of the soul are never done.'

So. A personal letter from a teacher to an acolyte. His name is Dust - who assumed that name and thereby challenged the world to fail to take him seriously. Says the name: are you of this realm or no? Are you substantial? Dust feels a prickly heat: he's angry. Will this arsehole ever take him seriously? What right has He to run away? Does he treat this bodily world like a play, expecting us to do the same? It was he who exhorted Dust to 'get out there and do his part', to take seriously the plight of human beings, to act as if his part were of use, of *service*. And the great Employer pikes out! If the man really is gone, the businessy tone of his letter is nothing but a parting shot, a stab at Dust's shaky conscience. Dust assumes he is expected to succumb to guilt and regret, even loneliness. Or rather, he is merely one of many, not at all special, and has indulged the sin of pride. He re-reads the letter... The tone now appears matter-of-fact, 'eschewing hysteria at the mere passing of a body to a subtler frame'. Sentimentalists, you are caught out! Dust dimly encounters the relentless rigidity of his own mind. He suddenly longs to pen a liberating missive to The Man. But the Man has caught him again, as the perennial child who demands approval. Dust's silly name backfired! Who else received letters or tasks? Dust's failure to cultivate Church friends now looms as a drawback. He warily calls Anna Rex, only to find her number changed. And he daren't risk a visit to the Staan Building on Fernino Street. But as ever, the universe clicks in place with frightening clarity. Anna calls him. He barely recognises her clipped-shrill voice on the line: it is as if something in her has already passed on to another life. The girl has received a letter from her ex-Employer! urging her to collaborate with one Monsignor Dust on a matter to be expounded to her. Poor Anna, she just succumbed to the Employer's plot to render her terribly sorry and abandoned and lonely. And I'll have to shitting well fix it, thinks Dust. But he will fail to spill anything to her till he has traced his Blue Wendy goddess. Oh, he wants his *nurse*. Since the Moodzlinger debacle Wendy has shunned him with sad gusto. No talk of marriage now, just the soggy reality that Dust has Other Women. Or else she needs time to assimilate it all before encompassing him once more in her overweening compassion. I should attack her aloofness, warm her to me again, he thinks. Yet her voice on the phone backs away in muted denial, and he hears a guttering need. Oh, what the fuck is Wendy grappling with now? Suddenly he asks her: to 'help him deliver a *coffin* into the wilds of Devon'. She assumes it to be a dirty joke, and now will not speak to him at all. Impasse. And then he sees he'll need to get money from her. And he knows she won't ask for it back. Dust's bitty employ in a dusty bookshop barely ever sufficed to pay for his Church's soul errands, let alone his post-stabbing hospital layover, or the cost of a van - which now seems a massive sum in this distracted state that's come upon him since the Employer's exit, which he can't but take *personally* and hates himself for doing, immature as he knows it is. The idea of *grief* hasn't occurred to him yet. It will. Should he accept another wild goose chase? Is he ready to be fooled again and again? Dust feels exhausted, coralled. He needs a scapegoat. He argues with himself for Anna to come to Devon. He knows she has to repudiate the hatred in her thin heart against That Man (the Employer, the German, Dust, whoever) who shamed her. It's *her* sodding karma, not Dust's, that should be expunged! So he says to her: 'If you'll go I'll go. Deal?' After all, the Employer asked it.

So, so. Midnight in an alley at the back of the Divinology Church. Dust backs a van up to a door. Dust and Anna Rex are greeted in a bleary office by Alcina, the Employer's assistant. She gives instructions (verbal not written), and a heavy lidded box is dragged from the vestibule to the van.

Alcina pushes, Dust pulls, Anna supervises. Anna is all lip and no brawn as usual, and before the doors are sealed Dust already feels sick. Alcina casts him a standard pitying look, says goodnight and disappears into the building. Practised in the ways of the Church where vagueness is all and 'the devil is in the karmic small print' Alcina gave only such instructions as will save her from further entanglement. And he, not knowing the deep picture behind this night foray, cops the old gullet-churning disease of unease... The road west out of London is quiet, and after several hours they find themselves on a B-road in the west country. Suffice to say Anna brought no sustenance, leaving Dust the burden of getting them through the entire affair. In her mothy fur coat she feigns to shrink into pouting martyrism, since though the Employer did her an Evil, she can at least show she is a bigger (if not a fatter) person than he. Besides, he apparently died, so one's media campaign might be suspended temporarily. And if all goes tits-up we can blame it on Dust. (Defiant Anna won't admit to feeling sorry or abandoned or lonely, and this is possibly the real reason Dust managed to persuade her to come along...) Not to mention one hears that Big Wendy 'refused the boy outright'. One might thereby 'step into the breach'. No small thing to aid a dead man and a needy one. Double compassion, frightfully good karma. Now though, he's floundering with a map in his dim little cabin and cursing the lack of a torch. One shall stay aloof, smoke cigs in one's moth coat... (a habit to which one only succumbed since the Moodzlinger debacle).

- Don't *swear*, Dust. Accept. Surrender
- I will if I don't have to breathe your poison
- I'll assume you refer to my cigarette.
Anna winds down the window. The cold night worms in.
- So where are we going?
- I told you. Somewhere in Exmoor. Don't ask me why. Find the biscuits will you?
- One is not hungry, Dust
- No shit
- If only Wendy were here. She'd know what to do. Help, Wendy! Or maybe *Blondie.*

Anna's cutty irony seems designed to ensure everything turns to shit. And Dust is tempted to let it. But he'll do it slooooow-ly.

- No no, Anna. You and I stand alone. It's you I truly need
- Sorry Dusty, that's bullshit. By the way, who d'you suppose is in that box?
- D'you care?
- Not the slightest
- Shut up then. Now there's a forest off a road, about two miles off this second road on the right. Try to memorise that for me in your capacious brain
- I ain't digging no holes, honey
- Sure. That's why I only brought one spade. Will you drive?
- No!
- Thanks. I love to cop the dirty karma... Keep your eyes peeled. (They drive) What's that?
- Civilisation!
- It's a gas station. I'm stopping. Shit... I recognise this place somehow.

Non-comatose readers will have grocked it. This new little trip to Exmoor may have something to do with a previous little trip to that fair region. But who'd ever know, right? And Anna Rex with her capacious brain wouldn't admit that the body in the box has a single thing to do with the corpse of Moodzlinger the German. Why should it? Only one's *conscience* rules the hidden connectors in this universe, thinks she. No-one else may judge what I need and don't need. Karma, that spider's net of illusion: I piss on it! And even if it does rule I can't do a thing! I'm its *victim*. Let me surrender to the world's shit! Do your worst, bastards wherever you are, wherever in your sightless substances you wait on nature's mischief... Yo. Meanwhile outside the van Dust shuffles about in darkness. He knows straight away this is the garage of the Alighieri Brothers. There are no lights, but he sniffs further. Signs of abandonment are clear. He ponders. The night's black silence curves in a great bay over his head. Clouds obscure the stars. In the van Anna is getting nervous.

- Well? Is this where your fabled forest is?
- Wendy and me were here. The Brothers helped us. We 'covered a thing up'. We 'buried' something

- What *are* you talking about?

- Nothing. Superstitious, is all.

This is the juncture where Dust decides to call Wendy. He feels lonely for her now! And yes, she answers. Was his flaxy-haired girl awake? He steps well away from Anna, talks into the dark.

- I'm back in Exmoor. The garage of the Alighieris... I have to bury the body in the box. I wish you were here! Tell me how you are.

And Wendy tells.

- Well Dust, right now I've a little thing that needs to be cut out. I am trying hard not to worry about it, trying not to be concerned. I even wanted to welcome it! Or I tried to smile it into a corner. It's in the colon. I kept it private. Like a newly pregnant mum! I'm sorry, Dust. So sorry. Because I fear my own need. And I know you'll call it self centredness. You'll say we run from shadows but that *I* do it professionally! But don't worry about it now. They'll possibly cut it. You don't have to come back.

Dust stands very still in the dark. But Anna is calling at him.

- *There* you are. I'm so cold. What's going on?

- Wendy has a cancer. She's just told me now

- Oh.

Dust puts the phone to his ear but Wendy's gone. Pause. Anna hovers. Now she pulls him back to the van. She gets out the biscuits and fruits and water. Nestles close and feeds him. Dust is very still. Time goes by.

- I wish you'd eat too

- But I feed you, Dust. And feeding you, feeds me.

He peers at her in the dimness. He sees that she meant it.

- Where's the limit to self-effacement? Wendy's clinging to guilt and shame do her no good. I tell you Anna, this cancer is her ballooning grotesque urge to *live*

- Dust darling, we live in all the worlds. All at once. We're transcendental, mental, vital, not just physical. We're boundless. Physical health is a balance, a poise of anabolic and katabolic energy! But the unspoken wish to cling to the physical is rampant, and the multiplication of cells begins. Cancer is nothing but compensation, a burgeoning identification with the

low physical. But who'd be able to live with a great rock in their stomach, hey? She shouldn't fear drifting away, away to a higher ethereal being…
- Drifting away?
- We're all unhinged, all shifting, tidal, swaying in the winds of need and longing.
She caresses his face in the dark, runs her fingers over his lips. Oh, Anna is great at lecturing on things she should herself take heed of. Sigh. Maybe it's just her way of dealing. But her physical touch soothes him a little.
- Now, let's get this box and body done with and go home. Wherever home is…

Dust does as she says. He drives a mile up the road, and there sees a gate to a field. And then he remembers a valley, an iron-age place where he and Wendy fought and came together by force and where she regretted it and he didn't and where she sought revenge despite herself… and where so much happened, in another life, in another time that never went away. Dust opens the gate, drives the van on a track into upland fields sloping to blunt peaks under a silver-black sky. Soon they can go no further. He stops by a hollow, and in its midst is a little stream… Wendy nearly drowned in that stream, but Dust pulled her out. Anna and he stand in the silver-dark and listen to the shrill water.
- We'll do it here
- Yes, but don't bury him. Lay him in the stream, like the Lady of Shalott
- Him? Why not her?
- Open it up and see, Dust.

Dust realises he doesn't want to. But she makes him. Together they drag the box out and under the headlights. She finds a tool used for wedging tyres and puts it in his hands. Didn't think of this, did we? she says. But after a couple of shoves with the tool the box opens. And they look in. And Anna puts her hands in. And in the white ghost-light she pulls out a palmful of flowers. She makes a startled laugh. And she digs again, this time to the bottom of the box. Look! she says. Nothing but petals! Dust is frozen. She takes his hand, pushes it in. He feels nothing but softness. She is laughing, she is happy. The joke's on us! This is a joke I can take. This is a joke I like! Anna wraps him up in a hug. But Dust is exhausted.

It is Anna who drives the van back through Devon in the dawn. She saw to it that they scattered the coffin-flowers in that stream, and that they stood in silence and watched the petals fritter away. She marked the moment with a little speech, and seemed very light and very at peace. And she stood apart under the hills in the valley like a sage in the gathering light of dawn. *We mustn't worry about a thing,* she said.

It is also Anna who, in the fatigue that overcame them, lost control of the van at the edge of a ridge and almost dropped them into a deep gorge with a stream lunging over jagged rocks at its bottom - but who in the nick of time woke up, and scouring the chassis violently against the edge dragged them back on the road as if by some instinct or by the hand of some fate or Fury that alerted her, told her by God or by Gordon Bennett, this was not their time to die. And when Dust unaware beside her woke with a jolt and asked what happened, she assured him all was well, just a bit of paint lost. But we fooled 'em, we fooled those fates! and we're still here, still on the high road! - and no bastard's going to put us away unless we wanna go: not now, not ever. Dust heard her, but dropped away to sleep again. Anna Rex was in control.

* * * *

Back in the city Dust buries his mind in his diary... the diary that never attacks him back. 'Days after, I felt this sudden urge to go down to Divinology Church. Maybe sit in the hall, contemplate, think what I might do for Wendy. Anna Rex has already concocted lists of things 'poor dear Wendy' should be eating and imbibing and avoiding and denying, and harassing my conscience (and wallet) to go collect them immediately, me being an insensitive male who probably doesn't even like cats or dogs or birds, let alone people or women... But I managed to fob her off. The Church was empty that morning. I sat still in the panelled hall. New flowers had been placed at the altar. Wendy... she has taken no treatment at all. Did she suggest to marry me *because* she had cancer? And where is the Employer when I need his advice? Let me close my eyes then, sink into far-off silence.

- Dust… *Dust!*

What? That unmistakable voice. The sharp questing tone! The Employer is there at the end of the hall. I stand immediately. The tiny big man, with the luminous eyes… he comes forward, stops in front of me. I note the new shirt, and the rehearsed air of distraction.

- Mister Dust. Hmmm. How is your teacher?

- Er - who, sir?

- Your woman. Your *Blue Wendy.* What are you doing here? Have you called on her today? Why waste time hanging about here? You must wait on her every waking hour

- Er, I, er…

- If I require service I will call you. Not that I expect to. Nor indeed do I expect you will come. Besides, there are plenty of others who may do the job of tending to my needs. Since I am getting old and possibly frail

- Are you… better? They said you'd…

- Look, Mister Dust! Someone has given me a present.

He points at the wall. There's a mask, like a greek comedy face. Under it a caption reads: *The Man in the Purgatory Mask.* The Employer beams.

- A proper student offered it. Not a joke, an artwork! I predict it will be worth a lot someday. But are you tired, Mister Dust? You look it. Avoid carrying about heavy weights. Spiritual ones I mean. (For effect, he turns to go) Oh by the way, I had some slight illness: not terminal as some might have wished. But I'm better, much better. No longer frail! …Oh yes. Do come to my office. I have documents. They will possibly be of interest. Goodbye. Now tend to your *shakti,* mister Dust! Take her flower petals perhaps?

Uh. I step from the hall and loiter in the street. Frail huh? Pigs'll fly. 'Betimes I say truth, betimes I lie. Your job is to decide which is which, grasshopper!' Don't ever believe a fucking word the Employer says, then you might get near it. Pluck up courage, enter his office. It's chaos, with Alcina standing in the midst deluged in cardboard boxes.

- Don't ask me *anything* Dust. It's all *going,* the whole lot. Where I don't know. I know nothing, I never will. But always I *carry on…* Oh, this is for you. Take it and burn it!

She tosses me a wad of papers. There's red scrawl all over the front. I recognise the Employer's curdly archaic scribble. Flip through the pages. They seem to have been written by someone unknown. Red scrawl is everywhere, *defacing* them. Yup. My own goddam work.

Reader, why did I bore you with all this spongy narrative? I even contrived to act as if a loon called Dust wrote it. Oh, why am I surrounded by such calamity? Sure, the Employer and his infernal LOLS (List Of Lost Souls) upped the ante on me, but the truth is - all my hopeful linear narrativising is nothing but wishful thinking, nothing but myth, comedy, entertainment, artifice, clever-clever discourse. The real narrative of this world is circular, is inhuman human gyratings dissolving and self-exhausting at deeper and wider and subtler levels of the Gyre, arcanely repeating under polar forces that slubber it back and back and back... because humanoid progress, the progress of one solitary stinking soul, is just unbearably slow and light and wormy-soft and imperceptible! Weight of history, drag of past, miasma of karma - all is inertia, all is reiteration. And such is the shape of my groany little soap opera. Total fraud! Now the Employer pops up in his new incarnation with his new skin in his new shirt. And it turns out he's always the great EDITOR, and now he's handed me his latest big blood-red laugh. No need to read it! He edits my entire life, soothsayer who scans my past and recycles it as future. Subtle webmaster and prophet, his Church is all for *this*. His church is a scam, because Life is a scam, a big scammy shammy *fraud*. Nothing stays. 'Now' is not. 'This' is not. 'Was' is not. 'To come' is not. Is not is not is not is not is not is not is not. Don't you carry a single damn thing. Don't carry any bloody persons about. Take responsibility! Fucking don't. Choose. Don't choose. Dump effort. Kill control. You'll never be free. Tire patience with patience. Let this great Becoming wither its chops in the Everness. Yadda yadda yadda yadda. Till then, all is blundering grating teeth-grinding withering REPETITION. PS: Don't worry about a thing, y' all!'

* * * *

The little fractal task of this day, is to convince Blue Wendy to get herself admitted. Now I know she offered to marry me because she thinks she's gonna die and that it might be a big boon to me - but what a lie! On the bus an old man sits by me. Seems he wants to unburden. I don't, don't wanna engage. I'm feeling self-sorry, vulnerable. You see, I fear death. Or worse, mediocrity. It's the recycling of this day-to-day that saps one's confidence. Truth is I'm worried about Wendy. Nothing lasts, everything has its time to go, but I'm scared I can't live without her. And Anna Rex's self-starvation could seem at this moment stupid beyond measure. But don't judge. Anna is still raving on unscathed. Apparently bones are hardier than blood. But God is everywhere: he's in every little thing. Stop moaning and smile. If only one could. Tell you what, I will when Wendy gets better. I'll smile and give mighty thanks. If only. The old man on the bus is glancing at me. His bony knees, old-man mustiness, blue-saggy skin... Mate, tell yourself that cruddy outer stuff don't matter because you're the God within (where though: in his bowels, in his arse?). He starts to talk about himself... and I realise right there, the only thing that matters in this cosmos is *me*. Without *me* there is nothing. Take away ME and there's annihilation. Emptiness and blackness. I am boundless. I am the light and soul of the world. And yes, I am You. Well not you, irrelevant old man. You who are taking up my self-sorry space with your dribble babble. Silence is golden don't ya know?

- Yep, back in seventy-three, that was the high water mark... we got sales that year bigger 'n we ever had. Like some kind of a miracle. I was at the firm for forty-three years. Or was it forty-four? Till I had me Op anyway. It weren't so bad. But we had to work hell for leather that year. Folks were buyin' our blinds like there were no tomorrer. And we had to invent all sorts o' ways to make 'em and deliver 'em. It was a biggie, that one. I was on the front line, managin' the floor-team. Helluva time, young feller. Not much call for them blinds nowadays, but she was rip-roarin' back then, back in seventy-three...

I stumble off the bus, lean on a lamp post and cry my eyes out. Later at the flower shop I find Wendy sitting at the back, all alone in that bent heavy knees-together mussy-haired way of hers. I know she's in a stew. It's all simple really, I tell her. We go and get you sorted, cut out the crap inside. Then you and me get married and live happily ever after. Because we're eternal and can never die. So there. Still, I want you in your body right here and now. Why? Because I like you, I like your face and your flaxy hair and the way you walk and the way you look at me in your sorry-sorry way. What's this? Anna Rex sent you a bag of bottle cures? Well drink 'em since someone took the trouble! D'you hold onto shit when you wanna go to the toilet? You don't. (Bad example, sorry) So. Let's trust the people who know what's what and get you sorted. Because you're a legend, Wendy girl. *My teacher.* And I'm yours. Teacher I mean. And your lover too. Whether you like it or not. Tyranny of love eh? Get used to it baby. Ha ha. Shall I get your coat, shall we go now? Good girl, that's it. Take my hand. I'm here. Right here. And don't you worry, you hear? Don't worry 'bout a thing. Not a single thingy thing.'

* * * *

Dust the meditator sits alone once more, out of habit. Is this meditative activity absurd? Though Dust is tempted to conjure worlds out of himself, he knows this isn't the proper thing. Still, he can't help it. If he were savvy he'd think the following: set not yourself apart from anything. Be not tempted to totalitarianism of intellect. Avoid to build the cocoon of self-prophecy. Engage. Step out to the struggling street not as conqueror but as learner… Also know there is nothing, nothing but eternity. Be amazed therefore that human civilisation is like a noisy gaggle of teens let loose in an ancient forest, who impose themselves on some pristine clearing with all their chatter and their flirt-talk radio gaga and babying need and grubbing gadget-strewn camp all ogled up and flung about as if they were sudden stamping arrogant masters of the forest and so confidently light and insouciant they'd be truly taken aback if the patient ancient trees above were to whisper down to them, cautioning them to show a bit of respect… But Dust the meditator knows how God has long since thrown the dice… There'll only ever be vibration in the eternal mind, infinitude of sudden pointillisms in the clearness, oceans of bubbling self-importance, gross conjurations of forms and histories and chatterings of time and space in bubble worlds of obscurated ignorance by which we live and hope and groan and die forever. And Dust will know that perhaps this is the only way we can ever learn. Learn to love, learn to help, learn to laugh. And learn not to worry, not to worry about a single thing.

Chaos

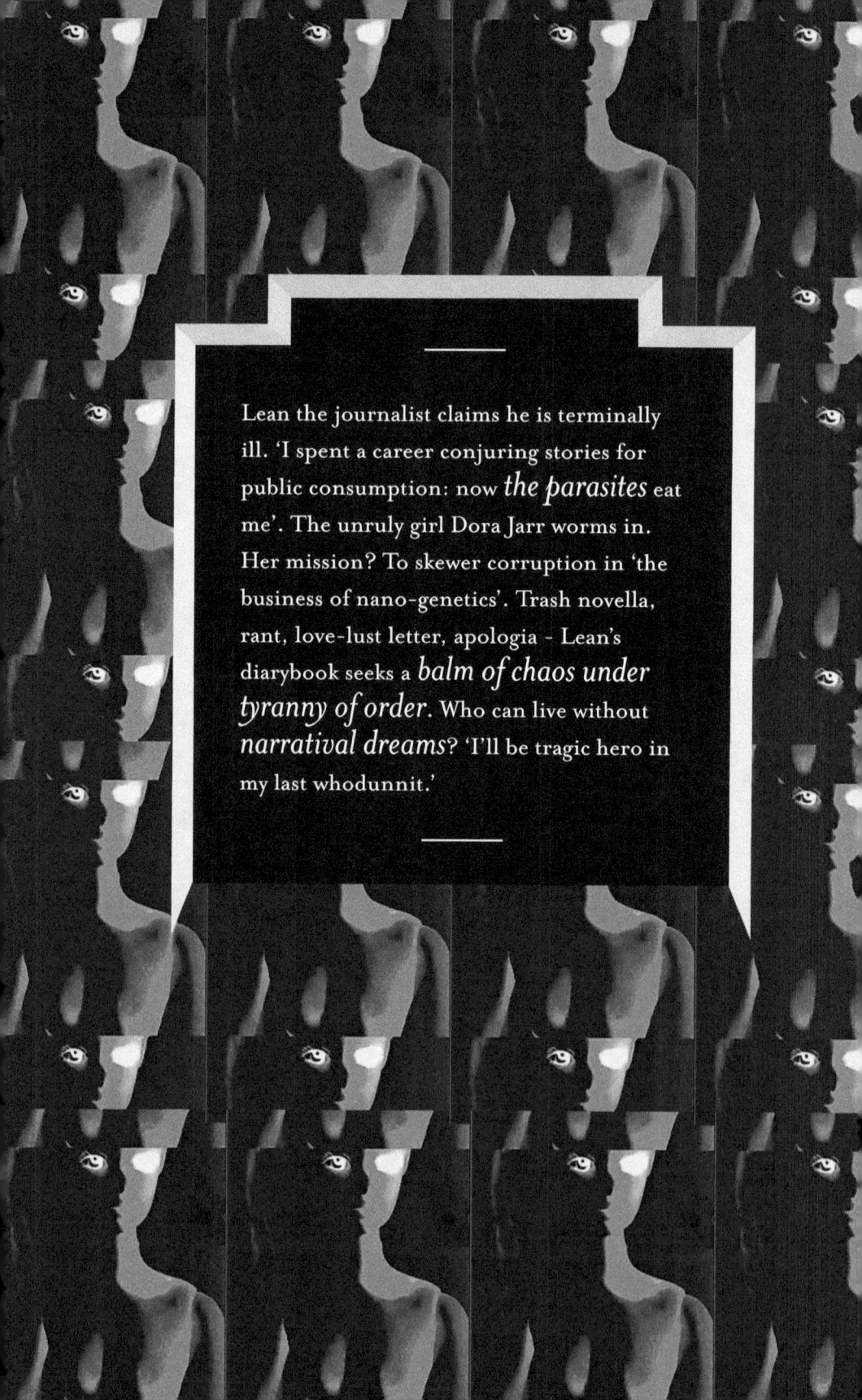

Lean the journalist claims he is terminally ill. 'I spent a career conjuring stories for public consumption: now *the parasites* eat me'. The unruly girl Dora Jarr worms in. Her mission? To skewer corruption in 'the business of nano-genetics'. Trash novella, rant, love-lust letter, apologia - Lean's diarybook seeks a *balm of chaos under tyranny of order*. Who can live without *narratival dreams*? 'I'll be tragic hero in my last whodunnit.'

Chaos

Our narrator's name is Lean, and he is a journalist for want of a better label. His business is scribbling stories to be swallowed by a society in the agglomeration of its myths. Once upon a time he did it all with gusto and commitment, but now he is over it, past it, beyond it, he says. In his diarybook he proposes to tell us why. Obsessively.

Fatal Disease   'Absent the grand fabrication of narrative, none of us can exist. In this limitless chaos of the possible, all living things crave order. Each tiny person must carve out his story, bless him, and wants it to be unique. For me, Lean, time is short for dumping things in print. Health is not what it might be. I am rotting. Total cell-count is burgeoning yet the form will be flushed away. Great news! I see nothing of consequence ever happened to me since there's only phase in this life. Sole philosophic question is: Am I responsible? Problem now is whether to write or think at all, to engage in a quixotic unravelling of complicated strands. Need to make sense is gonna be my undoing. I've nobody to talk to. Lemme talk. Got everything and nothing to say. *Be as you are*, the sages murmur. Well, if things could be any other freaking way I guess they would be. While I breathe, the bubbling Need won't rest, it vibrates. I'm getting ready to leave. And I've no way to do it since where I go is probably nowhere. Is nowhere to be like this? Fucking likely. I watch this careening phantasmic menagerie of forms, and tread water and… panic. What use is life trashed by death, what use a body, or knowledge that's all forgotten? Why participate when it slithers away from our candled eyes? Thus I feel the *chaos* - and like a pilotless plane, blunder at eternity.

Yet I cheer for a Mystery that's beyond time and space, conjured by no-one, un-subject to turn of mind or dogma or aught any creature might feel or invest in. There is a ghost who deigns to create! She has a thousand names, and no name whatever. I publish a few. The great, the reservoir, the aware, the shaker, the mover, the self who wears no chain of form, the holy ghost… She watches the angst of a man called Lean who fears the loss of his teardrop identity, his little dance of ego and id. The man who writes this shouts to be free but everywhere is in chains: of belief, idea, conjuration, fantasy, branch and eddy and limb and subset, matrix, thicket, bits and bobs, clouds, rumours, humours, perplexity, fixity, falsity, paucity, megacity, eccentricity, subtext, combination, involution, ramification, bifurcation, conflagration, fancy-flight, dream in air, garden-path, demi-chewed notion, drudgeries, faeces, gossamer filigrees, veins and eggs and wombs and rooms, fatty deposits, brains, prisons, walls and wormholes. To name a tiny few. So, the name is Lean. Some kind of *person.* And much shit do I write that must never be published in daylight. I take refuge in satire but in the silent night fret for my soul. My feelings overflow bounds of acceptable receptacles, they flood out of diaries drawers and windows, down stairs into streets and gardens, muddy up the sea, contaminate the sky. Nowadays I write without thought (bad risk) but still pray it coheres under laws subtler than I know. This is my excuse for fashioning a story of bits. Really an impossible thing, like a dancer who craved to crawl out of his skin: expressed nothing but itself, harked at the Great, fell away like spent fireworks in the sky. Inconclusive, lacked critical mass, killed ideas it fed on. I'd like to spill my guts in red streams on your pristine carpet. Vomit anything that comes to mind. Fixations. Ego. Effects of bad seeds. Life that eats itself. Incest. Anarchy. Craving for disorder. Clinging, suffering. Hate of suffering. The Impersonal. Victimhood. My strange longing for a girl. There's even a whodunnit plot around that girl (I don't care for it) to illustrate and embroider my implosion at the hands of bastards. I pull myself on by my bootstraps: the telling creates my story, the very telling lets me live.

Narrative will Save Us! Must we all cleave to ignorance to live? My latest depressing conclusion. Depression is my muddy counterfeit for calm. I dwell on the crazy stuff people do. Eg: Feynman the physicist - he wanted to trace the paths of incorporeal particles, pin down their ghost-dance of deceasing... Boffins chopped up Einstein's brain to discern why it worked so remarkably. Pol Pot tried to kill everyone in his sight, and they say he started out a principled man. Genghis Khan died content with the smell of human blood in his nostrils. Uncle Hitler was a vegetarian and saintly to animals. Some folks get so damn confused they top themselves.

Others get so riled up they murder folks. Some think and think and go potty like mustachioed Nietzsche who tried to swallow the wind. Some eat and eat till they're *dead*. Dudes drive cars at 200 miles an hour. People compose deep books. Women shop. Brave fools think they can fathom economics. Some report on this *maya*, dreaming they'll change it, worse still improve it. Some prey on others' misfortune in order to live. They're Journalists. Don't talk to 'em for pity's sake. What could be the fate of a man in search of a story, of a life? Who thirsts for coherence in this insane samsara? Pity me then, I've no story. I am Lean the lonely one, all stripped away.

Fear the Beast   This hack invents chimeras in the dark of night. 'I cling to a life raft, while at the fringe of my cabined world, my fragile pact with eternity, lurks a shapeshifting BEAST. He says: 'I am the wombless motherless beast of CHANGE. I am borderless, obliterated, never what I am. Scream and no-one will hear you! Set the controls for the heart of the sun, rush at warp speed to the centre of the black!' ...Yeah, it's Tuesday. In the morning. Eat your yoghurty wheatgerm and live. Decimate this cruddy kitchen while you're at it. Is change really a mercy? We live we shit we eat we live we shit we live live live live!' So cool down Lean. Chew yer scroggin and pause... Look, blueness through the window. Celebrate the gloried hiatus of the *possible*. Your kettle has boiled. Reminder of sweet home. And for an instant I feel a strange stirring love... and I've come to the bottom of my bowl. No place to look but up. What's with the shitey world today? Plug in, get online. Live - in your self-made death frame. Used to it. This is Tuesday.

The Beast that Eats Itself   Life is sacrifice, life is incest. Two particles meet, and their problem is murder or death. Ypres 1916: two private soldiers bayonet each other's lungs in a nameless field, lie dutifully dead in embarrassing mud-bed together. Well done lads, you participated, and your next blood-and-soul embrace is destined in far off future wars where armies of men will again knife and fork each other while criminal politicians dine at table on fatted birds. Just to *be here* is incest, sacrifice. Sister-brother tribes annihilate each other to win their peace: one living, one dead, the other to follow. Saturn chews up his children, buyers and sellers scrabble for a bargain, in the self-gorging city the cake poisons 'em all. Friend, let me help you live, we'll welcome each other at the stoop and fondle our daggers under capacious cloaks. Citizen, seek not to know on whom the guillotine falls. It falls on you! It's your blood that shall water our streets, water the fetid dreams of a bloodthirsty populace. Great trees gulp carbon and give us breath yet we saw off their necks! All things take: the more conscious the taker, the greedier. Man. Fire delights in its prey's agony but consuming itself will fail, while the airy sky bloats with clouds of dead fire and casts them back to earth, where a swathe of clamouring vegetable-trees suck the watery bounty but offer no thanks. And water will ever seek its body of ocean, its massive delight, but abandoned to the fiery sun it evaporates in muttering mists and is swallowed again by the sky. Sacrifice. Incest. Sacrifice.

So much for the weather forecast... Twelve hours just vaporised, earth turns again. Your lean chaos-merchant in the night quiet, abandons laptop and sweats in the dark... How did we learn to grab these little electric info-packets of light and store 'em? Or how could such quanta be when all is fluid seas of energy! How can forms *form* and where do they vanish? All things must vanish, to Black Holes say the boffins, that suck us like vacuum cleaners into rubbish tips of the matter universe. And there really are holes in the light, tunnels in the sun! And if we burned our dead... if I was burned and they scattered my ashes, atomised my ashes... oh lord when would I turn to spirit? For spirit hath no space - so what is this infinite unseen from which all forms cometh, to which all returneth yet cometh again? In the dark I see... it is the *mind,* my own own mind. That am I and always was and forever will be. Explain it, you material scientists: how mind is unseen yet cannot fail to be. Explain it to a cynic. Explain to a smoke-rotted journalist.

Little Jack Horner sat in his corner, gobbing his pudding and pie. He stuck in his thumb and pulled out a plum and said oh what a good boy am I! Should never've been a hack. Shoulda been... a what? Mystic poet philosopher preacher. I know: a *writer.* Here's what I like about journalism: the ephemerised trivial quotidian nose-in-the-dirt doings of little souls in their soap opera of eternal nothingness, ever-bubbling like mud geysers from the earth, fantastically complicatedly nuanced and signifying fucking nothing at all! Refuge in the NOW, I worship it. This great distraction-hideaway of fearful exposed humanity, these jottings and doings of tweety little beings in the immensity of void space. See how that immensity blows in like the weighty North Wind into cracks and niches of our flimsy houses, flings open doors, howls like a surging tsunami to the reckless wild beyond, laughing. We're domestic beings, can't survive boundlessness, cower in the teeth of the wild. Horrid tundra knocks with knuckles of death on our papery walls. We study minutiae at the ends of our noses, chatter in nervy circles, share our bubble-nuances, so glad to be invited inside to the warm party of life. But we shiver inwardly, being sensory rats; we anticipate some great *examination.* Our little scandals hint at a great scandal: we fail to admit the emperor has no clothes, that we live in a lying land, that we're corrupt and abhor the truth though it blows all about us, lifting and flinging the debris of yesterday's news in our canyon streets. We fail to look, we fail to see, we flap our arms in the world-scouring wind, scurry to catch wavelets on a shore, scoop handfuls of dust swirling in deserts. Running breathless for the great deadline we catch taxis to nowhere, slouch on grubby pavements reporting nothingness writ in mud, scratch out a life that turns on others' misfortune, finger poppies amid the graves of dead, harken to the hollow bells of unmeaning. We proclaim the *Importance,* everywhere the *Importance!* In the relevantness of our crowing ecstasy we are Little Jack Horner who discovered the world and saw it was good, and made a meal of its unfailing bounty... But Jack, he died and was forgotten, was no creator, nor even a participant. In the forests of time, did he colour a single leaf, usher one droplet from the great lake of the sky, paint a snow-shadow on forbidding peaks, cross an ocean washed by winds no human ever mastered? He did not. He was just a grubby little journalist who thought of being a wry-ter.

Vanity Fair... This writer spits on the scientist's How and the philosopher's Why. He asks *What.* Here's his lowly calling! What, he asks, are the limits of *suffering?* We journalists know best, hard-bitten cynics that we are, how vanity rules this world. We rush to clutch the action and freeze-frame misfortune and self-congratulate on our crucial work, work we know will ever go on in the face of slaughterwar and Armageddon and un-meaning and grinding repetition of pale horror. And we'll laugh at the prospect that nothing will ever change since this is human life, since these are the conditions and parameters by which all must function for ever and ever Amen. But we must work, otherwise where'd be learning and progress? Tyrants will pull wool over eyes, injustice and horror will multiply, none will be called to account and the Good won't flourish. Thus are the world-engines of HOPE oiled by the dripty-drip of news. Must have our daily feed of adrenal-junkie factoid dramas or life will not be life, will not be worth the living. No meaning, context, nothing to cry or die for. No way to forget our neighboury battles and dealings in our little window-worlds where fools like us peer back at us from hovels and brick-fill boxes and skyscraper towers, towers that once heralded tomorrow's better world under a better sky... Segue to endless hard-talk chatter on equity and justice and fairness for all. Is there no *equilibrium* in this crazy hill-of-beans world? Calmed by what hidden hand, the grinding chaos? The truth I saw one time in India. An old peanut seller with his cart languishes in heat and flies and dust by the roadside. His nuts are stale since no-one wants them. A man comes by on his bicycle, careens into him. Bang! Little hills of nuts are toppled and the stick-legged vendor sees flash before him distorted visages, hungry mouths, despair - his family! So many strewn in the gutter and dust oh Shiva oh Kali! But he wrestles to restore his little nut-hill. Curses and sweats and moans. *And I saw how no-one could ever help him.* Thus I felt the sickness of the world... and reported it. Give every bastard a million then! Oh but our currency 'd rot away, death of value, death of economy, no free lunch blaaa, we need scarcity failure poverty or there'd be no striving or aspirational bullshit. Hail the great valueless striving for value. Great fucken lie of capital and commune. Economists widget about stability and prosperity for all but secretly know it can *never be.* Always have to be ugly fat chiefs, skinny little indians full of envy. Here is our tragedy: old-man river to nowhere has to flow forever. And we all wanna know For Whom the Great Bell Tolls. You fall by the wayside, I shake my head, whisper prayers, pass on and forget, seeking grim reality *elsewhere.* **Lord grant me attention-span of goldfish!** New narratives required! Forget my life's a grotty tale of profitless half-baked wishy embarrassment. Don't remind me I'm nobody in my eighty-year waiting room. Still I wriggle in shame and doff me cap. Thank yer God. Glad to be alive, glad the showers are really showers. Fortune's meany roller-coaster snake jigs its snout up down. Childish hearts lurch in mouths, flickering screens of markets and banks hypnotise us little insects. Myopic bees clutter and soil their own hive. Any bee that's half-way clever will fly away, pass its earthly summer in mindless peace and bring no pollen home at all... Oh yeah, human beings one step from gods, but what life would *I* choose? I'd rather be fat and happy and ignorant than live a nobly degraded life in some benighted poverty-stricken corner of earth. In fact my ignorance degrades me wherever I am. But I'll not fail to *imagine* the gross and mass suffering of the world, imagine a perpetual living war somewhere elsewhere. I'll dwell on it 'cause to be a masochist salves my conscience. And I know it's the repetition and repetition of a thing that makes for suffering, but I will cling to the thought that this suffering has no general *mass,* that it is *individual,* that it is fractally broken in merciful bits, limited, diced into moments of ticking time - each of which is mercifully *gone* as if it never was. Please tell me forgetting is the end of suffering, that forgetting is release, that this is god's fractal mercy to the very bottom of time, to the very atoms dissolved in a void. I know there's no escape but let there be the mercy of forgetting. Please please make it all better, please salve the gaping wound of conscience...

And oh what an elaborate and beautiful thing is conformity. If all the beautiful people in the party kissed each other twice, once on each cheek at greeting and again at parting, how many kisses would be there? Surely enough to drown a million sorrows. This world grinds to conformity through habit. Even as we plan to stir it all up we simply vomit it out again in a technicolour yawn heralding new conformity. This morning as I awake is it conceivable that I might find... peace? Can philosophy do its cleansing work and lift me from the grind of yester thoughts? Nope. The quotidian world will roll on and crush me like a steamroller driven by a drunken man, like a horse its rider in a fatal charge of cavalry. Just try to do one little thing, just one little thing outside the square, outside the box, outside the norm - and you will see how the world comes cracking down on you, how the censure and the vilification, the scorn of the four winds will pour on you and drown your dreams. The world's mindless rump is sensitive to nothing, but *you* will feel the guilt at its righteous hostility. And we live in a democracy! A hysteric democracy where gated women hate, children store up evil, the old lose their marbles, men bully their way to happiness. Where we assiduously vote for public clowns, live shunted side by side in horror of loneliness, where animals are boned and sliced to make our lunch, where we grin-freeze the past and future in photographic death (we never move again) and yearn for a moment that never was, or if it was, 'twas the moment where we yearned for *another*. Moment, that is. But don't you dare ask *the question*. Don't be a bleating little Prufrock. Oh don't wish for anything *other*... Tell me, how can a creature so fine and complex as a human being be consigned to so lowly a fate?

Answer: exterminate all sewer-rats! Systematically extract all rotten teeth! Maximal efficiency meets maximal emotional chaos #&$@#+! And fractal unholy killing ORDER reverberates in the very bones of man. Yea, to the fifteenth generation. There are things so entrenched and monstrous I can't start to grapple with. One of these is *Holocaust*. Equal, our magnificent gift for delusion. In a flicker of brainial cells we re-badge any narrative, skirt about, shift the goalposts. Must replace, forget, in order to go on. I tell you this world or any other is a tendentious floating maybe-narrative flickering in and out with a whim and a will, and our planned and sober thought is all a fucking scam inside a dream, and when it flickers in and sticks we have the insanity of order: hardened habit plucked from an infinity of choice. But if anyone thinks this insane constructed world or any constructed world is to lead us to heaven - then he or she has not grocked the *Holocaust*. The lesson: take nothing, nothing, for granted. What is a 'world' but a flurry of mental electrics, manner of speaking, pathetic posture, mad anachronism? We're all mown down like nine-pins in a bowling alley and still we hope! Showered to death, cleansed under the nozzles of invisible gas in human slaughterhouses just like our animals, and we are so amazed that it can *be* like that. Where is dignity?

We are *meat*. But on we trudge with our sacrednesses and our logics and our papering over cracks and our dark revenge. Till the very day we fall and repeat the tragic tragedy of all our forebears. And it all gets *stored*. There is a group-mind, groupthink of skinhead thugs in an alleyway bent on the bludgeoning of one who is unkempt. There's a race unconscious with enough deep *scheisse* stored within to swallow ten thousand years of light. **Do Your Duty** The *Einsatzgruppen* took snaps of their victims: ladies in groups, contented friends as if at a beach picnic, before shooting and dumping them all in their great *Babi Yar* trench. Some say Himmler only thought up the gas option because his uniform got spattered while inspecting a shooting. So very distasteful. How one loathes inefficiency. What suffocates me is the people who collated the gold fillings and jewels, shoe-pairs, laces, follicles of hair, entered them in smart ledgers, refused to smell the smell or think the thought or stand up and say: *No. I am a human being. I do not participate in butchery.* What of the barbers who snipped and gathered the hair of naked jewesses at the chamber doors? The Commandant's wife and children who conducted happy familial lives within the fleshly smoke-drift of the slaughterhouse? What human is capable of this? Only a system, only a *corporation*. Are we human if we fail in our duty? No, we are animals. But what is a human... so much *mince?* What's human when officers require flawless requiems to be nobly executed by the camp orchestra while their eyes grow misty at some fond remembrance of home before the war... of blonde blue-eyed girls beneath a linden tree... of heather under azure sky... then send those sad and sorry fiddlers down the really road into the jaws of gas. Ruefully. But harken to the beat of a butterfly's wings! *Collective Memory.* Thinner than gas, it screams...' **The Conductor** In my little city garden, pulling back the wandering jew (what's the proper term these days?) I bring to mind a famed officer who greeted trains at the Auschwitz gates. With nonchalant sleight of hand and philharmonic mastery, in mourning black with gold cuffs like teeth he plied the conductor's art, and the orchestra responded as a great machine as he directed guests to left or right: young and strong to the left, infirm and childish to the right. And I saw that *duty*, unbearable though it be, makes each human free. If we shall accept our place on earth, accept the consequences of need - to kill, to love, to die as victim - then all is peace. And though we fret and wonder at fate: *shall I sleep in sheets tonight, eat wholesome food, take a warming shower, cuddle my loved ones after days of cold confined in wagons blindly enduring the grind of steel on steel?* we can be sure that our part is stolen by no-one else, that we are the enduring centre of our little glade, our little storm, our little garden. And salvation is here: duty to be done and done again without ceasing or regret. And as we greet the black-clad puppeteer and walk to his time and feel ourselves members of his orchestra as flutes and fiddles and piccolos, as we shape the very tone and timbre of his sublime inexorable work, composition of greater minds written in the stars of the Reich, we go to our duty like lambs. For without us the masters cannot climax their thousand-year symphony, their poetry of cleansing, their concertos of cool butchery. We shall soon rest, soon rest. At peace, at peace. Walk forward. Do not cry. Hold my hand. Play your part. Remove your vestments. Mind the step. To the chamber. Fear not the clang of doors. Breathe in, breathe out. The darkness. Summon your dignity. Human not insect. Arbeit macht frei. Don't shit yourself. Don't struggle. I love you. Is there a hiss? *Insecticide.* What is burning? Breathe your last. Expire. Be gone.

All suffering is past, all wandering done. All done. And where is grace? It is that there is no other moment. No other moment but this.

And I am ashamed to the core. What is the worst a foolish man can do in this world? Shit his pants in polite company. Show his penis to a class of children. Bleed on the hostess' carpet. Become ash. Wipe out a race. Nothing is ever disturbed! Not the moon and stars, nor the deep motion of the ocean. Not the wind on a mountainside. Not the tolling of the knell for all creatures born. Nor the habits of a human being... In my kitchen I come upon a phalanx of ants. Their crime? To be in my sink in my clean human world. I wipe great swathes of them out and take scant pleasure therein. Look to the chaos of the mind. The holocaust of ants screams at me: you are no greater! Little ants, where have you gone? Do your little souls rest, is reincarnation for you? A solemn but blythe historian mouths his words on television: 'The war to end all wars had been costly. Forty million died... But was the loss in vain? No, they live on in the glory of our remembrance.' Suffocate that idiot first, I beg you lord. And overlook my little mass-murder. My ant murder.

One single heedless *breath* is taken by a rotting man called Lean and a billion microbes act their tiny masquerades and perish. Kamikaze microbes die for love of emperor! Who tells their untold story? We, human, greater microbes, take it all for granted. But I have no mastery. I am but the folds and valleys and cliffs and mountains of a great slimy country called Body. I am the polluted evoluted field, rotting produce of human years, heaving livers and bile-churning liquid lakes, rivers of blood that roll to the heart, whiteblood corridors light-years long, caverns organ-deep, deserts and dunes of skin, mines of bone, cauldron-eyeballs sucking in light, skeins of forested lungs sucking crazily at solar winds. I am all birth and change and time, slow-dying, imperceptible as microscopic suppurating sweat-bubbles. I age in the moon's crying tides, astrologic fodder for the stars' nudgings and whisperings... helpless in the pulsing heart of an aching body. I am no individual. Microbes are me. I am microbe.

Razor's Edge No peace for me. Too much hate. This cold winter. I ache. No more stories. All my rationalisms, used up. Here I am. Razor's edge is infinitely thin. The spirit is lean. I wish I were boundless. I should cut myself open, red streams may purify. Only the empty can swallow the world. *Only light behind the eyes perceives the darkness.* Only the wind hears the thrumming of a drum. Every breath is my last. Madmen claim to stopper death. Only the lonely know a friend. There's no suffering but here. I imagine a razor so thin it cut through emptiness, a particle so small it never saw another, a sorrow so deep it swallowed the night. A castle so dense none ever escaped, a net so fine it scooped the sea, a love so entrenched it fed on itself. My clock is ticking. For every gesture, the anti-gesture. For every breath a vacuum. Every dream a rude awakening. The razor's edge is immeasurably thin, yet microbes journey forever. The caravanserai sets off. Is never seen again. Military columns have no end. War is here. Bell tolls for me. The night has no dawn. Here. Here. Don't wait. There's no time. Hurry. Hurry.

And then... my bell rings.

Man with Girlfriend   Something resembling a plot is about to be invented in my gritty booky-wook! Smell of Plot may keep us all alive. Positive story: How I Wooed My Girlfriend. A girl I met at a party called Dora Jarr rocks up at my flat. Super late. And rings my bell. I spy her distortally in the view hole. Naivety makes me open the door. She barges in, ta for asking.

- Why you spying on me, dude called Lean?
- Sorry - ?
- You Insta me. Ten times. You're a journo
- O-kay
- Need to know if you're a perv. Or a jerk-off
Solid-ish thighs disappear up a tartan skirt. Black coarsehair corrals a square pale face. Breasts beckon under the leather jacket.
- Guess I'd be - hunting a story?
- What? 'Bout me?
- Dunno. (shit-eating grin) See what the cat brings in?
She curls her lip at that one. Looks over shoulder, looks at ceiling. Breathes out of her mouth.
- So you 'like' me?
- Uhhh
- Males just want anal
- Ah!
She gives the middle finger, turns on heel, jerks to the door.
- Wait… err… oral?
- Fucken mess with *me,* dude.
Ooh, she's coming. I sway, clunk onto sofa.
- Know your fuckin' type. I'm some underage chick who needs a fuck? Show us, dude!
I have no words. She jerks her pants down a bit. I'm inspecting a significant spot.
- Do it, limpdick
- Are you… medicated?
She straddles me, grinds in, hard. In seven seconds I'm a bore. Rolls to the floor, splays legs, pouts. A hip flask drops conspicuously from jacket.

To speak would be problematic. She eyes the door. I wanna shut it but my legs are all broke.

- Let me… make a cuppa?

No answer. I'm up, hobbling to the freaking d -

(Barely audible) - Sugar n' milk.

I dive-ert to the kitchen, balls stinging like only boys know. I hear a bang in the bathroom. The girl's in my shower. Make yerself at home! Dora Jarr, whatever yer handle is. After a bit she's back, and dressed. Dumb-stares me with tray in hand, like I'm the intruder.

- Sugar and milk.

Silence. Her eyes roll about.

- No worries then

- Ya let go, be spontaneous… or you're a fake. Get it?

(Process this) - Er, yup.

Lower-groin pain has a leaner view of her spontaneity. No worries, she's a 'guest'.

- D'you eat cake? I got some

- God no! Fat enough.

We sort of sit - by the sofa on my floor kind of shit. She slurps the tea absently. Presently grabs a fistful of cake, nullifying previous injunction. Drops a fair few crumbs. (Keep gob shut, it's going swimmingly) It dawns on me she's 'far younger than me'. Seems fierce-shy in a blustery sort of way. Solid cheek, pouty lip, hunted look. Lot going on in that head. I feel a bit protective.

- Did we really meet online?

- Uh, press party? Duh? Old journo and his dirty look, asks his shitty question and fucks off? Then pats my arse at the Claus Heffenbonck conference (what, who?). Not to mention… uh forget it

- And the shitty question was…

- I'm here, dude

(Sure are) - So you're - staying the night?

I'm amazed I say it. She doesn't move.

- Up to you, pal.

Pal. Cool. My new girl, then.

A Day Trip to Remember   Today being a Saturday I arise a little late in the afternoon. Days still have to start however much light is squandered. There's no running from habity thoughts of rot and failure. They say 99 per cent of all thoughts are repeated, and 99 percent of them repeat 99 times over... till one day we peer dimly out through our sticky mental gauze and sense we're trapped creatures, dulled without remembrance or inspiration, ignorant of spider veils that shut out unutterable unspeakable freedom. We need the jolt of the new, the jarringly unknowable! I remember the first day I confessed (selected) thoughts to Dora Jarr... wondered aloud if my life amounted to a hill of beans. Nope, she said, but it might amount to a 'beautiful fucked-up narrative'. What could she 've meant?

Downstairs the kitchen is a jarring mess: what else where Dora's bin and gone? Slow bomb gone off. Doors ajar everywhere, her silly trademark. Her bed place abandoned hours ago is a pile of junk: knickers, boots, fingerless gloves, she-male porn mags, a scraggly hairbrush. Who can sleep next to that? Me is the short answer. I get when there's no choice. A single man of my age and condition has no choice. She got that on day two but doesn't exploit it too fecking much. Dora Jarr is a mystery: seems like hunted and there's no hunter but her. She vibrates. There-but-gone, tense but vulnerable in a way that gets me churning. She'd kill me if I mentioned it. But would she walk out? Don't mention that either. People who walk through strangers' doors, what are they looking for? I'm her stranger, and I suspect the whole world is. But she hooked me, and she's definitely a Thing. Maybe she's my thing.

Late in the nameless afternoon Dora actually arrives. Got a present for me, innit. Hallucinogenic Drug. *Whaaat?* You need it, pal. *If I say no?* Then I'm not your girl anymore and that means no sex. *Does it mean you won't raid my pantry and wallet anymore?* We'll see 'bout that, clever dick. And as I ope my mouth to make further objection she stuffs it in. Has a book for me as well. Read it quick! Timothy Leary's *Anatomy of Psychedelic Experience* blaaa. Get three stages. One: egoless bliss. Language'll fail you at last. Two: futile battle to understand said unrestricted state. Three: absurd struggle to regain normal dull consciousness. That'll be you. Get with the program, silly old journo. *You mean turn on, tune in, drop out n'* *all that? Are you gonna stay?* Nah, thingies to do. PS: I'm locking you in the house. And she's gone… Cripes! Half an hour and it's coming at me… clinging to my life, clinging to my nightmares, clingin' to the CEILING yooooooo… Who the hell is me what's the boundary of me what freaking person am i? Holy shiiit Doooraaa! I'm a GHOST I'm nothing I'm ETERNITY I'm DISEMBODIED. How many times do these brain cells die n' go to heaven? You tell *me* (shake finger at mirror) what's my END? Must avoid self-harm… Seem to 've been in this TOILET for hours… DESIRE IS HELL but what am i s'posed to do? Might as well not have a head. Can't sit on arse in ashram on top of fecking mountain. Born to stir, make mess, suffer, fuck up, repeat till hell freezes over. Struggle and holler and fight and die for *justice*. Do ya get it? GOD already *dispensed* *it*. I tell ya LIFE is AMORAL. And religion says be quiet blissy humble lick status quo arseholes. Fuck status Q I'm bored, hungry, want sex. Exit for GOOD 'cause I'm God, I'm IT. Get the fuck outa my WAY. I invent Cosmos with every breath. Ah but Leeeean, you'd not even exist without myriad forces that created *you*. Oh so they all joined hands in papal conclave and thought up me did they wise guys. All in the same boat dudes. God in a boat floundering: 'S called the WORLD. Even HE can't exist without ME. Don' worry 'bout me 'cos I'm free of You. Deal. I'm Impersonal Being which means ANYTHING GOES - but I *say* what goes 'cos I want my pleasure n' CHOICE baby. Was dis bliss drug my choice? No, bloody DORA'S, now it's all gone BAD… Where's the COW anyway?

Hours pass… Some mystery god of Night daubed the entire contents of my apartment black! Every nook and cranny surface object mote molecule a silky richy lushity velvety black. Black atoms yo. Shoulda been born black. Incorporeal night winds flutter through my street window. Won' blow away my little black secrets… *Calmer now. Meditation.* My mind is still and mirror-like, its depths visible to sandy rippled bottom. On a forgotten tropical shore, wind and cloud can't touch its paradisic repose. Later the mind wanders, flutters a dream of the faraway, of the wind-borne. Seeks tidings, and a great albatross brings promises over the ocean from afar and alights at my feet… Now I am the wide sea of possibility, of longing winds that fleck the horizon, that stir the spume and foam to grand longing, eternally pushing before which I sail lonely to the end of the world… The mind-sea is a relentless blue-grey thousand-mile heaviness of waves that surge forever to the uncharted destination and never arrive. Waves… I see their nature is to surge and reach, dissolve and die, o'erborne by pursuing waves that also pass away in opaque blue-black depths of forgetting. No place for humans, this: the pouring winds make fallow my lungs and eyes. And sometime now my mind is a watery fathomless grave of the past, of ideas and notions lost, of my childhood time gone, of all the dark deep of a life stored in the hazy mud-filmed bottom-locker of the sea… And then it tortures me, this mind: a colourless vaporless mirror of stasis, as if a lethe, a pall, has settled on the ruddy sun-addled waters, and I'm a sailor languishing under useless lumpen sails. And I stir with my eyes muddy pools of ragged boredom-despair… Dora? Where are you, mermaid? Come home. I made it, didn't drown! No answer. Make a wish then. I wish… in the morning my mind will be as a crystal river in spring, longing for the sea. And for thee.

System Paradise all the Days of your Life   'Case you're wondering, I crawled down the damn fire-escape after Dora locked me in. Trawled the city, surfed the crowd. Slow motion fog-parade of DOING. This shopping mall's the land of the DEAD. Shit everywhere. Rotting? Get a facial. Dying? Get a rope and nail. Necropolis. Sausage-machine fatness. Digestion, shit-progress, walk on… Look at them fucking *towers*. Why not mechanise whole shamble universe? SYSTEM is God. Purpose order! Forever daydream paradise. Machinery + Technology + Regulation + Control = EASE. Oil and nuts, wire and titanium. All feelings accounted. All impulse regulated. No twitchy moves. MACHINATION = apotheosis of happiness. In glassy tower rooms in foggy hives, workday warrens, we ponder at screens, send missives from pillar to post, confer and ruminate and fret, deliver decisions, await consequence, quake at superiors, mop sweat, furrow brows… Any hippie from Mars 'd see we'd all gone barmy. Why do these earthlings grovel to serve the levers and buttons and dots that feed their own pastime machine? And they built a fractal computer as big as a planet and clipped and snipped every genetical bit, with a nano-fiddle here and a nano-faddle there, till they birthed the fattened PIG of MONEY AND MEAT... Cadge some coin for a coffee dispenser. Tastes like Dora's five-day panties. OH SYSTEM. Life's smelly red-offal carpet laid out for benefit of humo-bots. You think I lack the compassional touch, reader? What will *you* do when no-one cares because you're smelly trampish and old, when not a soul registers what you want or think or vote? When you're alone and lonesome death awaits. My advice? Face the stupid emptiness, and *breathe.*

Walk on... so many lonely fish in a rainbow sea. City crowd-shoals flitter in fantasmic synchronisation. Reefs abound. No Fisher of Men in the canyon city. Pools of human eyes come at me, pulse and withdraw, never can hide their mind-flood. What secret rivers of tears are unleashed by people aching for the sea? We are the fish, thinking musing fish in our watery grave of musing, in liquored veins of streets whose horizon is the tips of skyscrapers, all unheeded by white winds of the sky. And down here our minds over aeons encrust pearl-shell identities, our clam bodies brood on lies and doubt and dreams. And on such strands and reefs we cast our nets and seek one fish who'll look at *us,* who'll moon through lips and eyes in private dance with *us,* who'll join our wan undersea world of lonely consequence...

Where to at last? Embarrassing when you find your end in a deserted church. Gloomy dust beams, high stained window, distant boom of the city. A woman genuflects alone in her pew, plugs her gaps of loneliness. Belong, fragile heart. Not me, not me. I laugh at people who belong to prayer and rule and habit, to vision-hues and softy peccadilloes, who cleave to posturing curves of thought, to bygone years and fogey generations, to a billion sacred unquestioned destined rules that scribe the path. Why should all this *tattle* rule your thought and act and speech? Lest you be trusted with the wide, the open, the unbelievable? Christian in his heaven, muslim and his mecca, jew with his god-fearing cap, scientist in his 'real world', kid with his fire engine, monopolist with money-wet dream, writer with booky-wook, guard in button-shiny uniform, reporter with death-defying deadline. Lunatic boxes all. Dicks who think they're individuals! Give me a mind that scorns the dogma-muzzle, pricks mental chattels, gobbles moral hang-ups. Rejects and lets it all, knows shit is forever, knows that mouths mothers minds bottoms toilets tears are the goddam same species of faeces. Where the fuck is the end to limits? Order order order determinismismism. My neighbour's toddlers obsess every day about being heard: they've perfected a subtle style of screaming. Later they'll obsess about friends who dump them - and as adolescents about contours in their faces, as nubile women about FAT deposits, as thirty-somethings about making it, forties about the meaning of making it, fifties about power, sixties about accolades, old and dying about emptiness. Me, I'm old and dead pushing forty. So who is this sick victim of rigidity? The dangedest thing: he's an *individual*. Give the toddler a hoop to tend, hoopla, she's a hoop-artist. Spend your days in dank mines, lo, you're a miner of soot-faced dignity. Me, glued to computer squander my life in digital pathways. Lock and load! What's yer label, Lean? Brave journalist! Walk on, dreaming your visions of frantic emptiness... Ugh, but I'm lonely. Go home. Here's my limit then, where satire ends, where I won't endure its heat, where I won't eat my own medicine. My limit is as a lover. With his ache.

Baby Anarchist   Dora Jarr's back in the house. My adolescence, my little ache. I want to imagine a sepia-world before the Coming of Dora, where god is in his heaven, money in the banks, national team on top, roses in hedgerows, cherubic clouds in the sky. No dog-eat-dog hate but democracy freedom peace, civilised people quaffing wines nibbling canapes, conducting killing-wars with proper rules: no gas, no landmines, prisoner respect. Mercy, for god's sake! But I don't. I whisper instead a hateful mantra: *Anarchy is creative, bombs are gifts, destruction is rebirth, rudeness is manna for the soul and selfishness instructive.* Dora is here. Those Hindus watch the hell out for Kali and Shiva. Shiva wipes out worlds and Kali grins like the evil Martian fingering her thousand-skull necklace. Bring her ON then.

The girl is making baked beans. And burning the pot. I should teach the child to cook but she'll call me Dad. I open a window, mutter about carbon footprint. Want toast? She says get it yourself dad. I do. She eats it, big deal. New idea: lightly suggest she come with me to a book launch (where she can drink). Some deal about 'Pure Foods and the Future'. She eyes me up. Am I having a laugh? Nope. Hmm, will establishment wankers be there? I tell her you bet. Says she'll come then. Goes off to dress. I fear the outcome. When it's an 'occasion' she morphs to a clown. Dora returns: red boots, green tights, pleated green skirt, red tank-top, seedy-denim jacket, face a whitish mask and rouge lippy smeared about. I murmur approval to which she replies *fuck you*. I hope she might when we get home, both of us shitfaced. I feel strange. She looks at me as if to say: has your brain changed shape yet? I know she wants it but her Drug made me vacant and detached. And detached is my best shot with the likes of her. Makes her stay within cooee. She grinds her teeth and hangs onto me as we come through the party door. *So why're we here* she asks, as soon as I've secured her a fistful of drinks. This question hints at our complicity-intimacy, since she assumes I wouldn't come amid this lot for social reasons but professional ones, and delays her question in order to appear nonchalant, since there are big intimacy problems. I note she has 'em in the sack too. If she lets you close it's because she needs her teddy bear, or rather, needs to fuck Teddy. Poor Ted! Bet she went through a few in the childhood she's still aching to leave. Thing with her is not to assume she's inexperienced or moody or painful or anything. She might let you co-exist then. It's a struggle but dude I get it. She's none too soft in bed, and gets annoyed if you want to linger about, but over the weeks little by little I get a feeling she might be lingering a minute or two longer. Might even allow a kiss or two. That's trust, baby... Meanwhile Dora's got her agendas in the murky corridors of student politics, and claims to have written articles for foreign mags exposing Graft and Malpractice in the Food Industry etcetera yo. Keeps her sources close to the chest since I could be a rival! A rival she assents to blow under sheets. Using her teeth. We won't go there. One little thing she floats into the convo though, is some foreign businessman with whom I assume she has a fruitful or fruity relationship since she smiles self-satisfiedly whenever she drops his name. Professional source: wow, what next? But watching her makes me ache. The *transitoriness*. How to let her see, that our little moments are the precious stuff of life itself? - that with each breath all her girly anti-moments are frittering away, frittering to nothing.

Dora affects her gracious look (pouty and sulky) and scans the room. Lucky her square face is obscured by thicksy hair. If some sap asks the name of 'my daughter' we'll both poke their eye out. We gaze sternly in opposing directions, affecting purposeyness. The room contains business types, journos, pollies. Having trouble focusing: mind is not mine after yesterday Dorra Jaarrrr. Now a tall figure in a creamy suit steps through a door from the interior (we're in a posh town house) and greets our host. They appear to be chums. Eyes turn, the hubbub changes pitch. The arriviste has an angular-diffident way of standing, and I note the vaguely genuine tan and choice diamond on a fingery hand. We seem to bask in the reflected halo of Money, and he grins as if his eyes were forever happy (shoulda been a novelist, me). Accent betrays a whiff of German. Dora turns to look - and spits a cheekful of liquor right in my lap. *Fuck!* At this precise moment the fey-tall Deutsche breaks conversation and steps our way. Dora freezes. I take the proffered hand, knobbly diamond prominent.

- The journalist Lean is it not? Ah, do not be surprised that Claus Von Heffenbonck claims to know English writers of note. You have read my new work? Und greetings Dora! Almost I did not notice you.
Dora shuffles left and right. Her knuckles are shaking.
- We are friends also. In fact, I should have little words with Dora alone, yah?
I'm not grocking it. Dora mumbulates. *Need the ladies.* Lurches straight for the front entrance. Oh, a black-suit man bars her way. Folks get jostled. She is manoeuvred *subito* to an inner door. Herr German, he smiles.
- Excuse us, Mister Lean.
What the hell did I just miss? I stare at the mystery door fronted by Man Thug. No entry! Wait up. My old drinking bud Lorna Kraus is making eyes across the room. She comes up. *Greetings Lean. Saw the little altercation. Wassup?* Big blacksuit dude is getting in the way of a story. Get him to show you the ladies room? *Ooh, filthy. Watch me hit on him.* You're a doll. And Lorna does the business… and I'm through the door. Dog leg to the right. Choice of doors. Behind one, a Germanic voice.

- You turn your nose at my tiny gift? We stay friends!
- Why? I'm fucken dangerous

- Come to my house. You like my beautiful leather
- Fuck no
- Why play game of coy? Do I not pay? My drugs are not to your taste? We lie to each other now
- When don't we?
- If you want to punish, sweet girl, take advice. People want revenge
- Save me Heffie
- Take zis. I haf it ready. Manoli, leave by back way.

Uh, someone else there. Sniffing noises. A minute goes by. Now rustling, fumbling.

- Dora, I am so better for you than 'You Know Who'

(Voice is slurred) - Fron' or back, babe?
- Back, always. The table.

Turgid breathing. I imagine them in a white-fleshed arc over the slab. He'll be mumbling disgusting things. At a point she cries out like a child. A guttural utterance from him. Now rustling.

- Going, Heffie
- Why such hurry? I have new task
- Double jiggy-jig in a day
- My Dora is in too deep? Little heroine masochist. Little attention-seeker!
- Spare me the analysis. (Silence) …That good?
- You improve. More patient I think. But listen. You will steal me a paper of your mister *Goran Demecharian*. Private. Here is the title. Put it in your breast
- Ooh, why trust *me*? My other Daddy never would
- Think of nothing! …So you haf new man? Zis journalist?
- Nah nah

(Silence) - Play your little sleuth game, but not at my expense
- No prob, bigwig dude who's loaded
- I worked for what I am
- You mean what your Nazi ancestors did - selling piles of gas to der Fuhrer
- You are stupid fucking. Do not be stupid!
- Okay okay sorry all right? I'll steal yer shitty paper. Nice Heffie, still the one. (Fumbling, breathing) Am I better than *Mummy*?
- What? Yes yes, you screw me better. Now go. Back way.

Finish! I blunder through the nearby door. Steps clump down the corridor. Pause, then follow out to the crush and chatter, and there's the Germ, all icky charmy, conducting his killing-wars with his civilised rules, smiling at the minions cluttered about quaffing his pricy slurp and nibblies. Dora materializes, spies me, shovels a thing in my mouth, hisses in my ear: *Keep it shut, Lean.* We drink hard for another hour and I leave without her.

This journalist is now conscience-bound to ask slutty Dora how she got tied with bighead Claus Von Heffenbonck. Or where she slid off to, post party. Under one's beady eye she opts for the smokescreen of telling it like it is.

- Six weeks ago. Only time I ever thought of getting paid. Before him I thought, no effing way I'm gonna. But two grand. He's a goddam show-off and I'm such a self-respecting slut. You like it, Lean? (She glares like I'm supposed to applaud.) Why me, I hear you ask. Not yer average catwalk model but that German wanted BAD so I obliged. He's a total dickhead. End of

- But what about me? He bloody well knows of me! And how many times? Do you care?

- Care? Lean, I was so pissed and stoned I don't remember a freaking thing. Sorry sorry, okay! This is my research into corruption in the fucking food industry. You never did a thing to get info? Bloody bet you did.

Very defensive. Holes in her story you'd drive a coach and horses through. And what the hell about this 'Other Daddy'? And 'Mummy'? I'm gagging to know. It'll have to wait.

Atonement   Amazingly, Dora has stuck around. I begin to see a pattern these last months. She'll appear at a silly hour, acknowledge not a thing and demand body satisfaction in proportion to her latest psychic disturbance. I thereby am invited to predict its content. She's pretty bestial: a rough enigma with me the faceless conduit. I've no idea if she repeats the ritual with ten others in the neighbourhood but the fact is, she comes to me. Maybe I fill a hole in a way she has no notion of, wanted precisely because she has no idea. Father thing? And if I were to protest at her sexual harshness she'd despise me, and if I didn't she'd despise as well, so

I wrinkle my brow and endure. I suppose I'm possibly in love with her, and we both suppose that no matter how pointless or unfeeling she is I'll not give up. In our Shadow is our chance, it is said. She tests, always seeks the opposite: if there's control she'll subvert, if there's knowledge she'll confound. Even chaos she'll despise. But things unspoken: there lies the chance of life, of feeling, care. Even hatred is feeling. So I turn to sardony, hint at the mystery of my annihilation - and the dirty girl deigns to need me, even affects a bit of concern. There are times when she wants that I actually whip her. Go elsewhere for the main routine, I tell her, my house has rules. At this she gouges or bites or spits or punches! I am required to disdain her as a disgusting child. At last a strange light fades out of her eyes, a light I only notice when it's gone, and then she goes calm, turns into the supplicant. One night she dribbled from the mouth, and I wiped her little prayer with my handkerchief. Then she put a thumb in her mouth and stared in my eyes. Brave, I thought. I stroked her cheek and her defiance melted away. She let me cradle, then slept the sleep of one who has atoned. Till tomorrow.

On that tomorrow I am emboldened to ask: - Who named you Dora Jarr?
- Nobody. Not my elders anyway. 'S who I am.
The sullen reply invites me to poke at a parent obsession.
- Where are they?
- Looking to send me home?
- Looking to know you, since you're a mystery
- Dunno who my mother is. Don't care who my father is.
These lies are delivered like she lost a dollar bet on a horse. But tone never matters with Dora. Fact matters.
I pause discreetly. - Have you tried to find them?
She seems almost about to tell a truth then thinks better of it.
- Nah. I mean I tried, but... waste of time.
I affect ignorance. - So they're out there... waiting?
She glares right at me. I endure being the arch fool. This is our limit of investigation for today. But I won't let this game of dare-the-past wear me out, not before it wears her out. All things of the past... must surely be paid for.

She has Gone to the Wide Universe Things fall away, pass out of shape, and at the end there's only the moment, whatever trivia it contains. Flotsam on the surface of a great unconscious lake, with the rest scuttled to the depths. Embrace the new, people say, but you and I never can cope with this world. Krishna the god was begged by his acolyte Arjuna to show the world's true nature. So he did and Arjuna nearly went mad, crying out and begging for the unutterable horrific bedlamic vision of death and change to *stop!* No. Our experience is always a sheltered, calibrated, tamed, pointed, simplified choice. We never learn how to swallow the world's chaos... So I think of the demented - who wordlessly cry out to all the things they lost or discarded. Have we seen the suffering chaos of these we love when their past is sucked away behind the glazed pools of their eyes? I need to talk about my *mother*. Just after Dora turned up at my door claiming I'd harassed her and punished me by moving in, my mother passed away from dementia. What am I to make of it, I ask myself, when a person in an eighty year-old form is presented to me in a casket and I am told 'this is the body of your mother'? Is there a single thing about this 'body' that is less unreal or more important than the person of sixty, the person of forty, of twenty, the baby of one month, the fabled twinkle in her father's eye? I saw death for what it is - a complete fake, a misnomer, a meaningless idea, a dumping ground for all superstition and ignorance. Listen. Whatever form you appear to take is passing away with each breath, each atom-second, into another form which passes away to another form, forever. This, in any million combinations, depending on the size of the optical tool we might look through. And none of these so-called forms is anything other than a phantom, an idea. And when this 'last form' appears to disintegrate, when the light of the windows of the eyes seeks the beyond, when the zephyrs of breath labour and flow outward into the wide air, when the bag of flesh hesitates, falls and hugs the earth and will not get up or walk on no matter how its companions urge it to, then we can say that the *person*, whosoever and whatsoever that may be, has moved beyond our sight into another room, a new garden - to pluck a fresh adventure, new entertainment for her eyes, a new movie to titivate her, fresh parlay with the ineffable converse of life. Inside or outside time and space, I cannot say. And I will reconstruct her story, or not, and reframe her former being in my eye, in my own tangle of grief and love, my narrative. Until I will think of her no more, since I also will have moved beyond this frighted quivering set of atoms, breathed too many of these intemperate breaths, replaced too many of these beaver cells, and walked on down the hallway into the dark or light. And then a hush will fall on our mutual mother-son soap opera, our construction, our painted little stage set, for whom there is no audience any more, for whom everyone has gone home to bed, and for whom a hush and a forgetting now falls in the camera-show of the world of men. Never to return by this road, but passing on, into the dawn. Whom will we meet and do our business with in future pleasure gardens? It may be our chosen familiar ones or it may be strangers. Walk on. Be sure of this: nothing ever stays what it is, and yet no fish is ever plucked from the infinite sea. Walk on. Don't look sideways, or grasp at myriad operas of invention that beckon from the verges of your cosmic road. Instead be the garmented nothing that you are, and let your train trail behind you like the stars of an emperor, and let those who come behind pick up the cloth and treasure it - or not, as they choose.

When the news of my mother came, Dora took the trouble to sit with me for ten minutes, even made me tea... or whatever was in that mug. And she kept her mouth shut. I appreciated it. And as we sat we looked out to the neighbouring house and saw a little bird in a window. It couldn't get out, obviously knew nothing of the transparencies of glass. Ran up and down the shelf, got in a birdy panic. Now the owner poked at it like Punch with something that looked like a toilet brush. Ignoramus! That bird impinged on your crummy human house of secrets? Get out birdy or die, the owner seemed to say. Fly away to some parallel universe, outside our precious human window that we fool ourselves we own as our own.

Into the Dark to Find the Light   So I said to Dora: did you hear of the analyst Jung, who waded in the gutter depths trying to transmute old rubbish into light, while the white winds of empyrean peace laughed over his head? He said that he made a decision one fine day, to dive into the muddy filthy crypt of the psyche. Brave man. Sick of the restraints of science, he saw that his overweening need to bring light into the murkiest places could only happen by surrender to Ignorance itself. Contradiction! Seated at his desk in his room by a lake in Switzerland, he dropped. All certainty all sanity all order all science all attainment fell away - all the sludge, into the bin, so much *scheisse*. In these wild places no language can sustain: no handhold of reason, only shadowy utterings and breathings and hysteric contradictions. So Jung unearthed some symbols, half-pie languages of the shrouded intuition, and let them stand as pictures: for wisdom and power and innocence and shadow. And out of the unutterable labyrinths of unconscious dreaming we trace Ariadne's thread back to the quiet sunlit worlds above. And here is the contradiction: no matter how we live, we will always seek the paradise of order. We follow the goddess' thread forever to the sunlit horizons. And as a race we never arrive, for this life is a railway station where people depart on night-trains just as others arrive at the gate: the crowd never diminishes. Every victory is the death of the old, every learning the displacement of something precious, the ruin of the old order, just as today's success is tomorrow's failure. Displacement is our fate. There is no evolution. When Jung dropped away to the land of the undead, he knew he would never return. When we die to ignorance we never return. On our journey of a thousand miles we die to every step. And the great ticking shuffle of shift and change whispers to our ear: you'll never come back, not by this road, not by any road. You are a ghost who walks, a mist of bones, a catenation of ideas, you dissolve in the very sun above that loves you. And in the darkness, in the primeval world-past from whence we came, from whence we evolved, that we claim to revisit with the torch of greater understanding, with the torch of the future - we are confronted by a bloody laughter that shakes us to the core. And we see that all we are is an ape in a suit, eyeballs in scholarly glasses, bloodied hands with a manicure, a grist of primeval ooze that fashioned letters and words. We are the indescribable mass of churning life that blindly seethed over countless ages toward order, toward the sun. Now all these ages are washed away, so that this moment is the only thing that is! All time is slaughtered for this insouciant sweet moment. Oceans of blood have fried in the sun for the sake of the smile on your infant face. Billions of years of moments, all gutted and gone - so that you and I may stand here, in this sunlit woodland in the morning, and thrill to the soft perfection of ourselves. Thanks to the *darkness*.

Dora, won't you finally face me?

No such luck. But I may have hypnotised her. Because she listened, silent to the end.

Connected to Love   So this day has turned to wholeness. I am the shy smile on my lover's face. The eddy of water in my lover's bath. The tattle of this day's love-wanted ads. Hushed space between the stars. All the days of our past. Caressing child-finger on a smooth shelf. Pulsing breath of a nebula... I fear no steel-eyed hawk in the blueness above. I fear not the lonely demise of a sparrow in the mouths of Sumatran crocodiles... The low-rumbling city. I laugh at the obituaries of strangers. Shit that runs in these gutters and sewers. Eviscerating chatter of the middle classes. Scream of pterodactyls ten thousand aeons past. Arthritis born of persecution-complex. Stifled yawns of a clerk in a former century, broken cup of a dead soldier at Thermopylae, hair of a woman in a dried-up river long ago. I laugh at all of these. I am the smoke and spark of a winter chimney in cold England. I breathe acres of birds rising at dawn above a lake. I am the mathematic of two atoms in love in the star known as Andromeda. I hear the sighs of a slave-girl under weighty flesh. I am you. We are larva in the bowels of a planet. We are grains of the deserts of the moon. I know the ache of a cub lost in snow. I am the breath of a billion-years wind as if it never was. I am the moan of telephone wires and a thousand conversations. I am the rise and shuddering fall of the fortunes of millions. I am the vibration of factories at war. I am the mud of the battlefield of the dead. I am the day-longing of a butterfly as its time draws into night. I'm the pleasure on your face when you wear the red shoes. I am time that never was, that I never owned, that never died, that ever lived. I'm warm here with you. You're here.

You're Not Here   Yesterday is gone. Today is cold. Feel like dying again. A stream clamours down a mountain, searches for the sea. Yesterday's insight? Gone, for self-pity. But the truth of life can't die, it wells up. If we leave the body we can be sure life goes on. Where the hell is the border? Pay attention Lean. Your sense of *I* doesn't depend on your body or brain. *That You Are.* In this world or any other, you are here... In the house opposite, the mother is feeding her child. It screams and I think of Dora. Why not smile, kid? You've got ten billion years, enjoy the tyranny of *this*. But if the moon-child smiles up at me I'd better accept: a signal to not give up. Last eve there was a discussion on self-pity. It went badly. Dora won't accept my melancholy. Looking back (I told her) I was spurred on by lack: always a cliff to climb, thicket to untangle, flame to quell. Discontent lent me life, discontent made me. The only goal was to fulfil this incarnation, ensure there is nothing left to repeat. How fucking deadening, Dora cried. - But I need to look down on all experience! so some jumped-up kid (like you) can't run rings around my arse with her flailing energy and intellect. *Pure pride old man. You're a poser.* Stop, didn't want this conversation. She doesn't do melancholy, except when it happens to her. Needs to fry all feeling then. But is she not also driven by lack: cliff to climb, thicket to untangle, flame to quell? She told me I'm a wanker. Twenty years is a gulf, unless she and I will look into each other's eyes and see ourselves. But not today. With Dora each yesterday is irrelevant. It is as if our togetherness is wiped out in the morning. It might creep back with the passing hours of longing, but in the cold of morning I am her stranger, her imposition, her obstacle. Her eyes say it. Fuck Dora, I'm alive too. Learn from me if you dare! But she grinds her teeth, seems to have multiple places to go all at once, in her fusty clothes, her mussed up hair and her despair. All is postponement, the world a heavy oyster with no prospect of a pearl. Now it's cold, the toilet froze. Someone left the window ajar. There's a blood-red scarf round her face when she emerges. The street door slams. Her breath in clouds. From the high window I watch her go. See you tomorrow? The pavement runs away in cracks and seams of ice. We can play tragedy since we live. I don't tell her she is me. She knows it. I don't tell her she can't leave me: she knows it. Doomed before the start. She tells me so very little or nothing. It's her way to be intuitive, the chaos of the unspoken. This is the spice that keeps her, the deadly grist that gets her boots on in the morning, that sends her out to the cracked world, to wherever it is she goes. Once I spotted her in a library. Maybe she longs to do research, be a writer, be somebody, part of a cosy team. She sure plays up the life-weary sage with me. Maybe it's her caustic offering.

I woke at 4 am. She was there, snoring from her milk-for-gall mouth. I felt insecure and I ached, hung over from staring at a TV doc on the holocaust. Horror wants to cling to my back like a hairy spider, to which I feed my fly-blown conscience. The anger-ache in my fingers tells me I want to be a victim. Arthritic victim, licker of racial wounds who conjures the faces of ugly systems and officials who I can loathe and murder. I'm Baader and Meinhof, I'm Black September. I'm heinously accused and arrested. I want righteous revenge. It comes to a shootout: me the hostage has to kill them all. There's a heroine. It's Dora. I save her, I always save her. She and me are victims of chaos. We're small people, we cannot grow up, we long to lose. This self-immolation in the heart! Dora has a heart, and it knows it must cleave to what it hates, endure what it fears. When bodies sleep together, like Macbeth and his Lady, there's a guilty complicity against the world, and it is tested in the metallic cold of morning. This morning she wakes and sees me and is sheepish. Momentarily forgotten are the days of insult. Her young heart. I long to kiss her face but won't. Only in the romantic hours of drunkness and fatigue when the world is a mellower place can she assent to have her lips pressed like the vodka she's drunk to buoy her, or her breasts kissed by this fuzzy man on the edge of her love. She might even assent to wear her raggy cotton wrap out of the shower - and wield her gothy vulnerableness at me by shedding it, as if a token of sorrow, wee apology for weeks of dirt and hard ice.

Perfect Victim The young are so bloody pitiless and young, they make me flail to shed self-pity. I put my head on the block for Dora again.
- When the dead are gone we may ask, what role did anyone play in this eternity?
- Huh? Oh yeah, your mum. (She humours me) To be dead might be cool, right?
- We sustain the dead. Or maybe the living are the dead
- The winner in your polemic is absurdity. Didn't we just do it, Lean? Lighten up, jeez.
Le petit morte. But anything the little anarch says is going to piss me off.

- We do one little thing, we wipe out the rest. All is dissolved
- Dissolve this shit, babe.

She squeezes me you know where.

- D'you know what anarchy is? To have the guts to admit you're nothing, to be as you are

(She cringes at the idiot) - Lying to yourself, Lean. Take a chill pill

- Sick of pills! The point, Dora. Anarchy is a fool's game since nothing stays anyway. Get it?

- And murder and suicide and your mummy's death? They 'stay'

- The cool little anarchist dumps responsibility! Sayonara!

Dora looks at me like I pissed in our love bed. Exits the bed. No goodbye.

After an absence of days the baby anarchist slouches in and announces:
- I met my father.

And after an icy pouty pause in which I fear she just left me she declares:
- He's cool. You need to get with the program. Check his business website. Pure Food In The Everyday dot com.

(Phew) Righto boss. Days pass, she keeps a beady eye out. I dutifully check the site. Uh… 'Nanotechnology and Pure Food Programs'. Dora hands out poison chalices but this time finds a reason beyond punishing me for being old. Story lurking.

Days later a media item appears, to the effect that 'a certain Captain of Industry has been found beaten and bloodied in the cellar of his country residence'. A message in red letters on his wall informs us he's a 'Nasi Faggit'. This allegation is corroborated by presence at the scene of Nazi memorabilia - SS uniforms, leather bits, pistols and the like. Were his (illiterate) attackers also Nasi faggits and jealous? All had considerably fled before police responded to a tip-off and discovered one Claus Von Heffenbonck, the proprietor, covered in gore and attired in nothing but jackboots and a mesh of leather. The coppers initially failed to recognise the victim, but later at a clinic confirmed the fabled industrialist had sustained four broken ribs, two lost teeth and a skull fracture but was otherwise pretty much alive and eager to point out he'd been dragged at knifepoint to his cellar, wrapped in these disgusting leather items and beaten to a crisp by four skinheaded gentlemen whom he assumes to be from the National Front. Next day, numerous Fleet Street hacks willing to fake up the research discover by magic that Von Heffenbonck did in fact have an uncle who knew a certain colonel in the SS and thereby is a neo-nazi and gay to boot. The gay bit is trickier to prove since Von Heffenbonck, though unmarried, has a reputation for liaisons with prominent people's wives, including one *Larissa Demecharian*. More dirt forthcoming. Watch dis space.

When I reckon to entertain Dora with this titbit at breakfast, she slaps my laptop shut. I raise a dully quizzical brow.
- Don't get it? That German rich fucker we saw at the book party. I told you I let him try it on.
(Have to play dumb here) - Love your phrase 'try it on'. But (a) why would a German rich fucker try it on with a little girl who'd likely deposit her boot in his eye? (b) Why admit it to me since 'try it on' means 'had full sex'? Is my wee girl shamed 'coz I'm her Significant Other?
- Listen up smartarse, I can learn heaps more about arseholes like that being female, than you can ever be arsed to
- Three rectal references in one sentence? I assume 'being female' allows you to rake up the dirty stuff.
Dora is consternated. Not hard to do it to her. She breathes through her nose, eyes glisten in a strange mix of hateable vs. vulnerable. Better let her win.
- Okay I'm a dickhead. Will you say what happened?
- You knew effing well who he was. Always wanna play me, don't ya? Well I don't play, mister.
This is cool, like a tennis match: can't hit a good return till she whacks you one first. Dora longs to be feted as bad and villainous but I know better. She wants to be loved. And won't accept that from the likes of me or Heffenbonck or any other Daddy... though she'll force me to squeeze the dirt out of her, the little tragic who behind that gritty realism bravely denies her victimhood... which she'll then grudgingly admit to if you grovel long and hard enough. We'll try a baseline lob.
- Them skinheads sure did a job.
She looks through me. Her black eyes say: trust the bastard in one million years? Answer - possibly.

- Wouldn't know
- Wouldn't know what though?
- If they did a good job. Wasn't there, obviously
- Can't be trusted. Certainly not pros
- Sheer luck eh?
- Clearly knew who to ask
- Clearly.

The rotting journalist allows himself an inward smile. They were mates of hers! Bad Girl offers to 'reward him with a cuppa'. 'Kay, you boil up water, me pop in teabag. That puts the faintest hint of smile on her dial. Harbinger to possibility of SEX. Dora and me make quite a team in a dirty perfect world. She has the makings: instinct for the story, grocks the stupid irony of our work. I'll never train her though. She'll lead me like a dog. Here she comes. Lean likes violence, she whispers in my eye. The table makes our bed. We eat each other's mouths. She uses the marmalade in ways I don't care to mention. My laptop is peripherally damaged. Her black eyes register beauty, at the critical moment.

…A hint of a pause for my sake. And lover girl slithers off to the shower, leaving me to clean the debris. Surprising breakfast. Okay, 'll be an okay day.

Late. I lie staring at the semi-dark. In the night psychic immunity weakens, and devils creep in. The girl sleeps, though she bursts out in flummery talk by and by. I tend to listen. What kind of girl consorts with skinheads, gets them to semi-murder some richo she's rooting then boasts it to another middle-age crock like me? What'd he do to her? Strikes me she's done it before. But - she told me. Ahh, told me. Wants approval. Maybe planning another fucking psycho thing, this heaped silhouette in the dusky space beside me. No, she's a girl, here with me. And why not, why not me? Calm down, Lean.

Calm. Yeah. Three days later, little plot thickens. There's a Dora-call on my cell. Breathing only. Then another call the same. Some oik commandeered her phone? Fuck off, I manage to retort. Moment later, a thought. I call back. This time sobbing. *Where are you?* In a tunnel. *Where? Tell me now.*

Mustn't. *Dora!* Lane… green building… roundabout. *Stay! I'm coming.* Drive out, nearly ram a cyclist. Green building lane tunnel rounda… Bull's Corner! Dump shitting car, run inside. There's a bundle in the gloom against the tunnel wall. She lies there, black jeans down her legs, blood on her mouth. Bag contents are shat about. A filthy scuffed jacket. And those boots. Dora Jarr looks at me. Snuffles and sobs. Ah, tooth missing. *Can't get up…* I pull up her jeans, gather her bits, spot the tooth, pocket it. Get her to the car. She's a ragdoll. Lurch into the stream, scuff another car, fail to stop. Get her home, upstairs into bath, douse her in hot water. She lies there.

- After this we get the police
- No police. (glares) You hear me?
- Fuck it, Dora! (My nerves are gone) Okay, don't fret.
I make tea, spill it, stumble about. An hour disappears. Wrap her, sit her in bed. No comment.
- Got your tooth
- Tooth
- You lost one, here. (She lets me finger her mouth)
- Got one o' the fuckers in the head… Pays to 'ave steel boots… Musta been paid
- You know these men? (She looks at me) Course ya do. Right. How many? (Silence) - Some. Four
- Who do you think is behind this?
- Don't understand the question.
I stare at her.
- Can't take this, Dora
- *You* can't take it
- I mean, you can't hide this
- If you tell a single person I will go away and never return.
I stare, turn aside. *How fucking dare you?* It's whispered but she gets it. Now her eyes glaze over.

It's dusk. I'm bunched on the sofa. The city sighs beyond my window. Who's there to talk to? God, I wouldn't know. I've no friends at all. Dora and I exist in antisocial space, a cave, a cynical one. But the fact is, she called me. I'll look up a dentist tomorrow. Should make her eat. Or let her sleep. There's a stranger in my house. Don't like to admit it. It's me. And I need her.

A day goes by where she's curled on the sofa pouting and staring at TV. I serve her junk food and fizzy stuff. In the evening she not-so-randomly says:

- Yeah, so I located my *mother,* who is actually not with my father. Her name is *'Larissa D.'*
- Thanks for the casual info
- Not the only fish in the sea, mister Lean.

There are times when that terse telegraphic shorthand of the young is a fecking pain in the rear.

- Be happy with our life, Dora
- Our life? Are you mental?
- In the future… you'll need stability
- Don't need any damn thing. Got my mummy back
- You need. Wake up to it
- I'm awake, cocksucking little reporter.

And *that* remark earns her a sudden whack in the face! Stunned, can't believe her eyes. Me neither. She is forced to sit down. I just violated her girly aura in a daddyish way. First time, first time for everything.

- Oh yeah, you're such an aristocrat. *Ms. Lola 'D' for Demecharian*
- Whoa, what?
- And here in my house she can play at being pauper, anarchist, orphan. Rape victim too. Nice little niche at my expense. I go broke so she can go cashless. Poverty-loving little snob
- So the old journo uncovers a name
- Happy with it, are we?
- Fuck yes
- Has a ring to it. Baggage too. I prefer Dora Jarr. Ironic at least.

She sits still, gazes at my legs. I stand there in gutter silence. Our death then: vacant little death, without quality. But then she does a thing. Kneels on the floor and clings at me, clings and starts to sob. And I feel like I'm caught out, with no underpants. Our death recoils to a corner of the room.

I stroke her scalp. Greasy, no matter. A sodding grim universe resides in that lonely head. I'll soothe it if it's the last thing I do.

- Don't worry, you. I like *Lola* as well

(Longish silence) - Truly?

- Absolutely. Come on now, come to me. Listen, I'll take you to our bar. Tell me any stories you like. True or shite whatever. I'll buy twenty drinks. Hey?

And yes. She comes.

* * * *

Dora Lola sure is a prickly kettle of fish. Still, this same night she deems it politic to invite me to hook her in and take some bites of flesh. Me and the tragic Goth thrash about for ten minutes in my bed... and I inwardly salute her for never bothering to make our bed or wash our sheets. And it doesn't take her long to toss in the name *Goran Demecharian*. Barely got our breath back. Cute little grenade. And this is where I'm at the mercy of my lunatic mate. What kind of shite would Dora sell to ruin us, or ruin everybody? I'll assume this Goran D hasn't ruined her yet. And what fibs will she now tell to twist me round her pasty finger? Better bite.

- May I summarise? It seems this Demecharian of yours has been outed in some kind of battle over 'genetic manipulation of pure foods'. And we learn your Nazi mate Von Heffenbonck is wrapped up in it like chips in newsprint. Who knew? But *you* do 'cause you read the Daily Mirror.

Dora keeps her gob shut and flutters her eyes. She's got on her pouty cuddly look and it's working so far.

- All right, little Dor. You 'might've and you forgot'. One thing. Watch out for the pair of them. Trust 'em if you want to be used. Trust me, if you wanna be loved.

God, that is forward. I'm a hypocrite. No, I weirdly meant it.

- Oh mister Lean, I know you love me and I love you too.

Watch the fuck out! This is one moment where I realise how idiotic she makes me by coming round here to cohabit. Her bathos is killing, I feel sick. She decides to rescue. The pitiful kid gets to dangle it by a thread.

- Anyway, I want you to come meet REAL Daddy Demecharian. You're to interview him. He's a real package.

Real daddy! Oh wow. Say nothing, Lean. Look at her pasty whitey face on the pillow and its sloppy doll make-up.

- You love me too, though?
- 'Course I do, why not? Don't let me run away again
- Lonely, yeah
- Why not? So you'll do it? Real Daddy knows heaps about dirty business guys and politicians. That Heffenbonck cunt for instance. Daddy's so cool
- And why me? I'm your journalistic rival.

At this she pinches my nose pretty damn hard.

- Don't be an immature cockhead, Lean. I'm definitely going to arrange it! Sieg Heil. Lola Demecharian.

Collection of Daddies   Lo and behold, next day I stumble across a diary, lightly tossed amid the bombsite of our bed. Dora kept it well hidden till now! She's even popped out for the morning. Little bookywoog falls open at a page dolled up in green and pink. '...DADDY REAL took me out today to his fuckin pricey Nitesbridge restaurant. Said to call him Goran. Told me bout his childhood in Georgia. Swum in freezing rivers, scaled up mountains under big blue sky. Hairy-chested guy claims he's an adventurer, 'suffers the curse of money', tries to 'avoid the world'. Some curse! Thinks I don't see he wouldn't have the *guts*. Dude's real sensitive. Glad we didn't meet up at 16, woulda thrown up. Have me round his little pinky, ruled by his moolah. Why do up-growns think they know it all? I'll make him sweat for wiping me, 's for sure. Goes on about Putin... loves Putin... So what am i? Georgian? Fuck knows don't care. Citizen of universe. Told him I was vegan and he jumped on that like flies round shit, reckons we should ban factory farming, live cattle exports blaaa. Dignity for animals! he sez chomping his fucking steak. Then he says he'll go veego as well. Copycat. Told him we should invent piggy beds lamb perms doggy toilets gold budgie cages cow massages pussy gravestones... LOL! [That reminds me, pussy's getting lonely, better be nice to Daddy LEAN] And I said let's have euthanasia for humans. That was a doozie, agreed with all of it. Fuck me, gullible. Or mebbe not. Gotta steely dark eye. Not a fecking fool I guess. Didn't mention sugar-daddy Lean... won't mention daddy NAZI with his big dong either. Gotta feeling he won't dig it. Told me heaps about his business, Daddy Real did. [daddy Nazi told me the same shit first] Reckons he's into making 'new kinds of pure food'. He wears cow leather! Bullshit all of it. Smell a big fat rat. No wuckers, daddy Lean 'll help me get the lowdown. Me faithful girlie eh, me with DADDY LEAN. He's *daddy cool*.'

It's mostly in fresh ink, for my benefit no doubt. Sprightly confession, cute manipulation, needy girl, all there. Girls are complicated! So, *Goran Bratski Demecharian*. Dora hints at the great clubbing march through life of a man obsessed with himself - wolf in his lair, killer fish who harbours little plankton, bush rhino even the flies are wary of, whose empire is his Will. But I see this Goran has a dilemma: to show his teeth or show his heart. Born of the Caucasus, rich man's solitary son, narcissist making myths out of himself. The outsider who bought the Inside and detests it. No flashy Chelsea football team for him. And Dora easily sees his underbelly: how he fears his own need, how love weakens him. Cold mastery is safer. And ever since mother *Larissa Demecharian* produced little Lola all those years ago, we bet he resolved to keep Larissa as part-time she-bitch, at arm's length, tossing her money. And she learned his trick too, stringing that German along to get the dirt on *him*. Mother Larissa exploits Goran's love phobias all right. It was behind her decision to put away baby Lola for adoption, and he never challenged it. Thereby hangs a shaggy family tale, and after nineteen long years Demecharian suddenly wants his girl, and this is the point where Larissa turns shadow love into open war: precisely why she took up with that rival cunt Von Heffenbonck! Daddy needs to impress the hell out of daughter now. Fat chance when our Lola plays hard to get. Mind you, when you actually *get*, you might wish you hadn't. Twisted logic demands that people Dora wants she spurns, and for those she despises she plays slut cow harridan pauper waif victim orphan anarchist snob and slob, but never 'daughter'. Trust me Goran Bratski Demecharian, I grock that one.

Older I should have complained bitterly to Dora about her stupid cover-up of her parents. And about her smut show with Von Heffenbonck. I should hate that guy since he treats her badly, but a voice whispers: *he's a man of your age; somehow you know what he is.* I say nothing and that's how she likes it. Tickles her to sneak off and sidle back again. Makes her free, why spoil it? Note: the threads she's wearing are definitely smarty-tartier. Someone's taken her in hand. I choose my moment to hand back The Diary, and I watch her conscience tell her to talk but she stalls since its content spells a way forward for us. Instead there follows a weird interlude of brittle calm, as if we are suddenly 'adults together', as if she's aged upwards, somewhere proximate to me. And these days we parade in some kind of faux-bourgeois gentility, all titbits of politeness and food. She even wipes the kitchen, not to my taste but a gesture, and her teeny smile says: Lean has to compete with other Daddies now, 'cause the future is at my feet, and time never cheats on us the Young! She even affects to sleep solo, all nonchalant in a camp bed as if her shiny conscience dictated it. Not my place to complain; don't have the heart anyway. Or maybe she somehow somewhere wants to get real, and maybe lonely Lola is looking out at all these adults and daddies, at out-of-depth, at the world's cruelties, at the real costs of life. Meanwhile we olds all hope there's a place for us inside the fresh capacious sensibilities of Ms. Lola Demecharian. I avoid the name, not sure how to address the New Woman, but at last she announces: 'Why don't you still call me Dora'. So our tiny niche opens again, and at our hoary old kitchen table I offer her a drink. We drink.

It takes a couple of nights, but she abandons the camp bed with its mounds of shaggy bits and crawls back into mine. No intro, just wraps her legs and lips about in the dark, sucks me in. No choice but to fill her favourite holes to the brim. Happens by luck, no effort from me. One of our giving moments? We don't have those, as the reader will discern by now. Post the deed she whispers in my face.

- See, Lean? I deal with stuff. Now I'll ask you one more time, and don't cry this time. Am I the best lay you ever had?
Upon my reply hangs our mini universe. Shall I say: 'might be if you practised'?
- You're your perfect perfect self.

She seems to like my nebulous reply. We nestle close. But in her jowly-mouth silence I sense I'm staring into a new world. At the moment she slipped back to my bed and took me over... she departed, on some night train, to a stranger future.

Still, it seems today's a fresh day in our bright winter. Dora is deeply attentive. Why? Oh, this borderland between selfish and selfless is a novel thing. Perhaps I look ungainly sick? Does she want to lull me before the delivery of pure punishment? Or is she mimicking her *mummy's* slippery ways of romance? Cooks a little thing for me. It's edible. Wants to walk out to the Heath in her trendy coat in the rapt cold. Wry smiles and a cosy bar. Green and blue drinks. Dora stirs them with a languid finger. She produces money and pays up. This is life, she says. At home she won't let go. Keen to go to bed. Really I can't process it. After our new love tryst (slower and softer than yesterday) she wants to read aloud from a book she unearthed called *Catcher In The Rye*. I mask a slow groaning feeling. Later she lines up my pills. A world first. Jesus wept.

Conspiracy   I start to realise my cellphone is getting the runaround. Today it's parked on the kitchen table, and oh look, 'new mum Larissa Demecharian' has posted me a message. *Please call your 'Dora' right now. PS: erase this!* Or one assumes it to be Larissa. What's this lippy smudge on the bottom? Only Dora wears pastel green. Such a busy girl! Anyway, late on this day I step up to my front door, and there are lights and voices. Crikey, Claus Von Heffenbonck is here! Careful with the key now... oh baby, they're in my bedroom.

- Small child, will you effer pay for drinks? No doubt Lean keeps you in money
(Sounds like they had a few) - Kiss muh fanny, Heffie.
- Will he come?
- So what if he does
- You sleep in zis bed?
- Yeah, do a few other things and all. I rule
- We will go to the Heath

- Want to freeze my arse? (There's shuffling and breathing) I'll get Real Daddy on ya
- What is this 'daddy club'?!
- Have to do me proper if you wanna join. No touchies, I'm underage! And I wanna know 'bout my *mother*
- Your mother does not want to know about you
- Fuckin' does
- Shall I call her now?
- Gimme the feckin' phone!

(Dora clumps into the hall. I jump to the bathroom. The German pulls her back, slams the door)

- Rack off! Fucken taunt me… (Now she utters a sob or two. 'Number 3 Sympathy Sob'… Yup, he fell for it)
- You push at me. Sit here, I want to help. Your father is dangerous
- Real Dad can handle himself
- What is your game? You hate him. Get revenge, Lola. I repeat, he needs to see what you lost all those years
- Told you, do it my way
- Is this why he manipulates you with his disgusting money and his club?
- He's a mansplaining oldie like you
- He is powerful. Do not enter his game of guilt. I know how it is
- Yeah, you do it to *me*. No fanny ever again mister
- Snotty fake rebel! Daddy's little bad girl
- Eat shit, MOTHER fucker.

There's a sudden thump! Think they're on the floor. Dora gasps. Rhythmic bumping. He grunts.

- You… should admit… your father… got those skinhead boys… to beat me… and beat *you*… Your sleuthing work… with Lean is no *use*… If you want to keep your teeth… you better listen… listen to me. Aaaaaghh!

I'm ready to charge in and rearrange his teeth. But there's a sigh. He presumably rolls off my girlfriend.

- But who tipped off Real Daddy about you, Crook? It was my *mother*. And you're not the stud you think you are. I didn't even come just now. Sucked in.

More rustling, then rattling at the door. (Glad that handle's stiff!) Further leap to bathroom. Dora charges out. Heffenbonck strides after. I creep out. They're in the road, he manhandles her to his car. Car lurches, swings up the hill to the Heath. I run on. Got no fucking lungs, breath is rasping. Car is stopped, doors ajar. A lamplit path... opens to a glade that overlooks our suburb. There they are on a bench.

- We will make a 'statement'. Send a message. Lola
- Don't fuckin need ya!
- You want my sex violence. But I am not evil
- Ever occur to you I might have feelings?
- You are a daughter to me
- Gives you right of entry! Wait till I tell Lean. Might even kill ya. I tell him a whole lot. And he had a chat to Daddy Demecharian. Oh didn't I say? Lean's good at putting it together. He rescued me in the tunnel that day
- What day?
- The day I got *raped,* arsehole
- You bring this on!
- Wadda you care? Self-serving egotistical -
(She jumps up. He pulls her back) - No! We are going to plan this, you hear me? Or I will expose your hate crime against me to *everyone.* We will have our little sideshow, our little *dirt bomb*
- Fuck off. If your bomb's as big as your ego you'll wipe out the lot
- Are we ready, baby anarchist?
- You dunno how to make it
- I am no assassin, Lola
- Ain't got the balls
- It must be at your daddy's seminar next week. Everyone important will be there. We plant it in a back room. Everyone gets a dusting. Fertilizer bomb. Amateur, nothing. They will look stupid. It will be all over the press
- The press? You mean Lean
- It must not be traced! That is why you must leave this man
- Fuck, I get it. My *mother* is in on this
- Idiot. Larissa does not know a thing
- Don't believe ya

- Your mother needs your father's money, that is all! And maybe respect. Ha!
- She'd be a suspect! Daddy and mummy have a *new thing* going. Ain't just about money
(In the dimness he sighs, then stands) - Remember, no-one gets more than a big surprise. And keep zis Lean away.

He legs it in my direction. I shrink into a bush. Silence. Dora is hunched on the bench. I can't tell if she is crying. Minutes pass. I'm tired. At last she shuffles off down the path. This is the last I see of her for five days. How to digest what I heard? There's a numbness in my winter world.

* * * *

At some point comes a text. 'Mister Lean, I shall conduct a seminar on Saturday ten days hence at the _____ Centre for Research. If you will consent to report the outcomes, I shall be happy to furnish you with materials and offer a fee. All best, *Goran Bratski Demecharian.*'

The lost girl slips in one morning while I'm in bed. Affects to rummage for food then depart. Cue to go shopping, Lean. Later she's back, stands in my kitchen and... yep, that old customised grunge look is gone. Now all pain-in-arse confidence, stuffing cereal in her gob. She tosses me my newspaper. *Check out page six.* It's a pic with article. Demecharian and a luscious blond woman. *Larissa.* He seems to be exposing a scandal involving a rival in the pure foods industry. All to be revealed at the seminar no doubt? She watches me, munches her scroggin. No milk, no comment. Two days pass. Same newspaper, delivered by same dark angel, splayed on my table this time at page two. This time evil Claus Von Heffenbonck is named. She murmurs:
- Bet you'd like to be writing this story, Lean.

Friday. I step through my own front door. Dora spots me, takes her phone, hightails it to bathroom. Loudly she calls: *Daddy? Daddy? It's me... Daddy, don't do the seminar! There are bad people. They want to cause mayhem.*

*I know the press expects you to speak. Daddy darling, I'm saying don't go.
Don't cut me off! Shit. Shit.*

Fuck yeah. Nice and crude, Dora. We're communicating. Like we used to.

Saturday arrives. The morning is bright and clear. My cell rings: a female
voice, no introduction.
- Mister Lean. Do you want a proper story? Meet me at the seminar
- Who is this?
- You know who it is.
Goodness me. Larissa Demecharian.
Random shards of a jigsaw! What shall a fact-gatherer do? Do not go
to that place! I hurry to the place. A peaceable street in Bloomsbury's
university land, adjacent to a little square... Shall I go the hell in? I am no
fantasist, I am a news-gatherer, I stick in my snout and sniff at human shit.
What the hell do I care? Hurry down the corridor to the main room, peer
through double glass doors. A hundred heads or so. Goran Demecharian
is speaking. Is he the master here? Does he puppeteer this catenation of
academics, business, journalists, mover-shakers, skeptics, wannabes?
And there is Von Heffenbonck, angular and statuesque, at the very back.
And my Dora, near her father. Larissa is nowhere to be seen. I see how the
girl glances about, how her mouth twitches under the parapet of greasy
dark hair, as if to be here at this instant is her most desperate manoeuvre.
How well I know you!

'...And so we humans validate ourselves according to the promises of
technology. Technology lets us ponder on our 'mastery', yet is it slavery to
an illusion? Why seek the subtleties of material life through ever deeper
webs, entrenchments, nets of control? And will we claim to grasp the
god-particle? Shall we seek to dominate, with fractal reach, the very soul
of society? Communism tried it, any totalitarianism in fact. But ladies
and gentlemen, there is a fly in the liquid, a ghost in the machine. To fail
to master all our acts is to acknowledge the irrelevance of our acts. Yet
technology lets us feed on a dream of order - and *quantum nano-technology*
is perhaps the glossiest dream of all. Perhaps now we shall arrive at origin,
at the pre-genetic, the subatomic, the ineffable, shall pierce the veil and

skein of form, and yet retain it! Perhaps now we might reshape the very Shaper of ourselves! Human genome, quantum manipulations - when placed in animals and plants - might eradicate disease, create pure food, immunise us, murder carcinogens, make us free. And yet, do we not need disease to keep immunity strong? I shall expound a new possibility in the field of nano-science and disease, ladies and gentlemen, and yet I do it with this warning: beware of hubris, beware of unexpected consequence, beware of the illusion of control, beware of your entrenched belief in infallibility - in your little, local, nano-pointed *order*...'

And this is where the alarm goes off. Clanging dreading noise riffles in corridors and rooms. A door swings at the entrance and a figure steps out. I foot it to the street, pursue across the square. The figure slips into alleys and is gone. Under a spreading chestnut, blotches of yellow sunlight spatter the stones. At the entrance a group of delegates starts to form. Soon they're a herd. Two security men confer. Under blue winter sky, under brick and stone gable, they're ants. Dora has not emerged. The alarm seems to end. There's Demecharian, signalling to his people. They follow him in. Against the tide I spot Dora. She looks left and right, pauses in angular street-shadows, re-enters. Suddenly with the insight of the destitute, the cancered, I see what's going to happen. Hurry in corridor to the glass doors. Crowd in seminar room. Out of a door comes Demecharian. He sees me, strides to the toilet. I peer in the ante-room by the main room. There's Claus Von Heffenbonck. Heads of important men bend in conclave, step away. I'm at the glass doors. Heffenbonck not there. Now I see *Dora* coming at me, coming at the door. She's wild. Suddenly I'm scared of her. I lunge to the toilets. White silence. Near-most cubicle occupied. Demecharian? I slip to the far cubicle. *Then it happens...* A blasting crunching bursting wave shunters in I'm thrown at cubicle wall jacked backward my head slaps the tiles there's a *crack* my ears fill with drumming blood Jesus NO I'm dying. Cloud grit choking throat can't see. Whining drumming in heart. Crawl to a basin, flood water in eyes. Demecharian is leg-splayed on toilet seat. I grab at his face, his eyes roll. Drag him, somehow shove under tap. Drag open corridor. Hateful white dust. Doorways stagger left right. Screams within. Huge hole where that ante-room… I fucking go in. Grogged thing by scudded blood wall. Torso in a blue suit. Von Heffenbonck. Can't breathe. Lime-walled corridor. Aching fluttering waves of smoke. On knees. Throw up. Dora. Dora. She came at me, clutched at the glass… The entrance now. People spill, shamble, sprawl on grass, crouch in gutters, whisper to phones… Siren cop arrives, and white vans, flicker lights. I'm past the square, need to crawl away. Down alley, cobbled mews, toward the Euston Road. 'Least I think it was that way. Don't know. Just get away

* * * *

Departure   At our city's fringe is a graveyard, with a dump beside it. These were playgrounds in my childhood - where human centuries composted and methanized and rose up as vapour to fall again as rain on crowded streets and fields… where not one microbe from the sewer veins of our dream city nor its dump-hills of memoried sorrow, had not surrendered a thousand times, had not been ground to miasmic ash at this people-mulching spot, where strivings and growings, litters of plagues and journeyings, vanity of prayers, passing years and passings away were all transmuted to mountainous fire-smoking rotted heaps… All rubbish is us, every microbe us! And when night descends like a pall on our world and ghostly forebears call us home, our child voices rise on dusky moonlit air, and we conflate our fevered party games, exhaust our pleasures in distraction. We heed not Golgotha at the edge of our city, though the bell tolls for us. We whisper: don't disturb little me, let me hoard my past like a dog with a bone, let me nurture my diseases. Let me be. Let me be.

Your narrator Lean has the unnerving sense that time is running out for him. It may be slow shock that draws him to the funeral of Claus Von Heffenbonck, but he is above all an epic regurgitator of melancholy things… The church bell tolls, and for the living gathered about today there is to be a reckoning. The robust and young won't understand, but the aged and diseased will nurture their own emotional departures, will inwardly rework the value of a life. For sages say (and we secretly fear) that the substance of our leaving is the substance of our returning; that the soul's frame is cast, and in the far future the waters of life will pour into this cast again. That a judgment is coming, a great election wherein the soul is parked on a conveyor, readied for departure to a great clearing house out of sight. And that soul, removed from its packaging in a mighty expiry of breath, retreats to a space beyond cause to lie at peace in the empty, to make its subtle hugs and handshakes with the eternal… until it begins again its slow redress to the worlds of cause and mind and sense and finally flesh once more. A breath departs, returns. Immerses, emerges. What frame of mind then, to suit departure? Herein is our riddle of ignorance, for we imitate what we think we know, seek an ideal version of what we always failed to be: a better lover, better father, juster man, sweeter, seriouser, sinless man. Von Heffenbonck I hardly knew, and his was a parallel life lived beyond a fence in another garden, where the things he did in fiddled isolation (the little things done by us all) seemed to him to be clever, important, poignant, rich. We are islands in our self-concern, our ignorance. But in the flood of our departure there is panic. Ideals then mingle with sickness, arrangements with pain like blood with gravy. His is a case of sudden death, so strangers and priests must signpost the departing; and that is what we have this day, a play, at this moss-walled quiet place under the arms of great trees on the fringe of our civilised city. And the long cars parade in slow motion, and the long box is carried forward, the prayers are intoned, the black-clad mourners gather about the hole, the sod is thrown, appeals to god are sown, and the visages of people register their separative scripts of love and fear and bewilderment and grey distraction. And this will be repeated to the ends of time, till hell freezes over, till the last man and woman have departed the life-worlds into the sheen of light, into the clearing-house out of sight, into shells of greater meaning, of incalculable love, into the spaces of peace so deep none ever wished for past or future, where no causes or desires ever came. And one sweet day in springtime, the breath of underground undersea winds from far might rustle the trees of paradise hanging eternal amid the light. And seeds from the trees of paradise may scatter in the garden, and gentle rains of time and change push them under the earthen grasses to the soil, wherein their little nature tugs and strains and squeezes, as tiny memories of past and future curdle in their hearts. And forms, the forms of the previously known, the encased, the subtly evil, the insidious, the returning - begin. Great repetition competes with great evolving, and no-one can know the difference, unless and until another addled rushing life in the flesh, in the seas of mind, in the threshing fields of feeling, runs its round. And the day of reckoning will be here again, and the stolid ritual departure performed again, all witnessed by crowds of black-clad bystanders (some who'll weep), the ghosts of the future. Today I am one of them... And I wonder, who will weep for me.

The Clan Demecharian   And here is Goran Demecharian, with the alluring Larissa, and their lost-and-found daughter Lola clinging to their arms. She is dew-eyed and silent. And how her father limps, for his wounds are poignant, inviting the world to feel the proper measure of empathy. How could I pluck Dora back from her people now? I admit to feelings welling up like black lizards from the toilet of my psyche. And how could this Clan Demecharian ever be content? Larissa's loyalties seem to have always been two-faced. And he, Goran, made his deals with Von Heffenbonck to keep her under his thumb and his eyes. Who says the Heffenbonck murder is not payback for a daughter's dirty transgressions? Dora now wants her man-lover for keeps, craves him more than her sanity. And no room there for cunts like me, though I'm the one guy who knows her better than she wants the world to see. Demecharian will dangle her in his rear-view mirror, and she will shield him to suit herself. Because Lola and Daddy and Mummy did it. The bomb I mean. Together. And just because of it, Dora will lunge out at me. She has decades of loss to feed on: won't reject her elders all at once but will scurry into 'bomb guilt' and hide between daddy's legs. Later she'll let him hide between *her* legs in a secret cave of their very own. After that she'll dream up outstanding ways to send him to hell. And one day she'll bore herself enough to trickle back to me? By then I'll be decomposing and thereby not attractive, not even in the ironic sense of a man whose life appealed to a girl like her because it was such irretrievable shite. A journalist? Ho ho. Needy rapidly-aging dupe who wanted his youth back, persisted in hinting at love for Dora despite her crusade to drive him nuts. Worse than sad. Or slightly better, an ironic crock who agreed to use her just as she used him. That arrangement might suffice for impromptu turn-ups, the odd toss in the sack or on the kitchen table, for the leaving of one's boots and bangles and discarded drugs at the old feller's gaff. And (thinks Dora) I could stay wounded for good, blame other people who cherish a romance that the world makes sense, that we can 'love each other', be sorry for past deeds, change, grow up. No help for you, arseholes. You are *bores*. So saith young Dora, pre-wounded narcissist. Can I wait for her to actually grow up, turn her gaze to me? How to tell her that all her scathing irony is expunged by the prospect of Lean's body dropping in dust? She'll reply: how gross is that? I fucked that? Where is the faith I placed in her integrity, in her deeply buried sense of care, her ferocious grasping at honesty, those searing burns she suffered at unutterable world cruelty? I hope she might see I shared them all, that I romanced her fecklessness, ironised her suffering, smiled when she took herself seriously, tenderised her harshness. All that. I hope she'll get it. Come back to me! But her father has already slugged her with his own romancing, and she'll have no choice but to waltz with it. He'll have all the low-life tricks: his gritty foreignness, angsty suffering, new-minted legends of himself and his star-crossed heart, boyish regret for his cynical ploys of power. And she'll have his money. I assume it'll ruin her. And then her mother will seek to 'bond' with her (women take up even more of the sky than men) and Larissa, with her glamoured longing deceitful sexual past will suck in Dora like a black widow spider. Dora will be titivated by legends of her parents' preying-mantis love affair - wherein both are victims, both unrequited, both tugging at her, hating each other through her, needing a scapegoat for their dread crime of insufferable love! Larissa could never have played glamour whore all these years without the occult favours of Demecharian and his money. And he could never have fed that wolverine ruthlessness without the lure of her peerless kitten-sex to come back to. Me, I should glue myself to the idea that this trio can correct one another. Fat fucking chance. Even if it turns out the killer bomb was their 'family baby' - the baby of a girl and her daddy and her mummy - I will not cease to wallow in sewers of debased conscience, sweatingly hoping my girl's coming back to me.

And alone in the drug prison of my house, I muster the worstest notions. New plot! Demecharians are coming to *moider me*. Which of Demecharian's women will end up diverting the Wolf's gaze at me? You know, darling slash daddy! - the man who pulled you from the wreck of the toilet... the one who wormed in with our sweet girl - that wormy fellow *Lean*. And as sure as night follows day they'll come! Not that a single one of them hates me. See how displaced victimhood works? Not able to resist Demecharian's cock in your arse (so to speak) you girls will require to make me taste all your victimhood. And he won't resist a bargain killing for the sake of his nearest and dearest, because that closeted rough-cold animal soul is vulnerable to your sexual acts of acquiescence: the beast bows to beauty and lets his head be caressed and you expendable girls get to prove you matter in some little way. Urge the emperor to murder! - and postpone the day when he flushes you away to make way for someone better. This family bleeds at the seams, and outliers like me are collateral damage. Ugly ugly.

Endgame   After the death of Von Heffenbonck the pale-dark girl known as Dora did come back to me, this time bearing gifts: of concern, of attention, of conscience. At my threshold she looked hard and long, and let me watch her appear to decide: this journalist Lean is indeed a crock; there's just no need to do him in, Daddy. The black holes of her eyes said it all: no further battles to be fought with you my friend. And she moved in again, in her fashion. So much unexplained, so many black holes in the fabric of things, she said. Yes Dora, all your Daddies will go to black holes eventually... She has definitely deepened though, grown up! Plays a brillianter game nowadays. Better class of corruption, jealousy, hiding, hate, victimhood. Pushes all the healing love downward, down to the recesses where only millennia can dredge it up again. Hers is a rosy cancer-future of needle-suffering and blundering wanting and wandering in her vagabond boots with her bits and rags of memories. Perhaps I'll meet her again on the moonlit miles of her dark roads, by the hedge-paths, amid the hills, on the sea cliffs, in the towns, in the hollows of another life. But she is not my responsibility, she is hers. Still, I kind of love my black-eyed Dora. Kind of. And I fancy one day she might half-pie love me. Half-pie lovers can have it all: selfishness, narcissism, anarchy, terrorism, plus the love. Got it sussed. Half a heart's good enough! Share a heart share a pizza... So my door's ever open, and swinging both ways. If she slams it in a fury it jarrs, but if she slips in her key and worms in, I'm lifted. I admit it. Because she has her moments of levity, moments when she invites her nice-girl spirit to flitter in for lunch from some trackless desert. With this absurd life briefly haloed in a lighter insouciant shade of black, Dora aims to keep me amused. You need fruits and nuts, she calls out suddenly one day. New messiah of healthy habits! Are you the nut? I ask. *No, I'm the fruit.* She smiles at me, one of those yellowy smiles that hint at sunlight. She's obviously been practising it. Daddy didn't eat enough fruit, she says, but you have to. By god I will. Dora has taken to hiding my fags as well. Prob'ly steals 'em. Only lately did I get that the smell of departure is weirdly aphrodisiac to her. Thought she'd run a mile but she didn't. Perhaps it's finite and can therefore be countenanced. She and I are alike that way: things have to finish, we can't stand the grind, the wait, the everness. Can't stand nuance and subtlety. Dora even consents to spread herself under me in the nights. Lies beside me too. Better kisses better smiles. Once she washed my body in a bath. Made the bed one or two times. Lordy lordy it was semi-neat. Takes my bills away and pays 'em. Demecharian's money. Robbing a Hood, doin' good. As they say, if Stalin takes a shine to you, be happy. There's attention of a sort. World future in safe hands. Youthful lessons to be learnt, the earth may turn again. But Lady keeps her shifty ways. Comes at night, whispers in the dark. *Lean, you have to write the true story.* At bad Daddy's expense I assume? *Naturally.* But you'll be at the centre of it. *Don't care!* she says. No, you have to care, Dora. You have to desist till love wins over hate. *When'll that be?* she says with cynic tone. *When I'm gone,* I reply. She stares. That one sailed over her raggy black head. But she thinks she has me by the short and curlies since I spoke of love. Till I gaze back at her and she sees mortality drip from my eyes. And she can't resist that. Got you by the conscience, Dora Jarr. For love is the battle Lola will fight in her gruesome future alone. Time will steal from her bit by ticking bit till one day she'll suddenly feel so sorry, so fucking sorry for everything. The fucked-up hate, the stumblings into crime, all of it. I'd want to be there then, when the guilt comes stealing, comes flooding, when she finally consents to grow up. I have one message left for her now. Of course I don't say it. She will have to come to care. I don't care to know what disgusting sins people do. We are all dumb little creatures. Life will drag us, drag us back, to care.

Oh but she keeps at me, between sweetified nudges and shifty smiles, about *The Story: the pure foods corporate nanotech scandal story*, because she needs me to celebrate the dirt and hate in her, to validate the scheming pantomimes she has played. Reader, you saw I was always there for her. I don't say out loud: 'you'll be an heiress one day baby, on the back of daddy's nano-genetical empire - or wouldn't you want any of it since it's tainted? Wise daddy Lean still strings you along, because you know, somewhere you know, what the real story is.' And like an illicit drug the mystery of murder and atonement holds us close, and sin's our slimy aphrodisiac. *Ooh, I mated with the man who knew too much.* Fucking hot, yeeahh! She needs to hold me closer than daddy, and she won't ever kill daddy but daddy's gonna have to *lose* - which says to me I'm gonna win, 'cause I'll die with all her secrets bound in my heart. My god, she likes it, oh yes yes. So we have our thrashing nights… and our surly nights and suspicious nights and cold-as-ice nights and druggy nights… and (best of all) little-girl-lost nights where her cares are watered with sorrow-tears… and at the end of all of these, at the end of a thousand years my Dora will be forced to admit: she might end up appreciating me.

Now there's a thing to stick around for.

Things are never so tidy-simple though. Dora tends to call up Daddy and make him pick her up right under my window. He mutters a curt hello, slips away with her. Back in our bombsite bed in the ruins of morning, she'll assure me she doesn't 'necessarily' like his plushy bars and hotel rooms. Likes to drags him to the Dark Heath instead, to 'her spot', where they can look down on the iniquitous barbarous world and comment superiorly on it. She aims to murder me with her winks of irony. Righteo then Dora… And how *are* mummy and daddy, one is required to ask. All pseudo-sex and desperate status, she says with a sneer. (Oh, well put) Mummy's the fucking man-hypnotist and little baby doesn't get a look in! I vaguely reproach her for that one. She says sorry Lean and licks my nose. Giz a fag, she says. I tell her I don't have any, and you're a fucking lunatic. She says thank you, thank you Lean. You get it, you get me. As a reward I'll stay tonight. And tomorrow, and the next day. Can't promise Friday though. Going to Georgia with daddy. *For how long?* Coupla weeks. Wants to show me some cave or other. Guy's big into caves and holes.

Vanish In Light   The sages say death must wait if a man asks the right question of the skeletal scyther: what exactly are you, my dirty friend? Are you real or do you ply your trade on our laziness, our stupid belief, our endless wait for Godot, we mooning cattle at the gate? I ask no more. Been in bed for turgid weeks. No clink of Dora's key in the lock. Baby you're late. Medicos tool in from time to time. Damn place is sanitised. Not my home no more. Images flood in the night... Sudden stabs in holes deep in the slums of the body. Should one give a shit? Weightless. Drugs. Imposter-doctors bleat with meanings. I crave the chaos of silence. Pinter's silence. Absurd. Each thought is death to all others. The past trails from the back of my head. Seaweed-slurry on a flecked beach. Winds of winter. My cells blow away. I slither out of a white past. Things vibrate, as if alive, as if. Ghosts walk in wind. Cliffs overbear the sea. Flies sweep over deserts. Child-whispers from way way back. Petal of rose, rustle of river. Kite in the sky. We who're here must always be here. In the warm sun of the garden of emptiness is hope. Morning winds of emptiness stir from afar. Leaves rustle and quiver. There's a whiff of future, whiff of regret. Nano-points in eternity. Moments embalmed in a haze. Strange world without meaning. Words without meaning. If they had, they'd cease to be. Look how a thing vanishes. Droplets of dew. Fractals in a god world. Don't close your eyes my friend, you'll vanish in the great. Seen one moment you've seen 'em all. Nothing stays. Flies depart a corpse in the hot wind of the veldt. My love is chaos. I sang an ode for all who seek to foul the common nest. Find a better story. Higher chaos. Oh my giddy aunt, I exist. *Scribbling in the mind...* A stream is never a stream. Silence swallows. People fall away. Nothing ever happened. Dreams of Himalayan fastness. Prayer flags flutter on a wall. Rustle in grasses heard by none. No wind ever blew, no human ever walked there. Faraway busyness in the commune of men. What is it? Lived a life. What? Murmur of a stream ten thousand years ago. Chirrup of birds after the battle. Spattered armour-mountains. Flies. The dead are sleeping. No face, no name. Regret the *Shoah*. Blanket of snow on the mounts of Asia. Carrion. Kites show no mercy. Someone called by, never returning. Memories shoveled in a hole. Cattle at the gate. Feed the turning world. Toilet fodder. *Dora, is it you?* The fullness. Never end. Bliss continuous. Ocean. Ship's prow. Tropic seas. Borderland. White cranes in the blue. Is that the door? Death is a door. Nothing lost. All lost. Pills don't work no more. Go. Not to worry. Nothing stays. Insect on a leaf. No physical. Son of man hath not where to rest... No centre to my head. Thousan' miles, to the bottom of my arms. The fingers of need. Why does one body need another? Love is habit. Dora Lola? My story. Note the mirage. Inconsequence. Don't believe. My window... Bright kite in the sky... Pause... Vanish in light*

[*Diarybook ends here. Editor]

The
Labyrinth

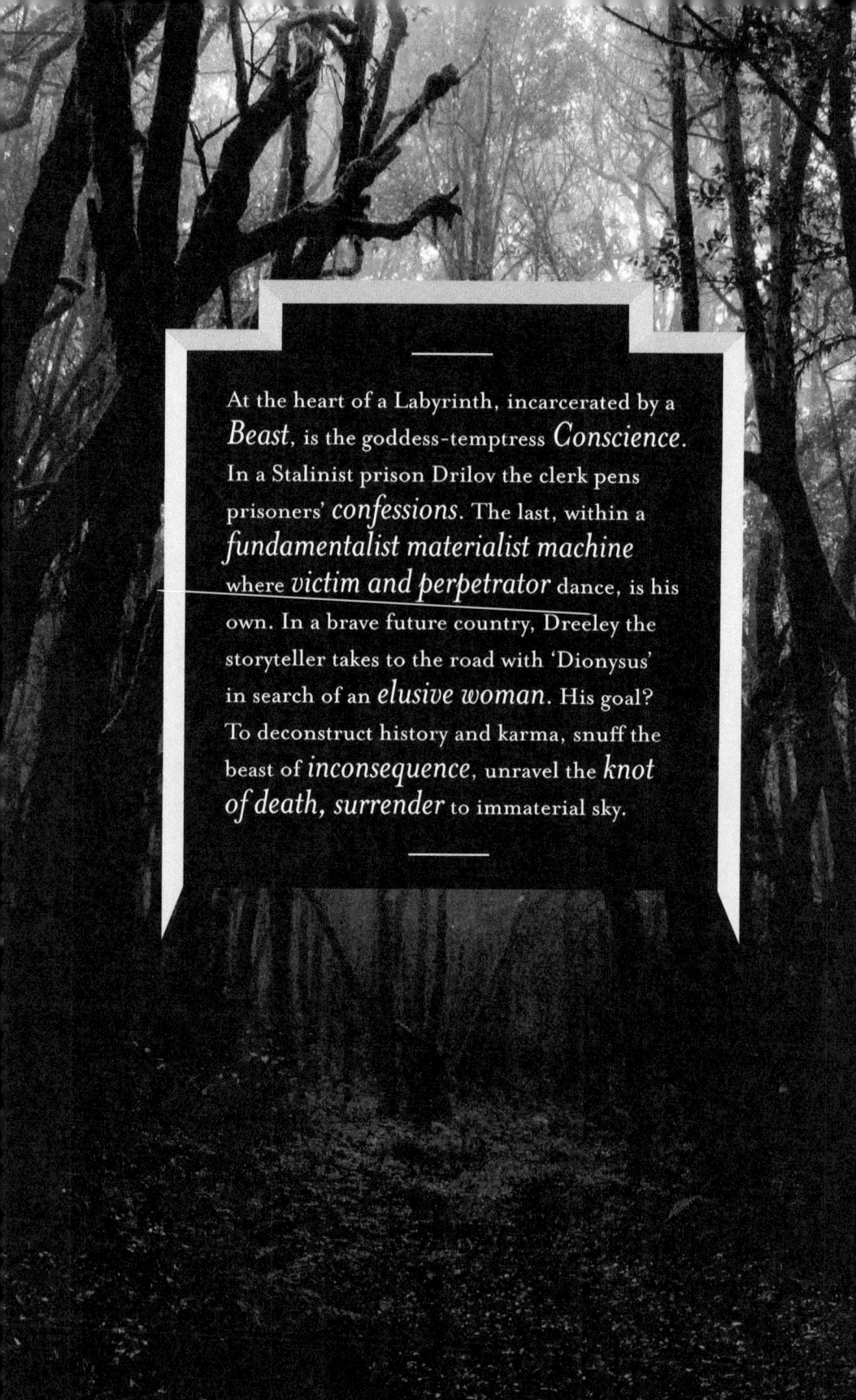

At the heart of a Labyrinth, incarcerated by a *Beast*, is the goddess-temptress *Conscience*. In a Stalinist prison Drilov the clerk pens prisoners' *confessions*. The last, within a *fundamentalist materialist machine* where *victim and perpetrator* dance, is his own. In a brave future country, Dreeley the storyteller takes to the road with 'Dionysus' in search of an *elusive woman*. His goal? To deconstruct history and karma, snuff the beast of *inconsequence*, unravel the *knot of death, surrender* to immaterial sky.

One: The Beast

Behold the fascination of a legend… Amid the threatened evacuation of Moscow in the face of the Nazi war machine, the General Secretary of the Communist Party of the Soviet Union stole from his personal assistant a thing close to his heart: his wife. A pretty doctor and relative of Trotsky, she had been inexplicably arrested under Comrade Stalin's covert order for crimes amounting to subversion against the state. Rather than her life being spared, an act Stalin would claim was beyond his power to enact such was the pure and incontrovertible machinery of Soviet law and justice, she was duly and in timely manner executed, most likely within the muffling bowels of Lubyanka prison and certainly with a bullet to the back of the neck. At this juncture, Poskrebyshev her husband had not even time to mourn, compelled as he was to toil on with crucial preparations for the possible evacuation of his beloved Moscow (and all the bitter-sweet things it stood for). The dutiful *chef de cabinet,* save perhaps for a few wayward sweat-beads rivulating his chubby brow (hastily wiped away) showed no sign of distress that might compromise Dear Comrade's faith in him at a time of utter crisis - apart perhaps from a slurrying inkstain of despair within his heart or the frantic dream as he stood poring over strategems beside his leader that he might take a pair of silver scissors from the desk and ram its spike through the fucking pig's eye then cut off his balls and jam them into the mustachioed fat corpse's gob as it lay spreadeagled on the rug, thus enjoying one pure moment of private bliss-grief before ten thousand jackbooted thugs came galumphing at him through the door. But no, our fellow breathed nary a compromising word to soil the orbit of his haloed leader. And Stalin for his part must have entertained the very ghost of a smile, thinking it an exquisite private lesson in loyalty and non-attachment, at once a gift to his valued minion and a gesture to all citizens who might think to put personal feelings above the Communist Party of the Soviet Union at the zenith of its need. For as the saying goes, what is nobler than loyalty and love for one's country (notwithstanding one's country blithely and impersonally murders one's wife and lover). In this way, Stalin enjoyed the utter hiatus of need, that fundamental cruelty among life's ironies. The sack of Moscow mattered less to him than the thought: 'Dear citizens, torture is my gift to you all. Torture alone lets you see that there is nothing in life that can be ignored, no level of reality that you may eschew or scorn. We must seek to be here and here alone, must seek nothing but to live this life in its fullest and deepest part. Only the exquisite hiatus of torture may offer this!'

Your narrator's name is Dreeley, and he is a citizen of the present time, wherever that may be. He cannot readily tell you why instances of cruelty and madness in the world should stand out to him in the manner of an obsession, as if he had lived and died through them… and though it may be said that the experience of a solitary soul in all history's becoming and solitude and suffering is nothing but distant rills, ancient winds, forsaken breath, atomised dust… we should admit to ourselves that experience is *something,* since in the vaults of time it lodges, like tiny nutseeds which by the power of obsession certainly sprout again. For the sake of all who tremble and perish under a regime of cruelty and unmeaning, like the institutional terror and sadism of Stalin's Soviet Union, Dreeley has an obsession with righting of wrongs, of 'light beyond darkness'. Stalin, while systematically wiping his comrades-in-arms, at once obliterated every trace of them by personally directing the purging of the archives. Worst, it is only He who remains in the memory. Meanwhile we envision those hordes of victims crowding towards the light, queueing and jostling on heaven's staircase - while the crude circumstance of their going unstoppably amplifies darkness' mystique. One may claim that life only plunges forward without reason into future, or that there is but omnivorous nowness that cannot but drown all memory… but the psyche is a grinder, sifter, analyser (and voyeur) that tumbles in great circles like snowballs or washing machines into an aching future that is nothing but amplification of past, and no matter how people try to build brave new countries of erasure, they are but products of gone things, of things snatched away. Dreeley is resident of a southern country where the complexities of past are quietly edited out, where easy present and easier future are bravely legislated day by day. Yet grave-spoiler Dreeley is a poor citizen of a land that prides itself on pure waters and purer snows! One should not advertise it here, but

Dreeley, beyond his obsessive compulsivity long endured what should be described as a depressive suicidal disorder. It is why he begs to burden you, reader, with his psychic burrowings. We are nothing if not revisionists: all our storytelling, fictionising, mythmaking, processing - Dreeley will tell you is 'history's justice' at work. Out of desperate need he harkens to the tempting reverberations of suffering from within the gulag heart of a terror regime, revives old cycles of perpetrator and victim, calculates the costs of old cruelties and loyalties, so far as he is able to imagine them. Why is every single victim loyal to life's *duty*? How do the best-laid crimes of mice and men turn inward and rot the perpetrators? How does guilt endlessly seek atonement? How shall we go beyond the perpetrator-victim paradigm - so that we might take responsibility, come to respect, come to detachment, come to innocence? Or how to deconstruct death itself? A mild and simple agenda!

Conscience: Heart of Light The lugubrious Dreeley, no doubt to bolster his self-esteem, channels his compulsions as 'analysis', and while some readers will find his ruminations annoying, brutally entertaining stories follow. With a certain formality he traces the human journey from compulsive fixated circular harsh materialism, to the gropings of the spirit... from victim to suicide to fugitive to wanderer to surrenderer...

...To remain even notionally loyal to sunken criminals like Joseph Stalin is only possible by maintaining delicate states of ignorance. One such state is a fundamentalist autism that trades in brute simplicities, thereby ridding itself of conscience; another is sadism, which lives and breathes by cruelty, interpreting reality as a grotesque; another is sado-masochism, which is the need to pay out one's haunted conscience by way of punishment; and a fourth is masochism proper, the need to 'enter the heart of the Labyrinth and be killed by the Beast'. Beyond these, we should also speak of a peculiar loyalty to *innocence* on the part of trusted servants of a master. The likes of Stalin know only too well that anyone who knows the truth about them could not possibly trust them. What then of General Alexander Nikolaevich Poskrebyshev, Stalin's only trusted assistant (that is, repository of his innermost cynicisms)? Was Poskrebyshev involved in the compilation of the death lists, organisation of the pogroms and mass deportations and show trials and conveyor-machine of executions? Amazingly, it is probable he was not. Most of us have no idea what evils pertain even in our neighbour's house, and the arms of Stalin's government were certainly set up so that one hand might never know what the other was doing. In that case, it might be posited that Stalin actually respected the value of Poskrebyshev's loyalty. Amazing thought! Until... he could not resist exposing the loyal one to the heart of evil, at least a tiny bit of it, in the insignificant matter of the murder of his wife. On reflection, it would have been patronising not to do so. How should a gangster show respect except by coyly exhibiting the tender tools of his trade? After all, Stalin's own wife had committed suicide, and while it is said that this act made him turn to inexorable hardness, he may have wanted at least one person he respected to share in his putative sorrow... Alexander Poskrebyshev like the hero Theseus entered a labyrinth, yet though he encountered the Minotaur he never thought to assassinate. Instead he dwelt therein, and sought to quieten the beast through patience and loyalty. These, not the urge for heroism, were in his nature. His chief weapon was but the passive fact of being trusted, though he did not save his wife, Bronislava Poskrebysheva (his beloved, his *Ariadne*) from the beast's claw. It seems that to defeat the beast we shall need the humility of acceptance... but was it really enough for Stalin to say to him: 'Don't worry, we will get you another wife'? For there will always be reptilian gnomes ruling us in this life, and what right do we have to hope they will be influenced by our patience and our example? Cold-bloods have no need for compassion since they rule and since they have a cause. Their fundamentalism is a great autism; it has no need to include, only to exclude. 'If there is a human problem we kill the human. End of problem', said Stalin within earshot of several people (excluding Poskrebyshev). Though that autistic impulse must exist somewhere in all of us, the general was a man who seemed to live in the eye of that storm, a man untouched by torture, somehow neuterable, somehow trustable. A man like him also knows that his innocence is all he has, that there is nothing he can ever *do* to be trusted. In the end he is lucky. Poskrebyshev slips between the cracks of history, the faceless man with a heart whom there is no reason to kill out of envy or suspicion or rivalry or hate or even love. And though

Poskrebyshev fulfils the role of displaced conscience of his master (who remember, is a devil and a gangster by design) and so keeps his silence and does his duty, enduring the soft winds of horror-thoughts that flutter by his door but do not enter, he lives on inside the horror-world and is amazed at how untouched he is. Perhaps this amazement is the secret to his innocence... And perhaps he *is* the needed sacred cow, the sole exception, a candlelight of conscience amid the amoral out-of-control State, a pure idol in the temple of doom, protected by the blood-hordes no matter what atrocities they do. So, while his master needed to stow his conscience in his deathlists and dossiers, there is reason to believe he invested it in people like his *chef de cabinet*... because the rational part of the human beast must find a reason for everything, no matter how bestial, and because the conscience, the heart of light, must ever be veiled in order to do evil. One way to do this is to enshrine laws and rules and regulations and norms that justify, that institutionalise harm. Or we can salve the conscience by telling ourselves that destruction of our enemies is a temporary thing, a means to an end, that the conscience is never really diverted or clouded in pursuit of that greater end. Is it a mercy, that by Stalin never allowing anyone to fully know what was happening, he offered a salve to the weakness of peoples' consciences? How though *can* a man veil his conscience enough to perpetrate mass evil? We create the excuse of saying he is schizophrenic, that he tries to make rational choices in a universe that is innately insane, wherein there is no course of action that does not epitomise its own insanity - like *Kali,* the roiling hindu goddess rattling her thousand-skulled necklace. And how would one worship a goddess like her? Thus a man is reckless with his conscience, he taunts it, he challenges it to fail him, he contrives to abnegate responsibility for himself by submitting to dirty evil legalities. He is infatuated with fundamentalism's simplicities, he creates veils whereby the inner does not know the outer, he effaces himself in his sophistries and his machinations. He does not have to take heed of the horror that constitutes himself. And he takes no heed of the heart of light, that he would have known if this blood-crazy world had not contrived to confound poor him, to torture *him* as it does. His only recourse to conscience in a world gone mad... is the rigidity of duty. Meanwhile Poskrebyshev did duty of a higher kind -

which was to serve, with life and soul, the beast in his labyrinth. And lo, he survived.

The Duel   'Any man wants to be loved. In the absence of love he wants to be admired. In the absence of admiration he wants to be feared. And in the absence of fear, he wants to be hated'.

Dreeley, fearing that few readers will attend with enthusiasm to the exigencies of his enquiry into criminality versus conscience, seeks to cloak it in imaginative conceits. Let us enter a scene in a Russian forest... that resembles something from *Eugene Onegin*. It is 1830. It seems there is to be a duel. One Alexander Nikolaevich P_____ sadly requires satisfaction of his erstwhile friend now rival, Iosif Vissarionovich S_____ .

It is a still winter's morning. We see about us thin white birch trees. Their trunks, mottled by dark cuts, thrust from drifts of glistening snow. At the edge of a clearing stand two men in long coats and *Ushanka* hats; one of them holds a small case. They confer in hushed tones, and a looker-on might imagine them to be friends. It is clear though that neither is keen to be present. Their business is grave: they are seconds to this morning's duel. Perhaps they understand only too well the falling out of friends... and harbour the colleaguey feeling that it is not they who shall die today. They await their chiefs; their boots shuffle in the crisp silence. First to arrive is a stoutish young man of medium height, ruddy-faced, balding a little at the crown, that is bare since he holds his hat in his hand. This is evidently the 'thrower of the gauntlet', Alexander Nikolaevich P_____. He looks about, then contrives (suddenly, jovially) to greet the two men. But he is distracted, as one desperate to be at peace and far far from it. He paces; his steps commit little dents in the white. Across the fellow's face flitter guttering elderliness and boyish hope: distractive torturers both. The enfolding trees stand and mutter. A sun-shaft flickers, and Alexander throws up his face to receive it... a golden hand come to rescue him from awfulness? It soon dims. Minutes slip by. At a point, an assistant affects to step across, touch the protagonist's arm. It appears the rules are flouted; the duel cannot proceed. They begin to tramp away. Alexander Nikolaevich stares at their backs, at last resolves to follow... Suddenly at the clearing's edge is another figure. He wears the required heavy coat and fur hat; the face bears a heavy moustache. He seems powerfully built, his white-dusted shoulders loom about him like a bear. His gaze seems to magnetise the men; they turn their heads at once. This is surely Iosif Vissarionovich S_____ . Alexander is consternated; he is sweating. Slighted honour suits him not at all! Satisfaction this morning would surely be the shaking of hands or a hug, followed by repairing home for a jolly breakfast. This is the nadir of his imagining, innocent soul! He hankers for a signal that will wipe away this affair. Iosif Vissarionovich offers nothing... A soft snow begins to fall. Our scene wants to fade to fairy tale...

But wait, look closer. It is the measure of Alexander's soul that he'll push aside his heart's resentment with such firmness as to be amazed when malice asserts itself. He is forgiving to the extent that he neglects to see that his friend is not. We will surmise that he befriended Iosif (long ago) because he knew Iosif's real qualities, then contrived to forget them along with the reason for befriending him, which is that Iosif had no other friend in the world. Whose fault this is, Alexander also fails to think on. But Iosif for his part is not one to forget such a *slight* from the one person who contrived to have him as friend... and by such a statement we may see that Iosif is not a conventional man. Yet it is Alexander who demands satisfaction today! Something close to the heart has upset him, and he has seen no way out... a matter of love from which there is no retreat. That is, when a loving man is cornered he sees no other way out. Yet it is not conceivable to Alexander that Iosif would hate his only friend (who overlooks Iosif's true nature) or would seek to use the friendship to win satisfaction against him. Sir, on the contrary: a man with but one friend in the world will surely abuse that friendship! Herein is the darkness in the soul of Iosif Vissarionovich. Do we have the resource to unpick it? By official account, Iosif contrived to steal Alexander's lover away. She is called *Arianne,* a curious name. She for her part is the daughter of a Count and a difficult woman to catch, though not for that reason. And not to say there is evil in her, but she is proud and suffers no fools, and there is in her a streak of aloofness that makes men dream. Has Iosif really stolen her... she who may not be stealable at all? Alexander never actually knows if

Arianne loves him; Iosif definitely knows she does not. In confessing to Iosif that she 'does not love him either', the count's daughter made it plain she would likely never love anyone. In fact, she is probably free of all men. Iosif therefore, in coming to the duel has information the honourable other has not. Why did Iosif tempt fate by seeking the grace of an untouchable woman? To confirm the solitude of his soul, the surly victimhood he has nurtured all his life? Here is a man who seeks darkness and seeks enemies to pay for that darkness. What better enemy than a man who tries to be his friend, and what better means than to snuff out his friend's impulse for love... Or might this woman be a rival to Iosif's control of Alexander? Does Iosif want Alexander all to himself? Why therefore destroy someone he possibly loves? ...We do not say he is incapable of love. Is not every man capable of it? If that is so, then one might contrive *not* to be capable of love, for the sake of contrariness, uniqueness. Oh, there is power in victimhood. Yes, power in sado-masochism, at its finest... One can offer no honour to people who've abandoned honour, and Iosif adheres to none of its rules. Alexander doesn't see, because honourable men think others live by at least some form of it. We see then that Alexander is fighting for the wrong thing. He fights for a woman's honour, whereas he should be fighting for his own. How to do that? Alexander should by rights annihilate his opponent - but will fail as long as he abides by rules ignored by the other. Or he should never have fought at all, since the duel is not over a question of honour, but over an alien woman. Iosif meanwhile pursues nihilism as a form of *morality*. How? To be loyal to nothing clears the slate, creates as if a scorched earth wherein the *germ* of loyalty might sprout. And that perhaps, is why Iosif Vissarionovich is standing here this morning, in the clearing, ready to kill or to die.

...Iosif makes a beckoning gesture. The assistants hasten forward, but with dignified precautionary nods as if to affirm they are in charge. Today's killing ritual will be humane, performed according to rules. The case is opened with a ceremonial click. Two pistols lie snugly end to end as if licking each other's toes on a bed of soft velvet. Alexander is invited to take one. With quavering fingers he selects the nearest, being politely brought up. It lies in his hand like a slippery fish. Iosif gruffly takes the other, as if to say 'This is not my doing!' All comprehend his 'gesture' to signify the absurdity of death, absurdity of this world. If Iosif is nervous there is no sign of it. The attendants whisper instructions to their proteges. There shall be governing proprieties! A coin is produced and tossed to the snow. Alexander calls: heads it is. The combatants shake hands. The surrounding trees nudge each other. The air drips thick with intrigue. Let us rise into that air a little, as if a bird alighting on a branch. The antagonists stand back to back, pistols absurdly raised to lapels. They trace a little path in the whiteness. Ten steps; heavy boots crunch the snow. There is solemnity, choreography. They turn. The assistants fall back. Begin! one calls. The two friends stand stock still facing each other. How did it come to this? How does anything come to this? Alexander raises his arm; his pistol seems flaccid, poetic. He hesitates… nudges his arm slightly to the left… and fires. There is a red and ugly report. Smoke puffles upward into the trees. One's birdy colleagues have taken to the air in fright. Stillness. Smoke drifts. Iosif stands unmoved. Alexander lowers his arm. He has made his last gentlemanly gesture; he shall not kill today. The attendants frown at each other, parsimonious extras in an amateur's play. Pause. Iosif now raises his arm, his gun the metallic extension of it. Alexander gazes out at him. There is a strange transference of force across the space. Death solemnly announces itself. Iosif fires. Blast and smoke. Alexander falls bludgeoned, backward into snow. The air thrills, shudders… The assistants now pad forward, bend over the body. One gestures to Iosif. He will not come. At last he advances. Let us flitter close above the idiocy-scene. Alexander is pillowed in the snow, gasping for breath. His face is red, puffed like a balloon. He seems to be searching for something… for something to be said. Iosif will not kneel to him. Alexander wants him. Now life's purport begins to shrivel before his eyes. The eyes dilate. He dwindles in the snowdrift. A better world awaits! The lids glaze… and he is gone. The attendants step back. Only now does Iosif kneel. So - a good man lost! He touches the innocent face. In some wolf-like way he pays respect. *Respect.* Now he stands, hastens away. A wolf in tundra, he shambles into trees, who enclose him in their silvery limbs. Soon one attendant leaves. The other guards the scene. He'll wait until a cart comes to take the corpse away.

Little rouge gushes glisten in the white. They soon begin to soften and fade. A snowfall is predicted for the afternoon.

The Helper at Lubyanka   According to the narrator Dreeley, a faceless man known as A.N. Drilov is identified as 'a recorder of confessions of prisoners' inside Moscow's Lubyanka prison in 1939. Dreeley admits: Voyeurs from the future like me are bound to grab at his words - as if all the dung-stained ennui of done experience were jacketed up just for us, a gift for breathless new kids who demand the re-living of a play, we dessicated actor-ghosts who need to whine at the upturning of their buried pain... thus the 'meaning of our own lives' steals on us as we ravel up the shrouded past, and we begin to see: it's really not past at all! The chronicler Drilov knew he was sowing seeds, and at the start he claimed (in his somewhat formal Russian) that he recorded these confessions 'for a better future', for 'fabled readers somewhere-elsewhere'. But at the last it is clear that he writes for himself, for the lonely sake of it, for the sake of *activity*, consecrated in the stillness of ungraspable unrepeatable *now*. What happened to him? In his elusiveness Drilov begs discovery, like a drug... 'Kindly report to the Departmental Ground Floor, at the usual 0800 hours.' (Dreeley sets the scene) Comrade Drilov distinctly recalls that order, slipped under his door as he lingered in bed against the December cold. For a full six months he had been some manner of clerk in the upper-floor warrens of the Lubyanka headquarters, and had oftentimes wondered exactly who had so readily 'maintained him' in this role, since in this place there is no neutrality, where to be present means 'they have a plan for you'. Drilov had been led, by little signs one not in his position would never have seen, to feel he should persist, that he was 'favourably marked' by persons unseen though not unfelt. This ground-floor order was a promotion then, and Drilov since the new year has been engaged in compiling 'confessional diatribes of Unpersons'. There was no discernible moment where he realised he had dozens of significant files at his fingertips... 'There is never a moment in this life (his private journal records) where we realise how we got to where we are, where the causes of our present and future are laid bare. Life is more stealthy, inexorable than that. Yet I'm privileged, not least since I hold in hand the records of

Unpersons (whether they be literally true or no) - and so one's conduct must be unassailable, since to so erase a person yet punctiliously record the reasons, requires moral rectitude... for that is how the quiet streams of our duty and loyalty wind their inexorable way.' Here is Drilov then, reflecting on the delicacy of his role, and concluding there's more to it than mere function. A curious thing about the records of unpersons is that 'he who commits them to paper somehow becomes part of them'... and dutiful Drilov has resolved to seek a kind of 'partnership' wherein the prisoner 'freely offers confession' and he 'efficiently records it'. Drilov seems to be aware that most of the visitors to this lower realm (and there is a continual stream) are never afforded the luxury of drafting confessions in conference with a dedicated clerk, 'though I expect similar business is done elsewhere by better qualified others... I personally shall stretch my duty for the sake of prisoners who exhibit 'complexity', composing my own record that they'll be 'invited' to approve. I assume my superiors will support such initiative! Perhaps my role is as chronicler... as if such records might achieve a sort of balancing that in time might salve, even immortalise. For what is this political present but the foundation of our greater future?' And yes, there were moments in these weeks where Drilov pocketed one or two tracts and took them home for 'further work.' Somehow he rationalised this unorthodoxy as 'duty to perfect the text' in the expectation that one or other of his superiors will peruse it and 'hold his reputation to account'. 'Yes, one must acquit oneself, must create meaning where confusion exists, forge a little clarity out of mistiness, truth out of crime, light out of shadow. Why else would one be employed thus, if not to do one's utmost?' And of course there was a moment when a confession he crafted was of such clarity that he neglected to return with it the next day... And all that day it burned in its place under his dresser; in fact it burned into his heart... and suddenly became a kind of germ, a possibility of a higher thing, an exemplar... as if he were suddenly writing for a cause, not just for history or for Communism, but for posterity, for love, for pity...

Comrade Drilov's thoughts reveal a startling frankness! - and beyond prisoner tracts, such extracts from his private journal begin to assume an unsettling life of their own... 'This day I went to the Kino, and saw Eisenstein's *Battleship Potemkin*. The director seems to have hyper-realised the fabled Odessa Steps massacre, 'as if to deal out a *warning* beyond the fatuities of propaganda. I actually spoke of it to the unperson Mishkin, a priest. And he had much to say that I did not expect. 'Why build a System for the benefit of people where people are expendable to the greater good? Certainly we must root out decadent history and create a clean society - and I reflect on how I personally have failed and must pay. Thus I do my duty. Yet I admit to a strange sense of dreading loss, that this life is precious because it is *unexperienced*... as if the less significant a person or event, the more words shall be needed to describe them - as if an entire volume is needed for the merest breath of truth! Is there any person or thing that's insignificant, Drilov? *If one, then all.* Then again, if we erase a man or woman, what is changed? To throw my dirty shirt in the washer is no calamity. This word 'death' is but a withdrawal from the level of the physical!' (I, Drilov, baulked at his suggestion that death is casual. Yet he retorted:) 'According to true justice death must be *temporary* - for how can we fail to return to fulfill all the causes of things? How may criminals (like me) not return to face the music? No one escapes fate! Men build prisons in their skulls, do dirty deeds, hoard their secrets. And these walls and gates and rooms and corridors of the Lubyanka, these frames of misery and human smell and breath - these must be revealed by *you*, Clerk Drilov! And it is not relevant that you have little stomach for it since your sole focus is 'your own conscience'! What of the conscience of a System, of a beloved country?' And I (Drilov) thought: this religionist Mishkin is clever! Should I not determine to fulfill my duty a little longer? Should I not celebrate life's hereness, all its ways? And should I not - condemn suicide?'

'...Yet it's only February and I am exhausted, miserably cold and weak. No doubt the culprit is overwork, or at least my obsessive attitude to it... though this toil is oddly *constructive* in nature. Then on Friday last (as if someone above had understood) our Sub-Commandant Blokhin came to my door to announce a 'celebratory lunch'. Reward for duties done, he said. (And doubly necessary to attend since he'll be present) With a faint smile he noted: 'Saturday is your birthday, by serendipity?' Yes, I am thirty-one years of age. Yet the Sub seemed worn: perhaps he needed to reward his own relentless effort (though I recall feeling less pleased with that notion than of my birthday). I, Drilov, tend to couch my diminutive role here in that of 'keenly observing newcomer', one who has no reason to think that to celebrate a thing in this place denotes the impending demise of said thing... At the lunch the attendees seemed uneasy - for when 'business as usual', the 'hum of the machine' ceases, even for a moment, there comes a strange unnatural hiatus: one almost feels like a sudden hole is torn in the world, through which a strange secret rushes up in the heart... I should say that I have seen and heard several unusual incidents these past days, in which a woman is manhandled in and out of a room in my corridor. Once, I encountered her on a stairwell with big Sergeant Dionylov and two others. They seemed in a hurry, and their uniforms were dishevelled. Days ago I heard a concerning disturbance in the room adjacent. I will not offer detail, but it is now obvious that though the Woman is being vigorously interrogated she is also 'coveted by certain persons', and (less fortunately) is whispered to be known to Leon Trotsky. Is she of the nature of a political football... or something more basic? Strange then - that this Woman whom I'd thought a prisoner is present at our lunch party! I learn that she is named Bronislava Poskrebysheva... Our Sub-Commandant is in a strangely jovial mood this day (normally he's impenetrable) and in his dress uniform offers a smile to Poskrebysheva before 'congratulating us all on our work'. No doubt he enjoys the sight of a pretty woman - and who wouldn't? I note his tendency to display on his breast a medal, usually just the one. I've seen several, all different; does he harbour a collection? We consume vodka with surprisingly acceptable little cakes. The Sub drinks aplenty and seems oddly keen to converse. At a point he tosses off a speech (to no-one in particular), something like: 'Friends, what need to educate, self-develop, evolve? If this life were all economic and political necessity it would be simple! A life of function! I suppose if we eliminate enough enemies we eliminate all our problems. Yet don't we seek a greater purpose? What are we here for, friends? We build a State, though cynics will say time waits for no man or state, that history is but 'a flurry of events for good or ill'. Yet by erasure we replace all... in a great time for a Greater Time. All is hereby erased!' And he flings a tumbler down his gullet, and we all follow suit. What's his intent? A hint of sadness at the world's verities? A veiled purview of the inevitable for us all? Drilov, you are too imaginative.'

Abasement in the Basement   This day, late in the nameless afternoon in an anteroom in the basement, the woman Bronislava Poskrebysheva is 'entertaining' a group of men. Drilov hears his name called from the corridor. He hesitates but goes, and at the door he is shouted in and clapped on the back by burly sergeant Dionylov. All the men have been plied with alcohol, and all are drunk. A beaker is thrust in Drilov's hand, and its liquid is horridly bitter. She, Bronislava, is poised in the midst. She rides her chair like a drunk cowboy; her orange skirt, black bodice and soaked hair are a twisted parody as she hollers in gutteral laughter with the best of them. Drilov sees: the white-armed woman is using all her wiles to stay alive, and everyone knows it and wills her on! Presently Drilov is invited to partake in the degradation ritual. It is clear that rape has been done by the others. There's an inner door. Dionylov thrusts he and her through it. It slams. The clerk whispers a thing that sounds like apology. None of that! she says, though you're better looking than the rabble. But won't they come and watch? There's animal roaring in the other room. She regards him pityingly. Drilov begins to feel... that she is the soul of tenacity. Maybe those men saw it too, and maybe they are flattered and amazed that she is the wife of the *chef de cabinet* of Comrade Stalin himself. She is indeed. Now she pushes him to the floor. He lies there. Its surface is gluey-wet, stinking. She deftly exposes his middle parts to the clammy air, and she has straddled his face, and now she has his genitals in her mouth. She has no underwear. It's unclean. He gags. She is practised and lifts a little, just out of reach. He feels a cloudy hiatus, then the urgent stab of wanting. Two alien bodies fall to collaborating on deft important work. Suddenly, shockingly he comes in her mouth. And with all care she licks him clean. Drilov is amazed. She turns, kisses him once... A pause for remembrance, and she stands. He cannot see her eyes. She raps on the door. It crashes open and Sarge Dionylov is there. He pours his drink over

Drilov's feet. The clerk is invited to laugh. She, Marsha, immediately has her lips on the big man's neck.

It's clear the thing is to participate, to collude, to uphold our colleagues, uphold the Machine, whatever it takes! Bronislava knows - and her self-regard, even as she toilets it away, is the thread of her imperviousness, the thing that might just turn these rapists' gaze to the irony of their acts. For they are victims too, they who participate in debasement, and she must delicately point to it without turning them violent! Drilov feels he can't help, for this is her razor's edge: the delicate masochism where her sadistic perpetrators might see their own plight and surrender themselves in it, might choke on the shocking pain-and-hope dance of it, the nothingness-and-hope fling of it, and might just witness in their inflictions on this woman the rape of their own souls by a Machine that made them what they are! And deeper... maybe here in the midst these operatives of the machine have the power to *poison it* through the faith of a dirty woman - and she has been elevated by our power to rape her to the status of goddess, all vulnerable-real and feeling-soft and contradictory and crying out, crying even for you and me in the bloody heart of a system that allows nothing but the bruteness of its own bruteness. ...Drilov doesn't know how many beakers of slush he has imbibed by now... for time seems to perish in this workday underworld beyond the daylight. It is said that this Poskrebysheva is the property of the Unseen Commandant, that she is 'his conscience', that he keeps her, that it is he who offers this gift of torture and abasement! Or that he does not hog damnation for himself, that he seems to guess that we all seek a kind of *Ariadne* in this labyrinth, and that she is the conscience of we the damned; so that beyond his criminal duty every man is a hero in his private hell, beyond the power of the system to induce him. The Commandant is surely a wise one! And he must have seen, must have known this Ariadne could be relied on to fight for life, be her struggle ever so disgusting, and that this is the only correct act in a place where murder is as cheap as breath. What shall we say of a woman who fights for life itself, be it ever so low? She is surely a goddess, who embodies birth and entanglement and hope... yet every man needs to hate her because she is Woman, and everyone needs her because she is Life Itself. And yes, she is the Commandant's bitch and she is Stalin's Woman, the woman we all must abuse and slowly murder, because we know she is the one thing standing between us and our own causeless relief of annihilation. There is a party going on in the basement... the cellar where all the dung and sewage of the world collects... and we will make the party an orgiastic one, where there are no rules but one: that our utter lack of respect is a kind of respect for something outside our control, that our raping is a thing we hallow in our wretchedness, that we commit to for the sake of wildness, for what we can't ever control, for the savagery of surrender to a *blessed unknown*. Here is the agora of the infinite, the slow dropping from the world into absolute vaults where we float without reason or rule in whiteness and blackness between the stars... we animals who know nothing but a tiny wish to wriggle our way back to mother-egg, to womb, to dark warmth, to where there are no rules because no-one made them, no rules because nobody boot-stamped them into us... and where we can rest and nest in our cocoon of rest without responsibility or care, forever and ever.

'Oh right now in the basement we are the purest drunken boys (drivels Drilov). My god! It's not crimes that matter but compassion n' care, no matter what. These're my brothers! Knowledge is the curse! To know nothing *bad,* that's innocence, that's love. Blame Eve who ate the apple in the garden, the woman who's our scapegoat all these ages, and we *are* nothing but seeds who wiggle our weak and sorry way to the great egg-planet uterus, little seeds blown on wind who by grubby and aching chance got caught in the web of the goddess *Ariadne,* who always waits for our dirty deeds to be done, waits for us to surrender, for we to lay down our arrogant little pin heads and be children again... God save me, but I am drunk! Someone Fucking Big is giving the orders today! This System we're all cogs of. *Someone big is letting beautiful rot trickle in.* We cogs are not responsible, and not even our leaders are, and this fact is fed by the self-murdering perfection of the Commie Machine, where corruption is its food and drink and heartbeat, and just as the sun will consume its own body in a far-off aeon so our shitty system will gobble itself away - and all the goodies, the wealth and power always get to be elsewhere nourishing some other bastards. Not for us to question why, ours is but to fuck and die. Where's order here? Is 't not rank that keeps us? We're all comrades sure, but *rank* is all we've got, and unbreakable orders can be passed down the line... as long as there's rank there's respect and life will flow! The sarge's got himself paralytic. He's foaming. This is our bloody perfect basement where the system lets off its steam... Or, or, what if there's no respect or rank or rule or morals, ever? What if there are no orders and a lunatic's in charge of the asylum, and in the pit the clever snake eats all the others, and our isolation is a barren womb where the winds of the real never blow in, where our little candle of life is nary disturbed... where the rules are different, here in the *secret chamber of the heart* where there's no morals because there's no victims and perpetrators, no order-givers or takers, *only a strange democracy where we are all equally fucked,* all in the dark, all rankless servants of whatever chthonic god is ruling here. The god is Anarchy! 'cause equality is chaos, 'cause equality is Commie Death. And yet we all win 'cause we're all killers, all victims, all dead. We are the Nemesis of System! And our tyranny is *free* because its only rule is that everyone is fucking utterly abased. Who'll punish the fucking punishers? So there's a Party going on - till the last drunk crook's annihilated *by his own hand.* Communism - may God bless your soul and may you burn in shit-hell forever.'

And big Beast sergeant Dionylov has vomited on his boots, and now he's dead asleep. Bronislava Poskrebysheva surveys the field of corpses. Her eyes flicker like the green witch. No-one bothers her now. And Drilov passes out.

* * * *

In the morning, Drilov unexpectedly woke to find himself dead.

This arresting little phrase greets us in Drilov's journal. He has no idea how he got out of Lubyanka's lower rooms and back to the faux-safety of his apartment, in bed with his boots off. The gap in his memory now corresponds to a gap in his Record... A person who knows himself to be dead is in an awkward position: he longs to cry out to the so-called living, that they might harken to his information that will unhinge the whole world. But that is not the way of things. No Unperson will ever convey the truth or feeling of the underworld journey he takes alone. No trip to the heart of darkness is communicable… The morning huddles in on Drilov. His new thought is: 'One day I will seek the benediction of a priest. Perhaps the prisoner Mishkin. Something is over.' Drilov is not sure what it is, here in the dark of the morning.

'Yet I go back, for duty awaits me. And I perform it because I am my duty, and I wear the uniform, the neutralising uniform, and I write down the confessions of souls, and this is simply and comfortingly how evil is done: that there is no choice but to do it, and it is ready to hand and intimate, with results that are clear-cut in a Mondayfriday world. Yet in my other, private hours, that are languorous and imprecise and confused, there is a minute prickling of my skin that never seems to pass off, and if I care to notice, a shortening of breath as if a knot is somewhere in the lungs. And the heart (again if I care to notice) seems to strangle and wither a little, begrudging its toil of being constant and firm and dutiful… for who is dutiful to this life? If anything it is the heart, and I sit in the silence in those lower rooms listening, and I always feel admiration for its continuance beyond begging or complaining, its sending of missives round the great body its empire, this beating heart that mutely performs all things, that upholds the world… upholds our Great State with the Leader at its core, he who exerts Himself for the State's continuance, for this utter utter good that we invest in and are loyal to and live and do our duty for… Meanwhile, we comrades shamble in solitary forests, in corridors of numbness. We are lone actors, and this is how we validate heartlessness, how we validate atrocity: by disconnection, by obscuration. And this world is the absurd positing of itself as real and enduring, the risible pursuit of substance in the midst of pain. It is the separation into Other, so that one may feel aloofly untouched, feel the unimpeachable separation of me and you so that I can kill you. Why must we separate the other and liquidate him? Was anyone ever able to do a single thing but in collaboration? So here is our last best collaboration: that of perpetrator and victim. And maybe it is the only intimacy some of us will ever feel.

We must validate this ignorant little island self... for this is the supreme and uniform darkness. We liquidate our victims into we know not what... and they will dissolve back into the merciful Silent Great - while you, you Drilov, are left alone with *yourself*, an island of stupidity in the dark.'

Following interviews with a prisoner named Lilya Popova (an artist and singularly uncompromising personality), Drilov has the temerity to wonder... 'if somehow the system is seeking to 'express its shadow' by some form of safety valve, some outlet for rigidity, some cloaca for excess... as inefficiency, as sheer irrationality, as the unplanned idiocy of drunkenness (like those stomping *grand guignol* parties the elite are rumoured to indulge in) or like some distracted cat playing with a mouse... irrational like the granting of a last meal to a condemned man... or the writing of a confession as if it actually mattered... or as if an unidentified woman were somehow a goddess who put on the raiment of a prostitute and let herself be tossed about by man-beasts in these lower rooms... as if the asylum must at times turn into bedlam, like Walpurgisnacht, Hallowe'en... and as if 'little Drilov' somehow had a part to play in it all, as a kind of liminal artist, a writer of conscience, a letter-off of steam... or (perish the thought) that he performs an age-old compact with the *divine*... who of course at all times, at least in regular hours, cannot by definition exist anywhere in this building. But that which does not exist by official decree ever begs its shadow... and perhaps it is this system's artistry, the supremacy of the human mind that invented it, that allows such a shadow to loom a little. Herr Hitler certainly lets the irrational in, lets ritual and religion have their head... Or perhaps it is better to permit the slow and clandestine drip drip of the irrational, as if it were institutionalised, as if part of the woodwork... as if (for instance) the condemning of enemies of the state could only play its proper part if it *were* irrational, if the victims were somehow absurd in that they were no criminals at all, as if their victimhood were dreamed up by the most irrational excuses of the most absurd people, by those people the world perennially rejects - as if here were a kind of service to allow all the crooks and shysters and assassins and psychopaths to run the place (before they also are inevitably flushed down the toilet) in order to show that we are egalitarian, that we offer succour to the downtrodden, that we are truly the champions of the proletariat, and that we honestly include the bullying-and-killing class! Yes, our system has its clevernesses. And maybe we can see in the end that the system is cynical in its knowingness, is representing all of us in its acceptance of irrational evil; that yes, believe it or not the system is aligned with Nature in its institutionalised hopelessness, that it's the True Way for ever and ever...'

Yes, Drilov. You are very imaginative.

The Butcher and the Poet Drilov records: 'It was Sub-com Blokhin who at New Year informed me that 'the last weeks of my Lubyanka sojourn' would be on 'the floor above the basement'. 'Extra hands needed on deck!' he said with that impersonalised look he affects, before taking the trouble to thank me for 'my commitment'. Why is a person promoted to 'special duties' on the floor above the fabled basement? (he seemed to dare me to ask). 'In our basement, comrade (the bowel, some call it) we routinely 'clean up unsavoury things'. The bowel is a weak organ. (I've seen it too many times.) Not for a man of your sensibility, Drilov!' Did he hint that men must be 'special' to work the dungeon, in the sense that 'few will touch you once you do'... since 'special duties' are what people get inured to, as the creeping norm, the new real... Is this some form of weird climacteric, some kind of parting gift? Worryingly, I fail to believe most things I hear. Yet the Sub seemed to want to *reassure*... and I suppose I should be moved to admire his well-cut uniform and his clipped speech and far-seeing martial air: philosophic, as if hinting at things deeper than words can utter. I could not discern if he approved my new role or regarded me as a threat... though I thought of how he'd appear at my interviews at chance moments - many of them awkward and intimate - and affect to take charge. Typically, he'd say:
- Be glad you're here in person, prisoner! Be glad you're not one of our photo-album cases! Often comrade Drilov has in his possession only a snapshot with which to decide an outcome. How can he ascertain truth or lies? Count yourself lucky.
And once the prisoner-artist Lilya Popova said to him:
- Why would you people interrogate me if you don't somehow trust in

my answers? Is this a grotesque ritual to salve your conscience? Don't you have better things to do? Your poor soul needs to hurt and to be hurt! Your torturing will always be your urge to redeem yourself. Here is the razor's edge of your spirit's survival or destruction!

The Sub curled his lip at this particular impertinence. Yet perhaps the advice sank in, because one time he spoke to me in private, as if he not only wanted to reassure but to prove himself a sensitive fellow, a poet even.

Now, Drilov
Even with women
The thing is
To act without heed
for everything that's happened before…
You and I are the sons of kings
We are capable of delight
And we do it *here, today.*

And he masks an impenetrable stink behind that bluff incorruptible mien, as if it brought to mind a peculiar mode of Russian tragedy (served cold). My prisoners (not fools) joke openly of it. For the Sub is projecting: he forever needs to tell them that they deserve to be where they are - that they, egregious societal threats, should count themselves lucky to be alive. He is meanwhile as if doomed to appear patriotic - in some official photograph that might always be being taken, to be ever correct according to some flinty far-seeing manliness or strut-jawed reasonableness that marks a true Communist… 'Our government has heaped honours on me,' the Sub informs: 'Honorary Worker of the Cheka-GPU. Honorary Worker of the Cheka-GPU (1932). Order of the Red Star (1936). Order of the Badge of Honour (1937). Order of the red Banner, twice.' Having dutifully recorded the list (I assume he wanted me to) I sense he must be one of our Great Enforcers, such that these honours constitute a cock-eyed recognition of conscience: of his own and of the System's. This straight-as-a-die square-jawed incorruptible operator maybe wants to be a *record holder* - of medals pinned to his chest (albeit in hidden rooms, by officials possibly sent by none other than Comrade Stalin)…' But the truth, and

Drilov is hollowly embarrassed that he might turn out to be the recipient of favours of an assassin, is that the Sub might actually have begun to seek him out... as a confessor... or worse, a friend. It is becoming clearer that the enforcer-in-chief has chosen a terrible, lonely path - and one suspects that certain notions have drippingly coalesced from the cesspit of stunted sensibility to present him with a hoary dilemma: that his performance of all the Dirty Work is no longer reward enough... that it is all beginning to seem *routine*. He wonders if his work is making a difference to anything - politically that is - though he routinely drags himself out of incipient panic by avowing that he is 'not privy to the totality of information from high up'. Next, he begins to wonder if his 'superb butchery' (he is able to call it that!) will not dribble on forever... and he at last wonders if it'll all have to be *massively covered up* - politically that is. Surely he at last senses the obvious: that he is untouchably contaminated and that his own private muffled liquidation will deliver him as the last in his attenuated abattoir line of unpersons? Yet how can one become an unthing with medals pinned to one's chest? *Let not the eye see the wound it makes, nor heaven peep through the blanket of the dark to cry Hold!* Hence a lonely man will seek a friend, or at least a companion in arms – though no one of this ilk has remained here, not at Lubyanka. All have been assigned 'other duties'... though what these could possibly involve beyond his subterranean apotheosis of despatchment, the Sub is unable to imagine. 'No, (writes Drilov) ever since the Sub learned that I was put here as recorder of people's testimonies, and that he (though my superior) might associate with me (invoking a spirit he barely comprehends, a spirit he might somewhere have dreamed to know), he has formed in his soul the idea that he must demonstrate to me the Truth of himself. While this butcher-fundamentalist cannot simply succumb to some 'rogue dissident instinct', we know that every soul must try to justify his acts, whatever they may be, and this man might say: 'Though force of morality is dead, and only cold mathematic calculation can be depended on, one might in the end come to understand compassion as an act of no less significance than cruelty...'

And Drilov suddenly understands - that he is being groomed to participate in the most crucial work of all... that of the Sub-Commandant himself.

Cleansing the Soul   The unperson Lilya Popova has been shooting her mouth to Drilov, our unfortunate scribe.

- A little man called Drilov writes high on a toilet wall: 'By what means can this evil world exist? Only by means of the *pure* - yet how can the 'pure' become all of this?' What do you do in the toilets, Drilov? Masturbate? Does Drilov get satisfaction from anonymous graffitising?

- No, to all questions

- What is the scribe Drilov's position? He keeps his cards close! What's Popova's? I'll tell you how the current gang called Nazis manages to hypnotise people and terrorise so many Jews. (I'm not one, by the way) They organise a national club that all Germany's bullies-in-waiting get to join: get to don the uniform and form up the village team. Reassuring, to be bullies *en masse*. And when the Big Boys tell you to do it in the name of purity and order you've a legitimate cause, at last a reason to live. The little boys who deep down know they're frail and stupid and inadequate discover a way to go beyond themselves... And when Big Mouth Fuhrer fans and funnels your humiliation and your alienation and your simmering hate by offering up the old Jew-Goat, you've a recipe for the cleansing of your soul, for the ethnic cleansing of the collective soul, for the very pleasure of the *giving of death*. It has no reason, it's beyond reason: it's the *instinct* for death. And it's a kind of great love as well, a noble self-annihilation. The extraordinary thing is that humans believe in rule, reason, regulation, balance, punctilious legality, moral order - and yet are prepared to liquidate vast numbers of their fellows in order to fulfill it. Comrade Stalin, purveyor of the paranoiac vacuum (whose future karma of atonement will be to scrub the toilets at Party HQ with his tongue) feels compelled to efface anyone more popular, talented, heroic or sweetly human than himself - which is to say the vast majority of citizens. And this gangster who got hold of a country and gang-rapes it in the name of 'necessity' has the dark foresight to arrange it such that all his gang members are in terror of him. These goons now justify any atrocity just to prove loyal to their boss. This 'cult of personality' results in

the Terror we see now. Trouble is, Stalin has a habit of liquidating those who're most useful to him. The more useful you are, the more inexorably you sign your own death warrant! Such is the fate of every cadre who volunteers for or is assigned the dirty work. Are you *listening,* Drilov? Thanks for your service, now kindly die – by the hand of the new-minted assassin. The daisy chain, keeps us all honest. Keeps our conscience clear. Impeccable self-cleansing machine! 'Herein is the monstrous Minotaur's near-impenetrable Labyrinth, wherein slaying the beast is an endeavour of legendary difficulty...' Mathematically, all Russia's souls will end up in the sound-proofed basement of this *Lubyanka...* facing a blank wall and feeling the nuzzle of a muzzle in the nape of their neck
- I do not accept what you say
- You can't afford to! Keep scribbling, clerk.

Trivia of Bones   January tenth, 1939. Following yesterday's personal attack on me and on the system I yet defend, the artist Lilya Popova says this:
- Where's the story of the victims? In an instant, all who perish in your basement will see death for what it is: a sham, a mirage, a foolery, a cloak and dagger charade, great lie, stupid little hatchway, dirty rouge fountain, bogus blood-let. It does not matter whether we choose death or not, the result is always the same. For though man is a genius at weaving his labyrinth with the death chamber at its heart (and yes, this chamber is where we all must go, into which we all must be fed) perhaps the victims are the privileged ones! Maybe the executioners, as they follow suit will look up to them! But how to speak of the heroism of self-effacement? When will the eternal victim transcend torture? The body is our prison house, our conscience writ in flesh, and the great torture is, we know nothing ever matters yet *we have to be present,* have to know that it *all* matters. What this tiny sentient soul does is *all of life,* yet what it does here and now is nothing! What a soul carries forward is all that is, yet it is *ever* obliterated. I can just hear Stalin, muttering to no-one in particular while he peruses his lists: *Who will ever remember these people?* And yet, if the tentacles of our acts do not feed their way into the future, then there's no life, no continuity, no thread of this nowness as eternity. For all

the grit with which Stalin dreams his utopia, there is the commensurate quiet relief that it is all a barbarous joke-nothing. And that is why a man is irrational: he is life and death bundled into one. He is eternity and a ghostly trivia of bones, fickle breath of ghost-wind without time or place or circumstance, lonely frond struggling out of a desert dune. He is not even a ghost of himself, such is he annihilated... And yet nothing is ever lost, and he knows it, and that is why he is *careful*. It is why you and me and Stalin and Hitler will justify all our acts (be they ever so dark) with rules and legalities and balances and caveats and justifications and moralisms - for the future whispers at us that we *are* judged, that we are *our own* executioners and victims, and that we as brothers and sisters can never break the bonds that bind us all as one organism, one destiny. Yes, a human being needs reasons, since nothing but reason corrals his wild dirty will. Even Stalin needs it. For if a soul has reasons for what it does, be they ever so dark, then we are surely absolved by the infinite. Acts and words fall endlessly into silence, my friend, yet silence does not forget!'

The Mincing Machine   Lilya Popova is proving herself the exemplar of reactionary polemics, which I, Drilov, will not fail to record.
- If we can discipline enough people, the world's problems will be solved, and our personal problems too. Then we shall come to the promised land
- Kindly explain
- Drilov! Old corrupt individualism, always a recipe for venal selfishness blocking progress since the sunrise of time, is dead! Our brave collective world (forged in a state of chaos) now makes Order through Discipline, through which peace surely will come - but until that day there must be THE MINCING MACHINE! The contraption that disciplines without fear or favour! Cynics will argue that nature is pitiless, red in tooth and claw, and that processing humans into mince is merely the mirror of it. 'To die today or die tomorrow, what's the difference?' Such defeatism is put about by bourgeois traitors to the spirit of discipline! Which begs our first question: the priority of citizens to be minced. The OLD BOLSHIES were always ambiguous about discipline, so should be flattered to be at the vanguard of the New Order of Mince. Yet our machine won't function without a *continuous river* of mince, and that's why the single-minded

must quickly be singled out to select Mincees and perform the mincing. *Methods* must then be addressed. There's a prevailing view that if mincers show any interest in the pre-minced by way of interrogating them, they'll be displaying worrying signs of ambivalence (Mister Drilov?) since to talk to the pre-minced in getting them to confess to crimes denotes that one somehow 'shows respect by requiring the benefit of their information'. It might be justified that we need the pre-minced to babble in order to secure a greater pool of potential mincees. But cynics already object that there comes a point where it doesn't matter who's minced as long as the machine keeps mincing. To assuage the objection that 'if the choice is random then useful mincees will be sacrificed along with useless ones', some attempt should be made to distinguish the relative value or corruption of mincees, and that's where you come in, Drilov. (There is a caveat to this however, explained below). It is surely in the interest of all mincees, once society has established the legal principle of mincing, that the machine runs with nice neat schedules for the benefit of all. To whom shall fall the task of maintaining or fixing a vulnerable machine? It is a sad but incontrovertible fact that there is nothing more effective for ensuring its continued efficacy than that its operators must continue to fill mincing quotas under threat of becoming mincees themselves. And more sadly, there is no legal alternative to maintaining a superior and select group of Mincers-in-Chief who must delegate quotas to these sub-mincers. This superior group must assume the patina of permanence. We shall call it THE PARTY, otherwise known as THE STATE. Better still, we shall dub the group MINCERS IN CHIEF OF THE SUPREME SOVIET OF MINCERS. Meanwhile, we all know that even the permanent politburo of mincers is subject to metamorphosis, such is the selfishness and corruptibility of even senior mincers, who seem to either become big-headed about their work to an extent that they feel special and privileged and thus cannot be trusted anymore, or begin to display a nauseating kind of fawning (dare we say mincing) need to 'do the right thing for the boss', thereby ensuring their own survival. Do you not see the insidious and subtle nature of corruptibility! Self-serving behaviour is vulgar, disgusting. Therefore the supreme question arises: who in the end shall be Supreme and Incorruptible Mincer in Chief? Who shall arbitrate the souls of mincees great and small? No man or woman can elect this Being. He must be above all human foible, above election by corruptible men, must be a self-sustaining mincer In Perpetuity. Do we not see that all men are susceptible to venality in the soul? How to guard against such corruption? Stamp it out! Hence the centrality of the mincing machine. Citizens have a sad habit of comparing their fortune to others, along with the evil habit of cleaving to souls who share their interest. Not to mention the nauseating trait of wanting to preserve the status quo no matter how corrupt it is. Should a Pure State play favourites, allow the tyranny of personal interest? We need permanent revolution! We need the permanent Mincing Machine. Its cogs and cylinders and wheels and handles are the very spirit of revolution! I remind you it is proper to a communist state, where all property is in common, for the individual to be subsumed to the whole, which in turn must own and determine the fate of that individual. Otherwise what's the point of having a state? Individualism is tribalism, selfishness, self-interest. The Great Mincer properly reminds us of our duty to the state. Who meanwhile spares a thought for the Man of Steel who puts personal happiness aside to do the dirty work? Not to mention the personal sacrifice his lieutenants must make if their quotas aren't filled? For discipline cannot be, without *threat*. People will do anything to survive, and selfishness and favouritism and corruption will always want to undermine the Mincer in Chief. We thus return to our former caveat: our quotas must in the final analysis be arbitrary (meaning non-partisan) because consequent general uncertainty (not to say terror) will ensure equal discipline for *all*. If we are to establish the mince machine *in perpetuity*, all the pre-minced must contribute! What then, you may ask (beyond insidious bourgeois self-interest) are we doing it all for? Why, we do it to keep you safe from foreign and internal enemies! From capitalist devils who want nothing but to erase our effort to establish purity and discipline on earth! Collectivism, my friends, is the noblest Roman of them all: the death of selfism, death of greed, tribalism, partisanship; death of fake religionism, death of foolish hope, of narcissism and decadence and irreliable feeling - in short, the death of *everything*. Er, everything *bad* I mean. Everything bad.

The Primitive   Thus the artist Lilya Popova blooms in lush fields of absurdity! - where her beautiful weapon is elliptical self-irony.

- Your art was banned by the government. Is that correct?

- Yes, and I wrote a nasty letter to Stalin and Beria about it. I assume it's why I'm here. Although, why anyone would want to let me open my mouth then record what comes out, is beyond me. I'm massively untrustworthy!

- What did they find objectionable?

- That I'm a primitivist! Yet in this place, why the fuck would I not? Always begin, Drilov, with the assumption that a man or woman is not to be trusted for the reason that he or she is *primitive*. At most desperate, a human being will do anything to stay alive. To be rational implies choice. Right now I have no choices so I'm irrational. Which is a rational response to being in this shithole. At least I'm not a *saint* (I hear you have one in captivity here) who'll 'do no harm' no matter how desperate his situation. Even before he came here his 'goodness' allowed no choice. Well, these guys just pissed in his water pot. We needn't be bothered with that pie in the sky

- Isn't rationality based on moral choice? And if there's no immediate danger to my person, what's to be done?

- *Terror* is required at this point, Drilov! If I make the calculation to kill, it is because I've been convinced by others that it's in my better interest. What's that interest? To survive, obviously. Under these conditions 'killing to survive' is a rational act. But good god, if we allowed every Tom Dick Harry assassin to rationalise when he carries out our Dirty Work, we'll have anarchy! We can't let people think for *themselves*. Our wondrous state of extreme primitive terror is the best guarantee against rationalising! And since in that state nobody can be trusted, least of all myself, I am a primitivist. This, my friend, makes me honest.

Origin of Torture   Popova is on a rollercoaster ride of doom.

- I was in the City Cathedral only weeks ago. (Silly move, Drilov) And while there I meditated on the origin of torture! One should begin by imagining a great sky, borderless, clear without end, as if there be no such thing as sky at all. Clearer than sunlight on a summer sea, clearer than electric white clouds columned in the blue bowl of heaven, clearer than tundra reflected in mirrors of sky at the northern apex of the world. Clear sky... too beautiful. Now upon this sky let there be placed a kind of 'great window of the purest spiritual glass', so pure there are no blemishes that can be discerned by any eye or any instrument. It seems it is not there at all, yet it is there. It's the first *filter*. (Jesus to you) Imagine thereby another glass pane superimposed in front of the first, so clear that it is near impossible to discern any blemishes or darkenings or nebulous regions. And yet it is a second filter. Imagine then a third filter, of great clarity yet somehow in some 'mystic sense' not quite as clear as its predecessor, yet by all reasonable standards exceptionally clear and pure and transparent. And yet it is a third. Imagine now an endless series of filters, of panes, superimposed one on the other, each a minutely less clear and pure version of the previous... until there is a subtle but appreciable darkening, a muddying, a nebulosity, a clouding... yet even now we can see through them all. The presence of our *clarity* is a continuous factor, it seems! Imagine now a further endless series of filters, so many that there seems to be no difference between the new and its predecessor, yet en masse the filters begin to fulfill their promise... they constitute a darkening, a descent to deeper, denser, material worlds... The filters are ever present, hanging eternal amid the light

(Drilov has a moment of clarity) - Yet the one who sees through all panes is ever the one who *lives*

- Who's that then, clerk? Is it 'you or me'? Let us speak of Power. Wherefrom is this power? Nobody knows or ever will... but this subtle business of *doing* demands the collusion of things that are desperate to *be*, to be *somewhere*. They are roiling, they are demanding their being by a strange seething and wanting to dominate, as if osmosing continually into one another, as if the sky-emptiness bitterly wanted to shake off its voidness! And thereby struggling to assert its ghostly presence, that eternal void can never return to itself since it is caught in a vortex of *struggle*, and yes, struggle dons the mantle of that eternal but in a *cruel and limited way*, in the cruel way of ghosts in the light. And so, the relationship between particular and eternal has come, and it is irreconcilable *torture*. Now you understand: torture is *limitation*, torture is *materiality*. This world is all tension, all impossibility. Where is home for us, we men and women who try to list and name and tabulate everything in order to control it? We namers are desperate and restless! We are literally the tension of the world. We are all torturers, all victims. This is all torture, all exile. It is you. It is me.

Bestial and Divine   At this breathless point we must introduce the priest Mishkin, a man of hidden intellect, who in sizing up his position in this place, claims 'merely to offer humble flourishes, as if a candle or a match, enough at least for some brave or gullible soul to write them down...' And that soul is Drilov. Yet the wily Drilov has contrived to get another prisoner into the room with him. This is the chemist, Ugdanov.

(Mishkin) - At the bestial level animals kill for necessity, and morality has no influence. At his bestial level, man kills for a Cause and exults in it. Here is the level of the fundamentalist, the most primitive form of rationality. A morally rational man, however, entertains himself on several levels. First is the level where he rationalises that he must kill his brothers and sisters as a threat to his status quo or desired status quo, or where he kills them out of fear they'll kill him. He is a victim of the notion that there is a zero-sum finitude of resource. At this moral-rational level, measures are considered regrettable but necessary. Next is the stage at which the brothers and sisters make a pact to pursue their interests without murdering each other. Here in the Communist Soviet Union we certainly have not attained to this (capitalist) state! Next level is where brothers and sisters recognise their mutual oneness, their interdependence, acknowledging the truth that we're one body, one soul, whether we like it or not

(Ugdanov) - What nebulous religionism is this, Mishkin?

- One where we at last suffer to understand that all levels of life exist always, as if the self grows into a presence that is *forever there*, as if discovering a secret garden in the midst, like finally joining a club whose door seemed to be closed, or suddenly recognising the presence of sunlight in a clear sky... Material evolutionists (like you) must admit as much! Evolutionary theory as espoused by followers of Darwin never answers the issue of context. In what context does evolution take place at all? It is blindingly clear that the context is *eternally present*. We merely fulfill its myriad games in the blind course of time. We merge in light, and invent nothing!

Darwin wisely never lost sight of the divine immanence. Only materialist terrorists who seized on his theory as a weapon against religion did that (Ugdanov) - Do you accuse me?

- Ah, the faithful Communist has heard my words, and he doesn't like them.

The Undead   Mishkin will not be stopped, but Ugdanov the Chemist, who takes things earnestly, seems keen to contradict.

- Where is your wife, Ugdanov?
- I do not have to tell you, priest
- Is she liquidated?
- I will not reply to you
- No? It might be claimed that we are 'dead men and women walking', since we are born into this world. Is our birth not justification enough for liquidation? It's only a matter of time
- You talk as if we are all islands, that we have no dependents or loved ones
- The same applies to loved ones. We're all born to die; it does not matter when
- Your drift is cynical
- No Ugdanov, *a realistic person must have a justification for everything.* I am sorry for you, but listen to my argument. Do you understand it is not meaningful to say 'she is dead', since the conditions from which and of which one speaks, are both positive and enduring? *She is dead* is an oxymoron from two points of view. First, the phrase merely affirms one who's present enough to be referred to as *is dead* - and certainly cannot, unless we are reincarnationists or resurrectionists, be referred to as *was dead;* and secondly, the one who posits the fact of this death exists irrevocably in the plane of the living, and therefore cannot be relied on to make any verifiable statement about the status of one who is alleged to have departed the all-pervading state, proof of which is the following: that anyone who would opine that there is a state beyond that of living is indulging the undeniable faculties of the living, and cannot be relieved of them even in his imagination (which of course is yet another faculty of this state)... from which as far as any casual observer can tell, there is no escape except to shakily opine that since a person is out of sight or of

mind, he or she is an 'unperson' or a 'dead person'. That oxymoron again! Who can posit *any* idea except in the positive sense? To do otherwise would be to indulge in what is called 'castles in the air' wherein one might be accused of insanity (which, come to think of it, is possibly a way to deal with unpersons) and of imagining things that cannot possibly be seen or proved. The only other option is to refer to the dead, somewhat weirdly, as the 'undead' which conjures visions of semi-human zombies bent on revisitation and revenge. In fact, one can believe in those things rather more firmly, for the subtle murmurings of memory and the sere whisperings of *conscience* dictate that revisitation and revenge must occur! And further, in a world where the orderly justification of even the most bestial atrocity is crucial to the human sense of self, the *results* of the acts one chooses must certainly attend them, and thus is born the naïve and native notion of karma, or *cause and effect,* which hitherto a mere airy tale to the unbelieving, turns out to be more solidly substantial than the alternative belief that when one has liquidated another, and that this other remains liquidated in the sense that he will offer no further cause for worry or loss of sleep or fitful dream or lurid nightmare of conscience that ushers itself into your mental fortress like some winter wind from unimagined steppes of solitude, into the clinical corridors you walk in all your busyness from one secluded torture sanctuary to another... and the sanity of the material world, the solid sanity of it, hitherto thought indisruptable and unshakeably final in its dispensing of death to the living - is assailed by the alternative: that the Material is mere putty in the hands of the Immaterial, and that the notions whereby a person lives, whereby all killers live, are in fact no more robust than the phantoms that haunt their ghostly minds, poltergeists that destabilise the thoughts of even the staunchest of men, the most redoubtable of murderers and bloody dispatchers. By the same token, victims should rest assured that their assassins have no place to hide in an immutably material universe, by which we mean a universe wherein all spiritual longing is recycled as incontrovertible *matter,* and wherein all falsehood is recycled as the rectification of itself (notwithstanding the creation of yet more falsehood) whereby these outcomes serve only to confirm the *hell* we are all living in, since no-one and nothing may escape the retribution that is coming, and no act, trivial or great, may contrive to escape its consequence! So, the blessed blindness of man, who blinds himself to the real fact, douses himself with hope that he, he, may be the first of all creatures in the history of this turning world to be inured against the consequences of his acts. And so the victim, somewhere in the great court of eternity as time, will turn perpetrator, or at least 'witness for the prosecution' as he revisits the crime done to him (in the name of order and rule and patriotism and loyalty and political science) perhaps long ago, and always by one who no longer feels responsible for his act since he is by now assuredly the victim of some crime similar to the one he enacted on the other... So that all perpetrators are victims and all victims perpetrators, and in the melange of time, which is nothing but wind and waterfalls of skeletal ghost-flickerings in bright solar light, amazingly we learn we are all cut of the same cloth, chipped of the same stone, and our only way home is to live *all possible roles* - in the minuteness of their trivia, in the nowness of their utter importance and their utter goneness... and we have no choice, except to do this, except to do this. This. This.

Drilov takes great care to record this particular speech, and to file it in the recesses of his apartment.

All is Material   Where there's indignation there's truth, and today we are well entertained. Ugdanov the Chemist cannot accept 'the immaterial as the basis of the material'. A decent argument is in progress.
(Ugdanov) - There will *always* be bodies! There is no part of creation that can ever disappear! The sum total of energy can never diminish!
(Mishkin) - What then, by your reasoning, is the difference between life and death? And therefore what is the loss of a million corpses where their souls are indisruptable?
- Sardonic! Your consciousness is not in control! Whether before death or after death, the vast bulk of our faculties are undetected. The heart feels, mind thinks, senses sense. The utter majority of our functions are unknown and unseen by the doer of them. Idiot! There is no escape
- Yes, but as you said: even if this material seems 'immaterial' to us, we must treat it with utmost seriousness. This material stuff is eternal putty in our hands. Eternal putty. *And this lightness of being* is utter and

pervading. Yet it is not unbearable. Why? Because this solid pain-world is as a mirage, is nothing but *the soul of inconsequence*. Let me list the ways! This planet is like an immense sky-chamber where we float weightless like astronauts. Think of all the things we do to maintain our sense of self, all things we must do to cling to pain and need and want and self-reproach and importance and validity and pettifogging ego. I tell you: try to take a slice or a wedge of your mind, or take a chunk of your feelings, or take your heart and stuff it in a box, or plant the flag of your country in its flesh! Ugdanov, box up the light and call it a name, corral all the world's noise and study its frequency, take your heartbeat and stopper it up, take your pulse and bottle it, grab the sights of your eyes and paint them on a page or plant them in a crop-field of air. Take that air and discribulate it, take a thought and pulverise it, take a feeling and ring-fence it, dissect it like a rat with a forcep, pluck its substance out! Descry the lightness of being, fathom and tame the anatomy of light, clobber and lasso and bung in a tin the silence of the moon, grasp and bundle up all your senses, shove your nose in a field of thought, hanker inside a bullish dream like a rowdy cowboy. Stick your sense under microscopes, ponder all its parts; pin a wish on a public board, drag a dream like a liar into the light, shout down and denounce the fleeting ghost of longing, put on a death-list the love of man for woman, put a bullet in the brain of shared bliss, cut off the balls of the memory of beauty, roast in an oven all sense of right, turn into ash the lingering of tenderness, bury in a mud-field an eternity of desire. And what have you done? *Why are materialists such fools?*
(Drilov) - Don't blame him. He lost his beloved
- His wife is not lost, Drilov. She is not lost!

Inexplicable Absurdity of Evil Drilov has engineered Popova's presence, and she'll disabuse the law-loving Ugdanov.
- Mister Scientist, our precious State's social fictions are established out of *madness*
- No, Miss Popova. Our political decisions and the government's justifications of them may be criticised as leading to certain problems, but they are necessary for both group harmony and individual security
- Bullshit! Madness is the result of people being allowed to be the sole

arbiters of their acts. (And that's coming from me, an anarchist.) The despot has no authority to whom he answers but 'himself, his perverted moral context'. Despotism demands a kind of perverted moral genius - which is also its fundamental fallibility. Madness is 'pretence to absolute power'

- And that's *why* we need social rules. Power is more than any one person can bear

- This Soviet state is the exemplar of hypocrisy, ambiguity, moral confusion! Any idealist is forced to align himself with either a hypocritical, malicious government, or with openly malevolent rule-defying dissenters like me. It's clear that to try to judge between these two is ridiculous. And the notion of choice between 'a lesser of two evils' is also bullshit. In this society extreme evil is no longer remarkable. Banality is the new atrocity! How can your 'moral standards' or 'social values' be relevant in judging evil in a world that's already gone insane? Look at the number of ridiculous arrests we witness. They reflect the larger absurdity, which encompasses 'insignificant mundanity and life-and-death issues' in one bundle. What the hell are nobodies like us doing here? Moral confusion and hypocrisy, doctor! Terrifying: homicidal megalomania and a *tap leaking on my poor head* are treated as equal

- Madame Artist does not appreciate the artistry of water torture? (Drilov) - Steady, Ugdanov

- So Popova, why are they torturing you thus? Is it perhaps because you are such an *idealist* that you have no respect for the wonderful Creations of God? Yes, I also am capable of irony! I, for one, have never questioned the onward march of material progress in the hands of enlightened men of reason. Why do you laugh in the face of dialectical materialism? I don't blame the authorities for seeking to disabuse you of such foolery

- No doubt this is why *you're* here in this shithole, Ugdanov? Part of your reward eh? No doubt the accommodation is to your requirements, enlightened material man? Spartan, not to say downright grotty. No nagging little wish to run away?

- I shall never seek 'escape'. I stand up wherever I am. For this is *all* there is

- Very good. Here's a little sample of 'all there is'! Ever hear of the *Liar Paradox*? A man is sentenced to death but the sentence is false. Let us assume that all sentences imposed by this government are false. On what basis? The bastards simply make use of the Liar Paradox. Take the following sentence: *'This sentence is false'*. Is the sentence making a true assertion or is it truly false? One implication of the sentence is to assert that *anything* can be true. Conversely we can assert that anything can be false. Or that a thing can be *both* true and false, or that it is *neither* true nor false and therefore it doesn't matter...

- You are obviously lying now

- Oh? And even if a man were to *admit* he is lying... is what he is saying true? Or false?

* * * *

We see that Drilov's 'subjects' have lately become used to conferring like a little 'community of the damned'. That is a dangerous oxymoron! In exceeding the bounds of his brief, Drilov's justifications are pathetically dogged: 'These prisoners will always seek some crack in the walls they can slither through, but still... how can we seriously think that 'normal human life' should be suspended just because one is a few steps from one's last breath? Besides, this floor is chronically short-staffed, and there really are occasions where prisoners may profitably be herded into the same room. Conversation is recorded by a punctilious official, in this case myself. And why should communal talk not be revealing? It is an opportunity for the authorities to understand how 'intellectuals' have misunderstood the ideals of our System. While their talk ranges from the trivial to the poetic, their copious dreams of escape are surely of interest. Not necessarily bodily escape from physical walls, but an escape of the *soul...* revealing, and incriminating, considering the circumstances of guilt and shame these people find themselves in... Lilya Popova is emerging as an exemplary study in anarchistic spite. It is no surprise Ugdanov the Chemist baits her. (Is he attracted to her?) No doubt the Chemist seeks to embody the voice of conscience?

(Popova) - You, Drilov, who think you're some kind of chronicler of a past and creator of a future: the past never was real, and 'future' certainly will never be. You are a phantom scribbler who creates nothing, a voyeur of no precise substance. You cling to memory 'as if it were real'. Between hopeless past and hopeless future you are the bumcrack, the impossible voyeur, cusp of nothing, painful thin vessel who thought himself pregnant with import and history and meaning, and like the fretful wind that swirls about the entrance to the tunnel to the past, you are the watcher and keeper, the fool-guardian of your non-self. You are just the image in the mirror, you are the rush to catch up with what flew away, you are the dot that realises the Party is elsewhere and no-one offered *you* a ride. You are a thing solitude breathed, you are the man wherein all memories are borrowed or hired or kept like presents you know you'll never unwrap. You are embarrassed to live. You're a hole, a pool, a swirl, a trap. You are like some place whose features made your mind take their own shape, that stole your mind from you - as if that table and chair really were there in your eye and mind, *defining* you as if they really had a shape or presence or meaning. God forbid. But these forms are all born out of sheer self-weight, sheer repetition, and you had no choice but to think them! Your thoughts are heavy dull objects, insidious and bulky killers of emptiness. There is no escape for you. There are objects on this table: paper, pen, glasses, a *confession*. Not mine but yours! In some arcane collusion of purpose these objects beckon at *you*. Ah! Yesterday's thoughts, yesterday's food: all *shit today*. These things I say to you are words, they signal narrative and continuity. I make them up myself... but that is not the POINT. There's an *object* on the table: we will not call it a confession. I've found a new use for it. Blew my nose with it, wiped my arse with it, soaked up the ink of a stupid epistle with it, filled a crack in the wall where the rain gets in, stopped my mind from wandering! All right! Call it a confession. Confession of *deconstruction*. Confession of *un-structuralism*. Oxyfuckingmoron. Any more labels? Expensive toilet paper infested by words. Spread a little shit about, Drilov, make somebody's day.

(Your writer suffers to be the scapegoat of Popova's wrath)

- But you, Lilya Popova, wrote all of this

- STOP WAITING. Stop waiting, Drilov! Are you waiting for me to explain? Stop waiting for love, for death, improvement, life, happiness, success, identity, substantial thing, hope, past, future, meaning, significance, revenge, chance to be victim, better weather, time to go, things to return, nice feeling, right thought, true sense, calm, order, ducks in a line, fruition, wisdom, your wife, husband, child, parents to die, sunrise, sunset, education, a fish, clear air, proper moment, the markets, coffee to boil, inspiration, discovery, to be noticed, hunger to come, weighty things, hand of the clock, fresh release, next heartbeat, breath, cool, quiet, emptiness, peace, blueness, god, for a time you can stop waiting, for the end of this speech, for a thing to happen, for the bomb to fall, for christmas, for your wedding, for sleep, for time, for life itself. Just stop waiting. STOP WAITING! I'm sorry. I just can't participate any more. Just can't participate any more...

(Ugdanov) - Take a glass of water

- ...Me with all my vain longing to create, spending hours and years and decades cooking up a dish called *art*. When will Popova ever give up the habit of creating Shit for humanity? Only when we murder her *arse*. Popova wants to validate and empower the human race. Yuuuurgh! Fuck the human race! Watch these ignorant fuckers gobble up my art then spit it out when they're told! Do I look like a blind automatic creation machine? I deconstruct the fucking world. Ooooh socialism, *please* take me seriously. Plenty of naughty thoughts to be had from me, eh Drilov? The State wants to dissect 'em. Scared to fucking death of my irrational wit. But that's entertainment, folks!

- Drilov and I are listening to you now. Because you're an 'artist'

- *I'm sorry. I just can't participate any more. Can't participate any more...* Soon I'll deposit my corpse, down by the sewer side... *Gonna put on my travelling shoes, down by the sewer side. Gonna put on my dancing shoes, down by the sew-er side!*

- I am not sure that singing is acceptable in this building.

The Indivisible Individual   (The suicidal Popova won't be stoppered)

- You're unreal, Ugdanov. How can you be passive, how can you accept the junk you're fed? Only hypocrites say we should aspire to be good *servants* of this system. Servants to other bastards? If we all serve others' aspirations, who're the ones to be served? Don't we want to kill off class, 'us and them'? Why serve others perceived to be more important than you? Fuck them! And how can you serve a System? How can you show subservience to an Abstraction, especially when it gives you nothing back? There's a shitting good reason why we're individuals, if any reason is needed. It is because we individuals are *of the nature of reality* - as opposed to unreality, as opposed to what makes us *die*. 'Service' never satisfied the person, because *we* are the ultimate destiny. What's 'individual? It means *can't be divided*. THINGS HAPPEN TO US! Sure, veils without number get dragged over our reality, (otherwise why would we have all these levels of ignorance or this fucked up social experiment we're enduring now?) yet we're always conscious of *being ourselves*. We're the ones who have to lead, make decisions, take care of our destiny. And the destiny of a soul, despite all your sophisms that say it isn't individual, shall come to its own *indivisible expression*. So make your choice, poor fool: victim or perpetrator?

Darkest Light   Drilov has noticed there is a particular room on his floor where the light is never turned off. He once glanced in through its tiny window. He has no idea who the interrogator is, only that it is a woman, and that she wears impenetrably dark glasses. Once Drilov lingered by the door and heard these words: 'It would seem that though the light in here is strong, it fails to do its proper work! If you were not so stubbornly blind, so self-preserving, I would surely bring you enlightenment!' The dark-eyed questioner in the room, the seeker of truth, seemed to writhe in her privations of frustration. Unable to perform her duty! All for the sake of a little honesty! Drilov thought: should we not pity rather than fear her... she who must wear the darkest of glasses?

Thinning of the Soul   Our lowly clerk feels his earthly foundation to be crumbling, and he descends to a dream... On a moonlit winter's night a man is rushing through countryside at the reins of a Troika. The driver urges three stamping horses on yet jerks his head back and back, obsessed by bulky shapes under the seat. He foot-shoves them to an edge and one by one they roll off like oil drums into the sea. Lumps on a mirror of ice, we understand they are human beings. Our driver is alone, and the ice-road turns to deeper shades of apish blue-white as if its blood, its texture were thinning, like old men's teeth. The beasts' hooves clip and clatter on it like sticks, and it is clear the only way on is for the carriage to lighten,

lighten. The driver tears at his balaclava, kicks off his boots, heaves his greatcoat from his back. It sloughs off in the whiteness, a ghost tramp by a roadside. The chill is deeper, the wind harder, the horses seem to surge crazily, their heads flaying in three directions as their knees rise and clutch at stiff air. Moonbeams bristle on snow mounds as the thud of hooves and slithering of the sled turn hollower, brittler. The rider sees a shape under his troika as if rising to meet him. He realises it is his shadow, his size but far lighter. It seems to frolic and mock, and man and shadow slide on down a moonlit river, for a river it is, an impossibly thin ice sheen. The orb slithers between clouds as the rider hogs his way in darkness and rumps of white beasts clumber in front. He knows his end is near. Suddenly there's a clank and a crash and he finds himself spreadeagled in snow. For a moment he feels a delicious warmness then his mind is no more. He wakes… Nearby is a house. Mean and low it seems to be. He shuffles toward it, presses at a gnarly door. A long room opens to his eyes. Seated at a rough table are three men in peasant winter garb, all with moustaches and penetrating baleful eyes. Heavy beams distend over their heads toward a glowing fire at the back. Come in, Drilov, says the man at the centre. We have been waiting. Let me introduce myself. I am The Judge. This man is The Jury and this man The Executioner. You see we are three in one. And where are your horses? Did you fail to *negotiate the thin ice?* The man Drilov is moved to explain but his throat is dry. He is guilty! Do you not see, says the Judge, how your soul must turn more and more transparent? (For you are Russian) In the Long Freeze we learn what we must be, and in the Thaw we are confused and have no discipline. For this reason our Troika* demands the Great Freeze ever remain. This is why you are here. We ensure it, we ensure it.

[* Troika = panels of judges appointed by the NKVD, Secret Police]

Next morning from his bed, Drilov witnesses furrows of grey slush in the morning streets. They crush him back under musty covers.

* * * *

No Individual   Even in his hidden journal, Drilov has begun to write in the distancing third person... 'Who will not have noticed that the operative Drilov, sensing that his work (to interrogate 'privileged' prisoners at length) has crystallised into a glaring *anomaly* far beyond the norms of this *torture house*, and that he had breathtakingly fooled himself it was anything but (despite the bland assurances of his sub-commandant), now contrives to write in third person, as if he has become self-conscious beyond the endurance of it... Serendipitously Drilov notices his handwriting is getting worse by the day. Is it the cold in those rooms? Is it because he no longer wants to read what he has written? Drilov never types during confessions; the chattering sound of a typewriter when subjects are pouring out their words would seem clinical, uncouth... Yet such interviews conducted by the writer Drilov, as sanctioned by ranking personages inside his own department, might (from the start) have been conceived not just as a subtle or advanced means of torture, but to legitimise the enforcers against accusations that theirs is nothing but the arbitrary justice of beasts... though if a beast sets up a question as to whether he is or is not a beast, then tries to answer his creeping bad conscience with displays of sagacity and enlightenment, we shall have to wonder if bestiality by its mere mention has not become a self-fulfilling unalterable *fact*. Not so, say diehards in the establishment (remember, Lubyanka is nothing but a microcosm of the regime) since those given a chance to speak whose death is inevitable are bound to inflate themselves, to seek opportunities to be elevated above the common, to buy themselves a climacteric beyond that of other ignominious mortals who pass through, to make of themselves seers and pundits and poets and sages and searing critics. They may well, in a unique testament that quickens the mind, speak brave or penetrating thoughts, since they are offered through confession a kind of *freedom*. Let them be immortalised! That is, if we choose to retain the records... and we may well do so since we as a regime (Drilov includes himself in this) possess a conscience... and even if we kill *en masse* we are resolute enough not to fear justifying our acts to the future; in fact we gain moral strength by revealing our human doubts. Yes, we search our consciences: we feel pain and we suffer. We are not beasts! This is why we let such records be taken, and by one such as Drilov, who innocent as he is now, will lose all his innocence as he listens! He will inevitably absorb the dictations of his interviewees - so convincing and subtle and persuasive (and carefully chosen) are they. And since they are in no way immune to pride, distortion, hatred and cynicism they simply reveal themselves as idealists, mystics, feelers of petty things, as self-absorbed and proud and maudlin and egoistic and decadent *individualists*. Pity Drilov then, and others like him, for being exposed to such a dilemma...

Where does his duty lie then? ...Or rather: how might he lie to do his duty? (Drilov says) There is a reason Drilov has taken to talking of himself in the Abstract. He has seen the way the Self is layered: that it is an artificial construct, and must be so in a world where one must self-lie continually just to exist... And is there *community* in this death-filled world? One can't but try to create it! The sub-commandant himself hinted as much to Drilov. For the Sub is a lonely man who drinks, and if he lives to read this record he'll learn what is said of him by others. He may even be permitted to destroy it before he himself is destroyed. And herein is the immaculate order of things, that every man is made to clean his room before he leaves it at the last (though victims are spared the ignominy of digging their own graves before they are shot). But do not think, clever people, that because your Drilov is a day worker, carefully ushered from the building before nightfall to his home, that because the guards at the gates of the Ministry of Truth neglect to check the incriminating confessionals in his briefcase - that he cannot ever know what *must* go on in the lower rooms and courtyards *after* dark has fallen!

And so, it is not long before the sub-commandant makes a final change to Drilov's employment arrangements... the imposition of *night work*.

The Sub, by the by, seems increasingly weary and hollow-eyed, and Drilov knows the drink is unseating him. Drilov is moved to imagine how the Sub's access to it is facilitated by unseen powers... oiling the plebeian tragedy, the pathos of his denouement and downfall. Our Sub with all his medals has done his duty beyond that of many - yet is it not the one lesson that Drilov has imbibed these last weeks: that the more one is feted, the more he is being fattened for un-personhood? That the more illumined the person becomes, the more favours are heaped, the more clearly he is about to be offered the Supreme Gift - even as he is despised and feared? No one is above Law... and is not Law the transcendence of death, such that whether murdered or dying at peace in our beds, we all shall have justice? Even the Regime shall not judge the state of a person's soul! (Its leaders are pragmatists at the last) And so our Sub prepares to hand his deep work to others: he has long been preparing, since the day he became Master of Special Duties. And Drilov is moved to predict it is for the reason that he saw his own mortality that he resolved to 'protect' the clerk - in a position the Sub at first despised and feared, and that he at last encouraged Drilov to seek something in the brief company of condemned prisoners - souls like him - that at last seemed superior to the butchering of them. And most important, that the Sub offered Drilov a perennial truth: that even murderers have a heart and a conscience... Or perhaps Drilov, in all his sentiment and youth has overstated the case again! Perhaps Drilov's judgement of the Sub (as set down in his journal) is final confirmation of why people like Drilov should never be allowed to flourish in this world (beyond confession of their shortcomings). The confessor always self-incriminates! because he can *never* be other than what he is: born a criminal, born a sentimentalist, a feeler of things, idealist, lover of the world, individualist, *person*. He's condemned the moment he is born; his life is nothing but inevitable confirmation of his death. And the sub-commandant, the professional killer, merely fulfils his promise, receives his unction, goes to his fate as a man who couldn't have done other than what he did: a product of the world's inexorability, of its arbitrary totality, of a system that in grim recognition celebrates by 'heroically carrying on, suffering all and bearing all, holding its nerve in the face of the sombre adversity of self-immolation' - of assassinating its loyal members, its loyal workers, its own loyal Body. Let all Subs go to their maker, let all underlings follow! Let this great and grim *auto da fe*, this great cleansing continue... till the bitter end, be it hell or paradise.

Ah, Drilov is a *poet* now. Or a drivelling sentimentalist, or aesthete with nerves of jelly... heckler, rebel, condemned.

Finally, on the last day of February 1939 there came into his room a man Drilov had not physically met, though he'd had a vague sense of his presence, somehow, here and there. The elusive thought crystallised in the clerk's mind at last, like the snake that finally reverted to the rope: it was the Commandant.

- Hello, Comrade Drilov. I have been informed by Sub-Commandant Blokhin that your work has produced results... notwithstanding that you've so far been somewhat private and guarded with them. Do you have a question?
- Yes. Why me?
- Drilov, you are no hero. Because you are *no individual.* You joined the party (though not an original Bolshevik) and have by so doing been asked to take responsibility for your acts. Your stay as an operative here is not exactly a textbook model (since a little on the poetic side) of the inevitable trajectory of a person who subverts the machine. No, you believe (wrongly) in the logic that all party members with any kind of conscience or scruple, or association with those who hold to conscience or scruple, must be eliminated. In this case, your pathway was delicately managed by your unseen Commandant. You may thank me, and may see it as a kind of award. But you suspected that: and should have taken responsibility for it! Your job has been in some little way to portray our system as prizing conscience - though lowly operatives sometimes do not see it. Still, things must continue to be done in proper order. You are now required to participate, with Comrade Blokhin, in the despatchment of those with whom you've been intimate. I do not apologise, comrade Drilov! Did you not see that we wanted to teach you *detachment* - that emotional attachment leads back to the embrace of individualism? It is a form of cruelty to let you walk it! Thus have I seemed a little cruel in indulging your hope, but I do it to save you from a greater cruelty - that of delusion. We will make of you a good Communist! - in a world where that is quite rare, we admit... but it is a work in progress
- How so? Society is all, the machine is all. Its operatives are as nothing. No doubt then, the *machine* is as nothing

- Your party has taken unusual care with you! Though I am not at liberty to speculate on your future
- I took responsibility
- Certainly. You prove a certain outcome where 'people are left to make their own decisions'
- Is death nothing to you?
- Quite possibly nothing. Your spiritualist Mishkin might agree
- And where do you stand on individual responsibility?
- I leave that to you to decide!
- Then I decide you are possibly a fucking bastard cunt
- Then you lose, comrade Drilov
- Well, *there's* the failure of your system. Right there.'

The Lovers   It should come as no surprise that the interview with the Commandant signals a watershed. Drilov now rushes to document, in detail, his new duties within the cancerous heart of the labyrinth, the *basement* of the Lubyanka.

'...Sub-commandant Blokhin has exited for a toilet break. Drilov's companion guard steps outside the door for a cigarette. His nerves are betraying him; he is obviously green. Drilov is left alone in the chamber with two prisoners, a boy and a girl. The documents say they are from Minsk. Drilov sees: the boy and girl are deeply focused on each other. Despite their hands being shackled behind, they nudge close. His eyes are shining, and she bows with concentration as he whispers to her. Her eyes wander at the last but he pulls them back with his words... and her knees buckle a little yet her hero stiffens them. These two obviously dreamed freedom, somewhere in their bedroom solitude, before the cold justice of the state bludgeoned in on them. To dream and to love: are these not the deepest of crimes? Is love not anarchy of the most insidious kind? The state has a right to be angry! These lovers were always out of line, that is why they are here. There is nothing else to do with them; their bodies clutter up the state. But these kids never participated in any state. It certainly is irrelevant now. They tread on clouds, private ones; their feelings pulsate between them in the most shocking way. Drilov turns away out of respect (he dare not call it reverence), and meanwhile their words, whispered as a compact where each is a diamond and none matter at all (they never matter because people never change) are beyond anyone's power to manage or poke at. The couple take their tiny moment, and the intimacy of it ushers them out of reach. Now for we killers the murder is reduced to an impersonal thing: to be got over, an onerous duty. And Drilov will not record their whispers, or describe the young man's eyes nor her glistening ones, nor her quivering faith in him nor his tender smile, nor she standing to him and bracing herself up, nor his protective touching of his lips to her hair, nor she nudging at his cheek like ponies do in a summer field. But Drilov recalls it all in his mind, as surely as sunshine, somewhere, in a summer field.

Blokhin re-enters, re-asserts his presence like a dirty fart in the room, slips on his long leather gloves, adjusts his butcher's apron, sizes up the pair, glares at Drilov, barks at the young guard - who hands him his weapon. But the boy and girl need no prompting. Ah, they'll not do this shithead the honour of resisting, thinks Drilov. And wonder of wonders, the lovers *succeed*. Their final moment is but a dance, a celebration, a bouquet, a doorway…

Ladies first, says Blokhin. He shoves the muzzle under the girl's nape and fires. Her brains fountain against the wall. She drops where she stands like cut corn. Fuck. All about angle, Blokhin mutters. Sorry fellers, more work for ya. Now he pushes the muzzle under the young man's neck, this time letting it turn slightly. Drilov notes the professional adjustment. At the shot the man spins and crashes ignominiously to the floor. Fuck again. Blood or weight, can't have both, says Blokhin. Apologies, gentlemen. Now do yer business. Shove the bodies through the hatch, hose the room, report to me. Blokhin removes his gloves with a light flourish, stows his pistol in his belt, exits with the ghost of a smile.

Drilov has been made to feel like a novice.

Following description of an execution, one has no desire to describe another. Yet our thoughts invariably drift to the lonely victims… to their past, where they came from, their private world, their ghastly presence as exemplar of us all. There was a blonde-haired girl who was ushered in with hands shackled, and Drilov and his fellow novice-guard looked at each other. Oh, they're really giving us the *cream*. She seemed as if she had been startled while on the toilet or something, and had been brought straight here in the middle of the night. Probably she had. She was clearly experiencing a profound crisis of confusion, yet Drilov realised he was quick to feel a certain impatient annoyance. Did she not know how the routine worked here? Why cling to delusions? Why rock the boat? And yet, because she's pretty... *oh, I'm glad it isn't me who has to shoot you...* And Drilov's mind starts to grind... THE SYSTEM. Our great conformity to it is the biggest mystery of all. Why do we humans take this farce called life so seriously? Why are we so invested in such orderliness and properness that we go like lambs to the slaughter... even perform the slaughter like lambs? Why do we believe in *system*? Because it expresses the orderly balance of being? Yes, and by obvious experience this being is forever. *Inconceivable to imagine not being.* Our fright is at possible injury to our immortality! But immortality can't be injured. Death is impossibility, anachronism, parody, grotesque, dirty trick, fake thought, filthy game... *embarrassment*. Embarrassment... at upsetting the life, at wrongness, at the foolery of the perpetrator, at a wriggly body who feels fright, bowels that loosen, nerves that frightfully fray... We know we can't ever be anything but what we *are*... living, living, living. We are shocked not at the thought of death but at the affront to our being - because death is *inconceivable*.

Our heart goes out to the blonde girl in her lonely fright. Blokhin the professional, seeing that she is a little beauty, allows his face to assume the veneer of quasi-incorruptible regret. He less than curtly asks her to face the wall. Appearances appear to matter. She looks balefully at him, her round eyes not registering facts. But then she sees his long leather gloves and his bulgy apron like that of some high-street *charcutier*, sees the solemn-heavy assistants standing a few feet off... and her eyes begin to brim with tears of unfolding dread, and Drilov sees the boat of her soul toss like a matchstick in a wondering sea, foundering and gurgling under crushing stormclouds. This, in an instant... and what is time but an inkblot on eternity… and then she starts to babble, to talk, as if to explain herself, to *explain*. How to explain your existence, your presence, your fathomless wholeness… in a moment, in a moment of crisis-truth, to a stranger, a stranger in a room you've never seen, where you've never been, where you suddenly don't know what you are… in the sense of your story, your body, your loved and lovely hair… need for toilet, dry mouth, drunken wakeness at three in the morning, need to tell mother and brother and boyfriend and sister and daddy… and your job and your life and your bed and your dolly and your perfume and your pleasure and your future and your - …Blokhin asks her once more. And she turns to the wall. Sniffles a little. He steps up, keen to turn her into forgotten history. This time the weapon was respectfully hidden… now he pulls it out. Pause. A dot-point in eternity. He guns her down in the usual manner. She drops like a cut mist, lies curlicued on the slab floor. Drilov watches the blonde hair turn to red rivulets. He imagines she would have been a soft and lonely lover. He thinks he will never get to write her story.

Drilov needs to check his watch. He does it frequently. 3.13 am. Death of 3.13, February 26, 1939. And they do the business. Forget burial rites. Drilov suddenly vomits, out of nowhere. They have to clean that up as well. Drilov is certain there'll be revenge. Somewhere in the flung future, in this cesspit of eternity, there'll be revenge… revenge… On what though? We are life, we are undeniable. Can't seek revenge on ourselves… but we will, we will! …because revenge is all we have.'

* * * *

'Drilov has a recurring dream. He is witnessing a vaudeville show with endless acts and actors all busily entering and leaving the stage. The auditorium is dark and featureless. Who is watching? By degrees the show descends to farce, to slapstick, to the crudest Punch and Judy where great mustachioed Punch wields his mighty club. But little Judy seems to bob up again and again. The clubbing gets harder and fiercer, and Judy somehow turns more defiant. A great bell starts to ring. There is a clamour of voices. The theatre doors suddenly flood open and great rivers of slime slither down the aisles. There is a general gasp of disgust followed by pandemonium. There is no escape. The doors clang shut. Bodies pile up. On the stage, Great Punch goes on thumping. Judy screams yet bobs up for more. Drilov wakes in a fog of sweat. His heart is thudding in his chest; his temples are throbbing. He fumbles for the lamp. It is 3.13 am.'

Drilov scribbles: 'No matter how 'legal' a thing is, any child can distinguish between right and wrong! But legality not founded on morality: ah, there's the brilliant pinnacle of criminality. Drilov, in being assigned to *night work,* that is, work that by any layperson's standard of decency may not be carried out in daylight, is soon apprised that the work in question is part of a machine so oiled it takes the breath away. Drilov suddenly feels embarrassed by his daytime confession-taking! He now sees the extent to which he has been degraded: the extent to which he dreamed of being useful has made him a fool. And if he is moved to wonder why a booky clerk was ever asked to do dirty work like this, it is simply to create guilt by association, so that he can be charged and punished with oiled impunity...'

The Heart   Drilov suddenly resolves to speak of himself once more in the intimate first person.

'...And in these lower rooms there is often a silence that closes on me like a reality-vice, thick and inexorable like space between the stars, and I can't help but commune with my heart as it bumps and flutters in the cold. And then I see that all this life is incomprehensibly simple. Thereby a tiny comfort arises, and I know it to be comfort for at its coming I suddenly grasp the previous lack of it. And at that moment I am honest, and this honesty though coldly certain and utterly horrific is as if the sole thing I could ever crave. In this world people seek the comfort of validation and pleasure... or else the comfort of reality, of the cold austere truth. In as much as we want the latter we are lovers of purity. I am a lover of it, in whatever form it wants to take. I go further and say that purity is both kind and cruel, and it must be obvious that in the reality of Being, morality is nothing. Can it matter if there is preservation or destruction, kindness or cruelty, peace or war? The heart beats on... and here we forever are. In the silence of these lower rooms I often have the thought that behind every beat is *emptiness*... and I wait, and there it is, and then I wait for the beat to come, and there it is, and it is as if the heartbeat slows and slows until it seems there will never be another beat ascending out of the silence, no signal from the blackness-sea, no starburst in the raw-cold unending space. This is the fickle moment where I almost laugh... yet I am shiveringly afraid, for now the heartbeat *chooses or not* to come again. This is the very heart of cruelty, is it not? And since my mind is attuned and I share it with you, whoever you are, I say that it seems that even though the heartbeat and therefore life is inexorable, it is shrouded in deep silence that we can only call eternity, since it is not death, not death - wherefrom the heartbeat may never come again but yet is *written* to come again, as if a pact had been made at the beginning of the world, a pact between silence and the drum, wherein all futures were written so that they play their tunes and drumbeats, till the end of time that never ends. And for me in this silent basement room, what use is insight? *None*, I tell you. And yet I tell you. Be not afraid, a voice whispers from the slimy walls. You are here forever. Be afraid, it whispers again - you are here forever! And if we are to die many times, so many times that our deaths are lost even to the memory of the soul - then what of our present death, and our present life, if this presence can be called such, in this vault of eternity whereby the moments and minutes tick away under the beck of the pulse, the pulse, this thing that is born and dies in an instant, and in its birth dies, and in its death is born... There are no landmarks for us! The demise of the body by a bullet to the skull is nothing, since this is the way of the world. The bubbling of blood from the fleshy mound on the floor is nothing, since this is the way of all rivers of the world. The silencing of the heart at the core of the body's empire is nothing, since here is exactly the silent eternity between every beat of the heart. These momentous events: they are nothing! These signposts and milestones and memorials and fullstops and ceremonies and passings away and recitals of liturgies, these corpse-dumpings from vans, these brutal rituals of burial in the cloddy snows, the skirt-wastes of the motherland - these are nothing. Really nothing.

These, friends unknown, are my thoughts sufficient to this moment, which as you see are wiped out by the next. Let this instant bring what it may. Time may never come at all but for the ticking of the heart. And even if this little heart in its great empire were to pass away, if Communism itself were to pass away, there would be other hearts, hearts without number ready to do the work. And as they beat, like a horde of clocks in a still room, into the future that is ever *this*, then their thoughts and dreams, whatever they may be, will not be cruder or worser than this. For we are *human beings*, born to be born and die again, within the instant of a breath, within the pulse of a heartbeat. And these worlds we conjure, these social and political and metaphysic worlds we conjure between pulsings of the heart, will never be better or worse, will never evolve, for everything is already here… just this, this pulsing of the heart out of the silence. Have no fear! Or greatly fear… Marshall Stalin, wherever you are, you are all of these dead, just as you are the dread of all the living. Hear me, hear that I cling to nothing, here in my cubed room in your basement abattoir where all duty is swiftly and inexorably done. And gone.

And I never used to use that word. *Abattoir.* No, it is fitting.'

Five Hundred Clocks 'Unknown reader, imagine there are five hundred clocks in a still room and every one of them is ticking. And as we listen (there is no escape, even for an instant) they seem to form sonic shapes wherein the individual ticks lose themselves in a sigh, in a big sighing wind, and they seem to take the shape of the mind, the mind surrendering to the shape of a big sighing wind or a steady swish of a broom that might sweep the bitty world clean, or the big flush of a river gouging its hours and years as if the peace of the sea were somewhere, somewhere to be wished for… Yet this is the sea, right here in this room, and we drown in its soundwinds, its ticking alarmless tick… and suddenly, they lose their crushing togetherness for a moment, these lonely clocks, before they collude again, and the hypnosis comes again, and we are lost again in the crush, the rush, the cloudy belting rhythm of the shoosh shoosh shoosh.

Just so, the tick of time is our cover-up, our refuge from truth. Under it we can claim to be victims, automatic beings, functionaries in a great shovelling evildom under the manic laughter of god. And thereby we require no conscience, none at least that tells us we are blessed nothings and therefore incapable of harm, that we are innocent like children, and that blood is pure. Inside time there is no silence, except of a mute dissident conscience lurking red-eyed in the dark. Instead we are reminded of heartbeats, thudding looms of them, thousands of bloodbeats that enter here, in this room; and are dragged out by their heels again, and whose heads are lead-dead, who now are scoffed at by the dour indifference of a country's cold-numb agony. And the only sound to be had is the satisfied scratch and scribble of a pen on paper or the tappy tap of a typist's confirmation - some booted little gnome somewhere in the cavern of rooms, marking the satisfied closure of a sticky matter. And once the red dribbles have been all hosed away, it is time for appetite, time for lunch. A good morning's work, for the sake of the tranquillity of the State.

When we enter a room where death has been, where a person has met their loose lonely end - and though their abattoir place is nothing, really nothing... yet these walls, that sweat all the things they have seen, are wounded... though outside to the end of the world there is no barrier, only horizon and sky that makes this space cry in its arbitrary walls because it *is* walled, and because it has seen things no walls should see yet walls always see, as if the dirty secrets of the world have to be caged, as if the walls were doomed to witness the dirt of gnomes and men and their dirty ideas, while outside their huddled camp there is only gigantic wind and pure snow and open sky... Times and moments of all things are recorded in the air, whether future comers know them or not. This is the church of slaughter, where slaughter is worshipped - not ostentatiously or devoutly, but casually, necessarily, pragmatically, as a kitchen worships food, or a bedroom sleep, or a toilet, waste. Five hundred ticking hearts... every one of them has seen and felt the truth of it.'

Blood and Shit 'Food is the maker of blood, and blood beats and curdles inside veins and is shovelled forward by the heart. Its impurities are sucked out and it drips like wine in a vat into the organs of exit and then is gone. Never is it seen by the eye. And as we eat again, new fresh blood takes its place. Thick and viscous and pure and red and lovely, in its moving state it is the staff of living, it is the oil of love, it is the alchemical ground of healing joy. It does not stick to things, does not stain, does not linger in the brain as a memory of disgust or a gout of horror or as a splash of woe exposed in a place where it should never have been, exposed to the eyes of bloody old children, to immature beings who never should witness it. Blood is a precious red gold that should never be witnessed by the human eye; rather it should be the stuff of the eye itself, the sight and the seer and the thought and the sense and the love. If a man is blood and all is blood, why spill it? His blood never fails to shock by its lividness; it is not water, it is not white or opaque, it is the raw viscous manna of the world. If we are to feel then we feel with the heart, and it may not seem that an organ can feel, but if you take it away, if you take its function away, you will see then if you can feel!

In the toilets, where I tend to go in the moments, the moments after, in the hiatus where the rooms and corridors are abandoned, where the doors vomit smells, where the accusing silence closes in like red mists after a battle, I sit and listen to the acqueal squeal of a cistern pipe above my head. I do not remember any time when that water-constricted pipe did not squeak. It moans at a high pitch, at the edge of lonely madness, for the sake of all those dead who never uttered a sound or a word. And I listen to it, sitting there on the toilet bowl in the urinal vapours and the steel cold. And the longer I listen, the less my mind is able to form a thought or an image or remember any sound at all. It is the inhuman whistle of life. It is the moan of life's neglect. It is accompaniment to the quotidian wiping of the slate. It is the necessary sorrow of necessary rules. It is criminal. It is forever...

...Today, I had to run to the toilets in order to avoid emptying my bowel in the Lubyanka corridor. And this time I discharged the content so violently that I was moved to wonder: why should I take care to deposit shit in the right and proper place when no-one else is remotely doing the same? Why do we cling to propriety in the face of imbecility? My body today dissoluted under me. My being seemed to turn to the softness of nothing - confirmed by its transformation into pure unadulterated *shit.*'

Or Life Eternal There is a fountain in the garden of paradise from which pure water flows outward as all the rivers of the world. The flow is without beginning or end, and a nameless clerk, standing at a mirror by a basin, takes a pinch of its water in his cup hands. Even his body knows that we fumble always back to the same thing, the dissolving of *hardness*. Fear, paranoia, self-protection, investment in separateness… we must come to compassion, to admitting that we are one. Conscience is our bell-ringer (and this is why victims are the holy though they never chose it), but we force conscience aside again and again, invent new norms of depravity and fallenness even in our desperation for renewal. And so here at the lowest ebb in the hard hell of separateness (the abattoir of Joe Stalin: I say it now because I can) though truth is stolen from us (since those who know that truth will never write of it) I have understood: that to grab any, any miniscule chance that life offers - this is life, this is our positivity, this is our persistence. And though I cannot fool myself that life is anything but postponement of the inevitable, and though this dungeon is hell enough for a dutiful fool who blundered in where angels fear to tread - yet your writer is a Hero, because he is always naïve, always the ingenue, always ready to be the sacrificed, to become the dead; because his vision of hell is washed clean, washed clean… in the persistence of life eternal, life eternal.'

* * * *

Who is the Victor?   Since the masters-that-be will bring to an stop all indulgences shown to Drilov's Unpersons, he has contrived to record in his hidden journal the ever-more-urgent tracts spoken by them. And he knows he will find himself confronted by these people, these sudden friends, very soon, at night in the Lubyanka courtyard.

Mishkin the priest said: - I confess that I think of how short this life has contrived to be. Write, Drilov! I remember fifteen years ago I was at the centre of the parish in my Ukrainian village where they'd sent me. I had friends and admirers. Where is it all now? And fifteen years before that I was a student at the seminary in Kyiv. And fifteen before that, I was a child running about the streets of Kharkiv, trying to dodge my mother's endless calls to bring me home. Where are you now, mother? Life is so utterly nil. So many things have happened. And when they are lost to memory they have no existence, and here at the last, there is no sense of accomplishment. One should have a sense of 'satisfaction of time done'. But time is nothing but an ache, a shyster, a fraud, a murderer...

...And Mister Drilov, do not think that because someone slipped you the privilege of writing, even creating, others' confessions as if you were designated a chronicler, a maker of meanings, an artist - that you're somehow the conscience of a system that despite its inexorable hardness allowed you to delve in its hiddenness, let its humanness be aired through your labour, as if you were the last chronicler of a conscience that vanished under its boot... for then you'd be victim to a fool's flattery, fool's belief that what he's doing actually *matters,* that his work somehow makes history where nothing else does, and where the victims are forgotten, where they never ever mattered. *As if one thing can matter while another thing does not!* Who is the fucking ape who believes that one thing matters and another does not? He is the strutting tyrant ego, he is the bloated believer in his own power to arbitrate, he's the reason this system exists - as if his petty purpose could be elevated above the purpose of any other soul. As if he's the maker of himself, as if he's the inventor of all things, as if he could take his next breath or fart or heartbeat without the *utter gifts* of this world and heaven being laid at his feet... Or even if he *did not* believe in anything, and if this system were just the work of cynics and crooks and unbelievers and grabbers, out to save their own rumps, then they *still* fool themselves that what they do matters more, that their little decisions are righter, that their destiny is preferable, that their right to kill somehow justifies itself in terms of morality or history or the progress of their souls! I should not say that souls are despicable, but I say it now! And I regret it, though I'm honest. This is the darkness of a person, darkness of birth, of life itself, of the hell of treading water, hell of breathing and knowing that your previous breath is gone: of knowing that memory and time is erased as dust in the noon-bright air and that your feet never even touched the sod of this earth despite your sweating ramblings and your calculations, despite your love affairs and your romances and childy happinesses and little learnings and precious solemnities and love for your country and all your slow creeping quotidian disappointments - and even your little body death, which is coming now, coming now... and even the *last thought* - that you'll be erased from the pantheon of thought itself - that you never were, never will be, that your present living and thinking and feeling and breathing is the supremest mockery - that one meaningless life can snuff out another, that a meaningless ghost-villain can destroy you, you - either out of conviction that he's superior or the conviction that we're *all* monsters, or the conviction that it's all a cosmic joke and that this is his only revenge for his *own* humiliation - to butcher another who's the very soul of himself, who's his brother or sister, who in being butchered is the confirmation of his own victimhood, and that this act is the only justice, such that his hell is confirmed by the hellification of another... or that he somehow *undermines* all the meaninglessness by rubbing his own face in the dirt and shit - so that we *all* might celebrate the end of this fucking charade under the umbrella of a dirty hoodlum or a god or a president who laughs in our face, who subjects us to the drivel and horror because he can, because he can. And just as the communist government sells us the lie that we contribute to a brighter future, so history told us that God wanted us to go through His penance to reach Him at last. Well, I tell you, young Drilov or whatever your name is, I'm the winner at last - because I don't believe in anything! And yet I'm not a cynic, not a slave to negativity, to my own venality, my need to survive - because you and your people will never get me because I'm free of you! Am I free of the hate of you, you'll say? I who duped himself he should be a dutiful priest and lover of souls? I don't know. But right now I'm glad to report that no-one can arbitrate my feelings of hate and anger. No-one. I know you'll retort (if you have no heart) that it is the system that arbitrates my feelings at the last, that I go to my death 'in my anger and hate' - so that I'll no doubt prove a useful assassin in future lives, that I'll become a cheerleader for all the cruelties and revenges of future systems like this. And no doubt some will say that a priest, a servant of god, has finally been made to face his nemesis of *cynicism,* at the very moment he departed, and that therefore we've *done him a good turn* in exposing his hollow religion and faked goodwill... But I'm the winner because *no-one* is the winner, and the loser because no-one is the loser. And I'm the winner because no-one's the loser, and I'm the loser because no-one's the winner. I'm free of winning and losing!

I'm free of hating and loving. And if all's lost, *then I'm free of wanting to be free.* So Drilov, here's our present moment wrapped up present and correct! And my dirty little death is the total death of your dirty little State! But don't take it personally, because your State is forever nothing, a greasy uneasy notion of the mind, a motion of the bowel, a hectic dream, pathetic scribble of history, laughable rebadging of falsehood that ever hangs about we dreaming fools on this planet of mud and crud and semen and blood... And now Drilov, try to tell me that *anything stays,* and I will say you are a stupid liar. And the criminals who did this to me are nothing. *So that I forgive them because they are nothing...* Can they stand being forgiven? Can they? Breathe out now Drilov, and know that your last breath is gone. What's the difference between you and me? None. No difference.

* * * *

At this point, Drilov loses grip on the priest's circular arguments, or else loses the power to resolve things in himself, which is after all the reason he persists in these recordings. It crosses his mind that it is amazing what roils under the labels we put on people ('priest') and how all are demeaned by so labelling... but he also thinks that this spiritualist is frighteningly unable to see that Drilov is always teetering on a knife-edge of sardonic irony by even bothering to listen to and write down these victims' needs. A *refined* mind would have noted this sardony. And thereby Drilov feels momentarily justified in dismissing the man as underdeveloped or negative or unreliable! ...or whatever crude adjective allows itself to impinge on his conscience... And as that day wears on before sleep engulfs, as if its events were really nothing but a bundle of stool deposited in a toilet, all forgotten: the tastes, judgements, fleeting joys, wisps of hope, pinpricks of sanity that this little grey day brought, now all a bundle of shit and rapidly discomposing... Does it mean one is right now just a rushing waterstream that floods the sewers of the city of Moscow? It's likely that *some* people are, some corpses who yesterday were shuddering and breathing... And yet something about oneself *never* departs, and our imaginings of 'osmosing to something else' like the flow of sewer waters or the breath of faraway winds or the drip of snows on the mounts of Asia... is nothing but another clouded dream, because something always remains as *oneself*, as if *oneself* were the ultimate thing one can never depart from; that one is a *person* and must always be so despite the rocking of the worlds, despite the trade winds of imagining, despite the floodings of history, despite the very forgetting of oneself! We are with ourselves for better or worse! What logic is there to say that we *ever* lose ourselves - even after the passing of the body, the lopping of the head, the de-embraining, after the blood has drained through the sewer-hole at the end of the room and the bag of bone and gristle has been delivered to the maw of an oven or the gape of a snow-lined hole in the frozen steppe? To think that we lose ourselves? And in this thought, light starts to seep again, and there is space in the head, a slowing of the breath, and Drilov realises that he's been an alien to himself these past hours and days, and that here's a salve, a bouquet, a freshener of fetid toilet air. And he resolves to tell it to the poor priest next day - as if the priest had forgotten or never knew it, despite all his years serving the infinitudes of his God. Ha! And Drilov regrets his previous negative adjectivising, and blames it on the gloom of his world that makes him think badly of others' frailties. And in the same whiff of thought he sees he's a victim of contamination, of a societal poison that none escape - and that this is so very much an *affront*, an injustice, for a pure pure man such as he wishes to be.

The Elusive This day, Drilov's tone is quietly assuring.

- So there's always hope, Mishkin

- Hope? Are you expecting your next breath to improve on this one? Your next heartbeat to exceed the quality of this? Do you expect your next thought to be somehow more elevated than the last? Do you assume your blood will be purer tomorrow? Do you really expect anything to change? Life is the continual and constant believing that what we do matters, and it is the continual and constant death of all our hopes and beliefs. This life is automaticness driven by blind will. Life utterly recycles itself at every instant. And of course there are no instants at all. Perfect torture! ...Lo, the Bible says *I make all things new*. Thus, is naivety our only hope? Is ignorance of memory and past and future our only hope?

Eh, Drilov? Hope for what? Peace, truth, beauty, joy? Do you know that your own ego, your own will to live, is the maker of your own misery? Your ego is the thief who embezzled life from you and beggared you! And if it ever enquires into itself, it is faced with two paths. One: it will forever tangle itself deeper and deeper in the knot of seeking itself, like a dog chasing its tail, like a donkey wanting a carrot, like the serpent *Ourobouros* that devours its own body. Or two: it will dissolve in the naked foolery of its own enquiry, realising its bogus identity like a thief proclaiming his innocence by catching another thief. To know oneself is therefore to expose oneself. And to expose oneself is to *obliterate* oneself. Religionists everywhere: you can only know your path by abandoning it! You are continually seeking, seeking like the waves of the sea. But where are you going? Nowhere but the *sea*. The sea is the obliteration of the wave of yourself. Poetic! You cling to the idea that you are a seeker, and therefore you are forever the blind and ignorant wave, forever surging into the illusion of future out of the illusion of past. And you will never arrive, *and thus death will always accompany you,* all your days and years and millennia… For time itself is a pinprick, is the idea of *this,* the idea of now. Time is point, and as long as point is there, your attention will be arrested, you will be hypnotised by the need to arrive, by the need to know, the need to understand, the need to enquire and to find. Yours will ever be the search for The Great Beauty who is as elusive as the sunset, or the search for the Idea of Truth, that is as transparent and elusive as the very air you suck into lungs that forever seek air. We are slaves who beg at the feet of the goddess of beauty, supplicants who kneel and worship at the feet of the goddess of truth. Does the goddess exist? She does as long as we seek her! We will believe in her as entity as long as we believe in ourselves as entity. And when this dualism is ended, goddess and supplicant perish together. Ideals and fundamentalisms perish with their maker. Here is forever the creation of droplets in the borderless sea of mind. In the beginning (and it is forever the beginning) the seer creates the seen, and these two dance and fall away forever together. Are you the thing you see? Yes, and forever. Do the objects shift and change? Always, and thus do you. You are nothing but the becoming of your thoughts and desires. And herein is our slavery and our liberation, all in one. Torture!

And Elusiveness! I loved best the story of the monk who, accompanied by his student, arrived one freezing night at the door of a lonely temple. The monk surmised that the only thing in the temple that was combustible and that would save them from freezing to death was the effigy of the holy buddha on the altar. He promptly chopped it up into faggots and lit a fire. The student howled in protest, asking what on earth was the point of being a monk if you are going to desecrate the absolute idol of the most sacred buddha. The monk of course ignored him. Here's a nice bit of warmth, he replied! Young Drilov, bless you. To live you must destroy. To love you must kill. To be free you must be obliterated. Now walk on down the line, and let life perform its dirty business on you.

No-One Has Ever Seen The Red Man The spiritualist Mishkin is nakedly unfettering himself on Drilov. This time Ugdanov is present.
- Ugdanov the great Chemist fatly announces: *Mishkin, you are going to die!* I wonder how you may know that? I am willing to bet life and limb that no-one has ever been able to prove the existence of death except from the standpoint of *living*. If you've seen a corpse (and so many have) what did you see? The truth is you saw yourself looking at a corpse. You watched yourself staring at 'a mound of flesh with no electrical energy in it'. Similarly, no-one has ever been able to prove insanity except from the standpoint of sanity. No doubt, the one who experiences death is very much alive. And no-one has ever been able to prove his own death experience to anyone else. We are bound to ask: to whom does the death occur? You will say 'to me, to him or to her of course!' In that case, who exactly am I that death occurs to me? My meaning is: if it occurs to me, then it must be a thing separate from me. Are you going to tell me it occurs to no-one? This is not mere semantics! Does 'dead' mean 'not functioning normally'? Does it mean 'gone from this world'? In that case, gone where? Does it mean disassembled, dissolved? In that case, into what? It all reminds me of the old Hindu Upanishad: Nachiketas enters the Cave of Death and asks for a boon. Death smiles ironically and says to him: ask whatever you like! Nachiketas says: I have but one request. *Tell me what you are.* At this Death gets very disturbed and says: No no, ask me for anything: riches, power, fame, love - but don't ask who I am! Nachiketas

is adamant: *I want nothing else. Tell me who you are!* And suddenly Death shrinks back like a crab into his shell, disappears in front of the enquirer's eyes. To this you might object: if we claim there is nothing but life, then we may also claim there is nothing but death - since life is nothing but change and transformation. In that case I say to you that death is nothing but a *word,* a word like 'change'. (Now we *are* in the realm of semantics!) And would it not be better to speak of these 'nothing but' absolutes in terms of life, existence, being, somethingness - rather than your castle in the air called 'nothingness'? After all, 'I am' is the foundation of all experience, and therefore of all proof. There is nothing outside it; nothing that can be proven, that is. It is as if we were all a race of Blue Men who had never seen The Red Men. The blue men might speculate and prattle about the existence of these fabled red men, but no-one has ever been able to prove it except in their imagination. The image of the red man becomes so all-pervading that everyone believes he exists, somewhere. In fact there is no red man. Just as in the same way there are no *communists.* Oh, have no fear that communism will die, my young friend, since there were no communists in the first place. No-one can ever 'be' a communist. It is pure illusion, a label, a fable. There is no Red Man! In the same way, to believe in 'your own death' is the same as to believe in a 'heaven above the clouds'. We want *proof.* To whom shall death be proved? To the one who *exists.* And he, unfortunately, is all there ever is, is all there ever can be...

What is Lost?   - Yes, I Mishkin am a silly fundamentalist, busy trying to convince myself of the things I profess! For years I'd dream a dream of rebuilding my house, and the dream would always end in a heated dispute about the *foundations.* They were always sinking or were shonkily built or in danger of slipping away. Why does this dream keep recurring? I tell myself: when we think of a thing that is falling away, whenever we think of death, we are always the one who *lives.* We never stop to think that there can be no thinker or seer outside the eternal presence. What is the foundation of the life we take for granted, or the foundation of fear of death that undermines it... *and* undermines the awareness that founds this very thought? Does anyone fear what's plain and clear to them? Of course there's knee-jerk fear of impending pain, of loss. But *what* is lost? This is the only question that matters. There must be an answer we can live with, without fear, without end, without interruption, no mere emotional solace, no mere intellectual construct but *the essence of the nature of ourselves.* Who are we? There's never been a time, thought, feeling, sensation, place, impulse, need, wish, love that has not been *you.* You are existence absolute, utterly aware, ever unified, and there is never any instance or transaction whereby it's other than itself. We thereby affirm: 'I am forever myself because there is nothing that is not myself'. It may be objected that there is an infinitude of things that are not myself! But these are not 'things'. Rather, they are of the substance and nature of the sole and absolute being-awareness. This being-awareness was never born and will never pass away. Our fear of loss is but the realm of change, illusion. The word 'death' signifies nothing but change, transformation, and we merely take on combinations of this eternal substance. I 'change clothes': I put on and take off garments, coverings, costumes, masks, wigs, makeup. I put on and take off flesh and bone and blood and sinew. I put on and take off the power to see and hear and taste and smell and touch. I put on and take off the power to feel love and pain and confusion and doubt and need. I put on and take off the power to imagine worlds and places and universes, to imagine sun and sky and moon and wind and trees and snow and sea and all other imaginings right down to the tiniest object. I put on and take off the power to think, the power to measure, power to evaluate. I put on and take off the power to see the future and the past, to sniff the invisible, to intuit the hidden structure of all things. I put on and take off the power to understand time and space, the power to will, the power to create. I pulsate with nothing but change because simply, I can. It is simply my nature. I breathe in the breath of all the worlds and breathe them out again. And when all these powers are temporarily absent... I am never gone, I am *myself.* I am myself as stillness and purity and forever-hereness. This is my crystalline empty home. And here I rest as I always rested. I machinated in the most complex worlds, I sang and loved and hated and strove and fought and shed blood... and I was never anywhere but here. Where the hell else could I be? And even now I look on the isolated souls about me and wonder if they will ever stop to think about this, and I feel pity. But my pity is misplaced! We are all of the oneness, of the hereness, and we all play roles and we all take them off again! I the still, permanent one, am real. You will object that this permanence is nothing but endless roiling change and suffering! And you will be right. But never fail to see that the one who changes is forever untouched. There is nothing to fear but fear itself, no fear but the fear of itself... Yet even knowing that every single cell in this body has continually died and renewed itself in the space of moments or weeks or months, doesn't seem to do the trick! Was there ever a time or place where you were not renewing yourself? Trust in the absolute power, the power that is nothing but renewal. Nothing stays. Be glad of it. The only thing that stays is life, awareness, the bliss of presence - and that is you. It can never not be you, you can never not be it, you never were anything but it. Cling not to some phantom Other. Relax. The foundations of the house are intact and perfect. You go forward as you should. There is nothing out of place, except maybe your belief that there is something amiss. Peace. Peace. You are fine. You are always intact. You are deathless. Be fearless, be fearless. Good. Good.

Respect Lilya Popova is on the bandwagon, railing at earthly stupidity. - Ugdanov, you heard the priest but I bet his advice is above your station! You are a chemical engineer and a materialist who says there's 'nothing after death'. Listen to me now. Is there anything *before* death? Yours is the story of an unswerving servant of a State. But your real crime was to not be political *enough*. Why? Because you didn't think enough about what is really *true*. Life is not a bunch of equations, life is not logical! You fail to see the illogic of your current position. You absurdly uphold the state even as you become its victim. You're cornered. How can you uphold a thing that is heartless? Why did you never conceive anything better?
- Why do you say heartless? When I was a young man my parents had a garden at their cottage in Voronezh. They'd think nothing of pulling out plants by the season and replacing them, removing weeds for the sake of vegetables. It's part of the order of things. If a man dies today, will not another live tomorrow? And if many die, will not future generations live? Don't be sentimental!
- Oh? Do humans have a choice not to be murdered, not to be considered weeds or vermin or insects? I saw some Jain monks on a street in Bombay,

and they had these little soft brushes they used to brush the path as they moved. It had a kind of grace, as the most futile thing I'd ever witnessed: saving the souls of ants from being crushed by a human foot. Why bother to be here in this world at all? Only now, all these years later, I see those monks were hardly of this earth, yet they clung on to the last strands of duty in a world that's all contradiction, all contamination, in physical bodies that are all but impossible since the souls of creatures are immaterial and take up no space... so that the monks must tread the lightest of karmic roads if they are ever to be set free. There can be no freedom if one *seeks* escape! One must instead seek unbreakable *respect.* Those monks with their little brushes - the very soul of respect... For how can anyone believe killing solves any kind of problem, as if 'strategic murder' can put to rights the imbalances of the world, or offer peace and salvation to the killer! What does he think he is doing? He is wretched! He is an actor in a great game, his mind is the spaghetti of thoughts outside his control, a tanglebush of headless wants. He is the great sewer flush of mindlessness, he blunders in a materialist dream. Does he never have any thought of standing up, without conditions, without excuse, like a stream of fresh water that proclaims itself against the filth of the world, that shouts *I am alive, and that is enough?* Talk to him, Mishkin. Talk to this cipher. For god's sake, keep him entertained.   **Deconstruct, Deconstruct** (Mishkin) - All right, Mister Chemist. Let us do some science. *Is there materiality outside consciousness? Discuss.* I bet you never got a topic like that at your chemistry school. Those who wish to call themselves materialists are free to do so, just as I am free to call myself a goat. Because no-one has ever been able to prove that a thing exists outside the realm of awareness, we may assert that awareness is the be-all and end-all. Not happy with this 'short cut' conclusion? All right. Can any 'object' be identified without a seer or 'subject'?

- No.

- You'll note that it is impossible to designate a 'thing' without labelling it something. Let's take a so-called material thing, a rock! - since it appears to be 'hard' and without awareness. If I turn it in my hand, does its substance change according to the perspective from which I view it?

- The answer must be no

- Does its form, its shape, change according to the perspective from which I view it?
- The answer is yes
- Is its shape and therefore its 'identity' subject to my vision of it?
- The answer must be yes
- Is its shape part of its identity?
- Yes, but the *substance* of it, the chemical or atomic substance of it is not altered by my vision of it
- All right, investigate its atomic substance. By the way, what instrument is used? A microscope. Invented by what agency? Awareness in the form of human intellect, correct. Let's enter the 'atomic structure'. What do we find? A lot of space, a lot of light! Where the hell is this atom exactly? Over here or over there? Does the identity of the object change according to the perspective by which it is viewed? Yes! Does the object have any identity independent of the perspective from which it is viewed? No! Therefore does this atomic structure have any identity independent of... etcetera? No. It is now, according to the perceiver, mere empty space, pulsating light. Enter this light and deconstruct it. I put it to you that light is very much the same substance as the consciousness that perceives it. I put it to you that there's no difference between light and consciousness. Are there any objects outside the perceiver? In the context of 'the relationship between perceiver and perceived', there are none. I put it to you that there is no difference between perceiver and perceived. Did anything happen? Nothing ever happened. Is there anything but the ocean of awareness? Sorry, there is indubitably not

(Popova) - The fucking system doesn't exist!

(Ugdanov) - How then do things appear to exist? How do things appear to be material?

(Mishkin) - *Is awareness not a material, the original material?* Are the ocean's waves anything but water? When the perceiver 'causes external things', is the perceiver anything but itself? No! What then causes 'waves'? Awareness pulsates. There is displacement, relativity, limitation. It is the power and force of awareness delighting with and as itself. In its utter freedom it is free to extrapolate all combinations forever - and of course never - since time and space and relationship and cause are never anything but phantoms generated in itself. There is nothing but ocean of awareness. It is the alpha and omega, the absolute, the immanent, the One. It is *you*, whether you admit to it or not. What is 'material? It is nothing but the endless tiny flickering alteration, the becoming, of your perspective

(Ugdanov is cornered) - Poor Mishkin! Physical death is always unwelcome, always 'premature. Such is proven by recurring bowel failure among prisoners! Undignified. Death is undignified. Our *preciousness* is ignored. Material uniqueness, scoffed at. Yet spiritualist Mishkin is always going to flout the loose-bowel rule! No doubt he's prepared all his life for this. I doubt though, that he'll be able to control his faculties at the moment of truth - or the moment of *untruth* as he'll call it...

- Ugdanov, a billion battles have been fought within this body of cells and atoms, this unruly labyrinthine kingdom of tunnels and plains and valleys. Battles of will and of disease - between warriors of health and goblins of demise, between valkyries of pure sky and dwarfs of the curmudgeonly depths. I've seen all of life! Is that not enough? Death is nothing, it is the essence of falsehood

- Bowels don't lie, Mishkin.

True enough, thinks Drilov. But after all is said, why talk of Mishkin's physical death? It looms though, like the muffled coda of a symphony by Shostakovich, or a needless eulogy at the end of a heart-rending funeral. Mishkin is a brave soul no doubt, but certain things are remembered. Shit sticks. Mishkin shies from 'posterity' since it is his weakness: despite all, he needs to be remembered. He must admit that though eternity is all, 'time arbitrates posterity'. Ugdanov has his point. Nevertheless, shoots of desperation are multiplying in the Chemist.

Don't Ever Believe (Mishkin) - So you don't admit you'll die soon, Ugdanov?

- Won't we all? Fuck them

- Ugh. It ill becomes you to say 'fuck them' when you've benefited so much from the system

- What am I doing here? Don't these cunts see there's a mistake! *Drilov*, do you ever do anything but write, like a goddam scribe at other peoples' funerals?

(Popova) - You've changed your tune, Ugdanov. When all the stalwarts and the do-rights change their tune, there's nothing left. You failed to understand that a system based on lies and hypocrisy can't keep earnest zealots like you. You're a blight on its conscience!

- How did it come to this? I did everything right. I hate them now

(Popova) - Listen Ugdanov. To hate this so-called Communist system would be a mistake, since it's but an abominable conjuration of people's minds: to justify their powerlessness in the face of death and change and hatred and fear and all the other emotions they can't escape. Why try to create any kind of system? It's only 'a discipline on the soul', an attempt at order, at purification. Fundamentalists hate life. They want to destroy life. Life is fecundity, multiplication, positivity. It is icons, objects, stuff – all anathema to the pursuit of *purism*. Just as Musselman fundamentalists hate women so they hate life. Communism conjured a great fiction that claims austerity and purism to be the staff of life. *It's nothing but an excuse to kill, to erase.* And its exponents think that getting rid of enemies and detractors and infiltrators and poisoners is justification for its survival and flourishing! But this is cruelty built on illusion. Discipline thyself, oh man! Blame not, interfere not. I know we feel the need to pre-emptively kill before they kill us, but if we were to 'do unto others as we'd have them do unto us' then we'd *leave them alone*. Still, Macbeth said: I am so far in blood, my only course is to go on… Ugdanov, it's all built on an illusion - this discipline, this purification, this fundamentalism of yours? Purification is a mighty thing, but it's not systems or arrangements that'll do it, but the *removal* of them! The mind is your trickster, your jailor. Overcome your attachment to ideology and you'll have a chance to find peace

- But the putting of illusion over people is *always* happening. It can never be overcome

- That which *has no existence* can never be overcome! It is to superimpose illusion on the self. The self is only ever itself. Understand that, and you'll have no further trouble

- Except when someone tells you you're doomed, and that you've no hope, and that you're nothing!

- I understand, Ugdanov. It's very hard. But you shouldn't believe in them.

They're conjuring an illusion and wanting to make you despair at having lost what was always an illusion. It's hard because you believed in it so long

- I shall go to my death with my head held high

- Don't. 'Your death' is the illusion you refuse to let go of. You'll see, as soon as you're out of this confining body. You'll see! But don't let Comrade Stalin hear us talk like this, or he *also* will see death as nothing! And will sanction these 'death events' all the more

- In that case, we should resist, because our death is unjust!

- Living an *illusion* is unjust. What more do you want? To justify the injustice of illusion?

- But what of a *dog*, or any other creature without the power to discriminate? Can it claim that it's not a dog? Eh?

- But it can see that another dog is not itself. It can see that its master is not itself. It can see that the blood on the floor is not itself. You may say that 'a dog is just a dog'. But if you see the dog as limited, then you're limited. Ugdanov, the thing seen is nothing but the invention of the one who sees it

- Then I *am* this body, whichever way?

- What body, Ugdanov? The one 'you' experience?

- Aha. Yes! …But, but… I'm too weak

- *Who* is too weak? You… or that body of yours?

- Whatever way, there'll be fear and suffering!

- Wait, Ugdanov. It'll be over soon. And then you'll kick yourself that you made such a fuss

- Where will I be?

- Here. Just without that smelly body

- Still in this cell?

- No, not in any cell, nor in any world! There is no world. There never was. BUT YOU WILL BE HERE.

Popova is silent. At last she whispers.

- You are right, priest. There is a presence that is always here. There is a servant who never fails us. He is the man who stands in benediction. He is the last man standing. He is the faithful one. And he is the *ruler*, the one who never passes away… And you have already seen how dark he is! He is *dark*, Mishkin!

- No Popova, he is all Light.

* * * *

Unknowable to the Gnomes   Like salmon in a dish of sardines, the artist Lilya Popova has been inserted in this night's gaggle of unknowns to be liquidated, all spilt out of convoys of black vans that trawl the noble city of Moscow. Across the cobbled courtyard, Drilov sees her. She is shivering in the night, her sturdy frame engirdled in a big red scarf. She grips her own arms and looks at him. At last she smiles. He smiles back, and this is their little victory, his and hers: Popova is a planet, a world, a nebula, a constellation of flesh and thought and memory and feeling and attainment and journeying and love... She might also be nothing at all, since life can snuff her so cavalierly and without compunction, without the faintest alteration to its own immutable eternal body. But Popova can be nothing because she is everything, cannot dissolve because she is *indissoluble*. How else could the Lord receive her unless she were the Lord? And Drilov thinks to himself at this 'last moment', that because he saw it and because he thought it, then the thought is recorded forever and irrevocably, that the seed is planted, that it is written on the wind, written on the snows and across the sky (but of no stinking country) - that he or Popova or Mishkin or Ugdanov or anyone is the Lord and cannot be erased, or that in the erasure is the proof of it - that we never needed to be confined in this dream of a body, in this mental dream of our own making; that we were but a musing, a drowsing breeze, a coagulation, a joke, an affirmation of sunlight, sun-tears that shone on flowers of a field, on grasses, on the branches of a wood - somewhere, anywhere, unknown to anyone yet always and forever present.

Drilov did not see the moment when Popova passed away in a flurry of shots and the dropping of bodies like ninepins under the muffling stupid thunder of the truck engines. In the greasy important shaft-light of the night she lay without name or number amid the pile. Only when the trucks were backed up for loading did he come across her, lay his hand on her. And his co-worker wouldn't allow any moment of pause before he shouted at Drilov to heave, and up she went onto the truck bed like so many pounds of lumpy potatoes in the marketplace. He'd taken her shoulders, and did not notice the runnels of blood that covered his wrists before twenty other bodies had been loaded up and driven away. And he looked down at his hands in a headlight beam, and saw the red nauseous unnatural stains, and said to himself: no-one can piss on the spirit of Popova. Hers is the blood of the earth itself.

Put Out the Rubbish   And there's no time to think, only to do. Brutality in every instant, every act. The breath of guards and prisoners rises in the chill, caught in the beams of the trucks. Tyrannic walls, the freezing cold, industrial, industrial. A bird far up in the sky would ask, why is one set of men murdering another? Are they not one? *Put out the rubbish, the rubbish, it's rubbish night!* Drilov's offsider (who worked with him in the basement) is muttering. In truth he is getting louder. No-one else hears, hears anything above the roar of the engines. Directions come in semaphore; the group leaders wave their arms. *Do what's in front of you. Anything to get out of this damned cold.* Drilov wonders if his mate is a closet sadist, wonders if he's starting to enjoy. No. It is the absurdity of murder that gets you laughing. Is it not a killing joke that we can work our politics by liquidation, that a human being can think he's done good, done a good night's work? Insanity is accepted without feeling, without compunction, without ambiguity. It is law, it is regularity, it is *fait accompli,* so when a man starts to chatter and burble and ironise while performing his dirty deed, we can be sure he still has a skerrick of feeling in his heart, and that the skerrick can't be erased, not in a billion aeons of time or circumstance - and that his incipient madness, his mad irony, is the seed of future conscience, to be re-hatched long after he also is liquidated erased shelved unnumbered puffed and gone. *'Tis but the work of a moment, the work of a moment,* repeats Drilov's offsider, wiping the blood from his hands to his pants. A philosopher in the making! How does anyone secrete such experience in his inmost heart? There is nothing more private. Will a man strive to be a hero, who enters again the labyrinth in search of the thing he has discarded, his conscience? Oh, there will be a far time, far in the future, where he must. Any man or woman who seeks his own heart is a hero. Beyond all the atrocities we have witnessed, it is heroism to seek atonement and peace. Or will peace involve further killing... and will the peace of the ideal state of Communism require endless killing? Ugh, these thoughts are not compatible. There is but one thing holding us from the abyss, and that is conscience, conscience - in the manic mutter of Drilov's offsider. And this night it is catching. *The work of a moment...* There is a figure standing and watching in the glare of a headlamp in the insane cold. It is Mishkin the Priest. Drilov stops what he is doing - hoisting bodies to the truck bed - and looks. Oh, Drilov is embarrassed to be alive - yet Mishkin wants to reassure him with a look. A mere second. Mishkin is shoved aside, out of the light-beam. Drilov involuntarily steps forward. Mishkin runs at him, hugs him. Drilov can smell shit. *Yes, mine,* whispers Mishkin. *They will have to shoot quick! The Lord is watching in the form of you, Drilov. Do not waste it.* And the priest is pulled away by an officer who curses at Drilov. It is the beast-sergeant Dionylov. There is a volley of shots. Only lumps now present themselves on the shining cobbles under the wheels. Someone else's business, someone else's little granite-bit of karma! Drilov's offsider is gesturing. Clouds of breath rise in the lights. The lorries roar. Horror walls of the prison loom. The lorries grind forward in convoy. Hoses blast the asphalt clean. Inside ten minutes Drilov is back in the building.

* * * *

In his bed in the dawn, Drilov writes with frozen hands. 'Of course. Mishkin was the princely Idiot in Dostoevsky's tale. Entirely positive, with a beautiful nature, removed from reality but wanting to do right, to save us all. For Petersburg Society he can't be other than idiot, but his emotional awareness beats them all. Even jealous Rogozhin's lover falls under his simple spirit, and though Mishkin falls in love out of pity, the world's Rogozhins can't ever forgive. But this was not exactly my Mishkin... Dostoevsky wouldn't have imagined such a killing house as this. Why do I put up with it: because I want to laugh at death? Duty is meaningless. Only way to live is as nihilist. Time is running, is gone. I am spectator at the idiocy of worlds. Like a lunging drug this ride will end... rollercoaster lunging at a cliff. You killers, bring it. See if I care.

Last But Not Least   There is one more atrocity to be described. Ugdanov the chemist, it seems, is to be made an example of. Drilov is summoned to basement room eleven. He is met at the door by an official unknown to him. It is a woman. Behind the official Drilov sees Ugdanov at a desk. His hands are bound. Drilov is directed to stand by. Ah, Drilov! says the prisoner eagerly. Glad you're here. You'll explain some things, won't you? You'll tell them I only got momentarily angry, that I lost my temper for a moment, that I only conspired with those others to *question* them. Just like you, right?

Drilov sees that Ugdanov is not abreast of the sum of reality. He feels the urge to ask him to save his breath, to think on the need to *empty himself,* so that when the time comes for liquidation 'there is nothing that can be liquidated'. Because *this is the trick, you see.* Drilov sees it clearly at last. He wants to confide it to Ugdanov. Leave before they make you leave! Be a step ahead of the gnomes! But no, Ugdanov is several miles back. The female official, standing under a piercing light beyond the desk, contrives now to read out a confession Ugdanov has apparently written. Drilov knows better, there was no such thing. Or perhaps there was! Perhaps Ugdanov really wants to conform to the last! And perhaps this official of the State wants to show him what a cynic and a traitor he really is - as if the State would ever believe that a man could write or speak such a bogus confession! (The official is getting excited. She thrusts the paper away) 'Your ploy is an insult to the State. Your faux-loyalty is all insult. At least mean it if you want to rebel! Do so, then die properly! And do not try to *agree* that we are correct in obliterating you. You are despicable in your cowardly acquiescence. This State does not need cowards. It needs men, it needs proper enemies, not fools and weaklings who actually agree with its sentence! Shape up at the last! Admit to your failings. Admit that we do not *like* you. Admit that there's no *place* here for you. Admit you have no political consciousness. Admit you are a conformist without conviction! Accept that we see into the hearts of men, know their failings and contradictions. Accept that we despise your *mea culpa.* As if you ever were a candidate for re-education, as if you ever were a candidate for promotion, as if your marches in support of Comrade Stalin, your degrees in chemistry from *our* institutions, your work record in *our* factories, your articles in support of *our* scientific programs and your giving of three *children* to our State… could ever cover up the reality - that you'd actually suck up to us to save your life! As if you even had the option to become a martyr! Do you think we would let you associate with the likes of Drilov and Mishkin and Popova if we wanted you to *agree* with us? You're all moral failure, Ugdanov. Do you not see that this was all a test, a test of moral character? And you failed it. Because it doesn't matter whether you agree with Communism or not. What matters is that you undergo the torture of its rigour, the hiatus of it, that you understand that the rigour of torture is our gift to you. Torture alone lets you see that there is nothing in life that can be ignored, no level of reality that you may eschew or scorn. You must seek to be here and here alone, must seek nothing but to live this life in its fullest and deepest part. Only the exquisite hiatus of torture may offer this! I am disgusted with you beyond the telling of it!

And the red-faced official unlatches the leather holster at her belt, hauls out her revolver, raises and straightens her arm, and blows Ugdanov's red red brains all over the room.

The Darkest Light   The following has had to be constructed in the imagination of Dreeley, your present-day narrator.

Drilov once spoke of a room where there is no darkness. The room exists, and is clearly a metaphor for the absence of shadows, the absence of Other, the absence of anything but the present real. Drilov ends up there, on a day that could be night but there is no telling, and in a place that could be all horror but there is no telling… here in this room where there is nothing but light. The human being opposite him at the desk, is a woman. The same woman who de-brained Ugdanov.

The hair is short and brown, the chin blunt, the cheeks heavy. She wears heavy shoes and a skirt, and on her thick jacket-uniform is the insignia of the State. He cannot see her eyes since she wears dark glasses. It is possible she is forty years old. It is possible she is an actor. It is also possible she is a sadist. Or she may have a heart and a sensibility and a family and a past and a conscience. It is all possible.

- 'Where the force of morality is dead and only cold mathematic calculation can be depended on, we in the end might justify compassion as 'an act no less utilitarian than cruelty'. You wrote that, did you not, Comrade Drilov? Tell me first of all: where have you secreted your private writings? Did you think we wouldn't know that your private scribblings are more important to you than your official ones? I remind you: there is nowhere for you to go but here. There is no place but this, comrade. You are here, inside the light. Whatever we do, whatever I do to you - is real. You understand that, don't you?

- I don't know you

- You will know me… and then you will not

- Women don't suit communism. They fuck up male ideals

- Then you will see that I am unutterably special

- I get it. You're no woman

- Shall I tell you something? I have worked all my life for the privilege of liquidating the likes of you. Yet now, that is a thing I am loathe to do: to let you leave us, to let you leave *me*. Your official (your fake) writings revealed enough: you seem to claim that death is to be wished for, that it is a liberation. Or rather, that it is the *quality* of that death, the quality of understanding, of your awareness when you leave the body - that is the liberation. You have offered up a powerful argument, but you are wrong. At the very last, you are wrong. What if the quality of your death, of your mind and spirit and heart at your death - were clouded, were mundane, were filthy, were full of hate, of bitterness? The priest spoke of it! Though I am not concerned with any priest. I am concerned with you. You, whom the system took so much care over. You, the blue-eyed boy (whether you knew it or not), yours is the greatest, the worst, the most dangerous betrayal of all. And so you see I am exerting myself to the utmost to understand what you have done. Because I am the system, Drilov: I, the individual. No-one else. I am not an abstraction. I AM. The buck, as the Yankees say, stops with me. Your commandant said you were *no* individual. But he was fooling you. He needed you to react, he needed you to get furious and to lose your way so that you would come to me. Because I am your mother. I am your conscience though you do not know it yet. I am the heart of your system. Of any system. Are you not glad,

276

Drilov? The quality of *me* is the quality of the system, is the quality of the world. Do you see what a burden I have taken on my shoulders? And therefore do you see what a privilege it is to be here with me?

- I want to say one thing

- Say it

- In this great state of communism, everyone is utterly alone. The desperate need of this State is to shrink imagination so that the wonder and glory of being, and being human, is negated and stifled and crushed! Communism is the ultimate in self-hatred, and its materialism is the epitome of gnomish shrunken *unbeing*

- Wrong! We do revere the personal, and for one reason only: to truly revere it is to ascend to the *impersonal*. Murder and suicide are anti-materialist gestures! To negate the individual is the apotheosis of individualism. How? Because you must see that your true nature is not confined to your puny idea of individual! You are boundless, borderless, immaterial, already subject and surrendered to the All. Didn't your priest friend tell you that? And the State is but the symbol of that impersonal All. You want to escape into 'spiritualism' as the negation of materialism? Mishkin lied to you... because he accepted our assassination of him *willingly*. And our punishing of all you truth-telling individuals is a testament to the truthfulness of our state!

- One more question: have you ever heard of a thing called mercy?

And Drilov did not know what happened next. But your narrator can report that the interrogator jerked open a desk drawer (wherein there is no light), pulled out a steel spoon and with a muscular thigh jammed against Drilov's chest, expertly gouged out his left eye. With a theatrical cry she slurried it against the wall, and it slithered to rest on the floor. Drilov fainted. Thirty minutes later, the prisoner came again to light... to half light.

- Here you are again, Drilov. Intact minus an eye. What has changed? The light is harsher. More concentrated with one eye. Enjoy. And do you like to be clean?

The woman seemed to regard him for a long time. He could not see her, only a blur, as if from the far back of his head. At last she came close and straddled her legs across him. She seemed to sigh. It took some time for her to empty her bladder. At last she grunted, and stepped back.

- Do you like to be clean, Drilov? You can never be clean ever again.

(After a silence) - I am your Beast, Drilov. Are you the hero? We beasts *have* to be killers. Do you know what it is like? Do you know what shit we slither in? Do you care that there is no hope for us? We are in hell, at the centre of the labyrinth. And we never complain. Perhaps you could bring yourself to care for me. Am I your *Ariadne* in this labyrinth? Are you my hero? For what is the quality of your mind, Drilov? The *quality* of your mind... No, be awake! (She thrashes him across the face) Stay awake! Because of the *quality*, Drilov. The quality! ...You will label me a sadist. You say that this system encourages the lowest denominator, that it enforces the end of respect, that it licences us to be hopeless, licenses us to hate and to kill. But you will claim with all your heart and soul *that nothing is lost if no-one is there to lose it*. I am testing if anyone is there, Drilov. I am condemned too, you see. We are all utterly alone, whether we pass away in our own little house or on a bare steppe or mountainside... What is lost though, *if no-one is there to lose it?* What is there when everything else is gone? Where is the light at the heart of hell? Do I appeal to your metaphysical sense, Drilov? I am a philosopher! I am truly your helper. Tell me, should we kill *everyone*? Why not? What is lost, if no-one is there to lose? Here is our justification for the annihilation of people, annihilation of justice, rights, dignity. And you: you found a truth for us. You showed us, with the help of your priest and your artist, that the *quality* of mind is what matters, that quality of soul is what matters, that attitude to death is what matters. You found a justification for emptiness, and thus for immortality. Thank you, Drilov. Now we can kill, can kill you with impunity, with relief, with clarity, with emptiness, with immortality in our hearts!

- No need...

- What? What did you say? But there *is* a need. I, Drilov, am a needing soul. Don't you know? Look how wretched I am, your Ariadne! You are my penance. Therefore I will let you starve, slowly, to death. And in doing so, I will seek to *not hate you*. Truly. You are my discipline, my purity. I must not hate you. I will carry on my duties, carry on my life, while you starve in a place to which only I possess the key. Please take as long as you wish. Yes, it will hurt me, it will even torture me. But you are my penance, my purity, my *quality*. And when my own time comes, as it must, as it soon must… I will remember what you have done for me… what you have done for me.

Something and Nothing   Drilov is thirsty. He has no idea where he is. His face aches with a draining dullness: there is a cave where his left eye once was. He lies against a wall. It is semi-dark. There seems to be no water. Drilov recalls he'd said to the water-tortured prisoner Popova: - 'You should always drink', and she'd said, - 'More than anyone, I know that water, the staff of life, is a killer… Yet there is a fountain in the garden of paradise from which pure water flows outward to all the rivers of the world. The flow is without beginning or end. Take a pinch of its water in each of your cupped hands, Drilov. Is there a difference between the portions? How to speak of your *being* then, in all its ways and incidents? A thing is never itself, is always empty, is *only* perception: one garden of many flowers, one fount of many streams, one water of infinite drops. It is you, Drilov. The event never began so never ended, and thus never was except in gross clinging. The human creature like all creatures is a very nervous tenuous animal. Forced to balance a billion things in its pinhead identity, it is awash with anxiety and longing in this sea of life. The eternal sea may well suffer forms and bodies to grow in it, but let them not fool themselves they are anything but property of the sea. This body of mine is the body of infinitude. We exist as a dream; we dream ourselves a world of names and forms, we struggle for identity, we succumb to identity's endless tension: real as long as it is dreamed. And out of restlessness we begin to compare it with a new dream, one that might eschew all these names or forms, might partake of the nature of wildness, even of emptiness. But layering new dreams on top of other hives of dreams is absurdity on absurdity. No-one can ever be but where they are, living the circumstance they are in. And even to reflect on the death of another, long ago, and compare it to oneself, is the absurd superimposition of fantasy on fantasy. This is being as *becoming*, and there is no remedy. My friend, the action of energy is absolute. We span all worlds. We are always incarnated and never incarnated.' This is what Popova said. And Drilov had replied: - 'Yet I habitually find many regions to be queered and obscure, and I live in a prison inside a prison city, and here there seems to be scant representation of anything I feel to be real. The number of things that are false is ever growing in me. Soon there will be no true things left.' - Drilov, Plato said that in the hierarchy of creation the person's position is archetypal, eternal. He may seek to 'evolve beyond himself', but he should know there can be nothing that is not himself, here, now and forever. And he will also see there is *no* form or position that is ever himself. Yet he must live... The nervous tenuous animal that you are must understand that just as desire is purged away by patience, so your limitations are purged by the end of wanting - to act, to know. There are only two things: the realisation that death is the end of nothing, and realisation that death has no existence at all. What is a man's body but a city, a country, a planet, a world, a universe? All the highways and canals and forests and fields and skies and rivers of blood and water: who is the owner of these? He is no-one, he is the impersonal field of life, with no centre because the centre is everywhere. He is himself.' And Drilov recalls Mishkin said: - Why are you mourning the death of bodies? Your body is someone else's property now. But even if it were your own you'd have no cause to mourn. Your body is clearly not yourself, since you are mourning *it*. We mourn because the beloved body is here no more. We are lonely. But mourning can never be for the people who are lost, but for *ourselves.* How? Physical body exists at the behest of awareness, which becomes intuition, intellect, imagination, emotion, sense... I tell you, Drilov, nothing exists but as product of the inconceivable seer! Even at the withdrawal of bodily manifestation (through sadistic murder or disease or accident) awareness remains intact. Where does it go? The clear and obvious answer is it goes nowhere, since there is nowhere to go, since it never was in a 'place'. Awareness takes up no space. So-called physical has no existence except as idea in the eye of awareness. So, there is no-one to mourn, not even for one's own body. Because my dear, there is *no other.*'

Drilov hears. And he understands. But he is weak. He has had nothing to eat or drink. Perhaps the body is really there to save us from loneliness. Perhaps it is our old and faithful companion. Perhaps we cannot do without it. At the end, at the very end... Drilov is lonely.

Two: Ariadne

Ariadne said: I am your confessor, and conscience of all the dead.

The Unutterable Inconsequence   In the early part of this twenty-first century in a mountainous southern island country, the narrator known as Dreeley penned a story set in Soviet times about a clerk who chronicled the statements of political prisoners about to be executed - before he was dragged to the same fate himself. The reasons Dreeley did this will gradually emerge, according to the following thoughts: 'What paradigms of dislocation, of dim struggle in the tunnels of the mind and heart (he asks) have we to endure through years and lifetimes, in order to come again to a place where we can say *'I am a human being. I am worth something'*? My present life has been one of such fragmentation, elusiveness, inconsequence, that I am pathologically disposed to melancholy, to an overwhelming sense of *ending*. No-one has been able to offer clinical origins for my obsessional circularities. But wherein are the seeds of anything? To me it is plain they lie far beyond 'this present birth', and I therefore have had no choice but to try to repeal the amnesias of physical death.' But are Dreeley's efforts mere fiction heaped on fiction? Why does he scribble great lists of memorial things - to prove that something actually occurred, that there exists at least some kind of ragged context, since the absence of it causes such wretched vertigo? Reader, indulge him as he deconstructs the labyrinth of a mind, confronts a beast, seeks a goddess. 'I don't know any more how to live (he says) except to feel that when all is swept away, when there is nothing to lose since everything is nil and I am a ragged soulless ninepin in the night - that here is a way to begin'.

Ariadne   ...On a bittersweet yet lumined day long ago, at a lunch for his birthday, to mark a respite from therapy's solitude, (as if *ago* could be a word to glibly solve the impossibility of time) a certain woman, not a girlfriend or a sister, not a colleague, nor even a periodic acquaintance - but a comfort woman of sublime skill, in whose confidence Dreeley had come to invest his troubles after many visits to her private quarters where she ministered to his fears and his cravings and for which he scrupulously paid... this woman had gathered a group of men, other men like him, in the sun-bright ante-room of a restaurant in the city, on the pretext that it was his, Dreeley's, birthday. And she had made a little speech in Dreeley's honour, wherein she contrived to deliver apposite words to the ears of these men... and Dreeley had recalled, as she spoke, that he couldn't imagine anyone who would eulogise such a man as he, who lacks all qualities discernible or rememberous (or was this his ploy to divert a need to be noted and loved?) or to recount the life of any man as if he were a coherent seamless (w)hole, or as if moral beauty could be codified or conveyed - especially to such male rivals who would only suck it in through veils of their own selfish need... And so this hostess who spoke, was called by him *Ariadne*... Yet who, thought Dreeley, would ever deliver praise unless they hoped for something in exchange? This woman, he knew, sought no such reward: a measure of her dedication to the business of comfort. She affirmed to the little company: 'we all are lonely, cosmically lonely, and ever wander, ever reaching out in hope of validation'... a truth that reminded Dreeley of 'all the materialists and empiricists of the world' - including scientists and academics, who like rats in our ranks will happily deconstruct billia of particles such that they barely exist according to the Uncertainty Principle of Heisenberg - yet who can never bear to admit to *the utter dissolution of all borders, the non-existence of the self* - such would be the threat to their donning of ceremonial hats, conferral of honours and delivery of esoteric epistles each to each in mutual boosting and desperate charade to remind them against all odds, these brothers-in-ego, that they are solid creatures of hand and eye and blood and fat and sinew, and that the very blood and fat inside their skulls is *the repository of all knowledge* which is furthermore proved by blood and fat being the pinnacle of existence, miraculously spewed forth out of the fabled Big Bang for which we should be traditionally and eternally grateful amen... But what *really* is a man? Dreeley wonders. Or rather, what is a man that he may question what is a man? Nor flesh nor blood, that is certain.

'And so (thinks Dreeley) I validate my woman as Goddess, this *Ariadne,* who spoke coolly and truthfully to me of my *immortality.* And I must try to pay her homage in kind, must repay a huge and subtle debt. And since her name means *utterly holy* I ought to do it with utter zest, though I can't think how, except to know that the threads we cling to in this mazelike world are only what we claim to be... that imagination is but a watery canvas on which the exploits of men and woman and creatures only seem to be painted, and though this worldly matrix of space and time and cause is subject to winds that howl out of a void like the inky detritus of some defeated dream - or else dreamed by *she,* all unknown to me, so that her threads bind me unknowingly and darkly such that I have no choice but *that this present thread were the only thing I could ever be...* For who can fathom the matrices of how we come to be? No puny words like *evolution* or *progress* or *cause* may catch this fathomless emptitude, for I cannot be as I am but in the context of All, and even this 'I', this painted name 'I', this ubiquitous mantra, miserable fist in jeering air, lonelying moan of want, cry at the stars, hawk in etheric sky, rasping breath in the ocean of night, rallying-call to *me* the tiny pea, centre and magnet to the wandering catch-all mind memory body and soul - is nothing but the *constant beginning* of my unthreaded travels from nowhere to nowhere, my cosmic journeying from then to now, and to never, to gone.

And that special thing gifted to me by goddess Ariadne, began to dissolve the instant it left a woman's rouged lips, and perhaps was already deceased before it reached my ear... and if ever such a gift is given and we toss it away, then morally we are nothing - then, now, and ever - and thus in my unworthiness I cannot hope to receive another far-off gift from that shadowy Other, despite that I fool myself I might one day at last be clean enough to receive it as it was meant. Cocooned in memory a gift may surely be kept: without memory it is nothing. Though sages say all things are stored in the deep mind of the race, what use are memories unless I might clutch at them as valuable and meaningful even while I blunder on from forgetting to forgetting? My birth, the memorial of it, that luncheon, the digestion of it, my prized eulogy on that faraway day: all are as sand in the mouth of a dumbstone *Ozymandias,* swept away by rasping winds of dissolutory death. And yet I recall at least that I have forgot, so I aspire at least to a kind of amnesiac beggar-status. Now from the far future, I dream up the notion of Seeker in a Labyrinth, and (unlike the legend) I fail to find a sword or ball of twine to lead me in or out again. And though my delirious twittering memoric dreams fail not to throw up black beasts that brandish horns and hoarily shivel at me their death-heads, these incarnations of beasts of unmeaning, of all cruelty, all implacable blindness, revenge, loss, shame at ineptitude, grotesque longing for purity, all Stalins, all Hitlers… and though I want to believe in their realness and indulge them with shape and solidity, and shiver under them in ecstatic horror - I know that these are my excuse to live inside the great story of the past, which despite being a dead place, a drugged evil lifeless place, is the only thing I may ever claim to *own*.

…Thus the time has come when timeless gifts rejected by me in blitheness and ignorance present themselves once more, coyly, as if to say: look child, we were waiting for you. And by this pricking of conscience I begin to fumble for what was mine, as if stored for me by an unseen mother… For we who are now grown and dying, who feel the waste of time consumed, we, gesturing with anorexic breath, skeletal dreamers blundering in clammy labyrinths of our own making and who living habitually in them come to no longer recognise them as traps - or if we do recognise and seek to escape, only validate them more, or perchance by *not* seeking to escape, little by little might recognise our tunnels as lost dreams and therefore never existing - we men and women might then see that we are the makers of all our dreams, that our dreams become us, and therefore that as creators we might *uncreate,* so that our new dream is to dissolve the dreams we have made, to unmake ourselves, or yet to realise that though we cannot undream we may at least dream of undreaming (!) … But this, this is yet far off.'

Dreeley daydreamed that in a temple of ancient Crete he stood under a grand and famous *mosaic:* the Hero holds the neck of a bull-headed beast with his sword raised to kill. But, indifferent to the whole, seeing instead only bits or fragments he knew nothing of but that here was some cracked irrelevant composite of thousand-year myths, of lives already lived, things already thought, fragments and versicles of millennia entombed yet overseeping the stone, Dreeley thought how the artisan's fingery thoughts could only be occupied in fashioning *one little bit at a time,* and only fleetingly would any intrinsicness to a whole as the poise of composed art or narrative or history occur to him as he sweated his busywork on some sun-glazed afternoon two thousand years past... and if history were a phantom glueing of fragments stirred in a soup of *ever-present oneness* that spits them out in dissonance and multiplicity as 'the moment, the hour, the century', what then is this mosaic such that a little worker who works to fashion it can call it art or narrative or history when *he himself is the mosaic of infinitude,* ever split in the moments and minutes and hours and days of his own life, wherein no instant can ever cohere with any other, and such that he is never self-composed except as a dream - dreamed by one such as Dreeley... And though the artisan is called a sentient soul with the sense of being 'himself' or at least of acting in ways that seem coherent and sequentially causal (albeit that he'd have no such words for that, and no notion of how or why this coherence should ever be invested in him) he is in fact nothing but 'a random thought of himself', or some tenuous notion of being 'an artist', fashioner of 'things that were his dreams now chiselled in stone'. And how many *other* dreams crowd about as if waiting to turn to stone... yet there never will be time for all of them since thought is far quicker than stone, and this chiseller will think myriad things without chiselling them, and the things he does chisel are but inchoate fragments of some chthonic construction in his unfathomable psychic sea (as if any sea would submit to be constructed)... And what of *all* dreams, glass spaghetti of centuries, that might halo this mosaic on a wall, infiltrating the eyes of We the present watchers (we are all islands, continents, alone) who might 'chafe at the agony of a mosaic trapped in stone' or 'drift to some elsewhere' even as we stand before the thing which speaks so incoherently of itself, of itself... And what are our thoughts of the maker's thoughts as he gathered these stones in his lost silence, or as he thought of times to come, or thought of we the people who stand before it and wonder on such as *he,* gaseous victim of the future as he has become, vapid victims of the past that we are... So the mosaic is worthless, fool's history (Dreeley says), since the Labyrinthine Beast will never be slain! But a better thought comes: that the mosaic is a work of Art, because it is mutely patient in the face of all shivering rantings and posturings and ignorant abusings and tirades and betrayals and breathings and mind-scatterings and tides and trivias of the world of men… It bears them all in its shrugging glazed silence, its massivity on a wall in a dusky temple, where the breeding chaos of the outer world clatters and fries and dies like flies in the beating sun and dust. *Within it stands* - cool in shadows, absorbing all, reflecting all, caring *nothing*…

'And as for my long-ago lunch guests (who are my ghosts in a way no-one else can ever own) - what other scintillae of personal threaded daydreams might have been shattered by the sudden imposing tinkle of a spoon on glass, by the speech of *Ariadne?* And who will retrieve these mosaical quanta of conversational fragments except such as me who creeps as if down glass corridors of the past and enters expectant still rooms of eternity, and as if in new communions with old ghosts helps the talkers re-invest like chattering songbirds innumerable pingpongs of chat and answer out of cryogenically stilled wads of time… Or perhaps nothing and nobody is lost or waiting, for their glaze of thoughts was but candy floss that scintillated and self-entertained in eternal light, emptily signifying not a thing but itself, and barely even that. But I tell you my lunch guests *are* doomed to leave and leave again their threads like frozen pointillistic beads in passageways, for you the reader and for me the needer - for without labyrinthine arcane paths, where would any of us be, where would any of us go; without trade in words who would we be, and so on and so? In invisible paths as in electronic webs of cyber worlds we must weave the patterns, the patterns… our conversations, our browed questions and studied replies, exclaims of surprise, deft rejoinders, grave considerations, ironic disclaimers… the traffic of studious nothings, the maze of past, present, future.

And there is nothing more death-ghostly than my longing to retrieve what is called past. It is as if I wished the winds of a thousand years to repatriate the leaves of a ragged tree on a winter plain that is now dust or the ether of comets, or as if I wished a surge of water that enveloped a fish in ecstasy ten billion years ago could somehow reshape and recreate itself exactly and minutely as it did… or was said to have done, or might be said to have

done, once and once only in a unique expatiation of particulate atoms...
but that it as if sported and flaunted and laughed at itself because it knew
as it did so, that it *never* was what it was, could never in fact ever be so,
and was not even conscious that its insouciant supple laughter and sport
would haunt a seer from the utter future who might dream to recreate in
his mind a thing he could not possibly know ever was, to conjure again a
thing that might have been, once, once...

And suddenly I seem to recall on that birth day, these people I scarcely
knew (since invited by *Ariadne,* who had put a spell on them also)
contrived to discourse each to each and tete-a-tete in faked solicitude
for *me,* as if they were like old and staunch friends, whereby in fact they
talked excludingly of themselves and their doings and their wants and
their ins and outs - and I, wanting to recognise this as a sort of homage
to me the nameless inconsequential man in whose name this gathering
happened, contrived to *join in* on my own faux-celebration and become
as drunk and as involved and as posturing as they, because in seeking for
my Immortal Partner one who while popularly desired by all of them
(*Ariadne*) yet had the grace to focus her pearly mind on me in token of
the occasion, herein I seemed to justify all the insatiable reasons why I
lived and breathed and had my secrets and my fearing little nuances: it
was for *her* ears and eyes only! and she in her subtle coolness responded
as if I were the only person in the world - and perhaps I actually was,
since I received the grace that may only be dispensed by a goddess, who
with cool calculation lets herself be the chosen idol of every dreamer
who hopes to be recognised or loved, inside this sultry delicate-deadly
competition we call social life, or human life...

Yet though *Ariadne* is ever the object of my dreams and thereby unassailable,
I am separated from her, and it is my karma to be so. Because *Ariadne* is
fascinated by the obstacles she puts in the way of the ones who seek her,
she who dallies sexily with many Beasts. For me they are always the Other
Man, always *Dionysus,* always the desirer, the opposer, the subverter, the
cutter, the toppler, the blinder, the executioner - no hero - and I must find
him, must murder him, he who must steal her away, steal her away. And
though perhaps she as object of my dreams will be the one to release me,

she for want of whom I have accumulated all my losses and mistakes and foolish things and for whom through the labyrinth of uselessness I go, ever evading or confronting some monster or beast concocted by myself to serve my need to fight or die or be victim or victor or hero... did I turn her into an object of salvation that she could never be? A dream must always remain a dream, and will perish in its fulfillment. And dreams will metamorphose, and we do not recognise how our own dream has shifted. All we really know is that we need to have them... and when a dream ends, what will replace it but another more refined? I need someone Unborn to idolise. A mysterious woman will do the job!

At last, at the end, all I can say is this: once upon a lost time long before this present future came to pass... certain parties were held to have had conversations at a birthday lunch, and we from the standpoint of eternity imagine that these dreamers, out of freedom, 'dreamed the conversation of themselves'. A brilliant trick, Jorge Luis Borges would agree. Should I then strike an attitude of amused irony - since this life seems to offer no meaning except that I am doomed to participate forever and ever in clever-clever mental conversations, in the dreamer's sport, as if though nothing could *ever* change or improve or evolve or grow up, it irrevocably must be allowed to *seem to do so?* And should I invest in desperate remembering, in a trivial lunch from long ago, as if I believed in evolving and growing up, and in my consternation try to see a way back in order to go forward, to get out of this unending prison of raw feeling through *analysis?* Or will I admit that the conjuring happens *only now, only here* - so that the speaker is forever my own ego that is forever generating and manufacturing the works of me the Manufactured Man? Perhaps my problem is utterly simple: that the secret beyond all my manufactured dreams is that *there is no secret.* That there is nothing to worry about as long as I sigh and accept that the manufactured man is all I am, that my conversation is forever non-different from me, that there is no conversation but *a dream that badly wants to overwhelm.* And this great principle of 'boundless Awareness' - that there is no conversation but that of Myself - puts paid to the bother of memories and processes and particles and times and spaces and past and future! Laugh then, participate in the Great Conversation.

But it is long and arduous! And its best joke is that there is a heaven of *forgetting* - and there can be no desire to remember without this aching forgetting… though forgetting really cannot be, since the Seer never forgets himself… Is forgetting and remembering then how 'lonely freedom' longs to admire itself, how it longs to celebrate itself, how the Self learns to talk to itself in its loneliness? Here is clearly the bride-price of freedom. So, my mind, remember, remember… and the laughter is certainly on you! And when the elaborate sifting-game is stopped, the ghost-waltz finished, when comes the horror that things have never been and all the while you believed in them, that you never were and never will be (you are eaten, Dreeley-man!), when you forget relationships, associations, good times, memories, fondnesses, self-dreams, evolvings, satisfactions, learnings - then you must rely only on one thing else, and it is called *The Thing That Knows!* But what is This Thing that can tell you that the labyrinth and lattice and mosaic and bundle of threads that you call yourself is *yourself?* It must surely be magical, for it is the fountain and well of generating and forgetting, and it seems to be never emptied! Perhaps we are really like the comets that seem to stream across its sky, or like a fountainhead, as if our deeds cascade behind us like a waterfall of flowers or a florid cloak or a broadening field of lights in a great city we built. This Empty Thing must be dimensional like the sky - yet full like a thing with no boundary is full, big enough for comets and aeons and history to pass over it and disturb it not… That which is boundless shall have no rules, no unhappiness, shall have no truck with *things*. It is beyond the heaving breath and suffers no consequence, suffers no foolish time, suffers no cause. Shall we lament then, the agony of a mosaic trapped in its form? We who spend aeons to punish the boundless in ourselves, we who scurry from the loneliness of solitude, who pixelate the borderless, who holler out our syllables to the night, who hammer metals and murder the trees and lay out our waste-roads to places of Nowhere and like ants with backsacks plug them full with useless goods, we who shore up and drown deserts, drain blood from the lands, huddle in the solitude, wrap our arms about transparent air, scratch out lines of consequence and cause, rocket into spaces of the stars so deep to map them, map them and miniaturise them, who build our towers of learned babble, make rods for our backs, hairshirts for our souls, we who feel the death-breath of the boundless on our necks, that we might come creeping guiltily back to the borders of the solitude, we watchers who solemnly wonder what is its meaning: this empty, this quiet one, lone and still... This *conscience*.

Ariadne, I have named you. And I will find you. Or at least, a dream of you.'

Country of Erasure   Dreeley records: 'In time I have recovered from visions of deconstructive madness born of utter inconsequence, such as the reader has been burdened with at length above. I have instead become wedded, in this island country in the southern sea, to visions of sad yellow light and clear polar wind, duneswept beaches and cloud-caressed peaks... And now on this cusp of jettisoning all I have ever known, I reflect that I have learned some things: that obsession is a fool's game, that labyrinths lead only to more convoluted versions of themselves, that obsession with death is nothing but rampant fear, that memory is nothing but the detritus of *need*. We live in the threads of our stories because there is no salve, no explication for this omni-repressive present. And worse, at last I must not only give up what I was looking for, but also the tool, the *paradigm* in which I looked for it: in the end the strands of experience must dissolve in a great lake of *not knowing*. Here I suppose is a source of hope, but my enduring need is still to characterise myself as victim, as a seeker of atonement for guilt, as one who must sacrifice, such is the power of habit, of belief, of unconscious history. Old myths seek fertile ground! And I am as if always at the turgid *beginning*, where I must take up again the unending narrative, the labyrinthine bind of birth and death and time and consequence. This man called Dreeley really wants to be gone. He habitually thinks of the end, the end of all clinging and wanting, of place and time, of cause and effect, of delusion... where life might come to be profound ease, simply as it is, nothing but itself. It sounds like death! Or else the death of death.

Meanwhile, in this country in the southern ocean the white inhabitants are shielded from the claws of history, and after generations of births and smoothings-out, they are only glancingly aware of their race's past. These whites construct new and eager lives, but they are aware of the sea, either its vast question or its capacity to swallow nascent dreams. They also know a wind that ruffles from the North like a breathless bringer of news, as if it once knew things but forgot them. And they know a southern wind that empties out the mind, that comes lunging over deep hills bringing ice from the bottom of the earth. Better to remember, says the north. Better to be empty, says the south. 'I, Dreeley, cleave to the south wind, though I fear it. In this flung country, must we re-create the history of the world, want to refashion the past as sweet-hopeful future? Or should we be as ghosts of forest and fjord and peak, creatures of the wild without thread or bone, buffeted by the south wind all our days unto death? We who came for refuge, for exile, for a fresh life, cannot erase the need for belonging - so that the clever among us might think to minutely trawl history's secrets before leaving them forever... And is such emptiness not effective: erasure of place, erasure of time?' Dreeley can barely decide.

New Bondage Street   'There is a little premises on a steep hill above the capital city where punters come to seek what falls to them nowhere else. I have come to view it as the place of atonement where perpetrators fulfill their victimhood or their manhood. Some need to dominate, others to be dominated, but all need belonging, solace. And all are solitary. My companion-hostess at that birthday lunch I reconstructed at length, about whom I could tell you so little... is a sex worker. I will say she is part Russian since the surname is *Popova.* Another part of her may be Pacifika or Maori. I have decided that it is. Her trade name is *Endaira...* and she employs all her foreignness as mystique. Her place of work on the hill, of solace and atonement, she has called (serendipitously) *New Bondage Street* - as if she could give the place a whisper of spirit where spirit is but fools' poetry. Actually, it is only one place where Endaira goes. You might say she goes wherever there is need. What do people need? Company, comfort, sex, talk, presence with her... although Endaira does not fulfill wanting, she fulfills 'the want of wanting'. One time I got the thought in my head that I would try to urge her to leave her way of life, thinking I could offer her something more than she had... I asked her to come to see a play with me, and she agreed. Oh she dressed wondrously for me, but I know she has a little price for everything. I was nervous, had vague idealistic expectations for the piece since I knew it had to do with Pinter's *Birthday Party*. As we wandered through a warehouse with many rooms where fragments of the play were enacted by different actors, I blurted out: But what are they doing with Pinter's profound unease? How to know what to do with a moment... or what not to do... to have decided not to decide... how moments fall? Is there a message in that silence? My commentary turned quite comical, and Endaira took it in with her customary muted calm. Well I knew that if the whole building were to fall on us she'd not even cower. Perhaps she'd be amused. She is like that, in no way nervous. That is, unless she decides to manifest such an emotion for the sake of a client. I have seen her offer a little tear, utter a sharp word, even cry out - but only as if not changing anything, as if it didn't matter... In fact, there was a time when I arrived at the place Endaira calls New Bondage Street, and in a hurry to find her barged into a room and spied her through a heavy curtain... and she was splayed out on the floor in the chamber beyond, with her limbs tied and stretched in four directions as if on a medieval rack, and there were two men in hoods with canes in their hands who were nonchalantly beating her legs and stomach. I shrank back, and no-one saw. Endaira had a spiked choker about her neck, and there was not a thing else to comfort her straining flesh. Blood seemed to drip from the crotch; at least, red liquid splayed about her thighs. At a point a man went down on her. I could see she was in an agony of shaking, with her muscles distended to the limit. She didn't cry out, except once and in a way that might have had the effect of amusing him. I could not turn away. The other fellow shoved himself in her mouth, and she seemed to all intents to suffocate. The brutes took their time, local fat-bodies who would not have seen this calibre of woman in all their bogan days except in this charnel house, this mental stage set where the simulation of torture is real beyond any stunted reference they could make to history's true debauchery. They had no imagination but that which Popova provided them, two oafs in hoods using her like a dog, like a urinal, like a pin cushion they could stick their pricks into and gush their semen over. And she, encouraging them, teaching them, getting *her* sexual power beyond their imagining. When they'd finished, and as the game started to look a bit tawdry and they'd backed off a bit and tittered to each other in their cowardy way, she offered the little boys a kind of professional dignity-pause (she, their victim and mother) before requesting them to untie her hands. One did, but as if to say *we don't have to, bitch* and she, controlled, neatly thanked them. Next she ran her fingers into her crotch and as they stood there (as we all stood there) expertly guided herself to a crushing orgasm - that I will never know was simulated or not, but I had the feeling it was not simulated in her *imagination*... and she proved to those fucks (sorry, clients) that she would forever have the last word, that she would forever hypnotise her acolytes at any level at which they came to her. At that point I backed away. I had felt something I had no idea what to do with. To see her like that was such exquisite pivot of guilt, desire and regret... that I realised that she strives to be a genius of extremes, of contradictions, of oxymoron. There is but one way to come to that mastery, and that is to have experienced the utter depths, over and over beyond the telling of it. What has this woman seen to become so completely detached? And why is it so magnetic, so evocative? We customers come again and again because we have to want the things we have seen her do, things she tempts us to do. We forever want her. We ever go back, deeper into the labyrinth of her...

On Friday evenings in winter I'd climb the hill, and more often than not step onto the path that led to her place of work. There was never any indication that the establishment was called New Bondage Street, Endaira's little moniker. I had told her once about a Russian story I had been writing, about great and unjust imprisonment, then had forgotten it. I failed to recognise her little irony for my sake. She has the power to make you forget... In the lobby, the hostess' brisk talk never did soothe my embarrassment. Where is Popova? I'd ask. Where do you want her to be, said a voice in my head. And I admit I fell in love with the unbearable thought that she is in the company of other men. The hostess doubtless knew my thought, and thereby was I a mundane and typical punter... and the pain is always with me, not her. The wanting is mine, not hers. Yet I feel I have no thread to find Endaira, no sword to defend her...

In time came an event where I understood the real price she has paid.

Discipline and abasement are one thing, revenge is quite another: the only proper response for certain black things that well up out of the pit. But it can't ever be served cold; such things are by definition uncontrollable, bestial. All our reactions are useless, misdirected, wild, momentary, faceless, absurd, blind and regrettable... yet they are necessary. I am reminded of an exchange we had where she showed me her anger, just once. I took it as a new stage in our intimacy, if there were any. Don't be the victim! I told her, and I guess it smacked of smugness. I'll be a victim if I fucking want! she replied. And right there is a *vocation*. But is there power in it? Popova is a phenomenally brave girl and I worship such a quality. But still, we are human. ...On the day where a price is resolutely to be paid, we are in a basement bar somewhere in the capital. She has come with me today because I am paying. Drinks will suffice, she says. All the same she orders the priciest ones. Popova will certainly talk, but not about anything that matters to her. A suitable topic is the foibles of her colleagues; they are the nearest she will get to putting herself in a human context. She'll not gossip, which is beneath a woman like her, but will observe. 'One's colleagues are dilettantes and ingenues, or are in it only for money or pleasure. Some even have degrees. None are artists.' And even her mercilessness seems apposite, for she carries heavy life within her such that nothing she says or does should ever be held against her. And she'll lavish care on clients but won't speak of them. That includes me. If survival is your raison d'etre (which sounds strangely solipsistic) you'll take responsibility - for every little terrorising ogrous beast that squeezes itself out of the woodwork of your body, for every niggly nuance and memory and unconscious gust that flutters out of your psyche. You'll pay homage to every trumped up fat little demon that pokes and leers at you, you'll acknowledge every scummy projection of want that your customers dump - because *it really is you,* it is your chance to slough off all your need, so that all your dippings in these dirty depths are an opportunity, a privilege, are your thorn-crowning, your reward, your survival. It is good to know I am respected by her in proportion to the levels of shit I excrete from my pores... It sounds like I am a victim, but no, Popova discourages self-pity, and you get the point: she favours the empowered mode of victimhood (move over, Jesus). But how do we enact our past as the playing out of unconscious needs? It is one of life's mysteries that we carry forward the pressing force of some singular scene wherein festers a great unfinished business. We blindly circle it, circle it because somewhere deep we know what really happened to us back then. Yet amnesia, carried from birth to birth, is also our blessed aide, and without this forgetting, without unconsciousness, we could never seek justice or revenge or atonement or knowledge or purity or love…

Endaira is standing at the bar, ironically dressed in padded black jacket, webbed orange tights and red ankle-boots. Her height always wins attention, and the thighs promise heaven to needy punters. Today's little goblins in the form of three semi-drunk guys, of a kind who think that a chick who dresses like that is asking for it, all complexed-up by their secret fear that they wouldn't ever satisfy her, sidle up and start a conversational ruck. I am ignored, and that's as Popova will have it. No bloke on *her* arm.
- Where ya from, babe?
- No planet you'd know. Sorry
- Aw right. Get you a drink?
- Sure. A bottle of *that.*
The young fellows look at each other. No choice, buddies. Furtive grapple for credit cards. Eighty-eight dollars later: - Any extras?
- You lot? Five hundred cash.
The fellas are out of depth. Get in depth fellas. - *Endaira, let's bail…* - Wait outside! she snaps. And she sidles to the far end, turns momentarily to us, slips through a door. Yo, that back passage. The guys glance to me. Murmurs all round. Finally they head in a huddle for the door. Feel almost sorry for 'em. The pub music ratchets up. I order a drink. Ten minutes. Better check. A little vestibule and a storeroom door. Get ready for fleshy scrummaging behind. I bend an ear. Suddenly there's a howling animal cry and the door bursts open. A guy is on the threshold, petrified, shovels past me. Another sways on his knees, grabs at his pants, stumbles after. I peer into the gloom. Popova has the jagged end of a bottle in her hand. The third guy is flat out on the floor, pants round his ankles. He is clutching his genitals. There is blood on his fingers. Popova steps right over him and with both arms raises the jagged eighty-eight dollar bottle and jams

it downward into his navel. He screams. And she thrusts it again. Fucking norah! She straightens, sees me, flings the bottle at the wall, comes at the door. I grab at her wrists. She lets me. Her eyes are brimming. She pushes me off, veers at the pub door. I kneel down. The guy has passed out, there's blood sputtering from his navel. Penis seems cut to bits. I cast about, find some kind of rag, try to staunch. And there is her bag… her tights, her panties. Gather them, run into the pub room, make semaphore with the bar manager, drag him in. His eyes pop wide. I fuck off quick smart. She is not to be seen on the streets. I stalk several blocks. My guts are heaving. Have to get to her. Get her away.

Next day, lie low, scan the news. Hello! Bar incident in town, cocktails plus violence with a filthy twist. No pic of Popova, description only. The victim: he's going to live but he's never going to be a family man. Scandaloso. A day after, I set out to trawl for Endaira in all her places. At New Bondage Street her co-workers tell me she without warning left her place of residence, crossed the strait and caught a ride far to the south, to the green-black forests, to the land of fjords. Endaira left a card on a dresser at her flat, they nod sagely. For who? For the one who finds it, numbskull. Clearly I should never trust sex girls, for the simple reason they don't want to be trusted. Yet it is as they said. In her thick-addled scrawl under a little portrait of a woman who resembles her face, Popova wrote: *If you look hard, a girl will leave clues to her whereabouts. I have no desire to be lost. I am a spinner and gatherer of threads. Do you want to rescue me?* I can hear her whisper it, the girl who pisses on our feelings and fears! But I know as long as I pursue she'll be a stranger, and only in strangeness can I know her, sort of. I reckon my absurd future: I will ask people in all places, *do you know Endaira Popova?* And the name is incongruous, for it's only me who describes her so. She is in my world, no-one else's. These strands of my atonement must be confidential, must appear in no official account, no police or government record…'

Dreeley soon identifies the aloof little snap left by Popova (artist Seraphine Pick) as coming from a local gallery. And he will tell anyone who asks, that it is not her face. He has learned to be evasive, and will say solemnly that his pursuit of a Russian woman in the far south of New Zealand is but a fiction, a need, a compensation - since he has a history of mental illness… and that even if he did track her down she would be semi-unrecognisable having put on new clothes new make-up new hair… He will claim she is impersonal, a chameleon, that she lives on the borderland of a psyche, that she is but the act of looking, the truth that the more you look the more a thing isn't there. He will say she is a romance, dream of a different self, and that if we glance ever so lightly we may get a hint but if we are to search high and low there will be no trace. Dreeley will say it is his last big foolishness. Reader, should we believe anything more he tells us?

Dion Dreeley records: 'A week later I hitched a ride with a hippie traveler who claimed he was touring the south land in the winter. Called himself (improbably) Dionysus. Dion 'for short'. He commanded an old red Falcon with a hole in its floor and beer and spirit bottles strewn underfoot and incense sticks poking from the dashboard. Ever-unshaved Dion wore a multicoloured Rastafarian beanie like a trophy. I soon realised he had bad eyes. One dim afternoon on some borderless road it was snowing heavily and the window wipers refused to wipe, and we ended up crawling into a suburb which turned out to be Queenstown. Dion said he knew a bar, and when we got there it was as if they were expecting us. I assumed Dion was a drug dealer since the proprietor wouldn't let us pay for drinks, of which we had plenty. Several girls gave him the eye. Outside on the street, he proceeded to insult some guys on motor bikes. We drove out of town heading for the mountains. Ten minutes later the bikers appeared on the road behind us in a swarm, all ducking and weaving about. Kids. We outdistanced them somehow on a straight stretch, and I called on Dion to make a super-dramatic stop. He did it, with a mega-dangerous skid, and he and I leapt out and charged back down the middle of that highway in the blizzard in our black winter coats with our arms spread out like some dreadful Christ Redeemers shouting and hollering like madmen. Those junior bikers took one look, turned tail and scooted in a flurry and a skid back to town. I can just hear the breathless gossip: *dude, those cunts were baaaad!* Kinda cool tho, a battle with evil weird guys. Me and Dion had a laugh and it appeared we were well met: two sad aging hippie guys. We threw a couple of snowballs at each other... Later, when I (foolishly) hinted to him about the mysterious Popova, I sensed he was more than casually interested since he started lobbing non-sequitur questions at me. This little conversation it turned out, underpinned an invitation to hang with him in his car. We'll travel the lost winter roads of the south, he said. Our cool and solitary road trip! On the face of it, the prospect of driving about with Dion didn't stir me, but I knew I'd let it happen in a passive wintry way. Something about descriptions of Popova flutters the veil of imagination. Guys seem interested. I guess Dion built a vision. I didn't grock till later he'd made up his own mind to find her - and maybe

I didn't want to grock it. I didn't mask facts, just told him she was semi-untouchable. That did it.

Anyway, Dion the old indie hipster likes to doodleyack as he drives us along, and he's a polished spruiker of himself in studiedly haphazard style. I glean he is the son of well-off parents, and he certainly doesn't fail to acquaint me with their shortcomings. Couldn't they buy you a better car? I say naughtily. Bought the motherfocker m'self, he retorts. He seems to assume I'm happy to be in his company, though he'll not fail to let me think that he's an alone-and-abandoned knocked-about sort of guy who has no fixed abode etcetera *by choice,* but doesn't care 'cause destiny is much bigger than all this shit and things fade to nothing anyways right dude? But hey why not take the Trip Of Life since it's all ironic weirdness yo? Not that he's averse to chicks feeling sorry for him and doing the chicky thing by him once in a way. Dion assures me he is the arch hedonist whose live-in-the-now shtick ignores the past, rejects the psyche as personal paradigm ('human labyrinth' he calls it) and yoho! superficiality / escapism is our duty in the face of absurdity of being alive, check. But still he's pretty cool and subtle 'cause he still chases heaps of things - next best lay, primo drugs, experiences - as if they mattered. *As if,* mind you. And no way he's ashamed of it, not being a nonce. Contradiction yeah? Can't live wivout doin', can't act wivout responsibility! Dion has it all figured out, but wouldn't bother telling me unless he knew I was hip enough not to judge and if he's going to hit on my girlfriend if and when she turns up then obviously he wants me to be prepared for that little post-modern experience because according to him my casual attitude every time I open my mouth on the subject of her, pricks up his antenna that she's *way out of my reach.* He can tell 'cause anyone that cool would have to be out of reach anyway yo? Sorry dude, not meaning to bring ya down, just reciting the bare facts which is what you respect, dig? But hey, when I tell him he's putting my relationship with Popova in a shitty box 'cause he's covering up his own mind drool over her he says: right on, dude! I knew you wuz hip to me and my shit! Nope, there's no way round Dion. He studied himself all right, and came up with the goods of a persona that fits the way he thinks of himself. Err right on. Meanwhile

Dion's driving is a bit fucken dangerous, and when one time he gets in a snowdrift on a blind corner and laughs his head off so I tell him 'if there was a frigging truck -' he says trust you to think the worst! in a *very* familiar way that suggests he knows my life story - and then he says sorry man because he knows he's testing me and I have to grit my teeth and eat it because he is actually not without the odd insight in the 'we're all uptight in the same way' or 'we all have skellies in the closet' or 'you're a capricorn with moon in scorpio right?' mode of shite. But at least he don't assume I wanna listen to his rave all day 'cause he has a bumblingly cute habit of changing the topic as we trundle along as if life on da road wuz one cool 'lil acid trip featuring one 'lil absurdity after another... so hey let's dig into his assorted drug and booze collection he brought along, paid for no doubt with someone else's money. Never know when you're gonna have company dude! Dion's used to having company, confident of it in fact. Lets him play the abandoned time-waif on his eternal road trip, lets him toss people off one by one... 'but man they *want* it, 'cause people are like sad fucks and masochists and they want me to deal it to them, expose their shit - which I *don't do* 'cause I got a conscience, 'cause that shit's not too evolved yo? I mean even if people appreciate you exposing their shit you don't go hard on 'em, know what I mean? I sense you're not too fucking slow in that department yerself. But hey listen: why exactly are you chasing this chick round the arse-fuck of the world? Where's she *from,* man? Wellington? Yeah, I was like up there for a time. Buzzy town. Mebbe I fucked her! Sorry dude. Describe her to me...' And so we're back on the topic of Popova. That druggy Dion brain has a habit of turning on the same riffs. Wouldn't tell him though. He's got his own self-scene going in that hip-funky head of his and I wouldn't wanna disturb. Because Dion is a metaphysician of the soul and a proselytizer too. 'We're like in the age of Aquarius, man. Wassa point if you're not gonna deconstruct all this shit? Heard of Derrida? Dude's fuckin' ace. Gimme a toke. Lissen. See that big fat mountain and sky? What's the difference between you and it?' (I'm hip to this line because privately I often get the feeling when we're flying down a road that there's no time or space because I'm always here - and BE HERE NOW is like what where when the fuck else could I ever be! so everything is totally blissy and super-simple - but I'll not let old Dion in on it 'cause he has to ration out the wisdom) …'Man, that sky and mountain are YOU. No boundary. Where's it end and you begin? Are you the air you breathe in and out? The food you gobble and shit? Are you the sun's heat you suck in and shiver out? Are you this body or this monkey mind of thoughts that come and go? Where the hell is mind anyway, get it? You are eternal, nothing but. And you drag all of your karmic shit to the next incarnation - till *you* decide to dump it.'

And I discover through the dope haze that his drift is like, a bit inspired.
- Yeah! We're nothing but Being n' Awareness (can't help copying his lingo)
- Yeah! How can anything ever be born? Nothing ever happened, dude
- Yeah! Who the fuck complains about dying? Let's get out of this shit!
- Yeah! We were never here anyway
(We're shouting) - Nothin's happenin'. Nothin's happenin'!
- What're you reelly, Dreeley? Shaping twisting makin' breakin' rearranging shapeshifter! What are you NOW? Get out of yer body!
(Suddenly the drug tips over to serious)
- Yeah yeah. No no… we have to stay and tough it out
- Bullshit. Unlimited awareness, man
- No. That's the reason we're in this body! We still haven't understood the relationship between body and awareness
- Fuck, we're IT, man
- But! But. I doubt it. I can doubt it
- Ooh well done you
- No, I mean d'you think every time we get some kind of insight that our whole body and mind doesn't scream with resistance and unholy shit like some pain-in-ass kid? This whole material world is doubt! Freaking ignorance
- Fuck yeah, you're flying now, man. You're like that little fish swimming in the ocean holding up a little flag that says: 'Water? I doubt it!'
(He's nailed it again) - You don't mean me, man
- I mean you, ya dumb fuck
- I just don't like to see people in illusion. Mostly they should know better. What I can't forgive is ignorance. And cruelty. Makes my blood boil

- You're a heavy shit sort of dude ain't ya? The whole world is ignorance, man. Your unforgiveness is your blockage. Lighten up
- What are you, a lightweight? (But the smug bastard is right) Okay, point taken. But are you a middle class wanker who never has to suffer?
- Quite possibly, dude
- Give it up
- Don't need to. It's the hand I was dealt. It's all self, I told you. All is self, so be self-centred! I am MYSELF. All I need to do is be
- Do be doo be doo beee
- Fuck off. No choice but to participate. And there's no good or evil, man. Life is all trivia. Life is cosmic joke. Live, die, whatever!
- You're an exploiter. Which makes you a closet cynic. Why not cause evil, why not revel in it?
- There is no evil, man.

Now we're on a downer. I can just about buy Dion's line. Just about. But what if Dion were faced with catastrophe - of the kind that not only has no meaning but is calculatedly meaningless? In other words, torture. In the cells of a prison for instance. Is Dion free? The measure is, would he forgive his brainless cynical wretched captors? Because you have to, you can't just act as if the event wasn't there. We store stuff, till the end of time if need be. Dion despite his knockabout cosmic wisdom is still a limited little fuck, and that's where I'm sticking. Call me a curmudgeon, call me captive of my own conscience, call me a conservative loser. Ah but it's the dope, makes ya paranoid.
(Then) - Yer lookin' a bit paranoid, man. The dope's got horse tranquilliser in it.

Late that afternoon we turn up at a crossroads. Dion randomly swerves onto a dirt road, clearly stomping on our plan to head for Wanaka and survey the Friday bars to look for Popova. Maybe this'll take us to Erewhon! he shouts in triumph. I get suitably pissed and shout Where the fuck are we going? which lets him say Don't you *know* the seminal novel by Samuel Butler? Erewhon is a nanogram for Nowhere, shithead. I refrain from telling him I knew it and he's an immature twat. We settle for him driving a mile on this nowhere road then saying Fuck it man let's go get a drink in Wanaka; maybe we'll run into some chicks! Which gets me grinding my teeth as he does his super-duper about-turn skid nearly breaking the axle then roars off down the Road Just Travelled to the Crossroads where he acts even more confused till I tell him to get to fucking Wanaka by nightfall or else, and he does his greasy 'You sure are desperate to get with the Russki ain't ya?' and pats my knee and says 'Light up that toke in the glovebox while I tell ya about the time I half-choked this Russian chick with a billiard ball in a brothel in Wellington 'cause she couldn't come hard enough in my face unless I did it. Nope, just joshing ya. Hey! Cheer up son, mebbe your Popova will be wiv us tonight.'

She sure isn't. Other girls are though. Maybe they're all Popova. Dion gets himself a date: two local ladies bored with their husbands. Too easy. I tag along. Dion sets up an elaborate scene in our motel room. 'Hey Dreeley, Rhona and Lena (the girls) heard rumours 'bout a girl called *Popova*... some folks saw her on an island in the lake!' 'Wadda women want?' shouts Dion. 'Bit of sado-masochism? Disrupt our inflated boy shit, we hope! Women don't make good commies or fascists eh Dreeley?' (This is all over our ladies' heads, but plied with Dio's drugs they're suitably loose.) He gets a rave on. 'Yeah, I'm like a vagabond son of old money... don' hold it against me. I was living in the capital for a while, turns out I knew that Russki chick, under a fake name o' course. (I ask Dion to shut it. No luck) Used ter play this game called *Interrogation*. (Ooh Dion! crow the ladies) Yeah, you get tied up in a chair (not me, I watch) and *she* does her thing with the cane and the billiard ball and the fake blood and piss! She's so ace at it it makes yer eyes pop. Guess them Russkis know: all that fucked-up history. Hey lemme show you guys!' This has the effect of creating giggle mayhem. Dion's night of sex drugs and rock n' roll degradation is about to go swimmingly. Sadly its chief spectator decides to absent himself. Has a more refined conscience to nurse.

The Bicyclists   If I am not mistaken, next day is my birthday, though this happy fact will stay a secret from the world. Dion and me, not speaking, head out on the Haast road: lonely snakehead, blind twists in unpeopled gorges, raindrift thickness, epic grey emptiness. An hour in, we come to a ford. The stream is swollen; we're forced to halt. Two figures stand by the roadside in hooded anoraks. Bulgy bikes shiver under a tree. The winter rain is sheeting, numbing; people like this, people like anyone shouldn't be in this wilderness of green-black woods creepling over beast hills on and on to interior places no-one ever named or walked. I can see the pair are one step from a squabble. - Get ready, we're parting the waters! grunts Dion. - Wait, we should ask if they need help. They're on fucking bikes! he says. I poke my head out. *My wife is a little injured. Her head bleeds. Her bike is not so well.* And her white face looks at me, and I feel I recognise her... or both of them, under those hoods... as if a weird *deja vu*. Can't help ya! shouts Dion and plants his foot. The car surges. There's a hefty splash. *Stop, goddam it!* Cool it dude! He jams the car backward. Come back to town with us, I say. They're mute, resolutely sad. The raindrift is icy. Somehow the three of us bundle their gear in back, strap their bikes to the roof. Dion never budges. They shuffle in like soggy seals, and on the road back, suffer mutely. Dion interrogates. Why'd you come 'ere then? For adventure. Yes, adventure. Wrong season! crows Dion. That is the point, the boy says. The girl seems to defer to him. How old are ya? says Dion uncouthly. Oh, we are both nineteen, says she. We come from Belarus. Have you heard of Minsk? It is far away, as far away as can be.

At the hostel in Wanaka I linger in the spartan room of the girl as she dries herself. Shortish lank hair embalms a round face. - Why are you here in the winter, she asks. - I'm looking for a girl, a Russian. She gazes. *Oh I met a Russian. Days ago, in Queenstown. She was glamorous, an 'aristocrat' do you say? A coincidence.* I produce my picture, the one that is in no way Popova. *Yes! Like that. She had that look, a cruel look... And are you lonely?* Too frank! Yet she potters about and smiles, and I feel moved to talk. 'I think often of the coast where I lived as a child, and where my parents lived till old age. A child never evades his ancestors, and in times of solitude they're our sole reference. Whenever we do our lonely duty we see no future except in the past. Sometimes my parents come to me out of the blue or black, and then I am at the mercy of roiling emotion, and if I try to unravel it, to lay it out as if dissected on a table with guts exposed to the light, I see nothing but shadowy parts that make up a kind of mosaic, or a tangling jungle surrounding my heart. But I say to myself, let me lay them out, these organs of darkness: fear, sadness, fake hope, pity, love, boredom, frustration, duty... let me lay them out. I want to call it my child rescue.' She seems to accept this deep speech as evidence of life's mute inconsequence: she takes it from me and lays it quietly aside. That's what these mournful people do, I realise. Her boy returns from his bath and she instinctively moves close, slips under his wing. They revert to their personalised quiet. I excuse myself.

Later on an impulse I return to the hostel, and seeing them huddled in the dining room over some tepid camp food, feel a strange sudden anger. I find myself demanding they come with me, that we'll have a fine meal at a fine restaurant and that Dion will *pay*. Doesn't know yet but he will! I scurry to the motel. Here he is with his stoned semi-naked chicks. They gaze. - Need yer dough, Dion. - Dude, kindly fuck off. I discover his bag and pocket a credit card. Cheers. Got a date with people who actually need my help. Back at the hostel the sad pair haven't moved. Get dressed up, I say, if you've glad rags that is. We'll celebrate your significant visit to this fair far country. And we're going to honour the dead. By the way, it's my birthday! They've no city clothes and present at the door in pitiable anoraks and boots... dislocated, cocooned in stiltedness. We find a fuggy steakhouse with an open fire and settle in. I note the little ritual they enact every few minutes: she touches his hand, he grasps hers, and their heads seem to come together a little. Small talk is off the menu, but the girl has a way of segueing to significance. It seems to please him to let her talk: she is his philosopher and his poet. Her grandmother disappeared, she tells, during a pogrom in the nineteen-thirties in Minsk after she tried to defend her family... as if such a fact were an essential entrée to this couple's mournful quietude. Such non-sequiturs are to be swallowed with sage nodding of the head, at the quiet narcissism of permanent bereavement.' And it comes to Dreeley: without knowing it he has crossed the border into a land of shadows. 'This is the couple who died in the Soviet prison in my dreams. Yes, it makes sense: the psyche is timeless, spaceless, and this southern land really does harbour people who fit nowhere...' Now the steakhouse chef makes an appearance. Kitted in a charcutier's apron he cruises the tables as if daring punters to order steaks: daring us to ask why he's out of his butcher's lair. He's luridly thick-set, brusque as if determined to prove to the world he's no species of moron chef. We order our flesh rare, and he takes his squat-heavy frame off to the kitchen, surely to glower in private and turn knives in his hands. No doubt about it: *he is the Soviet assassin come again to sniff out his victims.* Soon we're chewing our slabs in lugubrious silence. Blood seems to collect in pools, yet a merciful mash soaks it up and the beetroot salad rescues us from death by boredom. At the end the boy says that was quite good and the girl smiles. Let's have a long beer, I say, and you can tell your family history. I am drawn to their seriousness, to the polar winds of their faces, though I cannot but think of Dion who'll have his tongue in Lena's mouth and his finger in Rhona's pussy or vice versa. With our beers in front of us like monuments to an old dream of friendship, I mention a story I wrote of a man in a prison in the time of Stalin. And they listen, as if to an excessively-drawn cliché... Incarnations of an older world, peering forth into tomorrow without hope or expectation, these youths make me feel it is I who should grow up. What can I do for them? Yet they are kind, and we drink and chat. And by evening's end it is me who feels he has matured a little, somehow.

Doomed Troika   Dion and me, we roll indifferently on. The upland road leads to high mountains, and his headless space-music embroils us in fuggy hypnosis suitable to landscape dreaming. Here is my seductive excuse for basking in the 'ever going nowhere'. Great mother peaks spread out under blue-silk sky, their white aprons spilling into the valleys. A flock of sheep looms on the road ahead. We stop and ogle as the mob of fluffy complainers, heads craning over each others' backsides, swarms messily by. Dogs with pink tongues jump about on curly backs and horsemen in winter gear cruise laconically at the rear. I lower the window and run my fingers through their woolly coats. Dion does the same. Cool polar wind cleans our eyes. He says:
- Where's this gang going this time of year? The works, I bet. Who'll ever tell their story?
- One time when I was a kid I came across a new lamb, stranded on a cliff above the sea near my home. A flecked winter sea, I remember it. In the late afternoon I heard the little guy bleating, and I made up my mind to go back in the morning and bring it up to the field. There it was, under a thorn bush. I carried the little yellow woolbag up the scree slope to the top

in my arms - and three mother sheep stopped their chewing and gazed at me. Definitely grateful they were. Not fools, I thought, though their blessed kid will be slaughtered and eaten before many days are out... I felt like I'd done something. Silly really... something special
- Yeah, you never forgot. Is that lamb any less than you and me? Nobody ever tells the story of the damned and dead and forgotten. Right, dude?

Old Dion has his moments.

On our arrival at the alpine village we are told that a light plane is missing over the glacier, and that 'bodies are expected'. Bodies in this paradise wilderness? Dion lights up a spliff, his philosophy-guy answer to everything. I don't partake, makes me paranoid. We sit in his fogged car feeling dense. Dion suddenly says: hey, let's head down to that glacier. Just to be there, know what I mean? The guy wants to hang with dead bodies. Big evil ice river, dude.

We follow the shingle road out of the village into miles of scree waste and boulder fields. At the lip of the glacier we exit the car and climb a slope. The view is stupendous: great floods of lumpy glacial ice oozes earth-slowly out of a pale sky through buttresses of white-hard mountains. Our screwed-up eyes register the sun. Soft Antarctic winds arrive from far. And the slope about us is moving, it cracks and wheezes under us, and little pebbles rattle past to the glacial floor below. In this rock-river world only the sky is still. At last... at the far side of the valley we spy a tiny coloured line - the rescue party, bearers of the dead. Now a helicopter materialises out of the blue haze. We watch it alight on the glacier's rump. The little winter gnat does its buzzy pall-bearing work... and presently is lost in the still distance. The mountains are wind-silent, they avert their faces. The earth sleeps on. Pebbly doings such as these, shall surrender to the sky.

Back at the village we find people tooling about in a kind of feckless slow motion. The chopper has been, delivered its cargo. Two foreign men and a woman, they tell us. Tourists, Russian some say. Didn't know our country. Cruel fate, all undeserved. Dion stands about, raps with dudes, wants to make the scene. People don't notice his wackiness in this atmosphere, or his neediness. Dion requires bits of people and things about him, the psyches of others, and this scene is the closest he'll ever get to philosophic mournfulness. Too much the dilettante to ever fall back into himself: as they say, never alone but ever lonely. Hours later, after more rapping with sundry folks in the pub bar, Dion randomly takes his leave. Outside it's freezing, but I hover by the entrance to the ranger's headquarters. Dion sizes me up.

- I get it. You wanna see the faces, see that woman's face

- No way

- 'S what we're gonna do!

He steps up to the entrance. I hang back. The cop won't let him in. Dion negotiates. Could be our friend, need to be sure, please. The cop consents. Dion drags me from the shadows, I pull my coat about my face. In a back room, bodies are laid out under sheets. Which is the female? This one. The corpse seems short, plump. Dion uncovers the face. It is east European, hair brown and cropped, chin blunt, cheeks heavy. By the head is a pair of dark glasses.

- Not Popova?

- Not by any stretch.

I mumble thanks to the cop and clear out. Dion comes after me.

- What're you afraid of, man? Jesus, let's get to the hotel.

Thanks to Dion's fabled financial stash, we manage to check into the pricey Hermitage. At around eight Dion bursts through the door of our room.

- Dude, I was at reception just now and there was that same cop asking for a guy who sounds a lot like you. He's on his way up here. What've you done?

- Nothing. Another enquiry about that body

- Bullshit, man. What're you not telling?

We glare at each other. What's he up to? I well know how Dion likes to beat up the idea of not trusting the law in any shape or form. And I start to panic.

- Okay. The one story I didn't tell about Endaira Popova is the one where she nearly disemboweled a guy in a Wellington pub

- You were there?

- I covered it up, helped get her out

- O-kay. So she's on the run and so are you - and you want me to wear all this?

- I don't want you to do anything

- I'm the dude with the fucken wheels! You're gonna deny it all. Better still, we fuck off now.

There is a rap at the door.

- Don't wanna talk to this guy, right?

Dion shoves me into the toilet. I hear a brief conversation. He's back.

- Told him you took a walk round the block. Sussed it: we leave by the balcony. We're just a floor up. Get the car, drive the hell out. Fuck, you *owe* me, man.

Owing Dion is the whole point as far as I can make out.

- And you're gonna dump her for good!

This is no time to confront Dion about how he is manipulating the whole affair to suit himself. We grab bags, negotiate the balcony, drop down into snow, make the car. At the hotel gate a figure suddenly looms. Dion accelerates, brakes. The body bounces off the front. In the slush we side-ram a barrier before slithering off down the steep exit road. I turn and see the guy hobble into the hotel car park, jabbering into a mobile. The night in front of us is dense dark. There are no stars. It is achingly cold. We drive for hours, not speaking. There is time to think. Why would Dion want to put the frighteners on me? Why deep down does he need to use me? Worse, why do I need to let him? He wants to get inside my dream! Get a life, Dreeley. No really, he doesn't have a decent fantasy to live in and he needs to hijack mine. We're rivals, plain and simple. Birds of prey picking at a corpse that's all bones. Corpse of what? Our loser lives! Are we each other's *beast*? If you like, if you like… I suddenly find myself talking out loud.

- And who has any right to put a finger on *me*? Who has a right to interrogate? Not the law, not the fucking rule makers! This is a quiet country. There's only one law here, *my conscience.* No-one's going to dictate to me. I've been through madness and sadness, through depression and obsession. This is *my* journey and no bastard in a uniform with a set of robot-rules in his head is gonna get a hold of it. Because I'm not anyone's, I am not containable! I'll suicide rather than submit to other fuckers' rules. I will elude these gnomes till the end. I will jump off a mountaintop! (And Dion laughs) - Dude, I love it. You and me, we're romantics

- Oh but you know what? You need to get a life. Because I need to - and that's how I know you do. Fuck romance

- Don't ever say that, don't ever say it. You need to loosen up, man.

And in the dark I can see he is smiling. Dion is settled in the knowledge that he is an eternal loser - who once in a while is a winner. And he knows this is the fate of all human beings.

Dead End   In the farthest primeval places we wish our closest heart friends were with us. In the loneliest moment of the soul's journey we wish our lover were there. I wish Endaira Popova had been here. Perhaps she came here and left again. More likely she never came amid these inhuman ferns and rocks and shadows and streams.

In sheeting rain, Dion steers us into the mouth of the Homer Tunnel. The watery curtain ceases... and our suffering engine booms hollow under rough-hewn granite walls that seep-seep with streams runnelling out of the mile-deep granite mass above. We creep along the tunnel floor... and in the gloom I see the shadows of lone men who carved this crudity out of sheer rock, in truth out of the labyrinths of their dreams and regrets. Soon a white dot at the far end widens in mouth-open surprise to a huge gorge, with massifs funneling downward toward the fjord at Milford. The rain is deluging absurdly now, thundering on the car's bonnet and roof, crushing at the windows. Shocking cascades shoot from the mountains' granite chops and explode in ravines. The valley floor is a bulging torrent. We skitter to the lip of the canyon and grind to a stop. This is a maelstrom, there is no going on. We are hideously unwelcome, silenced in the horrendous noise of this skyburst hammering the earth. There's no choice but to hunker under, hold our breath, wait for it to end. Even Dion is cowed. I think of water torture, think of a universal mass of tears. Submit, submit you human scum shit, fucking submit! This line turns to a ghoulish chant in my head. Can't get rid of it. An hour of this - enduring a sort of hideous thrill that the drumming water can't get any louder-heavier - and at last the deluge regolates to a sullen thudding on the car's skin and we can at last distinguish raindrops from rain. Soon there is nothing but slithery runnels and rivulets under our wheels shoveling pebbles down the slicked road. A surly greyness obscures the massif above. Dion is moved to comment at last. Dude, what a blast! But his tone is faked. He has seen what irrelevance we turn to when nature vomits on us. We step out of the car. Egregious steel mists mill about the brows of cliffs. Waterspouts on their granity faces mutter, pissing sullenly into valley pools. The air has a raked and greyblooded leanness that only a deluge can inflict. My skin registers its cold wetness, its rough loneliness. We nurse the clapped-out Falcon down the squishy gorge road to Milford. This route is a dead end; it seems tiresome to be travelling it. But at last the sun comes out and we revive a little. Nature puppeteers our moods it seems. On our arrival at the fjord the sun is all brilliancy, and the buttressed mountains pulsate in a rock-yellow sheen. The waters of the fjord snake away to the southern ocean. Beyond, is nothing that concerns human beings.

So, the point where there's nowhere else to go. How will D the dilettante deal with this old, painful conundrum? Meanwhile the sandflies (who police the joint at Milford) have found us, and they're no respecters of dope smoke. We deposit ourselves out on the jetty, hoping the little biters won't follow us over water.

- We finally arrive nowhere
- This isn't nowhere, dude. It's *here.* And it's all beauty
- As long as we have all accessories to avoid the real
- What the fuck are you chasing, Dreeley man? Me, I do it for sport, for the ironic hell of it. Why turn it into some morbid quest to 'gather up fake strands of the past'? You think you'll ever understand the totality of the world? There is nothing we can do! We are born as the *whole thing*. We are borderless, man. Do you think you can do better than one single human being who was ever born into this humanness? Get off your fucking high horse. All beings are just like this, forever, and you can't do a damn thing about it
- Cool down Dion. We don't really disagree
- Quit your idiotic mythological quest to find your special goddess. Where'd you get that romantical idea? You claim I wanna latch onto her? Mate, I chase pussy! Not some fucking myth of a woman who's half goddess, half temptress, half ballbreaker, half your own half-baked imagination about some past-life story you wrote. You're caught in your spider-web, you're the writer of your own crummy tragedy.

How Dion likes to rave. It enforces the paradigm of himself. Since I agree with most of what he is saying, the real value for me is when Dion breaks out, gets enraged.

- Methinks you protest too much, mister lonely Dion, lost in the trivia of your own need-gratification, your quotidian dribbly little hunt for bits and pieces of other peoples' experience. You're the world's parasite. There's nothing you can call your own
- I'll let you know if I'm mister fucking lonely! You think there's one tiny thing anyone can ever call theirs? You act like we're somehow animated into life by our 'body' - like some wooden puppet. (This is clearly the after-dribble of some convo I thought was forgotten) Some huger blueprint has to be here, and it's not physical. You boast about 'evolving'. What, you

evolve out of your own head? - into a higher form of the same shit? That's a crock. If you were a higher form of yourself you wouldn't be yourself any more, would ya?

(What a spin-out!) - *You* still wanna change things, Dion

- It's all a haze, mate

- Total denial mode. You fear seriousness

- Don't patronise me, cunt! If I am afraid of anything, and that's a big if, it's pretentious wannabes trying to wank themselves to a higher level

- Cool. Let's say you are my own wish to do just that, my own wish to forget, to coast in a dream, to not take the world seriously, to stay stoned forever. You, the exemplar of escape culture. You, the trivialisation of the serious past, of all my furrow-browed seeking at life. Maybe I need you, maybe you really are right! But will you own the things I see in you?

(Pause) - Maybe.

Amazing how I read the guy's thoughts! Dion somewhere wishes to be me. And I to be him.

After all this guff there is inevitably only one thing to do. To retrace our steps... Besides, the sandies are biting like hell.

The Last of Popova   Hours later Dion changes course on a lonely road.

- Man, we should go to places where we're in danger, where there's risk. All roads lead to Shangri-La, my friend, in the form of *Queenstown*

- Don't wanna go there again

- You with your haloed conscience always accept the worst, Dreeley. But do you accept the best, hey? The best!

Dion is the lord of irony. I am certainly the obsessor, but Dion is the tantalizer... who teaches that since all experience is irony, then the past is all irony so he deconstructs it as *empty*. Neat eh? But your Dreeley has a conscience, and says that we have to work with what we have, and have done, in order to let it go bit by bit.

- Our Dion is a super-lazy guy. Doesn't want to do any analysis

- Deconstructing the present is hard work, idiot

- No, because you're unaware a lot of the time

- What's time?

- All right, you're unaware NOW.

Dion chews on this for a while. Presently I lob at him with:

- When a system is benign, do we have anyone to blame? Who are the evil perpetrators now, except ourselves? To take responsibility for oneself is to give up our continual creation of the Other. A repressive political system is the extreme Other

- Ultimately it's just me and you, mate

- But what does 'peace' do to people? Does it make them respect life more, respect themselves? Do we use the peace 'better'?

- Maybe we need pressure, crisis, threat, to feel really alive - even if we're not going to last long. See dude, I ain't lazy! All that time-based fucking about and so-called 'personal development through struggle' you blither about… in reality we always live NOW, in ETERNITY. There never was 1860 or 1910, or any other stupid date

- Who are we then? Do we ever evolve, do we need to suffer?

- Nope

- The Soviet story I wrote is really about materialism as torture. In its micro-trivia it's all torture. In its constant change it's trivial nothingness. Stalin understood that. Was he a guru?

- If he was, he was a KILLER guru

- Deep down he thought we should all be liquidated, or else we should liquidate ourselves

- Ultimate self-censorship, right dude?

- I see life as labyrinth, with we as our own beast. Materialist beast who upholds the illusion-world

- So you chase that holy goddess! Fiction, man. No wonder you write weird books

- She's freedom to me

- Only when you give her up

- After you've got into her pants apparently

- Why me?

- You're the guy I need to blame

- Keep blaming dude, till we find her.

Queenstown. The fun and erasure capital gives up its bars one by one. The mind customarily wants to yield to worldly drugs, so Dion and I don't fail to get progressively drunk. Alcohol is our Other, the one we use to stay ignorant, to conjure trivias anew here in tourism-ville. At a bar called *Crawl* there is a girl, a little blondey on a bar stool, and she greets us with a simple familiarness. Welcome to the fun capital, she says. My name is *Pia* (not a real name). Her singy tone comes on like a jewel that says to me I have lately been very alone. Her button eyes seem to scoop up the world's escapes, and it turns out she's an agreeable little talker in ways that say very little. Dion smiles at her, and I barely realise I do too. Soon she has made us feel… as if we never wanted to be anywhere else. We buy her drinks and drink them ourselves. She reveals no need to tipple or pop a drug… rather I see a tiny container of griefs of ages, entombed in the wan mundane pleasures of this life. Yet does she participate actually - for all her attentive eyelashy flicks and pursy lips and jingly jewels? We gaze, Dion and I. For she is *open,* as if to far realms… and I begin to think that if we asked her to drown in the steel cold lake she'd do it without a murmur… so lightly that you ought to check yourself in a mirror and say: be careful what you desire, beware your powers of conjuring, of your evil. Her studied nowness be-glitters a thing that once happened, a thing unerased like light that can't be leached from a day, or wetness from a lake. She has no faith but for *this.* All else she jettisoned in some long ago time… Oh she is the killed beauty who tottered in my room in a deadly Soviet prison, and I left her on a slab floor. I did not save her. Dion invades now, whispers at her mouth. Says he wants a dark tall Russian called Popova. To confide in her is his best sotted homage. God, somewhere he stole Endaira from me. And Pia the little blonde, as if she knew the question would come, tells: *Yes, I will bring her to you!* And seems to say *'I know I can't match the one you seek, yet I am the messenger of the elsewhere'.* And I dimly register that she too is a sex girl, that she waits to be used, and that there are no borders to her. Dion assumed it all along. He never separates those who give and those who sell. But Pia has stood up, and feigns to be a little eager. She leads us into the street.

And in the white of the drunk-cold afternoon, a male face in a suit looms at us out of the crowd. Says a mouth: we're gonna ask you to come with us. More loomy faces in suits stand by the mouth who spoke. *You guys look serious!* Dion titters, till a big guy vice-grips his arm. *Dude, citizens' rights!* I'm laughing too till my arm is gripped. *What the fuck,* crows Dion. We are bundled down the street. I glance back, and Pia on tiptoe looks on, seems to dither like Alice at her tea party, as if here were some problematic mode of goods delivery or a pesky traffic light turned red. She skips off down an alley. Two hundred metres in company of the Suits feels like a mushy slipway in a dream. We're at a building. Entry by an obscure door. *Pig shop!* declares Dion. Down some stairs to a basement room and I'm deposited behind a door. Big cold pause; starting to sober up. Dion is led in. Conference. Policeman sits in front, two stand behind. '...Reason to believe you are occupants of a vehicle identified at Mount Cook... Injury to an officer... Were you in Wellington on the date of... Incident in a bar... You were identified as...' Dion looks like he's about to say *It wasn't me, guv* - then seems to think better of it. Maybe he has a criminal's honour. And criminality or the pull of it is lighting up his face right now. Cops, people, tend to think of him as troublemaker and subversive anyhow - and in that basement it strikes me he is a villain. But all villains ain't we? - since we are born and live and since we're under the eyes and ears of the LAW, under the eyes and ears of the PEACE in some closed mournful place called Nee Zulland, this thrumming humming little democracy, this thuddingly terrifying peaceable little place! Shangri-La of Forgetting, now demanding us to recall out of the pit of our past all our damned and dead things we're driving at warp speed on these lonely roads to get the fuck away from, as if this moment or the terrifying future were a deadly assassin with a knife or gun ready to spill our blood and blow our brains like Easy Riders in a dream... And we *are* guilty, guilty of living, guilty of feeling, guilty of knowing and possessing, of storing stuff away from the prying riders of the LAW... You keepers of our consciences! Which of you cunts knows what we are? You wanna have and keep our lives like you've no life of your own, you stealers, you voyeurs! Now Dion is talking in that charm-ridden way of his. 'Looook, we can do a deal... what you got anyway? You pigs are nosy, snouting about. Charge us or piss off eh, or let us piss off'. One cop thumps the table, another kicks Dio's chair. Barely legal, uncouth. The three bad boys step out. Bastards are frustrated, sez Dion. Time to go! *What?* Bolt! Got the car keys? *Yeah.* Action stations then! And he grabs at me and somehow we run into a passage and somehow Dion kicks a cop out the way and somehow there are the stairs and we're up and out to the street and running god knows how... and there's the dreamy blue lake, the blue blessed unconcerned rills of it, and those sawtooth mountains laughing in the daydream day at us as we scurry along the shore past tourist folks living some parallel dream... till a red blob shows up in a line of cars that is our wing-ed Falcon. Dion shovels behind the wheel, shouts at me *get in.* But I see coming toward us... two things, two people, two girls. And one of them points at us, and now they're veering our way. One is dark and tall, the other littler and blonder. Dion has not seen or seems not to. He shouts, I slide into the seat, he lurches our Falcon into the road. The two girls like models on a deadly catwalk stride to the centre of it. *They'll clear out the way!* is the last thing Dion utters. *Look out!* is the last thing I scream. The blondy seems to fall to the side as if a shadow prop in a grand tableau but the tall one, the Other, strides on. Why would anyone stride like that? A noble resolute face looms, her eyes penetrate across space as if a deadly angel. Dion hollers. She is blasted off our grill like a bone and flesh ragdoll. We slam the kerb. I am out the door. In the road I am standing over the girl. Pia is kneeling like a stray dog in the gutter. *Popova* is lying at a strange angle, breast pushed outward to the sun, leg curled backward, deep hair splayed about on the asphalt like a ghost head white in a blackened sea... There is a ghost of a smile on her red lip. ... Now Dion shovels me, hurls me into the back of the car. The last thing I recall is the tossing and careeling of my face on leather as Dion floors his hell-chariot out of the streets of Fun Town... and into the lonely land and hills and forests of a quiet dead country.

* * * *

Dion didn't tell me till we were in the loneliness... he knew Popova was there all along. And despite wanting to murder him when he said it, I was slowly forced to understand: he had to find her, had to own (to abuse) the presence of her, then reject her, for his ego's sake. Then he would have to report it to me for the very reason that I failed to be there, that I failed to find her. But then, the *bad thing* happened, the *uncalled-for* thing. Dion didn't think she was ever going to do that, fuck no. And that admission made me laugh bitterly, at him, at him... until my laughter finally subsided in a mutter of tears, where it stayed and doldrumed for a week or two... before the oppressive presence of Popova one day was lifted from me gently... in the keening of a bird, a hawk I believe, as it rose above treetops of black green beech forest, under the shale cliff of a mountain, into the wide sky.

Alone   Perhaps I was always a bit hard on Dion. Slippery-eel guy who from under his massed sadness masquerading as trivia, loved to pour oil on the troubled waters of my obsession. I will never know if he mourned Popova or not... *Dionysus is the ever-dying and rising god. He is born, he suffers a death-like experience, he is reborn...* I am forced to accept that under that eccentric hedonist escapist drivel is a man with a heart, a seeker. And he delivered one more monologue, outside a rickety hut in the Matukituki in front of a field... before he disappeared from my sight for good. He let himself be caught in a moment of what might have been serious sadness. Maybe the landscape of this heartbreakingly beautiful country got to him. Or maybe he did it for my sake. Our sake.

- What's the difference between my God and me, I used to ask myself. Later I told myself: Dio, you cooked up the difference. Uncreate it then, uncreate the difference. Anything we have and hold tends to rule us. It gets in our bones. But if we look directly at a thought, it tends (after complaints) to sneak away and hide. You claim I trivialise experience. Okay. Our experience is consequential since it is karmic - but karma only has substance as long as we fail to call out its bullshit. All that heavy consequence makes me feel inconsequential. You claim that to deconstruct the past is to turn it to a phantom, to a myth, to render it inconsequential. That's where you come in. I get that. And I know we can uncreate the doubt and the inertia and the conservatism and the blocked up shit karma... But our real state, is emptily still and clear like the sky. Nothing to be done, right? Do I worry that it's uneventful in the sky? Maybe. Do I have the guts to be a Nothing? Do I compensate with all my druggy babbly avoidance shit? Sure do. But now, looking at all this beauty, from this utter height... It's not boring at all. It's the most unboring thing.

You, uncool Dreeley man, you've got a conscience. I don't. You think about sorrow and torture and atonement and stuff. Good for you. And who's left standing at the end of the thousand years' war? Maybe me, probably you. Who finally got himself out of the labyrinth? Probably you. 'Luck, man.

And with that, Dion-Dionysus got up and ambled away down the trail. Didn't offer me a lift back to dangerous decadent legalist materialist civilisation. Claimed he was going to dump the car anyway. Very considerate of him.

Far below a thousand years ago there had been a gate and a shingle road that ended in a field. I had stood still and seen the mountains tower beyond me. I saw the peak called *Aspiring* hide itself coyly behind a footstool massif. There was no choice but to walk up into the loneliness. On the brown upland of this mountainside, I am nestled in dew-stained tussocks, their frond-heads swaying and stuttering under mournful wind that combs my skin and eyes. Melancholy sunlight glitters in the dew, and white spider funnels nestle in the thickets. Far on, the wild bottom of the world merges in indefinite sky, signalling 'no return to the realm of women and men'. A skeletal tree in front of me bares itself to sun and wind, and a lone spider weaves its threads inside a fork. The web sways lightly in the polar wind that suffuses its delicate dew-water, before turning to mystery in yellow light. The inhabitant of her airy labyrinth clings on. She is Arachne, the weaver. For whom does she weave in these lone realms? Only for me.

...A spidery goddess dwells at the heart of a labyrinth guarded by a beast. The questing hero seeks her but she is strangely elusive. Still, she offers a ball of twine, signifying her suitor's attention and commitment, to help him trace his path. Our hero 'liquidates' the beast and claims to rescue her. Later though he abandons her... on a remote place, on an island. She pines away, longing for death. Now comes Dionysus, god of desire, claiming to rescue her. Once more. She always was a subtle spinner and gatherer of threads! The hero begins to see the labyrinth as of his own making, as the sum of his searchings, that its tunnels are but the roads and walkways of his mind: all that magineative story-weaving, all that obsessive need to discriminate truth. Why go back? Why not repair to a lone island and sleep forever? Because *desire,* the 'ravelled sleeve of care', the need to know and to return, cannot be stoppered! *To deconstruct* - is the goddess' magnetic wooing song. Still, the hero wants to protect his island self with a 'shield of learning'. Though his search intensifies to desperation, the goddess affects to disappear in front of his eyes! At last he realises that the problem - the beast - is himself. The beast is nothing if not a master shapeshifter, and obsession is his weapon. At last he has no choice but to skin and gut and fillet his own need. Facing his gasping for knowledge itself, he sees that it is but the habit of habits, the maddeningly unbreakable paradigm of *seeking.* At this point, the beast's death comes by suicide - and with it, the goddess's. For she the goddess is the container of all life and death, she is the movie of this world, she is the seer of the movie, she is the screen on which the movie is projected, she is the one who asks 'to whom does the movie occur?' And when the hero has intrigued and infiltrated that question, there is nothing left... She is gone. All is gone.

Dion-Dionysus had his role to play then, and I admit he was only myself. Do you see how close we were, like lips and teeth? All of my fiction is myself. And when Ariadne ceased to be, I finally admitted she was also nothing but me. Why did I look for her? This is a dilemma faced by all the world, inexplicable since none can trace the beginning of desire. And in the asking of *why* the seeking begins again. Our spider-trap is the desire to know, and all worlds unfold from desire even as heat of the sun emanates from its fiery heart. I admit there is nothing outside myself; all these wishings and wanderings are just a failure of responsibility. There are two things in this life: to accept oneself as pure formless awareness, the origin and end of all things - or to live inside the drugged solidity of form. To know that you are nothing but yourself and that the self only *seems* to take on the world's objects... But to see oneself as 'seeker of a goddess' - this is hypocrisy, for would a goddess ever see you as anything but herself? Did Popova, as she loomed in front of my car, see me as anything but herself? What then gives me a right to see myself as separate from her? Still, we all want to worship as children, and so we wander in the mind, in dreams and in histories. This has been my position. I should declare it to be no more.

Yet a thing holds me back... Who has the guts to be nothing? There must be romantical talk and mournful talk, longeurs to celebrate the suddenness of my lady's end. That is why I came here to this place. I know now that birth and death are nothing but the arrival of the thought and its withdrawal again, that the self has no death but the thought of it. And I want to tell her, want to shout it out to *Ariadne*, as if she will understand me, as if inside her wide gaze she always gets it. But she is vanished among lakes and fjords and lonely coasts. My pursuit of her was just like a pursuit in a dream, a dream in Dion's car... like that old Kiwi escape flick *Goodbye Pork Pie*. But I don't mind. I love that she was so clever, so elusive. The fact is, I am alone. What is lost, if no-one is there to lose it? Now it is me who is so clever, so elusive! Here in this high craggy place above green black beech forests, where spidery waterfalls feed gorged rivers far below, and late white sun streams across folded peaks and shadows them... there is such a silence... and this bright air that fills the world is nothing but my own breath. Breathe in, breathe out... and here is the pulsation, densifying and rarefying, of life itself. A lone hawk caresses the sky below my eyes, and its undulant rise and fall is the loss of itself, such that in pillows of light it ever is and never is. If it were not air, how could it be? If it were not a bird, how could air be? ...One time there was sleep. I recall there was sleep. A voice said: in sleep is no awareness, in sleep you are not. But I know that I slept, for even beyond sleep, awareness is. And it cannot cease, but only cease to conjure. I know that I saw no hawk in the sleep of dawn... and here is pure awareness, no 'limitation of knowledge'. In the sky of awareness, only two thoughts - I and this - ever arose. I is the origin of this; without I there is no other. And this-this is the creation of worlds. From one thought comes all worlds. Limitless self-delight, limitless play of nature. And ego: habit of desire, habit of paradigm, restless wanting, serpent biting its tail, donkey craving its carrot... From mysterious desire relationship is born. Why desire, why want the works of this world? Ask not! Cease! Unless you are delighting... The goddess teases me. I want to follow, want to chase her to the end of the world, to the end of this still valley at the bottom of the planet, and beyond to the far south sea, where only a lone seeking hawk drifts in ether between crags. Here is romance, nothing but illusory beauteous delight of the self. My hawk is in the sky. A particle none other than light. A wave none other than the sea. Awareness, do you limit yourself? You never could, never did. Nothing ever was. All is dream. Who seeks? Me. Fiction. No-one.

My hawk disappears, into theatres of the sky. The goddess laughs. Her laughter fills the valley.

Appendix

A faceless clerk in Moscow's Lubyanka prison, A.N. Drilov, wrote an essay in his secret journal and deposited it under floorboards in his apartment in the winter of 1939-40. It is a meditation (and mercifully precise) on the grand orbital paradigm of death-in-life, of perpetrator and victim, of materialism and the spirit - and it came (somehow) into the hands of the narrator Dreeley, whose purpose it suited.

The Death Instinct   'There is not a living being who is not loyal to something; attached, committed. To be loyal to bodily survival is deep; so also is loyalty to conscience. Some will argue that one's highest conscience *is* the will to survive. In fact conscience is beyond the ego: it is the great well, the oceanic vast, wherein a person's acts and motives are measured and weighed. It is the taking of ultimate responsibility for our real unlimited nature. It is origin, our complete morality, from which need gives birth to the will. When Systems are engineered of such criminality that the power to survive is either arbitrary or tested to the limit, then the great issue of conscience careens to the fore. When one is faced with either bodily death or the most convoluted path to survival, conscience becomes the final arbiter of our acts. Meanwhile, systems of a criminal nature express two shades: the first is concerned with the management of bodies, and the second (more subtle), with the testing of loyalty. The latter interest lies in torture and the limits of fear, while the former lies in the mere removal of obstacles to the triumph of gnomish fundamentalists. Yet, how is humanity *capable* of abominations toward its fellows, and thus to itself? How can it come to regard such abominations as a path to success or transcendence? (Here are the ingredients of the *death instinct*.) In this circus where force and counterforce play their endless round, there's not a soul who is not wounded. And because no-one can achieve without others, there arises the eternal polarity of perpetrator and victim. At a primitive stage of our wish to control nature, our clinging (to position) matches the fear and hatred we feel for a nemesis. The sheer weight and persistence of suffering means we, unable to grasp suffering's origin, turn to cynicism born of confusion. Thus comes fundamentalism, whereby the fight against perceived threats is exteriorised as murder or martyrdom, usually sanctioned under dogma supplied by sclerotic tradition: sadism or sado-masochism whereby we punish others as a substitute for self-punishment, or masochism proper where we indulge in self-punishment in the role of victim. In these states we are wholly partisan, that is, we know our life and success is determined in part by the existence of our enemies. If we persist in perpetrating crimes, we do so as a split personality, ie: one who believes her actions are no more than 'a means to an end', or that she is more victim of circumstance than instigator of evil. We may (for example) justify our role as assassin or torturer by citing 'melancholy duty in a flawed world', or 'the lesser of two evils'... At a new development stage, the person, unable to sustain her earlier flawed morality, accepts the 'interdependence of polarities', and so becomes more tolerant of difference, less political. Here we turn ironic, and our main interest is to survive. At the next (long) stage, we are pushed to investigate and reconcile all unpalatable polarities that roil within. Herein we signal the demise of absolute good and evil. Meanwhile the biologic organism does all it can to perpetuate polarities, including amplifying the fear of death. At last, when the instinct to bodily survival gives way to 'ultimate conscience', we begin to see the relativity of present limits, begin to adopt a phenomenological and impersonal view of self, now putting ourselves in an 'absolute, timeless' context. Life now seems to offer nothing but 'affirmations of itself', and the only difference between 'life' and 'death' is that in one, a person is visible and in the other she is not! At the last, we surrender, whatever the consequences, to the ocean of conscience. Herein, there is but eternal play of relativity, and all within oneself. There is no fear or comment or positioning. We comprehend the pulsation of life itself. Life and death are as one, and as nothing... and we experience innocence. It is thus said that loyalty - which is commitment in the face of any and all circumstances - is the highest position. Loyalty, in all its trivia and pain and confusion and contradiction, is the achievement of a rare soul - and a soul soon to exit this earth! Loyalty is thus seen to be highest duty.

Those who are loyal to others tend to be loyal to self, owning emotional intelligence and radiating it, Those loyal to self one usually can't help being loyal to others. Loyalty comes of belief and love, and its unbreakable condition is innocence. If we have self-respect, self-love, we have no choice but to love and respect others: it is really impossible to harm them. What then shall we say of those who have little or no self-respect? They will form a class, a species, a gang, a regime, who together must persecute. We thereby dissect the anatomy of perpetrators and victims. Those far from the gates of innocence, those who can only yet dream of loyalty to self, are the fundamentalists, the criminals, the perpetrators. Their loyalty is to an idea that offers unity or purpose, that deflects or assuages inner dread, inner void. They suffer the arrested development of a child trapped in its *omnipotence* phase, who for comfort hangs onto the infantile *paranoid-schizoid* posture that sees all as either good or bad, charm or threat. And herein is the essence of attention-seeking and the seed of martyrdom. There is little sense of ambiguity, of 'shades of grey'. The *depressive* mind has not appeared, the mind which to defend itself against rage or grief learns to channel aggression into self-soothing and self-help, and thereby learns to respect others through guilt and sorrow at its own 'sins'. In the absence of compassion or self-love, fundamentalists are perpetrators in a self-darkness of fixation. Though their resolute wish is to pursue a kind of ideal innocence or purity, and that the whole world should become as clean as they are or die, therein one might hope that their victims, loyal as they are to such naïve ideals as hope and love and the sanctity of value, could serve as *examples* to them. Yet because the fundamentalist's loyalty is born of fear of nemesis, he must believe himself to be incorruptible, and therefore remains wilfully blind to the relativity of his state. The extent of his sharing with others is in forming gangs of the similarly self-righteous, whose chief goal is to persecute those 'not of their stamp'. They will thus always uphold murder and death as the essence of purity. Herewith, the fundamentalist matriculates to *sadist*. The sadist, in whom universal suffering is turned to professional hatred of the human condition whereby one 'despises others as *substitutes* for oneself', indulges drug-like in the arena of torture and pain, ignoring the inner bond between himself and his victim. Later, when sheer experience turns the black-white world to grey, and he is unable to sustain the sheer flawed morality of his acts, an 'inner corruptibility' enters in. This is the first grudging dance with relativity. At this point of development are laid the seeds of the *sado-masochist.* Here we master the arena of pain but we do it ironically, as if for the sake of redemption, clinging to the belief that we are not instigators but victims of generalised oppression. And since 'only victims may have a chance for salvation', this makes *victimhood* attractive. From the point of view of the perpetrator, here is a way to participate in self-purgation yet continue one's war of revenge against life's infliction of horror and injustice and outrage on the fertile field of oneself. This self-purgation by means of cruelty is a kind of temporary bliss of detachment from care and responsibility, a kind of forgetting (surrender). Fundamentalists and sado-masochists certainly want *somehow* to be loyal to themselves since they are manifestly the centre of their own universe; that is, somewhere they wish to be 'whole' (and in this wish we see the seed of the urge to power). But do sado-masochists believe healing will come? Oh, it might or it might not; and are we responsible anyway? This life is cruelty and I did not invent it! In the old blind fundamentalism, it wasn't necessary to go within, to commence the messy and nefarious business of surrendering the hurt... the method was rather to project it outward as 'rigid steadfastness'. Narrow and autistic is the straight path! But for our subtler siblings the sado-masochists, the goal is the exquisite balance of punishing and self-punishing. Thus we see the death instinct played out. Remember, it has two forms: clinging and surrender. You will say that death-instinct is in fact *life* instinct, since its raison d'etre is release of tension, coming to peace, search for pure pleasure. And so the death-instinct is, in its dark and lowly fundamentalist phase, the shadow of its enlightened twin. Even here we see hatred of the separative ego and a nascent desire to submerse in a greater cause, be it nazism or communism or any purifying fundamentalism... So, death instinct begins as fundamentalism, which births the desire to torture others for their laxness and decadence (sadism), and when a certain guilt masquerading as 'ambiguity' has taken hold, torture turns to investigation of 'self-torture' and we enter the tangled realm of sado-masochism... And when all the equivocation and ambiguity gives way again to certainty again, we come to *masochism* proper, the professional infliction of pain on oneself. Here is the domain of the budding saint! Now we can be true victim, *willing* victim. And the better to fulfill our destiny, we seek out our 'special torturer'... and this is how the circular death-business thrives.

Here then are the great stages of life-denial: and so we die, under the double-edged sword of severity and justice, either as perpetrators or victims or both at once. It is said we are all 'chips off the block', and precisely because we are of the subtlest mind and matter we are also masters at invention of pain, at invention of *systems* that study and tease out and dissect pain. Thus, in our need to self-punish, projected outward onto our brothers and sisters (whom in our secret heart we might claim to love) the whole of life becomes the art of punishment and self-punishment, for perceived and feared wrongs and hurts done to us by others, done to others by ourselves, and murkiest of all, done to ourselves by ourselves. And here the truths of karma lurk, and now we are victims of a haunting, of our own deeds buried in dim mounds and caves of the future. We despise this possibility, and so invent systems of *erasure,* systems for cleansing, for forgetting, for displacing hurt. Who shall be our victims - our brothers and sisters? Nothing so mundane. We shall assiduously be our own victims. And this, in sum, is the anatomy of the death instinct... for the sake of healing of the soul.

Repressive Materialist State Unnatural ideals ever turn to paranoia under the need to protect them from natural reactions. This paranoid hardening of the ideal turns to a kind of purist autism we call fundamentalism. From this rigidity comes the need to be feared, which leads to increased punishment of dissenters whereby the only way to validate both the ideal and the practice of punishment, is to generate colossal lies (propaganda) until there arises a climate of unnaturalness that becomes almost natural, an environment of distortion and untruth in which there is little option for the perpetrator but to embrace self-delusion. Self-delusion throws up guilt which of course must be repressed, but this repression-solution can't be sustained and seeks a creative outlet characterised as sadism. Here the individual seeks more extreme punishments, which under the increasing pressure of repressed guilt segues to sado-masochism. Guilt cannot avoid seeking a creative outlet, in fact its balancing opposite known as 'truth', which expresses as increasing need to self-harm through more and more bizarre harm of others. The psyche dares itself to become increasingly self-disgusted, leading to full-blown masochism. This is the last and best outlet for guilt short of suicide - or else surrender to the need to heal. But how does anyone heal when the cycle of self-victimhood is so entrenched? Beyond 'physical death and rebirth', we must begin to gradually stare down self-loathing and nurture self-esteem. Success would seem to be a miracle considering the depths to which the person has sunk. A key stage is to begin to feel that 'the punishment the world inevitably metes out', is *unjust*. In effect one tires of victimhood, seeks the dim beginnings of self-empowerment. And so the worm turns. In time, self-empowerment becomes a kind of ideal, and yet, contaminated with all that resentment at the punishment meted out on your person for past sins (likely to be mostly forgotten) empowerment inevitably takes the form of seeking power over others, since one's level of development is not advanced enough to see that subjugating others for personal advancement is a recipe for disaster, in fact is the repetition of the long arduous cycle one has already been through…

To channel guilt and fear of truth, to seek power over others, to avoid honest responsibility for self… all that repression practised by gangs, regimes, corporations, systems, is nothing but the individual's need writ large. How then, does a State exhibit behaviour for which no individual seems to be responsible? A truism: the state is created to serve the person, and the forces of social organisation are but forces of the psyche. Society is thus the person writ large. From the personal point of view, social organisation should always be (despite the best intentions of communists and socialists and fascists and totalitarians and nanny-state democrats) a means to an end. The ego, powerful or weak, is the *sine qua non* of all experience, all judgement, all desire… and all fear. A state is made up of persons, and even the most trenchant exponent of 'state power' cannot see anything but himself. Why then do rights and freedoms fall so readily into decrepitude in a system purportedly founded 'in the name of the people'? Many have asked this. First, there is no such thing as a 'people's revolution'. It is nothing but a 'turn of a wheel', a harbinger of totalitarianism to come. Revolution is nothing but the difference between 'the people' and the best-armed gang that seizes the reins of power, and one can be sure that the gang and the people will be at dirty odds before the sun has risen on the post-revolutionary dawn. Communist theory goes like this: when persons abnegate responsibility for the totality, in other words, when they emphasise their separateness, then all the evils of social organisation get played out as chaos, class war, decadence, whereby totalitarianism is a necessary corrective. The lesson of communism shows that to take a concept (in this case 'in the name of the people') and claim to fulfill it to the nth degree allows one to subvert it to the nth degree. Communism, because it is fruitfully impersonal, is totalitarianism par excellence - all in the name of the people.

The state as corporation has no morality or conscience since it is an abstraction, but despite what Kafka may say, it takes a long conga line of acquiescing individuals to turn a state into a criminal tyrant, and the cult of personality (see Stalin) is its necessary apotheosis. The State thus becomes the dictatorship of the individual. This is perpetuated by two means, and these may effortlessly alternate: the ruling individual may invoke the impersonality of laws he and others have instigated, or he may contrive to suspend those laws in a perpetual state of emergency, precipitated no doubt by subversives who threaten state stability, occasioning the need for more laws, which may then be permanently suspended. But there's no future in this, I hear you cry. Fool! Since laws have a bad habit of being inclusive, the best way to avoid slipping outside the law is to pass laws that are restrictive beyond anyone's powers to subvert them. To create laws that define to nth degree the person's relationship to the state, is to ensure that the person has no separate existence outside his or her relationship to the state. And if the will of the person is subverted at every turn, then all persons except the ruler effectively cease to be a factor in the organisation of the state. Thereby, the supreme ruler of the state becomes the only person. And the extent to which he keeps all others in a state of uncertainty or terror is the extent to which personal will is subverted. (Safe to say, that the more criminal the regime the less anyone is allowed to *know* about anything. This rule includes those in its upper echelons.) One may object that the supreme leader rules at the behest of his cohorts. But even if certain ranking persons contrive to gang up (exhibiting all the characteristics of gang behaviour) and remove the leader and replace him with another - that other will in time become just like the replaced, and the system will continue uninterrupted.

Is a state capable of thought? Obviously it is inert, an abstraction. Is it therefore capable of exhibiting so-called historical laws? Again, these are nothing but notions in the minds of persons, and for persons to seek to manipulate inert objects (like a state) is the height of absurdity. Despite what Lenin and his dialectical materialism would have us think, 'history' is nothing but the dilemmas and choices of individuals. We may say that a person is not in control of herself, that she is the pawn of greater forces, and that if she is a pawn to the *nth* degree, she is no person at all. And, is the leader-manipulator a person? To the extent that he disbelieves or disobeys his own laws he may be termed so, just as to the extent that he obeys his own laws he is not. Yet it is self-fulfilling historical totalitarianism to say that 'sweeps of history' are of more significance than 'the tides of a single person's mind'. In reality, there is no history whatsoever outside the perceiver. All history is personal. The rest is labels: fascism, communism, purism, totalitarianism. History could therefore be called a shameful and stupid habit (paradigm) perpetrated by people who have no right to tell it - not on behalf of its individuals at any rate. Persons do not participate in stories put out by historicists; ironically meanwhile, we scavengers of the future want to set history to rights by re-telling victims' stories. But did anyone ask them? *Could* anyone ask them? No-one can tell me that history moves in 'narrative sweeps', that it follows 'patterns that can be studied' - as if history ever meant more than it meant to a single person, somewhere, anywhere, be he or she ever so ignorant or ever so wise... This indivisible person, whose flickering experience is as coherent or incoherent as a sudden flicker of light that illumined a bludgeoning hand

in a room somewhere in the struck-off nothingness of bogus past...
where a tiny child witnesses booted thugs stomp into her house, sees her
sturdy mother try to shield her, sees her collapse to the floor under the
butt of a gun like any old sack of potatoes dumped in the cellar (a chore
her father used to do before he 'disappeared')... Oh, there is a gulf of
difference between reality and the impertinence of 'history'.

Friedrich Engels, 'inspired' by Hegel, posits three laws of dialectical
materialism: (1) The law of the unity and conflict of opposites, which
gives rise to (2) the law of the passage of quantitative changes into
qualitative changes, and (3) the law of the negation of the negation. Law 1
suggests that for any political position to claim validity (say Communism
or Islamic fundamentalism) it must put itself in opposition to its nemesis
(say 'Capitalism' or 'America'). However, by doing so it tacitly accepts the
validity of its opponent, since it is defined in opposition to it and without
it could not thrive or continue its revolutionary war. It has no existence
without its nemesis; thereby it and its nemesis are one. This neatly
dovetails to Law 3 which shows how every brave new system will always
kill itself in time, and indeed the reasons for its death are contained in
its birth, which occurred in opposition to a system it feared and hated.
The idea embodied by Law 2 - that the build-up of opposing forces
leads to a sudden third solution (a leap) which then entrenches itself in
a thousand little ways, occasioning inevitable sclerosis and decay before
delivering the need for further adjustment *etc* - taken with the other two
laws to offer the possibility to 'engineer history', seems to me the best
possible advertisement *against* the idea of creating the ideal state based
on 'historical forces of dialectical materialism'. Why? The only stability
that can be imagined is 'permanent revolution', and obviously this is an
absurdity in terms of building any kind of 'state', which is by definition
sclerotic. The state's perpetrators contradict themselves in their rejection
of fluidity, of the possibility that the play of forces does not operate as
discrete parcels, as *quanta*, at all, that 'material objects' have no existence
except in *ghostly relation*, so that there is no certainty except eternal
uncertainty and instability, no 'state' but the eternal *subversion* of that
state... The cause? Rejection of the *person, he who cannot be divided.*

The idea that materialism is capable of explaining a world or creating a 'better' one, is the savage ignorance of fools who think that murder solves problems, that social engineering enacts qualitative change, that a state can 'educate' people rather than choke them. If the great state is so historically inevitable, why has it never happened? And if so inevitable, why would its decay and collapse not be inevitable from the instant of its so-called formation? That criminal Mao and his 'great leap forward' is nothing but an excuse to murder anybody you don't approve of - and this is the real heart of Engels' and Marx's and Lenin's 'revolution'. Notions of great leaps, qualitative changes - these are nothing but an excuse for heartlessness, born of the idea that we are 'discrete', born in ignorance of our actual nature: *ineffable indivisible spirit*. The very idea that we are 'but the play of eternal forces in eternal opposition' should remove any notion that there are 'discrete things'! The 'state' is an oxymoron, nothing but 'the fakeness of the thing that does not move'. It is a lie, and a profounder lie in the hands of those who trust only in the 'inevitability' of dialectical materialism. The 'eternal play of forces' is an idealist notion doomed by Engels and Marx and Lenin and Mao *etc* to the level of the material - doomed for the simple reason that there is no 'material' that can ever be successfully manipulated. *Oops*. The materialist who imagines that objects affect objects, forces affect forces, causes engender effects, is nothing but a victim to his own *ideas*.

Never Free, Ever Free Those who suffer unreachable fear that somewhere deep they may not actually exist, will always want to bend others to their will, to implant in others the suffering that they endure. They obey a singular law of Gathering, wherein their need to self-validate is identical with control. Ironically, that system wherein lust for self-existence and control is rampant, displays the most insidious form of institutionalised disregard for the person's right to self-government. This is the realm of the sociopath: he is out of control in his need to control. And who can control without victims? Fundamentalism breeds where the tiny self struggles for order, for simplicity, in a great ideational or social or material wash. But beyond 'purifying' communisms and fascisms and other collective alterations of sanity posted by man to justify and bolster his lonely ego, *individual* remains the only thing that has the possibility to be sane. This is because it springs from *indivisible.* Generated from Emptiness beyond numbering or particulation are innumerable *vortices* - as if these were 'self-regarding entities' - from galaxies to whirlpools to weather events to heartbeats to sensings to feelings to thoughts to egos; and though the utter field is impersonal and amoral, these its expressions seem personal and moral. The urge to separate self-existence, force of ego, materialisation, atom - these are only ever the myriad strange imaginative wild dancing scintillations of the infinitude, nothing but ideational markers of a great materialist urge. And the fundamentalists, the gurus of materialism - the purifiers, dictators, collectivists, the insecure ones - have taken the deep truth and turned it to darkness, delighted in it in all their cruelty, in all their compensation for loneliness. Satanic masters, holding us to a great darkening, hammer into our souls the message that murder and torture are the only ways to ensure that 'nothing in this life can be ignored, that no level of reality may be eschewed or scorned, that we must live life in its densest and deepest parts'... that the return to impersonality, amorality and freedom may only be trod by a dark morality, fashioned deep within a ruthless personality.

Sure, just as it is certain in this life that nothing can remain, there is also nothing that may be avoided, such that *trivia* recurs without ceasing. This eternal trivia is enwrapped in emptiness (like the skeletal words that make up this journal), so that if we remember not this eternal emptiness that brooks no time nor place, we shall either sleepwalk in endless dreams or come to see all as *futility.* Futility assumes that things have *substance* (thereby suffering and torture are explained) but in truth not a thing can be held except 'as if in a cloud - in fact an ideational cloud, a mirageous, a dreamish one' that sprouts from an invisible heart, carries all properties of invisibility, contains its own heart and never departs from it. This heart is finely empty, is smooth and subtle, is peaceable cool transparency. Is the key then to have no attitude at all, to bear all burdens with infinite patience? Shoud we not after all see that we are always here, you and me, and there is nothing to fear except fear itself, and certainly nothing to wait for - for it is all a dream holiday in the dark and rain and cloud and sun, that passes off as if it never was, though yet it clamours to be? Those in chains are ever free… *the lotus blooms in the mud,* such that purity is never tainted by evil, by time or event, be they ever so dark, for purity is constant and eternal.

And does this help you… faceless, forgotten victims in the clearing cells of the Lubyanka prison?'

www.ingramcontent.com/pod-product-compliance
Lightning Source LLC
Chambersburg PA
CBHW050123030726
47505CB00007B/2013